BLUE SKY
COWBOY
Christmas

JOANNE
KENNEDY

sourcebooks
casablanca

Published by Sourcebooks, Casablanca, an imprint of Sourcebooks
P.O. Box 4410, Naperville, Illinois 60567-4410
(630) 961-3900
sourcebooks.com

Printed and bound in Canada.
MBP 10 9 8 7 6 5 4 3 2 1

Also by Joanne Kennedy

Cowboy Trouble
One Fine Cowboy
Cowboy Fever
Tall, Dark and Cowboy
Cowboy Crazy
Cowboy Tough

COWBOYS OF DECKER RANCH
How to Handle a Cowboy
How to Kiss a Cowboy
How to Wrangle a Cowboy

BLUE SKY COWBOYS
Cowboy Summer

To Brian Davis, Jackie Littlefield Davis, and of course Alan!

Merry First Christmas to all three of you!

You are the best gifts ever.

CHAPTER 1

THE SNOW GLOBE ON THE DASHBOARD ROCKED AND SLOSHED as Griff Bailey's Jeep dropped off the pavement onto the dirt road that led to his father's ranch. The music-box base tinkled out a few hesitant notes, but they were lost in the racket of icy flakes clattering on the windshield.

Griff had picked up the globe at an airport gift shop, remembering how his sister loved Christmas kitsch. He'd set it on the dashboard in an effort to inspire his own Christmas spirit, but it was just making him sad. There was Santa, the most senior of senior citizens, frozen forever with one foot in a chimney and a heavy pack slung over one shoulder while phony snowflakes swirled around him. It was obvious the bag wasn't going to fit down the chute, and the jaunty, tinkling rendition of "Here Comes Santa Claus" was just plain rude. This Santa wasn't going anywhere.

Neither was Griff, in the long run. Like Santa, he'd flown halfway around the world only to find his life shaken and stirred by unseen forces.

As the wipers thwacked out their restless rhythm, he saw a light burning in the distance.

Almost home.

He was surprised to find his heart lifting at the thought. His sole ambition from boyhood had been to escape the everyday sameness of ranch life, with its early mornings, late nights, and chores that were never done well enough, soon enough, or fast enough.

So why was he coming home?

Simple. The last place he wanted to go was now the only place that would have him.

At least, he thought they would. As far as his family knew, he was still deployed. His dad and stepmom were on an RV trip in the Southwest, while his sister was honeymooning in California. He wasn't sure how long they'd be gone, but he was hoping for a couple weeks of solitude so he could shake off the dark memories that had smudged his bright military future. Bit by bit, day by day, he would become the man he'd been before.

Before what?

Ghosts of the past rattled their chains in the back of his brain, threatening to rise and walk, but he knocked his head with the heel of his hand and sent them skittering back to their caves. He'd deal with them later. Right now, he needed to concentrate on the road.

As he nudged the Jeep around an icy curve, he laid eyes on his father's house for the first time in four years—and slammed on the brakes, sliding sideways, feeling the tug of a snowdrift hauling him into the ditch. White-knuckling the wheel, he spun right, then left, and lurched to a sudden stop that slammed his chest against the shoulder harness.

Breathing hard, he stared at his childhood home. He'd expected to feel reluctance, nostalgia, even a surge of relief at the sight of it—but all he felt was shock.

The entire front wall of the house was demolished, with beams and boards scattered like matchsticks in the snow. He might not be a fan of ranch life, but the Diamond Jack was the one safe, unchanging place in his world. And it had exploded.

Unbuckling, he opened the door and fell to his knees. A low buzzing began inside him, blind bees bumbling for a way out. They were with him every day, simmering beneath any emotion he dared to feel, pushing for release in a roar of rage, a howl of fear, a savage strike at something, anything. But releasing them would make the outside world match the darkness inside him, so he held them in.

The docs ought to give him some credit for that. They ought to let him go back. They would if he could control it, so he followed their advice.

Breathe.

As he drank in the cold air, the buzzing faded and died.

Surprised, oddly empty, he rose to his feet and trudged toward the house through snow up to his thighs. It was slow going, but that gave him time to assess the situation.

There were lights on in the upstairs bathroom, his sister's bedroom, and the kitchen. That was all wrong. Nobody was supposed to be home. And what was that weird shape in the wreckage? Had it moved?

Holy crap. What is that?

It looked like an animal—one with beaming yellow eyes that reflected the Jeep's headlights. Had he started hallucinating now?

Apparently not. The creature proved itself disturbingly real by launching itself from the wreckage and loping toward him with an awkward, lolloping gait. Feet like paddles flung snow all around, and its drooling jowls flapped as it ran, revealing long, white teeth that gleamed in the starlight. Those teeth were the last thing he saw before it leapt up and knocked him to the ground.

Pressing Griff's shoulders into the snow with paws the size of dinner plates, the beast dripped a cold string of drool onto his cheek as its amber eyes burned into his with a passion for…

For pats, probably. Because it was just a dog. A big, weird-looking dog, but a friendly one. As a goofy grin spread across its slobbery face, Griff heaved it off his chest.

"Who the heck are you?"

The dog sat back and presented its paw as if introducing itself. Confused, Griff shook it, glancing around, and noticed a pickup in front of the barn.

"Shoot," he mumbled. "I didn't think there'd be anybody here."

The dog shimmied close and leaned hard against him, tossing its head back and almost clonking Griff in the nose. It gazed adoringly into his face, and he suddenly felt better than he had in a year.

It might be nice to have a dog around. Trouble was, dogs generally came with people, and he wasn't ready for people.

Riley James was slight as a ballerina, but nobody who knew her ever asked her to dance. She preferred a tool belt to a tutu, and her walk, usually in steel-toed work boots, was an ungainly git-'er-done stomp.

But rising from the steaming luxury of the Baileys' jetted bathtub made her feel like Venus on the half shell, or maybe Beyoncé at Coachella. Tipping up onto her toes, Riley raised her arms and twirled like a music-box dancer, then reached for a towel. She'd gotten herself profoundly filthy demolishing her client's front porch, and while that always made her happy, it felt even better to be clean. Wrapping her long hair in one fluffy cotton bath sheet, her body in another, she hummed along with Johnny Cash—her father figure, her man in black, the patron saint of recovery. The Man was proof that a life can change, and his songs were her Bible.

Glancing at the polished pink marble walls of the Baileys' elegant bathroom, she caught her rosy reflection staring back, all clean and serene.

That serenity hadn't come easy. Most of Riley's life had been gritty and dirty and sad, but for the past few years, she'd found sanctuary in the most unexpected place: small-town Wyoming. Here, the past couldn't touch her.

Not much, anyway. She'd heard the whispered rumors that still followed her down Wynott's cracked sidewalks. But she'd found a home at Boone's Hardware and a mentor in old Ed Boone, who had all but adopted her as a daughter.

The thought of Ed made her hug herself in happy expectation.

Tonight, she'd finally meet the rest of his family—*her* family now. Shifting her focus to the mirror, she decided to put on some eyeliner and blush so she'd look extra nice. She'd heard so many stories about Ed's sisters and their funny, fussbudget ways. He called them the Harpies, but he smiled when he said it. The stories always had the same moral: the sisters might be difficult, but they were always looking out for him because they were family.

Geez, Riley hoped they liked her. She'd spent her childhood watching wide-eyed from the outskirts of other people's Christmases, memorizing traditions, collecting images and ideas, and soaking up that precious, holy feeling of love and goodwill. Now she was ready to celebrate Christ's birth smack-dab in the middle of a family, one who knew her and forgave her flaws, because they shared a bond that couldn't be broken. A bond like blood.

Frowning into the mirror, she tamped down her excitement. She'd had high hopes before, only to have them dashed, so she had to keep her expectations reasonable—as in *low*. But her heart wouldn't settle down, so she spun away, twirling to Johnny Cash and nearly levitating with joy—until something hit the house.

Bam!

Holy cats, was somebody at the door?

Only if they can fly.

She'd finished demolishing the porch, so the door opened onto thin air, almost four feet above the ground. Plus a visitor would have to get past the Baileys' dog. Bruce was a big, old love bucket, but you couldn't tell to look at him. Half mastiff and half something undetermined—tiger, or maybe rodeo bull—he was a real guard dog, or so Heck Bailey said. Bruce inspired fear even in dog lovers, and she had no doubt he'd protect her if necessary.

Bam!

Well, not *much* doubt. He did have a weakness for Milk Bones—and for any sort of human attention. The love bucket was never, ever full.

Clutching the towel to her chest, she tiptoed down the stairs, telling herself there was no need to worry. In case anybody got past Bruce, Heck Bailey had shown her how to use the shotgun that hung above the door.

Her damp feet left funny barefoot prints on the stairs. She'd be sure to clean those up, clean everything long before the Baileys got home. She'd make sure…

Bam!

The door flew open, the knob slamming against the wall and knocking a sprinkle of chipped plaster to the floor. Clutching the banister, Riley watched a massive figure climb into the opening and stand, silhouetted against the starry, snow-filled night. It was a mountain of hulking male. Powerful muscles. Lowering brows. And beneath those brows, dark eyes focused and fierce as a beast spotting prey.

Bruce, Heck Bailey's mighty guard dog, stood beside the visitor, grinning from ear to ear and dripping drool, utterly failing his first test as a guard dog.

Riley glanced up at the shotgun and realized she could reach for it or clutch the towel around herself. Not both.

Maybe she wouldn't have that family Christmas after all.

Maybe she wouldn't make it home.

CHAPTER 2

FOR THE FIRST TIME, GRIFF HAD TO ADMIT HIS COMMAND SERgeant might have been right when he'd said something inside Griff's psyche had snapped. Because surely Riley James wasn't standing nearly naked in his father's front hallway to welcome him home.

"Bruce!" she cried. "Come! Sit."

The dog flashed Griff an apologetic grin and trotted inside to lower his enormous butt to the floor beside nearly naked Riley.

Yep, he was definitely hallucinating.

"Griff. It's you." Riley's eyes were so wide, she looked like a startled doe poised to run. "The porch… Um, it fell down. I mean, mostly. That's why I'm here. To fix it."

That odd, throaty voice was real enough. Griff almost groaned as it stroked his backbone like the slow glide of a bow. That slim body, that pale narrow face, those otherworldly eyes—there was something about Riley James that got to him. She'd always tugged at his loins like she had him on a string.

Which she did, in a way. How often had he thought of her in the desert, remembering his last night at home? Stars winking overhead, the quarry a dark mystery beyond the rocks, the flicker of the bonfire lighting her face, and the warmth of her hand in his. Those eyes, those crazy eyes, had drawn out all his secrets and dreams.

He'd thought of that night too often—and for all the wrong reasons.

"You should go," he said.

"Wow, thanks. Hi to you, too." She clutched the towel tighter. "I will, soon as I can, okay? Nobody told me you were coming. I'm n—I need to get dressed."

He nodded, strangely bereft. Partly because she was going to get dressed, but also because he could tell he scared her. There wasn't much that scared Riley, so apparently he wasn't hiding his issues as well as he thought.

"I need to get back to the store," she said. "I'm making dinner for Ed's sisters. They're coming in tonight for the holidays."

"Okay. You should probably hurry." Shoving his hands in his pockets, he hunched his shoulders. "I came here to be alone."

He wasn't sure if that night at the quarry mattered anymore or if she wanted it to. He did—but then, he wanted lots of things. A fifth of Jim Beam, a tin of Red Man chewing tobacco, and something, anything, that would make him forget what had happened overseas. None of those things was good for him, any more than he'd be good for Riley.

But those things he could resist. Her? Wrapped in a towel, looking so clean and untouched? That was a challenge he wasn't sure he could meet, so he needed to get her gone.

Riley remembered a long-ago night by the quarry and wondered what had happened to *that* Griff Bailey. The one who was strong but gentle. The one she'd trusted instinctively. The one who'd set her free.

Up until that night, her encounters with men had been ugly and short, but Griff had been different—sweet, really, and kind in a way that resurrected all her foolish dreams. She'd seen him ride a bucking bronco to a standstill at the local rodeo once and thought he might be the cowboy she'd always wanted. Not that she deserved her very own cowboy, one that came with a normal life and a family—but her friends had found theirs, and she sure wanted one. And back then, Griff had been an honest-to-God, true-blue, one hundred percent cowboy.

But something had changed. His presence filled the air with a strange, simmering intensity. She sensed fierce need and too much testosterone smoldering in his gaze. All this time, she'd thought of him as a protector, not a predator, but now danger came off him in waves.

She was through with dangerous men. She'd promised herself she'd never risk her heart—or her safety—again. So why did she have to press her legs together to still the fluttering butterfly wings thrumming down there, demanding his attention, his touch?

Shaking her head in disgust, she felt the towel around her hair as it gave way and flailed to catch it as it spiraled in slow motion down her back to the floor. Her hair was long, a shade of blond so ashen it looked silver. She knew men liked it, but she didn't want this man to like her hair or anything else about her.

His gaze followed the towel to the floor, then climbed back up the length of her, stroking her legs, tracing the hem of the bath sheet, and settling on the spot where those foolish butterflies beat their heated wings. Could he *sense* them somehow? She clenched her legs tighter as his gaze moved up over her breasts to where her hand clutched the towel and on to her face.

Twisting out a wry sideways smile, she hoped he couldn't see it trembling at the edges.

"Don't get all excited now," she said.

"I won't," he said. "Not *now*."

A slow smile wiped away his anger, and those dark eyes held her like she was another kind of butterfly—the kind they kept in museums pinned to a board.

What did he mean, 'not now'? Like…like maybe later?

Something deep inside her hoped so, which was not good. Not good at all.

Griff Bailey wasn't what she was looking for.

Not anymore.

—ᴠᴠ—

Griff shoved his hands in his pockets. He could hook an arm around Riley's slim waist, let that towel fall, and pull her close, but he saw the fear in her eyes and was sane enough to stop.

Not now, he'd said, and he'd meant it. But later? Later was up for grabs.

He took a step toward her. Her eyes widened, afraid, and that fear sparked a loss so keen he wasn't sure he could stand it. Once, she'd trusted him, and he'd known that was a gift she didn't give lightly.

"What are you doing here?" He tried to gentle his tone, but his voice came out raspy and rough.

Setting a hand on the dog's wide head, she seemed to find courage. "I told you, the porch fell down. I'm staying here while I fix it. Doing some other work in the house, too, and taking care of the animals. Nobody told me you were coming."

"They didn't know."

"Oh." She turned away, cheeks flushed. "Okay. Guess I'll change my plans. Go back to Ed's, or—or something."

She headed up the stairs. He wanted to follow her, but he'd been lucky to tame her once, and it clearly wasn't going to happen again. Back at the quarry, she'd acted brash and bold, but she'd been frightened as a fawn in the grass, and when she'd curled into him as if for protection, he'd felt more of a man than he ever had before or since.

He wished he could be that man again, but he could tell by the look in her eyes that chance was long gone.

"I'll be in the barn," he mumbled.

"Okay." She clutched the towel to her chest. "Um, this is Bruce. Your dad found him on the highway, just before they left, and um, he thought the dog should stay because…" She looked panicked, and he figured she didn't want to admit his dad had kept the dog so Riley wouldn't be alone and unprotected. "Because he liked him, I guess," she said. "His food's in the kitchen, and he sleeps in the house, not the barn, okay? On the bed. Don't worry. He's a good boy."

Griff eyed the dog. He didn't mind sharing his bed, but the dog wasn't the partner he had in mind.

"No funny business, okay?"

Riley sounded stern as a schoolmarm, and Griff wondered how to answer without making a promise he might not be able to keep.

"No humping," she continued. "And no pooping in the house."

He hoped to God she was talking to the dog.

Upstairs, Riley dressed hastily and gathered her things, hyper-aware of Griff's presence even though he'd stomped off to the barn. The disloyal dog had followed, abandoning her. She'd worried the animal was becoming too attached to her, but apparently not.

Cramming her feet into her boots and wrapping her scarf around her neck, she grabbed her backpack and racewalked out to her pickup.

"I'm leaving," she called.

The dog came to the barn door, but Griff didn't answer. That was fine with her. He'd figure it out, and hadn't he said he wanted to be alone? Let him be alone, then. She had stuff to do.

Her old Chevy LUV's engine churned uselessly on the first try but roared to life on the second. Her pickup ran better than it looked—a darn good thing, since its baby-blue paint was scarred with rust—but getting it moving was another matter. The bald back tires spun, caught, then fishtailed and spun some more.

Slow down. Breathe.

Putting one hand on her chest, she calmed herself, then eased the accelerator down, slowly releasing the clutch so the car glided over the snow.

Steering carefully down the long drive, she wondered what to do. There was no way Griff had driven all the way to this remote corner of Wyoming for an afternoon visit. He must be staying at the Diamond Jack, and that was definitely a problem. She'd been living there while she worked on installing en suite bathrooms for all the bedrooms.

Holy cats, that was a problem, too. She doubted Mr. I Came Here to Be Alone would approve of turning the family home into a swanky, five-star dude ranch, but that was what she was being paid to do.

The Baileys had asked her to house-sit while she worked, so she'd been taking care of the animals and picking up the mail, too. That had left her apartment above the store available for Ed's sisters, who had probably moved in already, which made her officially, if temporarily, homeless for the holidays.

She shivered. She'd been homeless for real before, and she'd never forgotten how the ordinary became dangerous and the darkness, once a sanctuary for sleep, became an enemy even as the light of day made her vulnerable, visible.

She glanced in the rearview mirror and saw the ranch spread out behind her. Dusk had fallen, and the timers had turned on the twinkle lights indoors and out, making the place look as pretty as a Christmas card.

Surely the season would soften Griff some. He must have had many magical holidays in that beautiful old house. Molly had decorated the place before she'd left, and Riley wished she could see Griff's face when he came in from the barn and saw the lights. The tree was decorated with heirloom ornaments like Ed's, only most of the Baileys' were obviously made by Griff and his sister as kids—Popsicle-stick creations, plaster handprints, and Styrofoam snowmen.

Riley had loved sitting on the overstuffed sofa in her pajamas once the day's work was done, enjoying the lights and thinking Christmas thoughts of angels and guiding stars, Santa Claus and carols. She wondered if Griff would do the same.

Probably not. He didn't look like a man who had a lot of Christmas thoughts in him.

CHAPTER 3

GRIFF STOOD IN THE SHADOWED MAW OF THE BARN, WATCHING Riley's little pickup fishtail down the drive. Her old Chevy LUV looked like a toy compared to the Jeep, and it was probably rear-wheel drive, but she'd handled the snow pretty well. Once she got to the main road, it would be clear sailing, so he might as well pack up the rescue fantasies flitting through his head. Riley was stronger than she looked. She didn't need his help.

Maybe you need hers.

Shaking the thought out of his head, he returned to the horse stalls. A few caged light bulbs cast a golden light on the barn's interior, and the frost-edged windows framed a twilit fairy-tale world that reminded him it was almost Christmas. Snow used to be just one more obstacle that made the endless chores harder, but right now, that didn't sound so bad. He'd missed snow. Hell, he'd missed chores, too.

A horse shifted its weight and his mind settled, soothed by the familiarity of the sound. Looking down at his hands, he realized his fists had been clenched so long they hurt. That happened a lot. Memories would surface and he'd struggle to shove them down, only to have more rise. It was like a video game, but one without levels or any way to win.

There were no cattle in the barn, which meant they must be in the pasture east of the house, probably sheltering from the storm in the wide loafing shed he and his dad had built. He needed to check on them.

"Cattle first," his dad had always said. "Every rancher knows the livestock has to be your number one concern."

Griff kind of thought your kids should be your number one

concern, but he'd put the goddamn cattle first all his life until he managed to find a way to live without cattle, cattle, cattle taking up all his time and energy.

"I'd be happy if I never saw another cow," he told the dog. "But dogs are okay. And horses."

Actually, horses were more than just okay. As he inhaled the sweet scent of hay, the musty smell of their breath, and all the less-desirable odors wafting from the stalls, his childhood came rushing back. He'd spent a lot of time shoveling those less-desirable things into a wheelbarrow, and the manure pile outside had seemed like a metaphor for his life, but now that drudgery didn't sound so bad. Ranch work might be hard, but it was routine and blessedly brainless. Wearing himself out might be the best way to clear his mind.

His mind apparently didn't want to be clear, because it drifted back to Riley. He remembered the way she'd looked in that towel, the way her eyes had lit on his, just for a moment. The way they'd answered his need with her own, he could swear. He imagined reaching for her, taking her hand, leading her up the stairs, and then…

And then the barn roof exploded with a percussive *bang* and he dropped to the floor, hands locked over his head, heart pounding, ducking to avoid the beams and shingles that would rain down any moment.

Bomb.

He could feel his brain shrinking to the back of his skull, trying to hide. The horses would need help, but he couldn't move, couldn't even lift his head. Everything inside him was boiling, buzzing. It was all he could do to hold himself together.

He squeezed his eyes shut and did his best to breathe.

———

Riley tapped on the side door that led to Ed's apartment behind the store. When he didn't answer, she opened it and stuck her head in.

"Ed?"

There was no answer, but a wash of golden light from the Christmas tree in the living room calmed her nerves. She'd decorated the place last week, heaping pine boughs on the mantel, decorating a fresh-cut fir with the red-and-gold ornaments Ed and his late wife, Ruth, had collected. Riley found the glow relaxing, but as she hung her scarf and coat on a hook in the hall closet, she heard a woman laugh, high and tinkling—false, but festive.

Some people try too hard. But don't judge. You probably will, too. These women mean so much to Ed.

What if they hate you? What if they send you away?

Riley found herself in a familiar place: hanging on the edge of a cliff, clinging to respectability with her fingernails, her grip slipping every time she allowed herself to remember her past and who she'd been.

But look at who you are. That was what Ed always said. And since these women loved him, too, they'd surely get along. Ed's parents had passed away when he was young, and they'd practically raised him. Riley had always thought they were the reason he was so mild-mannered and kind, and she had to love them for that.

Taking a deep breath, she made her entrance, hoping no one could see she was shaking inside.

Ed was in his ratty old chair, like always, looking a bit lost. The sisters stood nearby. Sharp-nosed and thin, they were female versions of Ed, but with hair coiffed so perfectly it didn't look real. They weren't tall, but they were very upright, as if they'd spent their teen years balancing books on their heads to perfect their posture—because they had. Ed had told Riley so, and she'd tried it herself, mincing around the room with one of his old-fashioned ledgers on her head. Ruth had died not long before, and he'd needed that smile.

The two women sensed her presence at exactly the same time and turned to look at her in unison. It was creepy, the way they mirrored each other, but Riley smiled brightly and held out her hand.

"Hello. I'm Riley, Ed's, um, helper in the store. I've waited so long to meet you. He talks about you all the…"

"Hmm." Carol looked her up, then down. She was the one with the blond hair, Riley remembered, and Diane was the dark one.

Dropping her hand, adjusting her Henley to cover her tattoo, Riley wished she'd worn something nicer. Or *bought* something nicer. Her work didn't demand much of a wardrobe.

"I, ah, came straight from a job." Her voice kept breaking. It did that when she was nervous and made her sound like a twelve-year-old boy.

"I thought you worked *here*," Diane said. "When we got here, Ed was doing *everything*."

Ed stood, wiping his hands on the thighs of his jeans. "Riley works most days, but I pitch in so she can do outside jobs. She's an expert at home renovation. Got her certificate and everything."

The sisters just stared.

Riley edged toward the kitchen. "Well, I'd better check on dinner."

Hopefully her coq au vin would thaw them out. Bustling into the kitchen, she grabbed an apron from a hook by the door, popping the straps over her head. As she tied it around her waist, she looked up and gasped.

There was a man—youngish, slight, disreputable looking—in the kitchen. He was emptying the liquor cabinet, lining up bottles on the countertop. Dusty and mostly unopened, they held weird booze Ed had gotten for gifts, like plum wine and black cherry brandy. Riley didn't drink, and Ed only had a finger of whiskey now and then, so the cupboard mostly stayed closed.

As she watched, the stranger took out the one bottle that mattered, an expensive anniversary bottle of Jack Daniels she'd bought after Ed's doctor had told him a drink now and then would be good for his heart. Ed, being Ed, had never cracked the seal. He'd said he was saving it for her wedding, and she hadn't had the heart to tell him she was living her happily-ever-after now at the store. Her life was as good as it was likely to get.

As she watched, the stranger cracked the seal.

"Hey," Riley said. "What are you doing? That's Ed's."

The man turned. She'd thought he might be with Carol or Diane, but he didn't look like their type. Pale, with a sickly sheen to his skin, he was thin in a wasted sort of way. A *druggie* sort of way.

She started to back out of the room, but then the stranger spoke.

"You must be that *girl*. The one who lives with old Ed." The guy said "girl" like he was saying "cockroach," and he made it sound like she and Ed were up to something dirty. That ticked her off.

"I work for Ed and rent the apartment upstairs," she said. "Who are you?"

"I'm Trevor. Ed's *grandnephew*." Rummaging through the cupboards, he found a glass and poured himself a massive draft of Jack. "So I don't *have* to ask Ed anything, because he's my great-*uncle*."

"Oh. Um, excuse me." Riley moved past him to check on the stew, acting busy so she'd have time to think.

When she opened the oven, the fantastic smell that wafted out told her Ed had put the dish in right on time, even though she'd forgotten to call and remind him. Her mind racing, she moved reflexively around the kitchen. *Open the stove, close the stove. Lower the temperature, get the foil, wrap the rolls.* Ed hadn't mentioned a grandnephew. *Open the fridge, get out the broccoli.* Certainly not one with, well, issues. *Close the fridge, find the colander. Rinse the broccoli…*

Ed walked into the room with Carol and Diane just as Trevor drained his glass. Riley wondered if Carol was his grandma or if he belonged to Diane. Her money was on Carol, because she was blond, too.

"Trevor, put that back." Turning to Ed, Carol said, "*We* rarely drink, of course. But it's a special occasion, especially for Trevor. He's been living in Denver, and it's so nice to have him with us. Plus we haven't seen you in so long."

She gave Riley a narrow-eyed glare, as if that was her fault, but nobody had stopped them from coming. They could have come when Ruth got sick or at least attended the funeral.

Ed touched his sister's arm as if pleading for understanding. "Riley's made a nice meal for us, and look at the decorations! I never could have done it without her."

"Those are *Ruth's* decorations," Diane sniffed.

"That's right. Riley and I met because of Ruth," Ed said. "Ruth fainted while she was running the store one day. Riley took care of her until I got home, and then—well, we decided to keep her." His smile was forced, but his words warmed Riley's heart. That was just how it had happened. "Ruth loved Riley like a…" He caught Riley's wide-eyed warning look. "She just loved her." He tilted his chin up, looking like a little boy defying his mother. "And so do I."

Poor Ed. His face was red, and veins stood out on his forehead. Riley hadn't seen him this stressed since Ruth died, and she worried for his heart. His blood pressure was a concern already, and she tried to keep his stress level low.

"Why don't you all go relax out by the tree?" she said. "I'm just here to make dinner for you."

As the sisters stalked out of the kitchen with their noses in the air, Riley eyed Trevor. He definitely had the pallor of a drug user—a frequent user. She should know—she'd been one once and fought her way out. This guy didn't look like he had much fight in him, although he was slurping down Jack Daniels like he was fighting sobriety—or maybe withdrawal.

She chopped up the broccoli, wondering how someone like him, with a family who loved him, fell into drug use. For Riley and most people she knew, drugs had seemed like the only escape from the unrelenting ugliness of poverty and abuse. That wasn't an excuse. There were no excuses. But at least it was a *reason*. Trevor probably did drugs for fun.

Gathering silverware, she paused. Four or five? Much as she'd been looking forward to this dinner, she wasn't sure she wanted to eat with the Harpies after all. Maybe she'd eat out here by herself.

No. That would only upset Ed, and besides, sharing a meal was the best way to get to know people. Folks were usually more polite when they ate, especially women of the Harpies' generation.

As she circled the table, doling out silverware, she tried to absorb the warmth of the Christmas lights, but their shine seemed brittle now, and the warmth of the fire couldn't get past the waves of hostility coming from Carol and Diane.

Lighting the red and green candles she'd set in a centerpiece of fresh pine boughs, she squared her shoulders. It might not be what she'd hoped for, but it *was* Christmas. She'd find the good in these people somehow, and maybe they'd warm to her—at least a little.

CHAPTER 4

GRIFF WOKE TO SOMETHING SMELLY AND WET SLAPPING HIS face. Reaching out, he patted straw beside him, then palmed a hard skull covered with fur. Running his hand over the bony contours, he remembered.

Dog.

It was Bruce. He was in the barn. It had exploded, right? But everything seemed normal, like nothing had happened. He could see stars winking through the missing shingles in the roof like always, and the horses were munching their hay.

But he couldn't have imagined that explosion. He wasn't *that* crazy.

He glanced over at the closest horse, a pretty Arabian mare. She was pressed against the back wall of her stall, her hide gleaming with sweat. Her nostrils were flared, and her ears were pinned—so something had clearly happened.

Griff sighed. Apparently, *he'd* happened. From what he could see, he'd imagined the explosion, then fed the horse his imaginary fears.

Closing his eyes, he clenched his fists and let them go. Clenched them and let them go.

Breathe, breathe.

He savored the familiar scent of the barn, let it settle his senses. Took in the sounds of the winter night—the soft breath of the horses, the cooing of mourning doves perched in the rafters.

Oh. Doves in the rafters.

That was what he'd heard. A covey of startled birds had burst from their perches, making a sound like a shotgun blast. Doves tended to do that twenty times a day, because their brains were the size of dried peas.

So was Griff's, apparently. He knew he was safe here. That was why he'd come. Although the hard work of ranching had been the bane of his adolescence, it allowed for an orderly parade of events. Life marched on, season to season, with predictable rituals he'd known since birth. Disasters were small—a failed crop, a runaway horse, a calf dead in the birthing. That was as bad as it got, and right now, he was fine with that—or should have been.

But if he couldn't deal with frightened doves, could he deal with anything? Maybe his commander was right. Maybe he was damaged goods.

"Tell you what," he said to the frightened horse. "This'll be our secret. You don't tell what a mess I am, and I'll try not to scare you again."

Clearly unconvinced, the animal pressed her haunches into the corner of her stall and rolled her eyes.

Well, that was that. Griff would feed the horses and turn them out, but he'd stay away from any training or riding. Horses saw inside a man, sensed intentions and emotions, and this one had seen the fear in him. He'd passed it on, and who knew how long it would take for her to get over it? Most of his dad's horses had been abused at one time.

He'd chosen the life of a soldier. He'd never wanted the ranch, not at all, and even if he wasn't quite the hero he'd hoped to be, even if he feared his own dreams and had come running home to hide, he'd never wanted to be a cowboy.

So what was he supposed to do with the aching sense of loss he felt when the horse backed away?

Ed Boone stood in the door to the kitchen, hands hanging limply at his sides. Riley didn't turn and smile, like she usually did, or invite him to help. She just kept scrubbing, her head hanging low over the sink like she needed to polish each plate to gleaming perfection. She was crying, he was sure, but she didn't want him to know.

Dinner had been a disaster. Carol and Diane had sniffed Riley's savory stew and refused to eat it because it had alcohol in it. Well, it did, but Riley had explained how the alcohol was all cooked out, leaving only the flavor of the wine. Which was delicious, by the way.

Trevor obviously didn't have anything against drinking alcohol. That bottle had been a gift from Riley, and Ed had wanted to snatch it right out of the boy's hand. He was saving it for her wedding day, knowing she'd someday find love and start a family despite her protests. Much as he'd miss her, he'd be glad to see her make her way in the world. It would be something to celebrate.

He guessed most parents and grandparents thought that way, except his sisters, who seemed intent on keeping Trevor close. The way they watched the boy's every move made Ed nervous, so he couldn't imagine how Trevor felt. The boy's parents had died in a car crash when he was barely a teen, but that tragedy was no excuse for his rudeness.

The kid probably got that from Carol and Diane. They'd certainly set a terrible example tonight. They always put on airs, yet their manners at the table had been no better than a farmhand's. Worse, in fact. Farmhands generally ate what was put in front of them.

That was what Ed had done. He'd even eaten those pearl onions, the ones that reminded him of eyeballs. Yeesh, they felt funny going down—but he'd rather eat eyeballs than hurt Riley's feelings.

He stood in the door to the kitchen, wringing his hands, longing to apologize but unable to find the words. There was a burning pressure in his chest that had built throughout the night, as if something inside him wanted out. He hoped his heart wouldn't act up again, but he was sure it would break watching Riley try so hard.

He cleared his throat and she turned quickly, as if she hadn't known he was there. Her hand flew to her face to dash away tears, splashing soapy water.

"Probably looks like I'm crying, huh?" She gave him a shaky smile. "I got soap in my eyes."

"You look fine," he said. "You handled that with real grace, hon. I'm proud of you and ashamed of them." He sighed and slumped against the cabinets. "They're difficult. Always were."

"It's okay."

"No, it's not." He picked up a dish towel and began to dry while she washed.

"I didn't know Trevor was coming, but he can use my second bedroom," Riley said. "I have it set up as an office, but there's that daybed."

"I think they're hoping he'll stay a while, though, and Riley, that's your home. He's got problems, I guess, and they think it would do him good to stay here."

"Well, they're right. You helped me with my problems."

Ed snorted. "You helped yourself with your problems, hon, and then moved on and fixed mine. Plus you're the one who made that attic so nice, and they've got no right." He sighed. "The Baileys will be back around Christmas, right?"

"Not sure." She dumped the contents of the Dutch oven into a plastic storage container and snapped on the lid. "But Griff's back, so it's kind of awkward to stay. I mean, there's plenty of room, but…"

"Griff's back?" Ed remembered Griff Bailey. He'd been a good boy, hard-working and respectful but quiet. Still, he'd be a man now, so Riley might not feel safe staying there. Ed didn't know her whole history, but he'd seen her fear when male customers came in angry about some product they'd bought. He didn't want her to have to deal with Griff, who was a big guy and just returned from the war. So he'd have to... have to...

He didn't know what he'd do. There was no room at the inn. Or rather, the hardware store.

"I'll be over there working all the time when I'm not at the store, so I can stay in the office like I used to." Riley flashed him a smile. "Remember? In the old days, before we really knew each other."

Ed was ashamed of those old days. Riley had truly been an angel to him and Ruth, but they'd heard ugly things about her, so she'd slept in the office rather than their home. It had taken them too long to see she deserved their trust and their love.

"I don't want you there, Riley. I mean, I want you here, but you need a better place to sleep."

She shrugged. "It's fine. You know I've had worse."

Now Ed's eyes were leaking. Riley should live in a castle of gold as far as he was concerned. Back when Ruth's MS had gotten bad, her care had exhausted him. Riley, a regular at the store, had quietly taken over, first in the store as a volunteer helper, then with Ruth herself, spending nights by her side so he could rest, doing all the private, womanly things that made Ed uneasy.

He owed this girl everything—so why couldn't he stand up for her? He'd needed to grow a backbone all his life, and if he couldn't do it for Riley, he was really a lost cause.

"You can't sleep on that cot," he said. "They might be the ugly stepsisters, but you're not Cinderella."

"You're right, I'm not." Riley barked out her funny, hoarse laugh. "Cinderella was a good girl."

"So are you."

"Now. But I wasn't always, and they know that. It's okay, Ed. The cot is fine."

"You deserve more." Tears stood in Ed's eyes, blurring his vision. "So much more."

She flashed him a crooked grin. "If I deserve it, I'll get it. That's the way the world works." She sobered and touched his arm. "Oh, no. Are you crying, Ed?"

"No." He turned away, swiping at his face. "Just soap in my eyes."

CHAPTER 5

Griff woke the next morning with a start. He'd been dreaming he was in downtown Wynott when he'd spotted three figures draped in black scuttling along the cracked sidewalks like beetles. They were dashing into doorways, poking their heads out, then racing to the next hiding place.

He'd chased them, making them scamper faster. Finally, he'd caught up with one and put his hand on its black-clad shoulder. The figure spun around, lifting its veil, and he saw—something. He didn't know what, because he flailed his arms at the sight and struck his hand on the corner of the nightstand. The pain woke him and wiped the image away. He could only remember it was something bad, something wrong. A corpse, or an animal head.

Dammit. He'd been sure home would heal him, but the desert haunted his sleep every night. Even here in the middle of a real-life Christmas card, he could swear he smelled the musty scent of canvas cooked in the sun and heard angry voices arguing in a language he didn't know. Hell, he could still hear them as if they were right outside. And he couldn't move his legs.

He jerked upright, listened harder, and let out a dry, mirthless chuckle. Those weren't hostiles at his window; they were his dad's tom turkeys, bossing their lady hens around the chicken house. And the weight on his legs? It was Bruce, who'd apparently disobeyed Griff's orders and hopped up on the bed during the night.

Maybe Griff could solve all his problems by training the dog better and eating those feathered terrorists for Christmas dinner.

Heading downstairs, he shoved a few logs in the woodstove and made coffee. Once he'd taken care of the horses, he fed Bruce and settled down to read for a while. He'd developed a taste for Louis

L'Amour paperbacks overseas, and he longed for that author's Old West, where there were good guys and bad guys, white hats and black. Every western woman was a paragon of virtue, every cowboy her noble defender.

He was thoroughly lost in that world when somebody knocked on the front door.

Riley. She's back.

He racewalked to the door, tripping on a throw rug and barely catching himself before opening the door. He stared out at the snowy landscape, confused by the white-laced trees. It had been summer in his book.

Plus there was nobody there. That made sense, though, since the door opened into thin air. "Down here," said a small voice.

He looked down to see Fawn Swanson standing in the snow, looking cute as a bunny in a puffy white parka with fur around the hood. Snowflakes sparkled on her eyelashes as she blinked up at him, smiling sweetly, and she held up an aluminum pan like an offering.

"Hey, Griff."

Fawn had the kind of wholesome, ranch-raised beauty that had made her Wynott's golden girl in high school—class president, prom queen, and the top of every cheerleader pyramid. The teenaged Griff had been dazzled by the way her heart-shaped face had lit up when she smiled, and he'd never tired of watching her leap and spin, cheering with the squad on game nights. Football, once a duty demanded by his size and strength, had become a mission once he'd noticed Fawn. But she'd been golden, while Griff, at best, had been bronze.

Oh, he'd had his admirers. Ranch chores had piled the muscle on, and he'd had some success on the rodeo team as well as the gridiron. He'd never had much to say, and he'd worried about boring his dates, but his silence had apparently made him irresistible. That was too bad, because he hadn't been interested in anyone but the unattainable Fawn. Every date had ended with a chaste kiss and a promise, soon broken, to call.

Fawn hadn't changed a bit, but apparently, he had—because looking down at her, he didn't feel anything except a vague, heavy thud of disappointment. Maybe Riley wasn't coming back. Maybe he'd blown it.

Fawn raised the pan a little higher. "I brought you something."

He needed to let her in, but it was a long way down. He could go down there and hoist her up, but that would be awkward.

"I hope you like lasagna," she said.

"Sure." He bent down for the pan, then pulled his hands away so fast she almost dropped it.

"Is it hot?" he asked.

"No, silly. I'm holding it, aren't I?"

Her laugh sounded like silver stars tumbling into a pristine mountain lake, but it cut off midtinkle.

"I'm sorry," she said. "I know it was terrible, all your *experiences* overseas." Her tone was gentle, like she was talking to a sick person, and her eyebrows angled up in an expression of—what was that?

Pity.

That was the last thing he wanted.

"It wasn't so bad." He set his book on the floor and took the dish, then stood there awkwardly. "Well, thanks."

She looked up at him from under shyly lowered lashes. "Can I come in?"

"Sure."

He glanced around, wondering how she'd manage. Riley had hoisted herself in and out easily, but he couldn't expect Fawn to be that tough. Riley was a survivor from the hard-knock life, while Fawn had been pampered to perfection since birth. Her dad was a successful rancher and her mom owned a hair salon with the dreadful name Wynott's Top-Knots. That was successful, too, despite the name.

"How about the side door?" she asked.

"Yeah. Right." Darn it, he should have thought of that. For some reason, the simplest things seemed complicated today. It was like thinking through mud.

When he let her in the kitchen door, she looked up, wide-eyed, as if she'd never seen a man before. Silence stretched out while he fished around for words.

Finally, Fawn spoke. "So how are you doing?"

"Fine."

She fluttered her lashes at him, lips parted breathlessly, as if she expected him to say something important. When he didn't, she flexed her mouth just the slightest bit, and a shadow of annoyance crossed those crystal-blue eyes. That didn't surprise him. He'd always come up short in Fawn's eyes.

Then the shadow of a pout turned into a smile, and he could swear the sun turned up a notch. "I heard about what you did over there." She wasn't quite meeting his eyes; she seemed to be looking over his left shoulder.

He turned, following her line of sight, and saw the dishes drying on the counter.

"Oh, that wasn't me. It was Riley."

"I didn't mean…oh." Fawn seemed shocked. "Riley James? Are you and her… Are you…?"

"What? No. She's here fixing the porch."

"Oh. Okay. Well, I meant I heard about what you did *overseas*. Everyone's talking about how you saved so many lives."

He swallowed the urge to swear. He'd never intended to pollute his hometown by talking about what had happened, but apparently the word was out. And judging from the shine in Fawn's pretty eyes, the word wasn't accurate.

"How did anybody hear about that shit?"

He probably shouldn't swear at Fawn, but he needed her to stop talking about his *experiences*. Nothing that happened in Iraq should come to Wynott. Ever.

"You're a hero," she said. "It was in the paper and everything."

"Sorry." He wondered why he had to repress a desperate urge to shove the former woman of his dreams back out the door and slam it. "Want to come in? Sit down?"

"Sure."

She followed him into the family room.

"What's that?" She clutched Griff's arm and pointed a trembling finger at a shadow beside the woodstove. The shadow had spooky amber eyes.

"That's just the dog. Riley says he's harmless."

"Really?" She huddled close to Griff until they got to the sofa. Sitting down, she patted the cushion beside her and smiled.

There'd been a time when having Fawn Swanson on his sofa would have been the culmination of all his dreams, but right now, sitting beside her made him uncomfortable.

"You're a hero," she repeated in a whisper as he sat down.

He stood so fast, she bounced back against the pillows. Shoving his hands in his pockets, he went to the window.

"Griff?" She followed him and set one hand on his arm. "Do you need to talk about it?"

"No. Sorry. I'm fine."

He knew he could use her pity to his advantage. It was clear she was expecting something more than conversation. But the mere mention of his supposed heroism made him sick.

"I'd love to get together when you're ready," Fawn said. "I know you've been through a lot." She ran her hand up his arm and down again, licking her lips. "I'm a really good listener."

The thought of dumping his ugly memories into Fawn's shell-pink ear made him nauseous. The whole reason he'd gone over there was to keep the ugliness from touching towns like Wynott and women like Fawn. Maybe that was sexist, but it was a primal urge he couldn't control.

He sure had a lot of those lately.

"Are you sure you're okay?" she pressed. "You can't close your-self off, you know. Don't bottle it up inside."

Who was she, Dr. Phil? He remembered the shrinks at the VA in Denver, the things he'd said to shut them down.

"I guess it's just not time," he said.

Fawn nodded sagely, biting her lip. "What about Sunday night?"

"That's probably too soon, too."

"I thought we could go to the Dawg," she continued as if he hadn't spoken. "Wayne wasn't getting much business on Sundays, so he offers two-for-one pizzas and dollar beers. I think it's going to break him, because everybody goes." She tittered. "And every-body wants to see you, so it'll be perfect."

He looked down at her blue, blue eyes and wished he could go back in time to when he'd been a less complicated person—one who'd thought *she* was perfect. He didn't feel that way anymore. He didn't feel much of anything.

Dang. If this war had made him impotent, he was going to sue the Department of Defense. He'd sworn to give his life for his country, but not that.

"I don't think I'm ready for the Red Dawg," he said. With that kind of deal on pizzas and beer, the place would be wall-to-wall Wynottians, and if Fawn had heard of his exploits, he could bet the whole town knew—or thought they did.

"Now, Griff." Setting her hands on those sweet, round hips, she frowned sternly. "You don't strike me as a man who dips his little toe in the shallow end of the pool."

"What?" Were they going swimming? At the Red Dawg? The place was already a senior center, a clubhouse, a grange hall, and a bar. Had Wayne managed to find yet another revenue stream by opening a public swimming pool?

"You seem like the kind of guy who jumps right into the deep end," she said.

"Well, yeah, but…"

"Good. Pick me up at five thirty." She wagged an admonishing finger. "Now I can tell you need some time to yourself, but Sunday, it's time to jump right back into life, okay?" She made a tearing motion with one hand like she was ripping off a Band-Aid. "You know it hurts less if you do it fast."

He wasn't sure what they were talking about at this point, but he did know one thing: he'd rather go back to the desert than go to the Dawg on Sunday. In fact, he'd rather stand up Fawn Swanson than go. Which was weird.

Why wasn't he jumping at the chance to be with his dream girl?

What the hell was wrong with him?

CHAPTER 6

RILEY MADE BACON AND EGGS FOR ED AND HIS FAMILY, THEN slipped out to open the store. She was sure Ed felt bad about how things were going, but although the cot was lumpier than she remembered, she'd slept fine.

She counted out the till, made change from the safe, then walked the aisles, making sure everything was shown to best advantage for the day ahead. She'd decorated the store for Christmas and was proud of her window display, which featured a life-size Styrofoam snowman wearing a hunter's cap and a Carhartt jacket, holding a snow shovel and waving a gloved hand. All around him were tools for taming winter: scrapers and emergency kits for cars, andiron sets for woodstoves, and an assortment of practical work gloves and woolen hats.

In spite of the snowman's welcoming wave, she suspected it would be a slow day. The sky threatened more snow, and the roads were already a challenge. So she was surprised when the bell on the door announced a customer before she was officially open.

Turning with a smile, she saw Griff Bailey, of all people, brooding and big as life. Her heart thrummed. Had he come to see her?

She tamped down that silly notion and kept her smile professional. She didn't *want* him to come see her, she reminded herself. This wasn't the old Griff Bailey but a new and not-so-improved version. The jolt of fear he inspired shouldn't be mistaken for attraction.

"What brings you to town?" she asked warily.

"An empty fridge." Scowling, he stamped snow off his boots. "There's a storm coming, and we haven't got any milk. Or beer. Or food."

"What do you mean, 'we'?"

"You're staying at the ranch, right?"

"No," she said. "But since I'll be coming back to town every day, I can pick up supplies for you. Just give me a list."

He grabbed a box of nails from a nearby shelf and frowned at it. He looked so fierce that Riley wondered why the nails didn't leap from the box and toss themselves on the floor in surrender.

When he looked up, his eyes were accusing under arched brows.

"Why don't you just stay? House is big enough."

"No, thanks." As warmth crept up from her chest, she turned away so he wouldn't see her blush. "And you're not going to find milk in here, you know." She fooled with the key lathe, plucking a blank from its hook, putting it back. "Or beer."

"I know. Just thought I'd check on you."

So he *had* come to see her? She tamped down a ridiculous burst of girlie excitement and called up something stronger: indignation.

"I'm not helpless, you know."

"Yeah, I know," he said. "I just want to know why you're not working on the porch. With Dad gone, it's up to me to see the work gets done, and I can't use the front door. You planning to get to it today?"

"Maybe." She frowned. Her body might like Griff Bailey—like him a whole lot—but he would not, could not, be the boss of her. "Your dad and I agreed on when I'd work, and you have no right to interfere." She jerked her head toward the window and the snow beyond. "Besides, it's too cold to work outside. I'll be doing inside renovations now."

"I was going to ask about that," he said. "Half the bedrooms are torn apart, and there's plumbing parts all up and down the stairs."

"I'm putting in some extra bathrooms." This probably wasn't a good time to tell him about the dude ranch plan, so she changed the subject. "But hey, since you're already here to get supplies, I'll probably stay in town today. No point in braving the storm."

Just then, the door to her apartment opened and the Harpies came down the stairs with Trevor.

Actually, they didn't come in *with* Trevor; they pushed him ahead of them, stumbling and reluctant. His hair was still disheveled from sleep, and his pallor had gotten worse.

"Can I help you?" Riley asked.

"Ed told us you'd train Trevor." Diane clutched her nephew's shoulder. "He needs to know how to run this place, being Ed's nephew and his only heir, but you've gone and started without him."

Riley kept her expression neutral. "I'd be glad to train him, of course. I just made you all breakfast first." She did her best to smile. "Now that he's here, I'll be glad to show him around."

Riley eyed Griff, who was watching the conversation like a spectator at a tennis game. His gaze lit on Riley, then the women, then the silent, sulking boy, and back again while his hands fisted and relaxed, over and over. He seemed angry, and she prayed he'd keep it to himself. She had enough problems with these people.

"Show him everything," Carol said. "He needs to learn."

"I'm not stupid," Trevor said. "I've been working in management, remember?"

Griff stepped forward. "Good, because Riley has to go."

"What?" Carol's eyes went wide, and Riley tried not to laugh. Griff dwarfed the two women, and they looked a little scared.

"She's working for me," he said. "My front door's four feet off the ground, and she needs to build me some steps." He grabbed Riley's arm in a proprietary way that made her want to smack him. "I need it done today, so what's your name? Trevor?"

The kid, who'd drifted off to finger the merchandise, jerked to attention. "Yeah? What?"

"You're on your own," Griff growled. "You got questions, ask your uncle."

Griff hoped Riley realized he wasn't normally this bossy. It was just that the two women got on his nerves. Everybody knew how much Riley had helped Ed when Ruth was sick, and the whole town wondered why his sisters had never showed up when he'd needed them.

Griff knew why they were here now. They must have heard Riley had made the store successful, and now they wanted a piece of the action. Hell, they wanted *all* the action for their precious "only heir," who looked about as enthusiastic as a death-row inmate—*after* the execution.

Shaking her arm out of Griff's grasp, Riley straightened her shirt and glared. Maybe he'd played the part of the difficult boss with a little too much gusto.

"I'm sure you can wait until this afternoon," she said. "As you can see, I have another commitment."

"Let the kid do it." Griff jerked a thumb toward the Only Heir. "My front door opens onto thin air. I had company this morning, and she had to climb in." Too late, he realized how that sounded. Riley would think he'd found himself a floozy. "Plus, I need help with that dog. He sat for you. When I tell him to sit, he just looks at me and walks away."

Ed walked in just then. His eyes were puffy and his thinning hair, still reddish despite his age, was sticking up around his bald spot.

"What's going on here?" he asked.

"You *said* your helper here would train Trevor, but she snuck down and opened the store herself," said Carol.

Griff was glad to see Ed straighten his spine.

"Guess we were too busy enjoying the delicious breakfast she made to do it ourselves," the old man said. "Thank you, Riley." He turned back to his sisters. "Trevor wasn't even awake last I saw."

"You should have woken him."

He should have woken himself. Griff waited for Ed to put the women in their place.

"Sorry," Ed said instead. His shoulders rounded again, and the harried look returned. "Riley, you go on and fix that porch for Griff. I'll show Trevor the ropes." He put his arm around the Only Heir's shoulders. The boy continued to look down at the floor as if he had the grace to be ashamed.

You ought to be. Mama's boy.

Griff took Riley's arm a little more gently. "Let's go."

He noticed one of the women pursing her lips as she watched them and quickly removed his hand. She looked like one of those church ladies, the kind who'd judge Riley if she found out about her past. Heck, she was probably judging her by her tattoos already. Riley was more covered up than usual, but he could see her sleeve tat peeking out from her cuff, and a feather from the tail of her phoenix waved just above her collarbone.

He liked knowing it was a phoenix and remembering the last time he'd seen it.

"Sorry," he said gruffly. "Just upset about the door."

Riley turned to Ed. "You okay with this?"

"Sure." Ed was okay with everything she did, and Riley knew it, but she always treated the dithery old man with respect.

"Just so you're sure," Riley said. "Because my first loyalty is to you. This store is always number one." She leveled a hard glare at Griff. "*You* need to understand that."

Shuffling his feet, he pretended to be cowed. "Okay. Sorry. But can we please go fix my porch?"

"Sure. I'll get my coat and tools." She ignored the sisters' pursed lips and narrowed eyes and gave Ed a hug. "See you later, okay? I'll be staying here tonight."

One of the women started to protest.

"In the office," Riley said. "There's a cot in there."

Riley might not know it, but she was staying at the ranch tonight. Tonight and all the rest of the nights these women and the Only Heir were around.

She'd probably hate him for butting in, but somebody had to stick up for her, and Ed obviously wasn't going to.

CHAPTER 7

THERE WAS NO SENSE CLEARING THE SIDEWALKS UNTIL IT QUIT snowing, so Wynott's plows hadn't been out yet. The blanket of snow smoothed the town's rough edges and rounded its corners.

Griff stopped at his truck, but Riley kept on walking.

"We should ride together," he said. "Snow's pretty bad."

The look she gave him made the temperature drop another five degrees. "I think I can handle it."

"It would make things easier. Plus we have to go to the store."

"There's no reason for us both to go. And it won't be easier when you have to drive me home later, after more snow's fallen, and then drive back."

"Okay. I'll see you at the ranch, then." He felt strangely disappointed. Had he really been looking forward to grocery shopping with a girl? He must be really hungry.

He watched her stomp off to her dinky little truck. If she made it to the ranch in that thing, he wouldn't have to find a way to make her stay. The forecast called for ten inches, and the Chevy LUV couldn't handle that.

"Need anything at the store?" he asked.

She turned and walked backward, facing him. She was dressed for the weather in a puffy white coat, boots that looked like buckets on her skinny legs, and a weird furry trapper's hat with earflaps that tied under her chin in a goofy, girlie bow. With her hair stuffed up into the hat, she looked even more like a kid than usual, except for those spooky, haunted eyes.

"Nope. I told you, I'm staying in town," she said. "You can take care of Bruce and the other animals, right?"

"I guess."

She grinned. "Come on. You've done it all your life. Did you forget all that cowboy stuff already?"

"No." She wanted to tease him? He'd show her teasing. Fixing his eyes on hers, he gave her a slow, smoldering smile. "I remember lots of things."

She turned away, blushing, and he relished a rush of triumph. For some reason, this conversation had become a competition, and he wanted to one-up her.

He wanted to do a lot of other things, too. Why hadn't his thoughts been this randy when he'd had Fawn Swanson sitting on his sofa? Maybe because he wasn't right for someone like Fawn anymore. Riley might be skinny as a weasel—*no, wait, that's not right; delicate as a ballerina, that's it*—but though Fawn was spunky and athletic, Riley was way tougher.

When she turned to walked backward again, the blush was gone. "I'm just glad *you* remember, because I've forgotten all about it." She grinned as if she'd won. Maybe she had, because he'd basically admitted he remembered that night at the quarry. That made him vulnerable, not to mention weak in the knees. Except…

"Forgotten about what?" he asked.

The blush returned. She looked away, then bit her lip and gave him a charming, crooked smile. "Oh, you know. Stuff."

She tried to toss her hair and nearly dislodged her ridiculous hat as her heel hit the drift that covered the sidewalk at the corner. Flailing her arms in the air, she sat down hard in the snow.

He hurried over to help her up. "Oops-a-daisy."

"Oops-a-*daisy*?" She brushed snow off her shoulder. "Is that a military term?"

He felt his own face heating and shrugged. "It's something my mom used to say."

Refusing his proffered hand, she rose with all the dignity she could muster—which wasn't much, considering she wore a hat that looked like a mangy muskrat, a coat that made her look like a marshmallow snack, and oversized Frankenstein boots. Tossing him a scornful look, she stomped off, and he wondered how she managed to look sexy in that getup. He couldn't see an inch of skin or even her shape, but he remembered what was under that coat. Her skin, her shape—even her scent.

He shook his head, dislodging the memory. He needed to keep his distance from Riley. She'd been broken long before he'd met her, and the last thing she needed was a broken man—which was what he was. That incident in the barn had proved it.

Turning away, he told himself he shouldn't have gone after her. There were other doors in the house, for heaven's sake, and nobody was going to get hurt unless he got drunk and forgot the porch was gone.

That was another good reason to keep Riley around. He'd been resisting the urge to anesthetize himself ever since he got home, and having her around would help. Not because she'd fix the door but because he didn't want to make a fool of himself in front of those haunting, all-seeing eyes.

—◦◦◦—

The old steps to the Bailey ranch house had barely survived the collapse of the porch, so it took Riley a while to move them up to the door so Mr. Bossy Butt Bailey wouldn't fall on his bossy Bailey butt.

"What do you think, Bruce?"

She'd been worried the dog would shift his allegiance to Griff, but his all-out prancing, dancing, slobbering greeting had eased her mind. He'd followed her everywhere since she'd returned, and now he grinned up at her with worshipful eyes while she tugged on the temporary railing, leaning her backside against the front door. It seemed a little rickety—a conclusion that was confirmed when the door suddenly swung inward and she fell into the house, tearing the rail from its moorings.

From her not-terribly-comfortable seat on the foyer floor, she glanced up at Griff, then down at the railing in her hand. "Guess I need to beef this up."

As Bruce took the opportunity to lollop up the stairs and park himself in Riley's lap, Griff's usual grim expression relaxed. He might have even smiled. She thought about getting up so she could fall down again, because he sure looked good smiling.

He put out a hand to help her up, but she ignored it, just like she had back on the sidewalk in town. He seemed to think she needed a protector, but she'd been taking care of herself since she was thirteen.

Maybe that's why you need one. Or deserve *one.*

Yeah, right. Men were never protectors. Not in the long run. They always used you in the end. And while Griff Bailey still seemed like a good guy despite his freaking mood disorder or whatever, he was still a man. She preferred Bruce.

"Sorry," Griff said. "I was just going to ask you…"

"It's okay. I needed to come in anyway." She stood, brushing off her pants. "It's, like, ten degrees out. Can't believe you're making me work."

"You didn't have to work. I could have used the side door, no problem."

She frowned. "Then why have I been slaving away in the cold for three hours?"

"I just wanted to get you away from those women," he said. "And the 'only heir.'" He glared as if their presence was her fault. "I thought *you* were Ed's heir. That's what everybody else thinks, too."

"Well, everybody's wrong. Ed's got a real family. And he's done enough for me."

Mumbling something under his breath, Griff turned away.

Riley hated it when people mumbled. "If you have something to say, say it."

"All right, I will," Griff said. "I don't think Ed's come close to doing enough for you. Everyone knows Ruth would have ended up in a nursing home if you hadn't helped out, and he would have lost that store to medical bills. So I don't know why's he letting those women treat you like…"

"You know what? Stop right there." Her temperature rising, she flapped off her gloves and unzipped her coat. "I helped Ed and Ruth because it was the right thing to do and because I love them like family. Not so I'd inherit anything. That's ridiculous—not to mention *none of your business*."

He just stood there, looking even more fierce and immovable. He'd stepped way over the line, shoving his big nose in her business, and she wished she dared to shove him away. See how *he* liked landing on his butt.

Not that he had a big nose. It was a strong nose, sure, but not big. He had a nice profile. Strong, and kind of chiseled…

Oh, stop it. He's good-looking. Get over it.

As if he'd read her mind, he let one side of his mouth quirk up in an almost smile. His temper seemed to smooth out along with his expression.

"You want something hot to drink? I made hot chocolate."

"Really?" Darn it, she loved hot chocolate.

"With mini-marshmallows," he said. "Pink ones."

"Oh, no." She let her coat fall to the floor. "How'd you know I love those?"

"I saw Cap'n Crunch and Lucky Charms boxes in the dumpster."

Her heart warmed. She could almost forgive him for being so good-looking and so danged nosy.

Almost.

CHAPTER 8

Walking into the kitchen, Riley almost tripped over the grocery bags strewn across the linoleum.

"You don't mess around when you shop," she said.

"I was hungry. And I don't want to have to go back." Griff grabbed a few cans and began stocking the pantry cabinet. "Couple of my dad's friends were there. Smacking me on the back, going on about… Well. Nothing." He shook his head, grimacing.

She cocked her head, trying to figure out what he wasn't saying, because he was suddenly very busy, grabbing mugs out of a cupboard, nodding toward some boxes on the counter. "I got you Frosted Flakes for breakfast tomorrow. They actually have corn in 'em, so they're healthier than that other crap. And you drink two percent milk, right?"

"Right. But I'm not staying here, remember? Do *you* eat Frosted Flakes?"

"No, so you'll have to stay and help." He frowned, and she could have sworn the light dimmed. "You can't go back there."

"I can go wherever I want."

"Yeah, right. Except your own apartment."

A tornado rose in her chest, spinning hard, scraping up emotions she didn't even know were there—anger, embarrassment, hurt—and making them hotter, stronger. Hurt was right on top, twirling hard and fast, because Griff was right.

The Harpies had taken over her apartment, and they were probably going through her stuff as they spoke, looking for dirt. They wouldn't find anything—her life these days was blissfully dull—so they'd probably make something up because they wanted her out. They'd get what they wanted, of course, because sadly, their greed was stronger than Ed's love.

All that stuff she'd told Ed about getting what she deserved was total hogwash. You got what you worked for, if you were lucky. If you weren't… Well, you got this. People moving into your space, shoving you out into the street. It had happened before.

"I can't stay here," she said, thinking aloud. "I barely know you."

Griff looked hurt, which was fine with her. Maybe now he'd stop bringing up what he *remembered* and making her all squirmy inside.

She wasn't about to tell him how clearly she recalled that night in his Jeep, how a random whiff of woodsmoke or sweet pine would bring back the soft light in his eyes, that surprising tenderness. There was a hollow just below his shoulder where his skin was soft as a baby's, and his hands had been surprisingly gentle when he'd cupped her head and kissed her. He'd met her eyes with something in his own she'd never seen before. It hadn't been lust or triumph or the need that drove most men. It had looked strangely like reverence—or at least respect. And it had made her heart go soft in a way it never had before.

Stop it. It was a long time ago. He's changed.

Leaning on the counter, he looked down at her, and she realized that even standing still, doing nothing, he was the dominant force in any room. And she flat out, no kidding, absolutely *refused* to be dominated.

"Seriously," she said, jutting her chin and meeting his eyes with a challenge. "I'm leaving."

———

Griff poured a rich brown stream of cocoa from a saucepan into a pair of mugs and added a heap of mini-marshmallows to Riley's. She pushed the mug away, watching with hungry eyes as the marshmallows wobbled on the swaying liquid. She looked tired, too, and he wondered how much sleep she'd gotten, holed up in Ed's office on a cot. The thought of it made him burn inside.

"Look, you can stay here. I promise you're safe." He spread his arms to show how harmless he was, but the sudden motion made her cringe, so he dropped his hands to his sides and shoved them in his pockets. "I know better than to start anything, honestly. I'm not fit for any woman right now, and I plan to keep to myself. Just pretend I'm not here."

Reaching for the mug, watching him like a wary animal, she took a tentative sip.

"You can't go out in this weather anyway." He nodded toward the window. The rising wind lifted filmy, white snow ghosts from the new-fallen powder and waltzed them across the yard in looping circles. Two whirled around her truck, which was already hubcap-deep in a drift. "And you can't sleep on a cot."

She shot him a glare that would have been a lot more effective without a pink, sticky marshmallow mustache. It would also have been more effective without the fear in her eyes—the fear of a cornered animal. He suddenly realized he'd been barking orders, scaring her.

"I can sleep anywhere I want." She slid off the barstool a little too fast and took a single staggering step before she grabbed the counter, going pale. He reached to steady her, then dropped his hand and did his best to soften his tone.

"Did you eat lunch? Or any of the breakfast you made?"

She shook her head, closing her eyes for a moment. He moved toward her, ready to grab her shoulders if she fell, but she skittered backward, and he realized he'd made another move that must have looked threatening to her. Bruce rose and stood beside her, letting out a growl so low it sounded like distant thunder.

"Sorry." Griff held his hands up, palms out, like a criminal under arrest. "Just let me get you some lunch. Something more than cocoa."

"No, I'm fine." She seemed to rally, color returning to her face. "I just…I just have to go before the storm gets any worse."

Before he could think how to stop her, she'd made it to the foyer, shrugged into her coat, and jammed the hat on her head.

By the time he caught up to her, she'd already climbed into her truck.

"Seriously, Riley." He bent and leaned one arm on the truck's roof. "You can't go out in *this* in *that*."

"What, because it's not a Ford? I'm so sick of hearing that. There's nothing wrong with Chevy trucks."

She had to know that wasn't what he'd meant. "I don't care what make it is. It's two-wheel drive, has the clearance of an LA lowrider, and all four tires are bald. Plus it's so rusty your feet are liable to fall right through the floorboards. What year is that thing, anyway?"

"1972." Riley patted the cracked dashboard. "It's a classic. There aren't many of these babies around anymore."

"Yeah, because they all slid into ditches and rusted away."

Sticking her nose in the air, she turned the key. The car growled like a mama bear, then growled again.

Rawrrrr, rawrrr, rawrrr.

Jamming the key in harder, she shoved the accelerator to the floor and cussed a blue streak that surprised him even as he smothered a smile. Maybe she'd stay after all.

"I need a jump," she said. "Can you pull your Jeep up?"

He wanted to say no, because what if the truck stalled somewhere on the long, lonely road to Wynott? But she was gripping the steering wheel and shaking it as if she could somehow bring the truck to life through force of will. There was a wild light in her eyes that made him realize she'd feel trapped if he refused to help. She liked to play tough, but he scared her.

As he slouched off to get the Jeep, he thought about pretending to screw up so she couldn't leave, but a woman who knew more than he did about power tools could probably use jumper cables, too. If he wanted her to trust him, he needed to be honest. She wasn't stupid. But she was definitely scared.

Not that she'd ever admit it.

———ᴍᴧᴧᴧ———

Yanking the hood release, Riley hopped out of the driver's seat and tramped through the snow to struggle with the latch. Once she got the hood up, she stared down into the Chevy LUV's ancient innards, wincing at the crystalline crust on the battery. She could hardly see the terminals.

Griff's Jeep roared up behind her, making her jump and hit her head on the hood. She'd had the truck forever, but she'd never gotten used to the way the engine compartment opened from the front.

"Ow."

She rubbed her head as Griff connected the cables to the Jeep's battery and handed her the other end.

"Thanks." Standing on tiptoe, she stared down at the Chevy's crusty battery, searching for the plus and minus terminals. She thought about asking Griff, but if he helped her jump the truck, she might go all Blanche DuBois and accept the rest of the help he'd offered, including staying at the ranch.

She probably should. There was plenty of room, and it would save her from further enraging the Harpies, inconveniencing the Only Heir, and traumatizing the dog, who had his nose pressed to the front window up at the house. He was watching her with sorrowful eyes as drool ran down the glass.

But although she knew Griff was a decent person and she believed he wouldn't hurt her, there was something in the depths of his eyes that reminded her of something from her past. Something bad. Something that told her to run, fast and far.

CHAPTER 9

GRIFF REACHED PAST RILEY AND USED AN OLD SCREWDRIVER to chip some of the corrosion off her battery.

"Thanks." She swallowed hard, unnerved by his nearness.

"You might try pouring a can of Coke over that battery." His breath tickled her ear. "It eats off the rust."

"Seriously?" Riley felt sort of sick thinking of the Coke she drank every morning. If it could clean off that mess, what must it be doing to her empty innards? No wonder she didn't feel good.

"Seriously," he said. "But don't worry about it. You should just stay."

She turned away, but his gloved hands were gripping the raised hood on one side and the edge of the truck on the other. She was trapped, and he was very, very close. Too close.

So why did she have this wild urge to get closer still? Looking up at his face, she saw... What *was* that? It didn't really look like anger. It looked like... Was that fear? Maybe he wasn't asking her to stay for her sake. Maybe he didn't want to be alone.

"Riley?" His voice was husky, almost a whisper.

"What?" Her heart was beating jackrabbit fast. Her earlier dizziness returned, along with the butterflies—darn those butterflies.

"You can't go."

Did he mean *You can't go* as in *I need you to stay*? Or did he mean *You can't go* as in *Your truck won't make it home*? Or was it *You can't go* as in *You shouldn't be sleeping on a cot in Ed's office*?

She scanned his face for clues, but all she could see was his jaw set hard, his eyes inky and unwavering. His body, inches from her own, wasn't yielding, either—but hers was. Everything inside her was warming, pulsing, yearning. Her body, her mind, her heart—they were all beginning to transform, to shape themselves a new way, making room for this man.

Geez, what was she, a teenager or just an idiot? Griff Bailey was trouble. Even *he* knew it. What had he said?

I'm not fit for any woman right now.

He was right. There was a good man in there somewhere behind the grim set of his mouth, his clipped, barked orders, and all those waves of testosterone, but it would take a while to dig him out from under the layers of pain she saw in his eyes. And who knew what might happen along the way? Damaged people did hurtful things.

"I-I have to go. I'm sorry. Ed can't run the store with just that... just that kid."

"Yeah, the Only Heir isn't exactly prime material."

He was agreeing, right? So why didn't he move? His gaze melted, but he still had her trapped. Didn't he realize how oddly intimate it felt? If she breathed too hard, her chest would touch his—and boy, she wanted to breathe hard.

He looked down at her mouth, and her foolish heart squirmed while her sensible self was whipped away by the wind that spun playfully around them, ruffling his hair and dunking snowflakes down the back of her collar.

She shivered, and he tensed in response. Maybe he *did* realize how intimate this felt. Maybe he *wanted* it that way. Was he going to kiss her?

Heat flared in his eyes, but then he shook his head. She thought she saw something like regret cross his face as he pushed away from the Chevy LUV.

"I'll start the Jeep."

She slipped back into her truck and waited. As the Jeep roared to life, she turned her key again, but though the engine made a few promising noises, it still wouldn't start. She tried again and then again. Finally, he slid down out of the Jeep and came to her door.

"Move over."

She didn't know why he'd have any more luck starting it than she did, but she obeyed, then immediately regretted it. Her truck was small; Griff was not. The man ruled a room just by standing still. In a truck cab, he took up all the air and left her gasping.

The butterflies weren't gasping, though. They were fluttering like fine ladies at a soiree. She squeezed her thighs together, but they wouldn't stop.

He cranked the key.

Rrrr, rrrr, rrrr.

"Shoot," he muttered and tried again.

Rrrr, rrrr, rrrr.

"Dammit." He spit the word out, harsh and sudden, and smacked the dash with his hand.

The truck might not have jumped, but Riley did, inside and out. She had the passenger-side door open before she had time to think and one foot in the snow, poised to run. But where the hell would she go? She was trapped.

She pulled her foot back in.

Stay quiet. Stay quiet. Don't draw his attention.

She glanced at his face, hoping for a hint. Should she joke him out of his anger? Or would that just make him madder? She could try being pliant, obedient, but then she'd end up staying here with this angry, explosive man.

The fear wasn't the worst part, though. Beneath it ran a river of sorrow for the man who'd treated her with such tenderness, the only man she'd dared to fantasize about. He'd gone off to save the world, to do the right thing, and been hurt in a way that had made him somebody she feared.

As he turned the key one more time, she braced herself—but wonder of wonders, the engine caught and roared to life. She hadn't realized she was holding her breath until it whooshed out of her in one long, shaky sigh.

"Better let it run awhile," he said. "The battery... Riley?" He was looking down at her, concerned.

She struggled to think of something spunky to say, but she was shaking so hard she couldn't even think.

"Riley, what's wrong?"

"Nothing. I was... I was worried about the truck, that's all."

He stared at her a moment and then seemed to collapse in on himself, as if his anger was draining away.

"Oh God, Riley, I'm sorry. I just... I lost my temper there for a second."

She waved the words away, giving him a crooked smile. It probably looked ghastly, but it would have to do until she could get him out of her truck.

"Darn truck. I don't blame you." Her laugh sounded even shakier than the smile, and she gave up the facade. "I have to go, though. Now."

"I'm not like that. Not usually." He looked down at his lap. "It won't happen again." He looked up. "Stay, Riley."

He seemed so contrite that she wanted to trust him again.

But she wouldn't. She'd rather take her chances with the rising blizzard, her wonky battery, her bald tires, and her two-wheel-drive transmission than even think about staying.

The Chevy LUV wasn't a great option, but right now, it was a safer bet than Griff.

Griff watched Riley's taillights shimmy down the drive and saw her fishtail, catch traction, and fishtail again. Obviously, his assessment of her driving skill had been optimistic. And wrong. He took a few steps as if he could catch her, then stopped.

Everything in him wanted to jump in the Jeep and follow her. He could stay back a ways, make sure she made it to town okay.

But he'd already scared her, idiot that he was, and following her would only make it worse.

He'd go inside, read, maybe watch some TV, and put her out of his mind. She was a smart woman. She'd be fine.

Her hot chocolate was still sitting on the counter, the marshmallow mountain slumping sadly to one side. He set it in the sink and looked around. Signs of her presence were everywhere—a fuzzy blanket draped over the sofa, a book splayed open on the end table. There was a stack of DVDs beside the TV, along with a portable player.

The big dog lifted his head with a hopeful look, then sighed when he saw Griff was alone. Griff sighed, too.

He picked up her book and couldn't help smiling. There was a cowboy on the cover who for some inexplicable reason had taken his shirt off while working in a corral. A coil of rope was slung over his shoulder, and his face was turned away so all the viewer saw were the hat and the muscles.

Yep, that was what Riley needed. A cowboy like the ones in Louis L'Amour—an honest man with simple needs and simple morals. A man in a white hat who rescued women and soothed their fears. A man who never, ever lost his temper.

He went upstairs, wondering what else she might have left behind. She was sleeping in Jess's room. That was clear from the rumpled covers and abandoned pajama pants she'd left behind. They had dancing dogs on them. He smiled, picturing her padding around the house, hair tousled, ready for bed, and something stirred down below.

He could pack some of this stuff up, bring it to her. She might need it.

Then again, as long as her things were here, she'd have to come back. So he'd just call, make sure she made it okay. He didn't even have to talk to her—he'd just call Ed. Back off a little. Give her time to forget his temper tantrum.

Why, dammit, *why* had he smacked the dashboard like that? Sure, he'd been frustrated, but he knew Riley had had bad experiences with violent men. So why had he opted to become one of them at the worst possible time?

Because you can't control it. Which proves she was smart to leave.

Sighing, he headed back downstairs. As he loaded the woodstove and started a fire, he gave the dog a pat. "We'll give her fifteen minutes, okay, dude? Then we'll call Ed and make sure she made it home."

The dog's tail thumped the floor, but he still looked awfully sad.

CHAPTER 10

RILEY WAS HALFWAY TO TOWN WHEN THE TRUCK LOST ITS grip and spun slowly off the side of the road. She was headed toward a massive drift, but she'd be okay. It would cushion the impact, and she had a shovel, some kitty litter, and a few old rugs for traction.

The pickup slid backward into the snow, then suddenly tilted and slid some more. There was apparently a ditch under there, because she found herself staring up into the sky, the truck canted at a 45-degree angle.

She wasn't sure kitty litter could handle this, but she had to try. Trouble was, her door was jammed against the snow. She threw herself against it, again and again, and by the time she managed to crack it open, she was so tired, she nearly fell when she tried to slip out. Not that it mattered. The back tires were sunk so deeply in the snow-filled ditch that she doubted she could get to them.

It's two-wheel drive, has the clearance of an LA lowrider, and all four tires are bald.

She hated to admit Griff was right, but getting the front tires cleared wouldn't help. It was a rear-wheel-drive truck.

Climbing back in, she gripped the wheel and pressed the accelerator gently. The tires spun uselessly.

Sighing, she slumped back against the seat and listened to the Christmas songs pouring from the radio. That was what gotten her stuck in the first place; the Waitresses had been singing "Christmas Wrapping," and she'd been singing along, surprised to find she remembered all the words. Lost in the song's sweet story, she'd stopped paying attention to the road.

She hadn't been paying attention to her gas meter, either. There was less than a quarter tank left. Why hadn't she filled up before she left town?

Because you were busy mooning over Griff, that's why.

She could probably walk the rest of the way. She studied her surroundings, squinting through the falling snow. Reddish rock outcroppings bordered the road on the east side, sagebrush somehow clinging to every nook and cranny. The fields beyond were dotted with bulky Black Angus cattle, their dark hides dusted with white. The long vista to the west was broken with more red rocks, including one in the distance that looked like a castle.

Steamboat Rock. She hadn't gotten far. Even in good weather, it was a very long walk to town.

She sighed. Surely somebody would come by. In the meantime, she'd warm up the cab, then turn the engine off so she wouldn't run out of gas.

Five minutes later, she was singing along with Mariah Carey, wanting nothing for Christmas but *yoooooou.*

After a dozen more Christmas songs, she was asleep, and the engine whirred softly under the blue Wyoming sky.

―――

Griff woke to find the fire had dwindled to glowing coals, and the house had grown cold. The book he'd been reading lay forgotten in his lap, and darkness cloaked the world outside the windows. Bruce lay on his side, fast asleep.

Rising, he wondered idly what time it was. Probably time to…

Oh, no. Riley.

He'd planned to call Ed to make sure she'd made it home.

"Bruce," he said. The dog lifted his head. "You should have woken me up, buddy."

He hurried to the phone, wondering when he'd started holding a dog responsible for his mistakes while he scanned the list of important numbers his dad kept taped to the refrigerator. A hard-ware store was always important to a rancher, right?

Sure enough, *Boone's Hardware* was listed halfway down.

Dialing the number, he listened to the tinny ringing and thought of all the dangers that could have befallen Riley on the way home. She could have gone too fast, slid on ice, and hit a guardrail. She might have taken a turn at speed and flown off across a snowy field, the truck rolling before it stopped, upside down, with Riley dangling from her seat belt. Or she could have…

"Hello?"

Ed's voice sounded creaky, as if he hadn't spoken for a while. And he probably hadn't, with those women around. Probably couldn't get a word in edgewise.

"Ed? Griff Bailey."

"Is everything okay?" Griff could tell the man had immediately shifted into worry mode. He might be a bit weak-willed, but there was no doubt the man loved Riley like a daughter.

"I was just calling to make sure Riley made it home."

"Riley?" Ed's voice rose at least one octave. "No, she's not here. Should she be?"

"Yeah, she left, um, a while ago. She's probably on her way."

"You let that little girl drive home alone in this storm? I hope you loaned her something decent to drive, at least. That truck of hers might as well be a sled."

Griff sighed. "That little girl does what she wants, sir. I couldn't stop her. But don't worry. I'll go track her down."

"You'd better. What time did she leave?"

Griff was wandering around the house as he talked, and now he glanced up at the clock in the kitchen and jerked involuntarily, stunned by the lateness of the hour.

"Um, a while back. I'd better go after her. I'll be in touch."

He clicked the phone off so he wouldn't have to answer any more questions. Dammit, he'd slept far longer than he'd thought.

It was nearly eight o'clock, and Riley had left—when had she left? Hours ago.

Shoving his feet into his boots, Griff shrugged into his barn coat and grabbed a pair of gloves from the radiator in the mudroom. They were toasty warm, which only reminded him that Riley might be freezing somewhere out there.

She must have stopped at a friend's place. She and Sierra Dunn were close, so she might have decided to stay at the group home Sierra managed. Staying with six or eight energetic foster kids would be better than going home to Ed's sisters.

But she'd told him she was going to Ed's. And he'd let her go.

You let that little girl drive home alone in this storm?

Bruce followed him out to the Jeep, leaping into the back seat as if he'd been invited. Griff considered sending the dog back to the house, but the animal's quiet dignity hid a stubborn spirit, and he'd yet to obey one single order from Griff.

Jumper cables still trailed from the Jeep's gaping hood. Cussing himself for leaving it open, Griff unclipped them, tossed them on the floor beneath the dog, and slammed the hood. The engine roused on the first try, and the big tires churned steadily through the snow, which was still falling. There were at least eight inches on the ground, and the drifts were downright dangerous. They'd already hidden all signs of her passing, so he couldn't track her.

He stared into the vortex of snow rushing toward him and thought of that night at the quarry. He'd created memories with Riley on his last night home that had lasted him through every deployment. She'd been a lot more sure of his heroism than he was. She'd said he was brave, trying to save the world, when the truth was he'd just wanted to escape his father's ranch.

How many times had he called up the things she'd said, the look in her eyes as she'd said goodbye? He'd gotten through basic training by trying to be the man she believed him to be. Hell, that had gotten him through his whole career.

She'd sent him all those messages, too, on WhatsApp. Newsy notes about Wynott, gossip about people he'd gone to school with, even family news. His dad wasn't exactly tech savvy, and Jess and Cade had been too busy with each other. Besides, he rarely answered anyone; often he'd been too preoccupied with staying alive. Riley had been the only one who seemed to understand that. She'd been his lifeline.

He'd never told her, and now this was how he thanked her. First he scared her, thumping his fist on the dash like that, and then he let her hare off into the snow like he didn't care.

Ed was right to be angry. No decent man would have let her go.

The Jeep slid, reminding him to pay attention to the road. He stared into the swirling tunnel of falling snow illuminated by his headlights. As he rushed into the vortex, the Jeep seemed to be the center of the universe, but that was an illusion.

The center of his universe was out there somewhere, stuck in the snow, maybe hurt. Maybe worse.

CHAPTER 11

GRIFF DROVE SLOWLY, SCANNING BOTH SIDES OF THE ROAD. There were two faint depressions that might be tire tracks under the snow, and he hoped they were Riley's. He turned on the round PIAA lights on the Jeep's roof. Two lit the road ahead, while one on each side lit the verge. They were designed to spot suicidal deer intent on leaping into the road, but they'd help him find Riley if she'd slid onto the shoulder or, heaven forbid, rolled down an embankment.

He concentrated on the tracks, noting where the mystery driver had skidded, recovered, and driven on. It happened several times before Bruce rose from the back seat and whined.

"What's up, Bruce?"

The tire tracks had been getting clearer, so he was catching up to the mystery vehicle that might be Riley. As the dog whined, Griff saw where it had slipped, slid, and slipped again. Then there it was—the rusted blue hood of Riley's pickup, its crooked grill dented and cockeyed, the square headlights staring sightless at the sky. He hit his horn, hoping Riley would toot hers in return or flash her lights, but there was no response.

The dog whined again, and Griff suddenly noticed the cold biting into his hands, his face, his heart, in spite of the Jeep's heater.

"Let's check it out, buddy."

The dog didn't wait for Griff to open the back door. Clambering over the back of the console, he nearly knocked Griff over as he leapt out the driver's door and into the snow. Humping his back like an otter in the snow, the dog porpoised through the drift to paw at Riley's truck.

"I'm coming."

The drift was nearly up to Griff's hips, and it wasn't easy to fight his way through. The dog had given up his otter moves and was working more like a bulldozer, tossing snow on all sides.

"Riley?"

There was no answer but a deep bark from the dog. Griff waded farther, then slid down into the ditch, which was invisible under the snow. It was as if the wind and snow had carved a new, illusory landscape that hid all the familiar features of the road he'd traveled all his life, creating new hills and valleys where there'd been flat, open land and covering ditches and dips.

When he reached the truck, it wasn't running. He squinted, seeing no figure behind the wheel. Yet there were no tracks coming from the truck. It was as if she'd been abducted by aliens.

Kicking away the snow, he staggered on, almost falling again before he reached the truck and yanked open the door.

She lay across the bench seat in the glow of the dome light. Her silly hat had fallen to one side and her long hair was draped across the torn upholstery while one arm dangled over the edge. Tinny Christmas carols wafted from the radio, but this didn't feel like Christmas. Not one bit.

He touched her cheek with the back of his hand, his heart thumping. She was barely warm enough to be alive. Her lashes fluttered, but she didn't wake.

He swore quietly. What if he hadn't found her? She'd have frozen to death, sleeping out here like this. Why had she shut the engine off? He touched her shoulder, then, when she didn't respond, gave her a shake.

"Riley?"

He eased her over onto her back and was alarmed to see how white her face was.

"Dammit, Riley, wake up."

Tears sprang to his eyes. Riley was no fool. She'd been home-less for a while in Denver and knew better than to sleep in her car on a night like this. If she'd let this happen to her, it was because her survival instincts had been blunted somehow. Or because she didn't care.

Those women...

This was their fault. Riley had come to Wynott with nothing and had worked hard to build a good life with Ed. She'd saved the old man's life, no doubt, and now those damned women had brought their precious Only Heir to take it away.

Their fault.

He banked his anger, saving the heat for later, but a blue flame of guilt leapt from the ashes. If only he'd been kinder, gentler. If only he hadn't hit the truck and scared her. If only he'd been more persuasive, more careful, she'd still be with him, back at the ranch.

The thought made him dizzy and sick. He eyed the truck, wondering how they'd ever pull it out of the snow, and realized why she'd turned the engine off. With the entire back half of the truck buried in the drift, the tailpipe had to be stuffed with snow. If she'd left the engine running, the cab would have filled up with...

The music changed to another cheery Christmas tune, though Griff could barely hear it over the dog's racket. Bruce was barking loudly, rhythmically, with a wild urgency.

Griff ran a hand over his face, trying to clear his vision, organize his thoughts. He felt kind of sick. Nauseous.

Oh, no.

Fear gripped his heart like a clawed hand, squeezing hard. He looked down to see the keys, dangling in the ignition, then up at the gas gauge. It was on empty.

He felt sick all right, for a very good reason. Riley had run the truck out of gas trying to stay warm, and the cab had filled with carbon monoxide. If he had come along just ten minutes later, he doubted she'd be alive.

He tugged her onto his lap and touched his finger to her neck. There was a pulse, thank God, but not much of one. Taking her in his arms, he lunged out of the truck, then fell to his knees. He pulled in deep breaths of clean, cold winter air, holding her away from the snow as best he could.

"Breathe, Riley. Breathe. Fresh air, okay? Breathe."

Struggling to his feet, he clasped her to his chest and followed the path the dog had plowed through the drift. The footing was slippery, and he bruised his knees repeatedly as he struggled to hold on to his burden and stay on his feet. Bruce bounced in front of him, turning to shout that rhythmic, desperate bark whenever Griff fell.

By the time he reached the Jeep, Riley had started to stir. When he set her in the passenger seat, her eyelids fluttered, then blinked open, but her eyes were blank and unseeing.

"Riley?" He raced to the driver's side, climbed in, and hauled her close while he cranked the heat up to full and flicked all the vents in her direction. "Riley, talk to me."

She stared at him, her eyes still blank, and he thought about calling 911—but his phone was back at the house.

Dumbass. Could you mess this up any worse?

Get driving. Just GO.

Warm air blasted Riley's face, but she didn't want to wake up. She'd been nestled in a warm, dark place, wrapped in velvet—smooth, soft, smothering velvet. She hadn't wanted to wake up. Not now. Maybe not ever.

Blinking at the hot air blowing in her face, she reached up and shifted the heater vent to one side and noticed a bubble on the dashboard with a Santa inside. He was climbing into a chimney, carrying a sack full of toys, and snow was falling all around him.

Santa had never visited her. Of course, she'd never lived in a place with a fireplace. Either that, or it was like her mom had said and she wasn't good enough to make the "nice" list.

She'd been good this year, though—well, pretty good. As long as Santa didn't talk to the Harpies, she might make the list, and Griff had a fireplace. Maybe Santa would come to the ranch.

Wait, what was she thinking? Santa wasn't real. She was all groggy and mixed up. Like she could have sworn *she'd* been driving, but now she was slumped in a bucket seat, perched high above the road, leaning against—who was that?

Glancing up, she saw Griff, his profile outlined against a window rimed with ice. Outside, the sky was deep navy blue, and a rising moon bobbed along in the window.

Griff looked down at her, his eyes alight with something—something nice. Fondness, she thought. Affection.

"Hey," he said softly. Behind him, the dog whined eagerly.

Bruce.

What had happened? Last she remembered, she'd been running away from Griff, and she'd left the dog behind. But now here she was, all snuggled up like the man was her new best friend—or something more—and the dog was in the back seat.

Her stomach flipped over. Maybe she'd been drinking. That would explain her sleepiness, her confusion, and the sudden wave of nausea. It would also explain why she was with Griff when she'd promised herself she'd stay away from him. It hadn't been easy, but she'd made a firm decision, and she usually hung onto those.

Funny, she didn't feel drunk, just sick. And she'd never gotten so drunk she couldn't remember what she'd done. She'd wanted to sometimes, but no such luck.

Her stomach turned again, and she tried to sit up. She might not want to be Griff's girlfriend, but she didn't want to throw up in his lap, either.

Bruce thrust his big head between them, twitching his eyebrows to look first at her, then at Griff.

"She's okay," Griff said to the dog. Riley liked the way Griff talked to Bruce like he was human. Like he deserved respect. That was the cowboy part of him, the part that was good with animals.

"Just rest," he told Riley. "You're safe, okay?"

"Okay."

Yeah, right. She was safe in Griff's Jeep, with no memory of how she'd gotten there. Had she slept with him? She hoped not. If she ever slept with Griff Bailey, she planned to pay attention and remember every second. Plus if she had, had Bruce been there? Had he *watched*? The poor dog would be scarred for life.

Then again, maybe Bruce could tell her what had happened.

"Bruce?" she said. "What did I do?"

"You slid off the road," Griff said. "Are you okay? Did you hit your head?"

She forked her fingers into her hair and searched for bruises and bumps. "Don't think so." She wrinkled her forehead, struggling to remember. "Where's my truck?"

He thumbed back over his shoulder. "Back there. You got stuck in a drift."

"Oh." She felt like she was thinking through molasses, but events were starting to come back to her. "I couldn't dig out, so I thought I'd wait for someone to come by. I was listening to Christmas songs and singing to stay awake, and then…" She scratched her head. "I guess I fell asleep anyway. I feel weird."

"You fell asleep with the car running."

"Oh." Now she understood why he'd come to her rescue. She must have called him. "So I ran out of gas."

"Which was a very good thing."

"What, so you could come and save me?" She remembered now that Griff hadn't wanted her to go. He'd made fun of her truck, tried to order her around, and then something had happened, something that scared her. "I know you like playing knight in shining armor, but I could have frozen to death."

"That would be *one* way you could have died." The man could go from fond to mad in a heartbeat. Those eyebrows came down, his eyes went hard, and all of a sudden, he was a scary guy. A flash of memory startled her—his face flushed, his fist rapping the dashboard—followed by a sense of tremendous loss.

She remembered now. He'd been so kind to her, so tender. But that man was gone.

"Your truck was backed up in a drift, with snow blocking the tailpipe," he said. "If you hadn't run out of gas, you would have died of carbon monoxide poisoning. Hell, you almost did."

Her brain was so foggy that she had to parse each word, figuring out its meaning before moving on to the next one, and by then she'd forgotten what they were talking about.

A few words caught her attention, though. Like *died*. And that long one.

"Carbon monoxide?"

He glanced down at her and nodded, then reached across and took her hand as if he had the right. She wanted to pull away, but her fingers were freezing. Cupped gently in Griff's palm, they seemed to be electrified by his warmth.

"Ow," she said, puzzled.

"Hurts, right? You almost got frostbite, too," he said. "Of course, that wouldn't have mattered if you'd *died*. Do you get that?"

"Oh. Yeah, sure." He seemed to think he was saying something momentous, but she didn't really care. "Can I go back to sleep now?"

"Sure," he said. "Just promise me you won't take that death trap out in a blizzard again."

"Death trap?"

"That truck of yours."

"Oh. Uh-huh." She had no intention of following his orders, but she really wanted to go to sleep.

"I'm taking you back to the ranch, okay? You don't want Ed's sisters to see you this way." He gripped the wheel tighter and glared into the darkness. "They'd probably think you were drunk."

"They probably would."

Ed's sisters. Jeez. She'd forgotten all about them. The last thing she needed was for them to see her stagger in hanging all over Griff, so to heck with it. She'd have to stay at the ranch tonight and trust him to behave himself. She had a vague notion that he'd saved her life, so she might as well.

"All right."

"Good." He pulled his hand away and she almost mewed, but then he reached over and put his arm around her and pulled her close. He was so warm, and then he took her hand again. "Now you can sleep."

"Good." She snuggled down into the velvet darkness again, resting her cheek against his shoulder as he breathed in, out, in, out, so solid and calm. His sweater smelled like a fire in the fireplace and pine boughs on the mantel.

How could such a grumpy guy smell so much like Christmas?

—*∿*—

Griff concentrated fiercely on the road, biting his lower lip until he tasted blood, clutching the steering wheel with one hand while the other held Riley close to keep her warm.

He had to keep her warm, of course. And he was holding her hand so her fingers wouldn't freeze. Just because his heart lifted whenever he looked down at her pale, drawn face, that didn't mean he was taking advantage of her. He hoped.

Fortunately, driving in winter weather was one of those skills you never forgot, like riding a bike. If he hadn't had a passenger, it would have been fun. How many nights had he taken the Jeep out in a blizzard when he was a teenager, searching the dirt roads for stranded motorists? Once in a while, some overambitious four-wheeler or foolish tourist would press a ten-dollar bill into his hand for the help, but that wasn't why he did it. Rescuing people had made him feel good.

He felt pretty good right now. Riley had shed her ugly fur hat at some point, and her hair smelled like flowers. His mind flooded with thoughts that were sweet but also wrong, wrong, wrong. Once again, he wasn't worthy of that sweetness, or her trust.

He'd done his best to hang on to their night together at the quarry with care, like an image preserved in the crystalline water of a snow globe. The Jeep, pulled up to the far brim of the quarry, the bonfire of the party a distant glow. The moonlight on her face, her hands, her body. The way she'd answered his kiss, hesitant at first, then hard, with unexpected passion. The way she'd trusted him.

Unfortunately, the memory had been soiled by his time in the desert. The men around him fed off each other's loneliness and desperation, and their stories focused on sex, not romance. They were each determined to be manlier than the next man and to show no weakness. Those who clung to love were joked, joshed, teased, and ended up joining the others in their coarse, manly, miserable ways. Everyone claimed to be a Casanova in a former life, and nobody admitted to having a heart.

So he'd found himself thinking less about Riley's amazing eyes or her sexy voice and more about her scent and her skin. After a while, he'd started fantasizing increasingly X-rated scenes with her in the starring role, even though he'd known deep down he was taking something from her without permission. He'd taken something precious from himself, too, and it would help to pay her back with kindness, friendship, and trust. He might be too broken for a real relationship, but he vowed to help her any way he could.

He carefully turned into the long ranch drive, holding her so she wouldn't shift with every bounce of the Jeep. Her warmth set his body on high alert, so he did his best to think about other things to distract himself—cow patties, barbed wire, turkey wattles—the unsexiest things he could think of.

As he pulled to a stop at the ranch house, the blaze of Molly's thousand-and-one Christmas lights cast a welcoming golden glow across the snow.

"Christmas," Riley muttered in her sleep. "I love Christmas. I decorated at Ed's. Did you see?"

He patted her shoulder gently, wishing he could take her there. "Those women aren't exactly Christmassy people, though, are they?"

"No." Her forehead furrowed. "Don't know what I'm gonna do."

Just in that instant, as Griff parked the Jeep, he knew what she should do. He'd keep her here, take care of her. They'd have a real Christmas, just the two of them. He'd have to do some planning. Molly had decorated the house, but there was more to Christmas than that.

He looked down at the Santa in the still-wobbling snow globe and tried to see hope there and the holiday spirit he'd need if he was going to give Riley the Christmas she deserved. But Santa had one foot in the chimney and one on the roof, as if he couldn't quite commit, and he was still weighed down with that gigantic pack.

Griff was going to have to find his hope and holiday spirit in his own heart, and that meant digging deep, because it felt as heavy and full as that bag.

CHAPTER 12

GRIFF STOKED A HEARTY FIRE IN THE FIREPLACE WHILE Riley, a little groggy, shuffled off to call Ed.

"I'm fine," he heard her saying. "Just tired, that's all."

He wondered if Ed had noticed the slight drag in her voice left over from the poison she'd inhaled.

"I'll be home tomorrow, when the weather clears," she said.

After some small talk, she hung up. The dog rose from where he'd been snoozing at her feet and paced behind her to the living room. When she sat in the chair by the woodstove, Bruce lowered himself down beside her. He didn't seem to want her out of his sight, and Griff felt the same way.

"You're going back tomorrow?" Griff asked.

"Of course," she said. "I live there."

"Right. In your apartment. So Ed's going to clear his sisters out of there?"

"Don't be like that," she said. "I can't afford to be mad. I need to like them."

"Why?" he asked. "They're not making any effort to like you. And let me tell you, Riley, it's not real hard. You're pretty and smart and sweet. You take care of Ed as if he was your own dad and never ask for anything in return. And here you are with me, even though I know I scare you…"

She started to protest.

"No, I know you're not scared of anything, but I scare every-body. Hell, I scare myself, except when I'm with you. You make me feel almost human."

She stared at him, eyes wide with surprise, then melting into pity, and he realized he'd said too much. Frustration always made him dump the contents of his brain on whoever happened to be closest, and judging by Riley's stunned expression, he'd said something stupid. Shifting uneasily, he waited for her to stop staring and speak.

"*Almost* human?" she finally said. "Griff, just how bad do you feel?"

What? Had he said that?

The question, her concerned expression, his worry for her, and exhaustion from wading through the snow—it all unmanned him, and he felt the appalling sensation of tears, hot like acid, stinging his eyes. Clenching his fists, he fought against them.

They could not fall. They could not even exist. Others had suffered far more than he had. He had no right to feel sorry for himself. No right at all.

"Don't twist this around," he said. "We're talking about those women. I'm trying to tell you to stand up for yourself, and now…"

Now you're acting like I'm the weak one.

His throat closed up, and he couldn't speak. He had an absurd urge to kneel before her, to rest his head in her lap and let her stroke his hair. He had an even more absurd urge to cry. But that was out of the question.

Without a word, he got up and left the room.

Riley waited to see if Griff would come back. She hadn't meant to insult him or anything; she'd just been shocked by what he'd said. Something in his tone had told her the words came from a self-hatred so deep it had scarred his soul.

She knew what that was like. There'd been a time when she'd felt less than human herself, and the road back from that dark place had been long and hard. It hurt her heart to think of Griff dealing with that after all he'd been through. Then again, she wasn't sure he was actually *dealing* with anything, the way he kept to himself and shut everyone out.

He had a softer side. She'd seen it, back there in the Jeep, along with an unmistakable look of longing—and yet he held himself apart. Even holding a civil conversation was an act of will for him.

She squeezed her eyes shut, ducking her head and rubbing her forehead, reminding herself it wasn't her job to fix him. She'd probably just make him mad, and she'd experienced the damage angry men could do. So far, he'd held himself together except for that one explosion in the car, but she needed to be careful.

Or did she? He'd just saved her life, after all. And while he might think he'd changed so much he was hardly human, she was still pretty sure the cowboy she'd admired all those years ago was still in there—the guy who'd talked to her so long before making his move that night at the quarry. The guy who'd been so concerned with her feelings when they'd made out in the dark, who'd stopped whenever she'd asked him to and made her feel safe enough to let go and find a level of ecstasy she hadn't known existed.

She wondered if he realized how much he'd changed her. Knowing she could be that safe with a man, that free, had given her a new kind of hope, and she owed him for that. That was why she'd stayed in touch while he'd been overseas, even though she'd known nothing more could happen between them. He was a Bailey, with a respectable ranch family that went back generations. That kind of guy wasn't looking for a girl like her—not long-term. But she was pretty sure he could use a friend.

She and Bruce sat and watched the fire for a while. The glowing embers formed tiny cities beneath the logs, with craggy brimstone buildings under the leaping flames. Orange lights in the fragile towns of ash blinked on and off, and then they'd crumble and fall.

"It looks scary, like a city in hell, doesn't it, Bruce?"

The dog sighed and leaned against her legs.

"So the people who live there escaped the devil, and they're hiding in the coals. They're building a new town, a safe one, back there under the log." She sighed. "But they're doomed, buddy. That log is gonna fall."

She huffed out a laugh. The fireplace was starting to look like the real world to her. Every time a person found a safe space, reality came crashing down like a burning log. The trick was to keep moving and escape before disaster struck.

Speaking of moving… Where was Griff? She'd heard him going up the stairs, but he hadn't said good night or anything. Had her question bothered him that much?

She stood, relieved that her head seemed to have cleared. She felt almost like herself now—a little sleepy, but well enough to brave the stairs.

"You stay, Bruce."

The dog laid his head on his paws and settled down with a soft groan of protest.

Upstairs, a faint glow emanated from one of the doors—the one that led to Griff's old bedroom. It was open, just a crack. He'd have closed it if he wanted her to stay out, right?

Right. But she needed to be careful. Maybe he'd left it open as some kind of clumsy signal. Maybe he'd gotten naked and was waiting for her. Guys did dumb stuff like that, and although he'd been respectful, there'd been a light deep in his eyes she'd recognized.

She tiptoed quietly into the bedroom to find him curled on his side, the bedside lamp glossing his wide shoulders and sparking off his tousled hair. Without the angry crease between his eyebrows, the implacable line of his mouth, the jut of his jaw, he looked surprisingly different—and if a man could be beautiful, that was Griff. Handsome didn't cover it. He looked like a sleeping giant born of angels. Like one of the Nephilim, she thought, from the Bible.

But even giant angels got cold, and the warmth of the fire definitely wasn't reaching this room. Creeping to a closet across the room, she hunted for a blanket.

She found a few clothes hung by category—shirts, then sweaters, then pants—and some shoes and boots lined up neatly on the floor. There were plenty of blankets on the bed, but they were all beneath the sleeping Griff.

Sitting on the side of the bed, she reached out, tentatively, and pushed a shock of dark hair back from his forehead. She suspected he wouldn't want to be seen this way, with his defenses down, but she couldn't help staring. Something in her heart yearned to soothe him, to find her cowboy angel under all the layers of pain.

She huffed out a quiet laugh. Something in her heart yearned for a lot of other things, too, but she'd learned to give it a stern "no" when it asked for too much. Her heart—or was that her libido?—was like an untrained puppy that tended to get overexcited and wanted to jump on...on certain people.

"No," she whispered.

Griff stirred and her heart fluttered like a startled sparrow. What if he looked up and found her staring at him? He'd think she was some kind of creep. But then he shivered, ever so slightly, and folded his arms around his chest like he was cold, and her foolish puppy-dog heart quivered in response.

Danger, she thought. *That puppy is out of control.*

Reluctantly, she dragged herself downstairs and put a couple more logs on the fire like a responsible housemate. Then she headed up to her own bed in Jess's room, careful not to look at the inviting fan of light that stretched from Griff's door.

—∿—

Riley didn't know when she'd fallen asleep, but she woke to the moon riding high in the sky, flooding the plains below in a mysterious, silver light. What had woken her up? A low call. Some sort of bird?

She sat up, staring out the window. The tall pines that grew beside the house tossed their frosty Muppet-monster heads while the wind roared around the eaves. Stars hung peaceful and unblinking behind the moon.

She was starting to settle down when a hoarse shout shattered the silence. She leapt to her feet, heart hammering, reaching for Bruce with one hand and finding him beside her. True to form, he'd followed her upstairs and stood beside her bed with his ears perked up, staring at the door.

Should she race toward the noise to help or run away? It must have been Griff. It sounded like he was fighting monsters in there.

Well, if he was, she was going to help him. Hunching her shoulders, she folded her arms across her chest, shivering in her worn pajamas. The floorboards froze her feet as she trotted across the hall to find Griff lying with his back to her, facing the wall.

As she entered, he let out a groan.

"Griff? Griff, you're dreaming."

He curled his body tighter, folding his legs to his chest as if to protect himself. His eyes were squeezed shut, his arms folded.

She didn't want to wake him; she wanted to get the heck out of there. He might wake up flailing, angry, looking for something to hit. It wouldn't be the first time she'd been that convenient something when a man needed to release some hallucinatory rage.

But this was Griff. She owed him.

Steeling herself, she sat cautiously on the side of the mattress. When he didn't react, she took a moment to collect herself, breathing deeply, thinking calm thoughts. Setting a hand on his arm, she tensed, half expecting him to roll over with fists flailing, but he only twitched. His mouth worked for a moment, and then his face seemed to relax.

She'd done that. She'd stayed, she hadn't run, and she'd helped him. Her heart was still thrumming with panic, her muscles twitching with the need to move, but she stroked his hair from his face until the anger and fear flowed out of his features and he was her giant angel again.

Bruce sighed, circled a few times, and lay down on the braided rug by the bed. Closing his eyes, he dropped instantly into a deep doggy sleep.

Riley hadn't slept much, and the poison gas from the truck was still fogging her mind with a heavy fatigue. She wanted to stay and make sure Griff was okay, but she was so, so tired. She needed to lie down, just for a minute, and what the heck? He'd never know.

Easing down beside him, she lay on her back, staring up at the ceiling. It was freezing in here. How could he sleep without a blanket? Apparently, his internal furnace was set on high, because he kept her warm even as she did her best not to touch him.

Shivering, she grabbed a corner of the quilt and rolled over, wrapping herself like a burrito. She ended up snugged tight against his back, warm at last. Hey, they were friends, right? She'd just rest for an hour or so, and go back to her room before he woke.

Wrapping one arm around his waist, she tucked her head into the back of his neck and slept.

CHAPTER 13

GRIFF WOKE TO A COTTON-CANDY SKY, LOW CLOUDS TINTED pink by the reflection of the rising sun. As he stretched cautiously, he realized a lot of his aches and pains were gone, along with the tension that had plagued him since he'd gotten home. Best of all, his mind felt clear, with none of the hangover feeling he'd had for months.

He started to rise, then realized he wasn't alone.

Darn it, the dog was too big to sleep in the bed.

He turned, started, and paused, propping himself up on one elbow.

Riley lay beside him, her pale face sweetened by sleep. Her lips, with that delicate Cupid's bow in the middle, were relaxed, slightly open. Long, pale lashes shaded her cheeks. In the pink and gold of dawn, she looked like a fairy maiden, enchanted by some sleeping spell.

Where the hell did that come from? He hadn't even liked fairy tales when he was a kid. Jess was the one who always begged for those silly stories. He'd been more a Frog and Toad kind of guy.

Apparently he liked fairy princesses better than toads now, because everything in him yearned to reach for this one, pull her close, and make love in the morning light. He wanted to bury all his pain inside her, let her warm his heart back to life.

And why not? She was here, wasn't she? Her room was across the hall. Why was she here if she didn't want him?

She opened her eyes, and he watched her work her way out of sleep like a swimmer rising to the surface of a deep, dark lake. Her eyes were soft and gentle as a doe's and filled with compassion and understanding.

He wished, with a sudden and unbearable need, that they could stay like this forever. She didn't have to touch him or kiss him or make love. She just had to look at him like that. He felt warm. Right. *Blessed.*

Then her eyes widened, and he saw the snap of awareness as his presence registered.

"Griff." She jerked to a sitting position, her body suddenly tensed for flight.

With a grunt, Bruce shot up beside the bed from where he must have been sleeping and joined her in staring at him. The dog's slightly crossed eyes made him look kind of goofy, and Griff almost laughed.

"Hey." He did his best to look harmless, which wasn't easy. He had the perfect face for a soldier, with features created for emotions like anger, disapproval, and hostility, but he needed to erase all that, because while he still didn't know why Riley was in his bed, he wanted her to stay.

"I was just… I have to go," she said, wrapping her arms around her slim body and shivering. "I came in because…" She scanned his face and seemed to come to some decision. "Because I was cold. I don't know how to turn on the heat in my room."

He almost snorted. He was pretty sure Riley could install an entire HVAC system without a manual, so she could probably manage the thermostat that was right beside the door, in plain view.

But if she wanted an excuse to curl up beside him, he wasn't about to take it away.

"Maybe it's broken," he said.

If it isn't, maybe I can break it somehow.

"So I have to go," she said. "I have to, um…"

She glanced out the window. The snow must have continued to fall all night. His father's fence was buried halfway up the posts, and the cattle stood in a miserable, white-dusted knot by the barn.

Her eyes widened. "Your dad told me if the snow got this deep, I should call Jeb Johnson to come feed the cows."

"We don't need Jeb. I'll take care of them." He flashed her a smile, hoping it was gentle enough to soothe her fears, but her eyes stayed wide and frightened.

He didn't know how to soothe her, so they'd get up now and escape this room where the shimmering warmth of their embrace still hovered in the air. They'd both be safe then—for a while.

—∿∿—

Riley was flipping an omelet when the front door opened. Griff entered along with a snow-covered Bruce and a swirl of white flakes borne on a puff of wind. Stamping snow off his boots, Griff shrugged off his coat, then tipped his hat and smiled.

Oh my. Riley almost dropped the pan, because there he was—the cowboy Griff she'd been looking for. It wasn't just the boots or the snowcapped black felt Stetson. It was the way he was moving—with casual grace and confidence. And the way he was smiling—free and easy and *real*.

Toeing off the boots, he chuckled as snow cascaded from his shoulders and the brim of his hat.

Griff. Chuckled.

"Did you feed the cows?" she asked.

He shook his head. "I'll need your help for that."

"Okay. Want an omelet first?"

"Do I ever."

She tried to smile, but it trembled at the edges, because what must he be thinking? He'd woken to find her curled up next to him like a lost kitten at best. At worst, she'd come across like a floozy hoping for some action. Either way, she was hardly showing him the fierce, independent woman she'd vowed to be, especially since she couldn't tell him she'd gone into the bedroom to take care of him. He wouldn't want to hear that.

"How were the horses?" she asked.

"Good." The smile widened. "You know that one bay?"

"Bay?" she asked.

"That's what we call a brown horse with black legs."

"We?" She arched an eyebrow.

"Horse people. Cowboys, I guess."

She nodded, swallowing down her foolish cowboy dreams, and served the eggs while he settled himself at the table. She'd been worried she'd made too much, but judging from the way he tucked into the food, he'd worked up an appetite.

"That bay Arabian and I weren't getting along too well, because… Well, we got a bad start."

"I noticed he seemed kind of scared," Riley said. She didn't tell Griff the bay had been her favorite or how much time she'd spent soothing him when she'd been feeding the horses. "I named him Spook."

"That's about right." Griff laughed. "He let me get a halter on him. Major victory. I turned him out with the others, and now he's kicking up his heels like a colt."

"The others seem so steady."

"They probably had their share of problems, too," Griff said. "My dad's always bragging about the bargains he picks up at auctions. The truth is, the horses he buys are just about wrecked, but with a steady hand and some patience, they've got a chance at a decent life. They're never bargains, though."

Humor danced in his eyes, and Riley did her best not to stare—but it transformed him. Made him look younger, more approachable. *Safer.*

"He ends up spending more on vet bills and training than he could ever sell 'em for," Griff continued. "But it's sure a good deal for the horses."

Riley felt a rush of fondness for Griff's dad. Griff had never gotten along with him, but Heck Bailey had always been kind to her. Come to think of it, she was probably a lot like those horses. No bargain and just about wrecked—but saved, just in time, by this town, this home she'd found.

"That's nice of your dad."

"Yeah, well." He ducked his head and concentrated on his food. "He's a lot better with horses than he is with people."

"I see him at the diner sometimes." She slid her gaze sideways to see if this was a safe subject. Judging from the way he was ladling eggs into his mouth, he wasn't bothered by it. "He seems to do okay with people then. He flirts with the waitresses, but respectfully, you know? And he tells those awful jokes." She couldn't help smiling at the thought. He told the kind of jokes little kids tell, and half the time, he was the only one who laughed, but it didn't seem to bother him.

Griff shrugged. "I know. Everybody loves him. But somehow, nothing I did was ever good enough." His face darkened with a memory. "I don't mind being bossed around by my superiors in the military. Lives are at stake. But the cows weren't going to explode if my roping wasn't up to snuff."

"Yeah, I don't like being bossed, either," she said. "Ed lets me do my own thing, and that's the way I like it."

"Nobody needs to boss you," he said. "You work hard. That's just how you are."

She flushed and glanced his way. His eyes were fixed on her with that look again, that *fondness*. That was all it was, but holy cats, he sure looked good in that hat. Suddenly, she needed a steady hand, just like the horses. *His* steady hand.

She needed to stop thinking like that. Sleeping beside Griff had been nice, but those shouts last night had reminded her that he'd come home with issues. Deep-seated issues that tormented him even in sleep.

What had happened to him? She knew there'd been an explosion. The local paper had reported that two of his men had been killed and several injured. Griff had carried the wounded out, risking his own safety repeatedly. She didn't know how many lives he'd saved, and unless he talked in his sleep, she'd probably never know. She sure wasn't going to ask him and make him relive it.

But right now, looking at his bright eyes under that hat, no one would ever guess there was any darkness in him at all.

"Once we get those cattle fed, I might spend some time with old Spook. See if I can get him used to me handling him."

"That would be great. Your dad said I shouldn't let him out of the barn, but you know what you're doing. I hope you can help him."

Or he can help you.

It was pretty obvious the horses were already helping him, making him her cowboy again. Well, not *her* cowboy. But the one she remembered. Even though he hadn't liked working with his dad on the ranch, even though he thought he'd been born to be a soldier, she'd always known he was cowboy to the bone.

"If the snow holds off, we'll see if we can pull your truck out later," he said.

"Okay." Her heart did a happy little flip. He was mellowing, becoming his old self. She wasn't afraid anymore. Cowboying was good for Griff. And when he was like this, she could believe he was good for her.

"I'll call Ed," she said. "Let him know I might be here a while."

CHAPTER 14

ED RACED FOR THE PHONE LIKE A TEENAGE GIRL EXPECTING A call from her crush—if the teenage girl was secretly seventy-two years old and hobbled by arthritis. His heart was thumping hard and he almost twisted an ankle, but he made it before Carol, who'd started answering the phone as if she owned the place.

Glancing at the screen, he saw it was the call he'd been waiting for.

"You okay, sweetheart?" he asked.

"I'm fine," Riley said. "Great, actually."

"You want me to come get you? Roads are better today, and I think the Ford would make it."

"Oh, you and your Ford."

He couldn't help smiling. They had a running joke about his old truck versus her toy pickup. "It's not stuck in a drift," he said.

"True. But I think that was the driver, not the truck."

He laughed. "I can't believe you admit that."

Carol came in from the kitchen where she'd been rearranging the cupboards. He'd asked her not to—they were the way Ruth had left them, and that felt sacred to him—but she'd ignored him and had spent the morning bustling around making disapproving noises as she tore the kitchen apart.

"Who are you talking to?" she hissed.

"Riley," he whispered.

"Well, I need you," Carol said.

He shook his head, pointing at the phone, and she frowned, then stood there, tapping one foot and listening to every word he said.

"Ed?"

He turned his back on his sister. A small rebellion. Baby steps.

"Sorry, Riley. Carol had a problem. We're good now."

He'd always tried not to lie to Riley, but that was a whopper. He rubbed his chest, trying to soothe the ache.

"Do you need me for anything?" she asked. "Is Trevor helping you with the store?"

"There's not much to help with. We had a run on snow shovels yesterday, and we sold just about all those Muck boots you brought in. That was a good idea, hon," he said. "But since then, nobody. The roads are too bad."

"That's kind of good," she said. "Gives Trevor time to just wander around and familiarize himself with the stock."

"You'd think so." Ed didn't tell her the boy wasn't out of bed yet. She'd just worry.

"Well, if you're okay, I think I might stay here after all," Riley said. "It's a big house, and Griff's been... He's been really nice."

"That's fine, hon. You sure you're okay there?" He knew Riley's blunt, bold facade hid a sparrow's heart, beating fearfully behind that determined walk, that harsh laugh.

"He's a gentleman. Don't worry."

Ed found himself squinting, as if that would help him hear better. Didn't Riley sound a little different? And was she really staying because Griff was a "gentleman," or was something going on between them? For her sake, he kind of hoped there was. Rumor had it Griff had done himself proud over in the Middle East, and Riley needed a hero.

She sure wasn't going to find one here. He couldn't even face his own sisters.

"You call when you can, okay?" He turned and faced the wall, shutting out the grim-faced Carol, who was standing with her arms crossed, looking sour. "We miss you."

"You miss my cooking." Riley laughed that laugh, and he missed her even more. "Put those sisters of yours to work, okay? Don't go back to eating peanut-butter toast for dinner like you used to."

"I won't. I think the diner's opened up. We'll go out for a good meal." He turned to face Carol, meeting her eyes with all the rebellion he could muster. "Wish you could join us."

"Don't worry," Riley said. "I'll talk to you tomorrow, okay, Bud?"

"Sure." His heart felt pinched and painful. Riley always called him "Bud" or "Buddy." It was a pet name, and she said it fondly, but dozens of times, he'd wanted to tell her to call him Dad instead. He always lost his nerve.

"Love you."

Riley hung up before Ed could respond, which was just as well—because how could he say "Love you, too" in front of Carol? She seemed to think he and Riley were having some kind of torrid affair, which was ridiculous. *That would be incest*, he wanted to tell her. But the words went unsaid.

"Now that you're *finally done*, I need to talk to you," Carol said. "I'm concerned about Trevor."

"What, because he isn't up yet? Boy likes his sleep, that's all," Ed said.

He didn't say the boy was lazy, but he wanted to. At the store, Trevor either skulked around doing nothing or sat in a corner messing with his danged phone.

"I think he has a fever," Carol said. "It's probably the flu. He isn't himself."

"Let him sleep then. I won't need him today."

Not that he didn't need help. There were paint chips all over the paint counter, and nails and screws were filed in the wrong boxes. A Sawzall somebody'd opened was still out of the box, the Styrofoam inserts abandoned on the floor. He'd asked Trevor to clean it up three times.

If the boy was sick, it would explain a lot, like the sweaty sheen on his skin, pale under a rash of pimples. His hair was greasy and lank, like a homeless person, and he faced the world with a cynical attitude and a smug smile Ed wanted to smack right off his face.

Oh dear. That was no way to think. Trevor was his nephew, and if he was sick, he couldn't help it.

"You want me to check on him?" he asked his sister.

"Would you?" She sounded relieved, which surprised him. Normally, she thought he was useless and made sure he knew it.

He headed upstairs and tapped on the door. This was Riley's space, and he'd always tried to respect her privacy. She'd given him a tour after she finished renovating it, and it was amazing what she'd done, but they were together enough in the store, and young folks needed time to themselves. But when his second knock went unanswered, he walked in.

Riley had made the place so homey. She'd haunted the Goodwill in Grigsby and had added pictures on the walls, throw pillows on the sofa, and a whimsical statue of a cowboy on a rustic coffee table. She said it was the nicest place she'd ever lived in, which was sad because it was just an attic apartment, hot in the summer and cold in the winter. The bathroom was tiny, with a cramped shower, and the sofa was a slightly ratty antique she'd picked up off the curb on garbage day. He'd offered to buy her new things, but she loved to find rejected pieces and clean them up. Then she'd act like it was Christmas because she had something new.

There was no response when he tapped at the bedroom door. Cracking it open, he stuck his head inside and almost backed away. The room smelled like sweat, dirty hair, and something else Ed didn't want to think about.

"Trevor? What's the matter here? You sick?"

The boy sat up and stretched, grimacing as if something was hurting him.

"You want me to call a doctor?"

"No!"

Well, the boy could talk, but he was shivering uncontrollably. When Ed tried to put a hand on his forehead, he jerked away as if threatened.

"I don't do traditional medicine," the boy said. "Just natural stuff."

"Well, okay. What do you need?"

"Nothing." The boy looked sullen. "I called my friend. He's a... He's a naturopath. He's coming up from Denver."

"All right." Ed backed away, relieved to shut the door and leave Trevor and his smell behind. Not for the first time, he regretted inviting his sisters for the holidays. Then again, they'd invited themselves. He hadn't had any say in that, either.

Well, they'd always been independent. Never needed his help. So they could deal with their boy themselves—though Ed sure wished they wouldn't do it here.

CHAPTER 15

"You ready?"

Riley tried to nod, but she was so bundled up, she could barely move. The temperature outside was close to zero, so Griff had insisted she borrow some of Jess's winter wear. She'd put on tights, long underwear, and leggings beneath her corduroys. On top, she wore a thermal turtleneck, a long-sleeved Under Armour top, and a flannel shirt, plus her puffy coat. Her long scarf was wrapped around her neck three times, and still the tasseled ends trailed loose. All this sartorial splendor was topped with her furry hat, with the earflaps tied under her chin.

Griff looked at her critically. She realized she was no fashion plate, but she'd figured the cows wouldn't care. Apparently, he did.

"Lose the scarf."

"It's warm. I need it."

He opened the hall closet and rummaged around until he found a shorter one. "Use this. You get that long one caught on something, you'll get dragged, or worse. Tuck the ends into your coat."

Sighing, she removed her scarf, which Eleanor Carson had knit for her out of something she called "confetti yarn." The festive colors always made Riley smile, since Mrs. Carson was possibly the least outwardly festive woman she knew. The scarf proved you couldn't judge people by their faces. There was often another person inside, a sweeter self in hiding from the world.

Riley put on the shorter scarf, which was both ugly and itchy, and gave Griff a sloppy salute. To her surprise, he burst out laughing. She'd meant the salute ironically, but she didn't think it was *that* funny.

"You salute like that in the service, you'd have to drop and give me ten."

She would have done it, but if she dropped, she'd probably bounce with all these clothes on, so she stayed at attention. Grinning, he adjusted her arm and hand, then stepped back, squinting.

"That's better. At ease, soldier."

She loved this side of Griff—teasing and easygoing, even a bit flirty. Maybe he'd turned a corner. Maybe their little town, the breathtaking country around it, and the pleasure of being a cowboy again would turn him into the man he was before. Yesterday, his face had been haggard, with bags under his eyes, but he'd slept well last night, and it showed. Had she done that?

Yeah, right. The VA shrinks in Denver couldn't fix him, but you can.

"What's the matter?" Griff was looking at her quizzically. Had she actually been standing there staring at him, frowning? And for how long?

"Nothing." She shook her head again, hard, and her hat tilted rakishly over one eye. Griff smiled again as he straightened it. She found herself smiling back, and it was so *nice* to look into his eyes and see happiness instead of that brooding darkness.

Suddenly, he bent down, tilted his head to get under the short brim of her hat, and gave her a kiss. Not a sexy kiss or a deep one. But a good one, and on the lips.

On the *lips*.

It lingered just a moment. His mouth was warm and surprisingly soft—something she remembered from that night at the quarry. When he pulled away, she longed to haul him back to finish the job.

"Sorry," he said. "You just—you just look so danged cute, that's all." He turned away, clearly embarrassed.

Did he mean cute like kid-sister cute or cute like sexy cute? She had no idea. But it didn't matter, because suddenly he was all business, as if it hadn't happened. The man was giving her emotional whiplash.

"I got the flatbed loaded. We'll drive to the far side of the pasture if we can and feed 'em there."

"What?" How could he just carry on as if nothing had happened? The kiss had set off a powerful string of images that had swamped Riley's rational mind. She imagined him ravenous, then tender, then taking her hand and leading her to the bedroom, where he'd take off her hat, and then the scarf, and then...

And then five hours later, he might actually make it to your underwear. Which won't be good, because you're starting to sweat under all those layers.

Blinking, she reentered the real world. "Can Bruce come?"

He thought a moment. "Sure, but he'll have to stay in the cab."

The flatbed was parked in the turnout in front of the barn, and sure enough, the bed was stacked high with square bales of hay and straw.

"Do you want me to help you dump the straw before we go?" She had to raise her voice to be heard over the wind, which blew the few strands of hair that had fallen out of her hat across her face. She raked them away, but they came back, sticking to her cheeks and mouth. "That's bedding, right?"

"Nope. They'll eat it. It's not supernutritious, but digesting fiber keeps their blood warm."

"Oh. I guess I don't know much about cows," she said.

He grinned. "Cattle."

"Yeah, right. Cattle."

Bruce leapt onto the bench seat, and Riley hoisted herself up after him, feeling strong and adventurous. She was a woman with a big dog and a hot cowboy, and she was going to feed *cattle*, not cows, from a flatbed truck. It was something new, and she loved learning new stuff.

Griff cranked the ignition and off they went, bumping over the frozen ruts in the driveway to stop at the pasture gate. Riley hopped out of the truck without a word and ran to the gate to wrestle with the chain. Once the truck had churned its way through, she swung the gate shut and hooked up the chain again. That was one thing she knew about ranching: always close the gate.

As she climbed back into the truck, Bruce greeted her as if she'd been gone for a week. Griff waited until she'd fastened her seat belt before bouncing off across the pasture. The drifting snow hid the landscape, and she wondered how he knew where to go.

Apparently he didn't, since he cruised right past the cattle, who were huddled by the side of the barn. They watched as the truck rumbled past, their shaggy faces frosted with snow, their pink noses questing the air hopefully.

"Hey," Riley said. "They're over there."

"I want to feed closer to the creek," Griff said. "If I do it up here, they'll just make a mess, plus we'd have to carry water."

Glancing in her side mirror, Riley saw a few cows leave the herd to plod reluctantly after the truck. The others milled around a bit before falling into line.

"It's like a parade," she said, putting an arm around the dog and bouncing happily in her seat.

"It is, isn't it?" Glancing over at her, he smiled warmly. She smiled back, though she probably looked a mess. In the brief time she'd spent wrestling with the gate, snowflakes had piled up on her hat, her shoulders, even her eyelashes, and now they were melting and getting drippy. It actually felt good, because her cheeks were hot from the exertion.

He finally pulled to a stop. "This'll work. 'Scuse me."

He dove toward her side of the truck, and she prepared herself for another kiss, but he was aiming for the glove compartment. She was partly relieved, partly disappointed as he rummaged around among a mass of papers and tools. Bruce managed to give

Griff a friendly slurp before he found what he was looking for: a bungee cord.

"Watch this." He hooked one end of the cord around the steering wheel, just above the crossbar, then stretched it to clip the other end onto something under the dash.

"Come on." He jumped out of the truck, and she did the same, signaling for Bruce to stay. Much of the snow had been blown off this section of the pasture, so it would have been easy to walk if it hadn't been for the wind, which cut to the bone despite all the layers and forced her to claw at her face to manage her hair.

Most of the cows retreated as Riley and Griff came around the back of the truck, but one shaggy beast stomped up to Griff and butted him lightly with an arching horn.

"Look out!" Riley wasn't afraid of animals, and Heck's Highland cattle were mostly tame, but their wide horns still made her nervous. She put one foot on the bumper and hopped up onto the back of the truck, out of their reach.

Griff laughed. "I was thinking you'd need help getting up there."

"'Course not." She grinned down at him. The butting cow was nipping at his pockets now, and Griff casually swiped it away with one arm before hoisting himself up to join her.

"Dad's got these guys too tame," he said, but he was smiling, and she was, too. The hairy cows looked like toys, with long, red hair obscuring their eyes and soft, pink noses.

Griff stood on the flatbed, fists on his hips, gazing at the land all around them. He was squinting slightly in the sun and had a satisfied expression that reminded Riley of an explorer who'd just conquered new lands. She saw his chest rise on a long, deep breath, and then he smiled.

Holy cats. The man. The hat. The way he looked out at the land as if he owned it clear to the horizon. She was pretty sure it was the other way around, and the land owned him—or at least his heart.

He ducked down to shout in her ear so she could hear him over the wind. "I'll put the truck in low gear, and then I'll jump out and help you back here. The bungee cord will steer it in a circle, and we'll pitch the hay out as we go."

"You could just drive," she said. "I can pitch the hay."

"Nope." He flashed her that grin again. "That's the fun part."

Apparently her lower-belly butterflies were immune to the cold, because despite the icy flakes pinging off her face and gusts of wind that tried to knock her from the truck, they were fluttering like mad. She clenched her legs together, trying to make the butterflies stop without acting too weird.

Naturally, he noticed she was standing like a wounded pigeon and gave her a look of grave concern that made the butterflies swoon.

"You okay? You need to, you know, *go*?"

Riley blushed. "I'm fine."

"Okay. Go stand up by the cab and hold on."

Scrambling over the bales, she found a spot just behind the cab where she could hold on to the truck's roof for balance. Hopefully it would go slow, because this was bound to be a bumpy ride.

"Oh, I almost forgot." He pulled out two pocket knives. "For the strings." He leaned over and cut one of the strings that held a bale together, then knotted it into a bundle he tossed into a bucket that hung to one side. "Don't let any of the strings get loose," he said. "We don't want a cow to eat 'em."

She took the knife. "Got it."

"Great. Get ready, then."

He jumped to the ground with the grace of a cowboy dismounting a roping horse, and as he climbed into the truck, Riley was as ready as she'd ever been.

Ready for anything.

CHAPTER 16

GRIFF SHOVED BRUCE OUT OF THE DRIVER'S SEAT AND SLIPPED the truck into low gear. "No driving, okay?" he said sternly to the dog.

He rejoined Riley on the flatbed, and the two of them got to work cutting strings, throwing them in the bucket, then separating the flakes of hay and tossing them into the snow.

The cattle caught on fast and so did Riley. Her cheeks were pink from the wind, her lashes damp and spiky from the snow, and her crazy muskrat hat was coated with snow and ice, but she was working as hard as any top hand Griff had ever seen. She didn't need his supervision, but he couldn't take his eyes off her.

The truck was going at just the right speed, crunching through the snow in a wide, slow circle. Bruce was sitting up in the driver's seat, and it was comical to see the truck lumbering across the field with the dog behind the wheel. They hit a low spot once in a while, which made the flatbed rock and forced Griff and Riley to stand spraddle-legged for balance. The first time it hit a gopher hole, Riley let out a little scream, but when he'd grabbed her arm, she'd turned to him, laughing. He wanted to fall off the truck and take her with him.

They'd land in the snow, together, and he'd kiss her... No.

He wasn't ready for a romance—but if he was, he'd want it to be with Riley.

That explained why he hadn't been more excited about Fawn Swanson on his sofa. He'd been young and shallow when he'd had that powerful crush on Wynott's golden girl—so shallow he'd been too busy picturing her naked to think about who she was or what they'd talk about. She was a nice girl, but she'd been too interested in his experiences overseas. It was like she cared more about *what* he was than *who* he was. He might be a soldier, but he was still Griff Bailey, the guy she'd ignored all her life.

Riley was no cheerleader, no golden girl, but she had an inner strength that didn't match her fragile frame or her ethereal looks. She was stomping around the flatbed like a happy kid, hefting the big bales and tossing hay like she'd been doing it all her life. She had a shine to her that didn't come from cosmetics or clothes but from her heart.

He'd pulled himself out of his reverie and bent to their task. He was tossing a bundle of strings in the bucket when something smacked him on the shoulder.

"Gotcha!"

He turned to see Riley scooping snow from the top of the cab and packing it into a ball. Scooping a cold handful of his own, he tossed it her way, making sure it flattened harmlessly against the front of her coat.

"Hey!" she yelled. "No harassing the help!"

"You probably didn't even notice that with all the clothes you've got on."

"Oh, I felt it." Strands of her hair had escaped her cap to swirl around her laughing face. Tugging them aside, she shouted over the wind, "I felt it in my soul, and I'm deeply, deeply hurt." The next snowball hit his chest dead center.

Narrowing his eyes, Griff grabbed more snow, a generous handful, and stalked her, rocking with the motion of the truck, smiling an evil, thoughtful smile.

With a girlie squeak, she danced to the other side of the hay bales.

This isn't safe. What if she falls? Those big wheels wouldn't stop turning.

With a quick move, he grabbed her sleeve and pulled her to him, intending to tell her to be careful, but she made a quick move and slipped snow into his collar that slid down his back, chilling his spine.

It was cold, but he didn't mind. He'd worked up a sweat, and he was sure she had, too. So surely she wouldn't mind cooling off as well.

He pulled her against him, laughing as she struggled, and put a handful of snow down the back of her neck. She laughed, leaning into him. There were way too many layers in the way, but that somehow made it easier to smile into her eyes and push her back against the remaining hay bales until they stood face-to-face and body to body.

She looked up at him, laughing, and what could he do but kiss her?

He'd kept that impulsive kiss in the kitchen light, but this time, when his lips touched hers, the wind suddenly dropped into a barely there breeze. Snow tumbled gently from the sky in the sudden hush, and it felt like Christmas, right there on the back of the truck. No lights needed, no presents, no shining star. Just Riley.

Her lips were warm in spite of the cold and as delicate as the rest of her. He savored them as gently as he could, shifting his position so she wouldn't know how much he meant this, how much he wanted her. But she made a sort of mew, and suddenly her arms were around his neck and her lips opened, letting him into her warmth, and he knew she meant it, too.

He had no idea where the truck was at this point. Curtains of falling snow created a private space just for the two of them, and as they rocked on through the mist, he wondered if she was as surprised as him at the way this felt, the way they fit.

They might never have stopped if the truck hadn't hit a gopher hole and nearly bucked them off. Laughing, Riley put a hand to her mouth where they'd kissed a little too hard. Her lips looked swollen and pink, but she was okay. They stood there staring at each other, grinning like idiots as they rocked with the motion of the truck, neither knowing what to say.

Finally, she cocked her head, regarding him for a moment with sparkling eyes. Then she shrugged and got back to work.

So much for that. He scratched his head, watching her bend over a bale and cut the strings, focusing on the work as if nothing had happened.

As he joined her, he wondered if she'd mention the kiss later or just pretend it never happened. He wondered if he'd get to kiss her again. If there'd be consequences.

He sure as hell hoped so.

They finished off the hay and he took her arm again, just to get her attention over the din so he could explain what they'd do next, but she turned, surprised, and gave him a look that nearly knocked him off the truck. Her eyes were wide with curiosity, her lips parted, and her complexion, normally pale, was rosy with vitality. He wondered if she thought he wanted to kiss her again.

If she did, she'd be right. But as her eyes met his, he remembered to worry about what she might see. She had some idea of the darkness he held inside, but he worried it might cast a shadow over the glow she carried with her, and that would be wrong. She was a creature of light, a fairy princess, while he was an ogre, returned from the wars with a black and tarry soul. Ogres had no business kissing princesses.

And soldiers had no business framing life in terms of fairy tales. There he was, thinking like a preteen girl again.

He cleared his throat. "I'm going to move the truck, make another line with the straw on the way back. You need to warm up?"

She shook her head quickly, like he was crazy. "Oh no, it's more fun here."

Jumping off the flatbed, he clambered up into the cab, shoving the dog aside as the truck rolled on. Removing the bungee cord, he steered into a tighter circle before tying down the steering wheel again.

Exiting the cab, he headed for the bumper to find Riley already there, holding out her hand. He took it without wondering how a slight, slender woman was going to hoist his bulk up onto the truck, and a half second later, she'd tumbled off the flatbed and into his arms.

—∼∼∼—

Riley heard Griff hit the snow with a soft *whump*, and a second later, she landed on top of him. She couldn't help letting out a scream as he grunted with the impact.

He was lucky she was wearing her puffy coat. She landed like a giant marshmallow and bounced.

"You okay?" She tried to look concerned, but she couldn't stop laughing.

His grin was like a cautionary flag, warning her he was thinking dangerous thoughts about snowballs or kisses or—or *her*.

"I'm fine," she said.

She tried to rise, but he held her tight. "Did you do that on purpose?"

"What?" She gave him her best wide-eyed innocent look. "Jump off the truck and knock you down? Would I do something like that?"

"I think you would." He rolled them over so the length of his body was pressed against hers, and *oh*, it felt good. He looked good, too, but she couldn't fully appreciate him since her muskrat hat had fallen over one eye. She wanted to tip it up, but she'd somehow lost the use of her arms. Fortunately, Griff did it for her, apparently so he could see her better. Why was he looking at her like that? He looked so serious.

He was going to kiss her again, but kissing was fun, right? Not *serious.* Sure, she wanted to rub herself against him like a cat, and the butterflies in her nether regions were applauding the idea so hard she went warm all over, but they were just friends.

With his hips pressed to hers, she could feel him growing hard. There was tension in his face, his forehead wrinkled as if he found her puzzling, and she wondered if he could see the shadows of the butterflies' beating wings in her eyes.

She was pretty puzzled herself. For example, why was she even *thinking* of kissing him again? But then again, why didn't he go ahead and *do it* already?

"All right," she said. "I *did* do it on purpose." She jutted her chin. "And I'm not sorry."

CHAPTER 17

RILEY WATCHED GRIFF'S FACE TRANSFORM WITH A SLOW smile, as if he knew she'd been picturing them rolling in the snow, kissing with all the hunger they'd built up on the truck. Her thoughts hadn't gone any farther than kissing, because she couldn't figure out what would happen next. It was cold, and there were cows. Hardly an ideal place for whatever it was those butterflies wanted.

She should make it a joke. With that in mind, she scooped up another fistful of snow and dropped it down the back of his coat.

"Hey!"

He pressed down with his hips, pinning her to the ground. Twisting as if trying to escape, she hiked up her pelvis and felt the ridge that pressed hard against his zipper. All the butterflies fainted at once, and she closed her eyes, savoring the heat that flowed from his arousal, letting it spiral up to hijack her brain. It swirled like a warm fog, making her feel deliciously helpless.

She closed her eyes and heard him gasp as he moved against her, his palms pressing into the snow. She was no longer in charge of her own body; the fog was in control, and it made her move against him in return as the heat rose more, more, even more.

She opened her eyes and his gaze slammed into her, the meeting of their minds as intimate and heated as the joining of their bodies. There was something in his expression that was almost predatory, and it took her breath away. He moved again, longer, harder, and she let her bold, careless self take over, her body daring him to do it again, again, again.

He did, and she almost lost herself completely, right there in the cold snow, in spite of all the layers of clothing between them.

Squeezing his eyes shut, he lifted his head as if struggling against his own version of that warm, swirling fog. Riley closed hers, too, clutching his sleeves in her fists and biting her lower lip.

When they opened their eyes again, it was as if a spell had been broken. Griff was Griff, and Riley was Riley. She wondered how they'd return to their casual friendship now that they'd discovered this secret force between them. She worried there'd be no more kissing on the truck, no more teamwork. No more joking and teasing.

Now you've ruined everything.

She was just sitting up when Griff made a quick, feral move and shoved a handful of snow down her shirt. Down the *front*.

She shrieked, then laughed, struggling with the zipper on her coat as he scooped up another snowball's worth. "*Aaaah!*" she screamed.

"Good enough." Grinning, he tossed the snow aside. "I just wanted to hear you scream."

"*Aaaah!*" she cried again.

He laughed. "Was that a free bonus scream?"

"*Aaaah!*" She needed to say something, do something, but she could only shriek. Finally, she squeezed out some words. "Behind you!"

"You think I'm stupid?" He began scooping up snow again. "I'm not going to fall for that. I'm going to…"

A strange expression crossed his face, probably because he felt hot breath on his neck—or smelled it, because Riley did. It smelled like hay. Old hay. Half-digested hay.

A large, shaggy head loomed over his shoulder.

"*Mrrrrroooooah,*" it said, enveloping them both in its warm, fetid breath.

Griff turned and laid one hand on the cow's broad forehead, shoving it away. "Moo yourself. We're busy here." He looked down at Riley and gave her a grin that made her insides squirm. "Now, where were we?"

Snuffling, the cow backed off, but a few of its friends had gathered to see what was going on. They stood a few feet away, shifting from one foot to another, staring at Riley and Griff as if waiting for the next act of a play.

"I thought you guys were eating." Griff rubbed the back of his neck. "How are we supposed to have a snowball fight with so many umpires?" Scooping up more snow, he tossed it toward the cows. It hit the lead cow in the middle of its forehead.

The cow blinked.

"Shouldn't we get up?" Riley tried to keep her voice from shaking. She wasn't afraid of the cows—not under normal circumstances. But with a whole herd of them staring at her while she lay prostrate in the snow, she felt a little vulnerable.

"I suppose." Griff stood and held out his hand. She let him pull her to her feet.

"Thanks." After brushing off the snow on her pants, she shaded her eyes with one hand and peered through the mist and falling snow to see the truck rumbling along. It was almost to the end of the hay row. A couple bales of straw had apparently bounced off the bed, and a small circle of cattle stood around plucking out a meal.

"I'll get those." She patted her pocket, where she'd put her folding knife. "We don't want them to eat the strings."

"You're a fast learner." Griff followed, which was kind of a relief. She was being spunky, independent Riley again, but interrupting the cows' meal didn't seem like a great idea. She'd just as soon have backup. She was cold, and she was nervous about the cows.

But at least those danged butterflies had quit their nonsense.

Griff and Riley pitched the rest of the straw off the flatbed as it rumbled toward the barn. Once it was empty, Riley sat on the back of the truck with her legs dangling over the edge. Glancing up at Griff, she pulled at the hem of his coat, motioning for him to join her.

And why not? The truck was headed in the right direction, back to the barn. Why not just ride a while, if that was what his cowgirl fairy princess wanted to do?

She'd taken off her hat and was brushing the snow from the mangy fur. Her hair flew in the wind, and snowflakes gathered in the strands around her face to make a sort of snowy halo.

Cowboy fairy princess angel.

Griff took the hat and finished the job for her, but he didn't give it back. Instead, he stroked her hair back from her face and held it so the wind wouldn't whip it into a tangled mess. He'd had a notion to pile it up inside her hat, but then she looked up at him, suddenly shy, and he realized they were close, so close. Again.

There'd be no regret this time. Sometimes a man had to listen to his gut, and his gut was telling him he and Riley would be good together. Not just this afternoon for a roll between the sheets, but *together* together. He still wondered if he'd be good for her, with the issues he'd brought home from the war. But she took pride in being an independent woman who did what she wanted, so shouldn't he let her decide?

Nesting his fingers in her hair, he tilted her head back and told her, as clearly as a kiss could, all the thoughts he'd had while they fed the cattle. His thoughts about her spunk and courage. His thoughts about how she made everything, even hard work, fun. His thoughts about how she was the prettiest girl in Wynott, bar none. She kissed him back, and when they finally pulled away, it was time for him to tell her.

Tell her what?

Before he could speak, he looked up to see the side of the barn looming up ahead. He had to leap from the truck so abruptly there was no time for words. Which was just as well, since he wasn't good at words anyway.

As the truck rumbled toward the side of the barn, he raced to the cab, leapt inside, and stopped it just in time. The sleeping Bruce looked up, annoyed, and Griff glanced at the rearview mirror to check on Riley, worried the sudden stop might have unseated her, but she was riding the truck like an oversized snowboard and looked just fine, which was quite an accomplishment in a puffy coat and astronaut boots.

She shot him a grin and a thumbs-up, and he started to wonder if he'd read that kiss wrong. His hands were still shaking, while Riley seemed to have moved on to her next adventure. The girl knew how to live.

Once he'd parked the truck, she jumped lightly to the ground and opened the passenger door to unload Bruce.

"Lazy bum," she said. "Sleeping on the job. I was almost attacked out there." She thumped his ribs as he grinned up at her. "You would have let that big, shaggy guy molest me. You didn't even bark."

Griff lifted his head from the straw he was sweeping off the flatbed. He needed a haircut, sure, but had she meant him to hear that description? Maybe he should apologize. He hadn't meant to attack her. It had been a joint effort.

Just as he opened his mouth to protest, she looked up at him, paused, and barked out that sudden, hoarse laugh of hers.

"I'm talking about the cows." She knelt and took the dog's face between her hands. "Cows could be dangerous, okay? You can't sleep through cow attacks."

She kissed the dog's flat head and stood, brushing dog hair and straw off her jeans. She was probably waiting for Griff to say something, and he wanted to. He needed to say something that would make that kiss count, that would tell her he'd meant it, but he could only stare at her openmouthed like a shaggy old cow.

She laughed again and looked away. "Come on," she said. "We're burning daylight."

"Uh, yeah." Griff was so much better at kissing her than talking to her. "I need to go check for strays. Dad didn't give me a count, so I need to make sure no cattle are caught in drifts." He waved toward the stalls. "I'll take Jess's horse. He's a trouper in the snow."

She nodded and headed for the house with a careless wave, ever the practical, git-'er-done Riley.

He should have invited her along. He could have let her ride Jess's horse, and he could have taken one of his dad's. They could have taken their time checking the drifts along the fences, and on horseback with a job to do, it would have been easier to talk.

But it was even easier to run away.

CHAPTER 18

RILEY UNBUCKLED HER TOOL BELT AND GLANCED AT HER watch. It was almost six o'clock.

Dang. She hadn't seen Griff since he rode out on Jess's old horse, Buster. He'd claimed he had to hunt cows, but Riley remembered how he'd looked, standing on the flatbed staring at his father's land. She'd expected him to take a while, but if he wasn't back in the barn by now, she'd have to go look for him.

She was reaching for her coat when Bruce let out a low *woof*. Glancing out the window, she saw a car pull into the drive.

"Calm down, buddy," she said as the car door opened. "It's just..." She squinted. "It's Fawn Swanson."

The butterflies folded their wings, their fluttery hopes dashed. Griff had mooned over Fawn for years. Even that night at the quarry, he'd been watching her, waiting for her to notice him. Riley was sure she'd been his second choice.

She pasted on a smile as she opened the door. "Hey, Fawn. How are you?"

"Good." Fawn peered past her into the house. "Where's Griff?"

Riley shrugged. "I'm not sure. He went out riding earlier, and he's not back yet." Her smile turned genuine, thinking of Griff and the horses. "He's really enjoying the horses."

"That's very good news." Fawn's brow wrinkled, and her eyes took on a pious look. "I know he needs something to help him through this difficult time."

That was true. In a way, Riley had been thinking the same thing. So why was she so annoyed?

"He needs more than horses, though," Fawn continued. "He needs people around. Friends. That's why we're going to the

Red Dawg." She glanced at her watch, frowning. "I said five thirty."

Riley nodded, swallowing hard. It sounded like Griff had a date with Fawn tonight, which made it awfully rude of him to kiss Riley the way he had. Three times. Twice like he *meant* it.

The butterflies were on their backs now, their wings still, their legs waggling weakly in the air. "I'm sure he'll be back soon."

She tried to picture him in the crowded bar, but her imaginary Griff insisted on sitting in a corner booth, alone. He even unscrewed the light bulb that hung over the table so he could sit in the dark, and he was still mad he'd had to come.

Except he'd be with Fawn. He'd probably do anything for her— even mix and mingle.

"Do you want to check the barn and see if he's back?" she asked.

"No. I'll wait." Fawn edged past Bruce into the living room. She glared down at the sofa where Riley had left her romance novel, her fluffy pillow, and the soft blanket printed with frolicking bunnies that obviously didn't belong to Griff.

With a little moue of distaste, Fawn placed the pillow and the blanket on the floor and took possession of Riley's favorite spot. The look she shot Riley smacked of triumph—or was Riley imagining that?

She really ought to sit down and make small talk, but she had no idea what to say. If Fawn had come in to the hardware store looking for some power tools, she would have had plenty to talk about, but Fawn was into hairstyles and fancy fingernails. There was nothing wrong with that, but they had nothing in common.

"I'll go out to the barn," she finally said. "See if he's back."

"Thank you," Fawn said stiffly.

Riley couldn't imagine how Griff could be late for a date with his dream girl. Had he forgotten? Or was something wrong?

⌁

Dumping the curry brush he was using to a bucket, Griff led Jess's horse, Buster, back to his stall, glancing around, wondering if he could just hide.

His stomach had done a slow, sickening flip when Fawn's car rolled up. He'd forgotten all about their date. He'd even forgotten today was Sunday.

And he'd just kissed Riley James three times. Not to mention that tumble in the snow.

He watched through the wavy panes of a smudged barn window as Fawn marched up to the house, wondering what was wrong with him. He'd wanted a date with Fawn all his life, but watching her now, he felt like a hunted animal.

Tugging his hat down over his eyes, he remembered her comments the other day.

You probably need somebody to talk to.

You can't close yourself off, you know. Don't bottle it up inside.

It's time to jump back into life, okay?

She meant well, but those helpful admonitions sounded like threats right now.

He'd met women like that before—women who wanted to save his tragic soldier soul. He knew how to stave them off; a few dull stories of long patrols usually lost their interest, and if that didn't work, a guy could just get crass with a few off-color stories.

He had one foot on the ladder to the hayloft when Riley's slim silhouette appeared in the doorway.

"Griff?" She squinted through the dust motes that danced in the light from the windows. "Fawn's here. She says you have a date."

"Yeah, *she* made that date. I didn't. Can you tell her I'm not here?"

Riley stared at him as if he'd gone crazy. "Didn't you hear me? It's Fawn. Your dream girl."

"Yeah, well, I changed my mind about that. Um…"

His throat suddenly went dry, and his eyes welled up. He had stuff bottled up all right, and right now most of it was about Riley, so he sat down hard on the bottom rung of the ladder and bowed his head, hiding his eyes beneath the brim of his hat.

Geez, what a doofus. Tell Riley she's your *dream girl. Tell* her.

His dream girl shrugged. "It's no big deal, Griff. I've always known you liked her. But you'd better get inside. She's pretty mad you're late."

"I don't… I don't…" He groaned, dropping his head into his hands.

"Hey, I realize the Red Dawg on dollar-beer night's a lot to deal with." She sounded chirpy, encouraging. "You could get a six-pack and go out by the quarry instead."

His heart twisted. Didn't she realize that was *their* thing? Doing it with Fawn would be like blasphemy. He needed to tell her that— but instead, he rolled his eyes. "Then we'd have to *talk*."

Punching his arm like a buddy would, she grinned. "Then the Red Dawg's perfect. You won't be able to hear yourself think in there. Plus you can get a buzz on."

He nodded miserably. He'd been worried about hurting Riley's feelings, but it was obvious that she was over whatever had happened between them.

"If you really want me to, I'll go in there and tell her you're not home yet, but judging from the look in her eye, she'd mount a posse and go after you." Riley laughed, and the hoarse, sudden sound sent a squadron of doves blasting from the rafters. She jumped, startled, but Griff didn't.

Hey, he was getting better.

"I'll be right there," he said.

"Great. I'll tell her."

Fawn's voice rang in his head as he hung the grooming bucket on a hook.

I heard about what you did over there. You're a hero.

She had it all wrong. Whatever she'd heard had been filtered, washed, and sanitized by the military, because he was definitely not a hero. How could he be, when he was afraid of a five-foot-nothing hairstylist with a dimpled smile and a tinkling laugh?

CHAPTER 19

"HE'LL BE RIGHT IN," RILEY TOLD FAWN. "HIS HORSE WAS sweaty."

Fawn gave her a skeptical look.

"The sweat froze because it's so cold, and then he had to chip the ice off its hooves."

"Won't all that just melt?" Fawn asked. "He knew we had a date. I'm here to *help* him."

Riley swallowed a pang of jealousy. She'd hoped Griff would turn to her for help, but then, he'd probably heard she'd barely survived her own problems. She was the last person anyone would ask for advice.

When Griff walked in, stamping snow off his boots and shrugging out of his coat, Fawn rushed right to him. *Right* to him. Riley wouldn't dare invade his personal space like that unless he asked. Or unless he was asleep and didn't know she was there.

"Griff!" Fawn grabbed his hands. "Are you all right? Riley said you might have gotten lost! I was so *worried*."

Riley's mouth dropped open. She hadn't told Fawn that Griff was lost. And Fawn hadn't been worried; she'd been furious. In fact, Griff had better toe the line for the rest of the night, or his first date with Wynott's sweetheart would be his last.

Griff looked down at Fawn and tried to feel the way he was supposed to—sorry because he'd forgotten their date and worried because she might be mad. He should be turned on, too, because she was wearing a low-cut shirt that would have had the old Griff drooling. But all he felt was annoyed. He'd been looking forward to a quiet night with Riley, sitting by the fire together, reading. His doctor had told him that was the kind of thing that would heal him: quiet times with family. Not nights in a crowded bar.

Sorry. Can't go. Doctor's orders.

Maybe he could pull that off, but of course Fawn would want to know more, and he didn't really want anyone to know he'd seen a doctor or spent three months in a military hospital trying to tame those buzzing black bees.

"You'd better get cleaned up." Fawn wrinkled her sweet, tip-tilted nose. "I can tell you've been riding."

"Right." Griff glanced over at Riley.

"Don't worry." She was trying to be game, but she looked like he'd sent her to the executioner. "Fawn and I'll catch up while you're gone."

"I'll be quick."

By the time he got downstairs, Riley was seated by the fire with Fawn, who perched ramrod straight on the edge of her chair with perfect posture that emphasized her generous curves. Her eyes flashed with the triumph of a cheerleader whose team was trouncing the competition. Riley, on the other hand, looked limp as a picked daisy too long out of water. Griff figured he'd look like that by the end of the night.

He gave himself a mental slap. He'd wanted Fawn with an almost desperate longing for most of his adolescence. Now, *she* wanted *him*. He ought to be overjoyed.

"You look great." She jumped to her feet. "I like that shirt."

He didn't. He'd apparently bulked up overseas, so he'd had to borrow one of the shirts his dad wore when he worked pickup at the rodeo. Striped in loud colors, it was too garish for a man accustomed to army green and camouflage.

"See you later, Riley," he said.

Riley looked at Fawn, then bit her lip and nodded.

He wanted to tell her, right there and then, that she shouldn't compare herself to Fawn. Sure, Fawn came from an old Wynott family and was a cheerleader and a beauty queen. And if you didn't know her, Riley might look like more of an outsider, one who'd come to Wynott with nothing but a bad reputation.

But that was *what* they were. When you looked at who they were inside, Riley won hands down.

"Have a good time," Riley said, her tone flat.

"Thanks." Fawn looked up at him as if waiting for something. He finally realized he was supposed to put his hand in the small of her back and usher her toward the door. Glancing back, he saw Riley staring after them. Her eyes looked sad, and a gong rang inside him.

Wrong, wrong, wrong.

But he couldn't see a way to stay. He'd tried to hide, but Riley herself wouldn't let him, which was a pretty good hint that those kisses hadn't meant much to her.

They'd meant a lot to him—but how would she know? He was leaving with another woman—one who was her opposite in every way.

CHAPTER 20

The Red Dawg was humming when Griff and Fawn arrived, but a hush fell over the crowd the moment they entered. As the swinging saloon-style doors flapped behind them, the dim light from the Tiffany shades over the pool table caught the gleam of dozens of eyes, all of them looking their way.

Somebody clapped and he almost bolted, but nobody joined in, and the applause faded to a scattered ripple. There was a hoot from one corner, a "booyah" from another, plus a rush of words as a few people rose and came to greet him.

Most of the folks were older men he recognized, along with some guys he knew from high school. Several clapped him on the back, and everybody shook his hand. Their words blended together, and he was unsure of who said what.

"Heard about what you did over there."

"Griff! Long time, no see, buddy!"

"Hey, soldier. How's it going?"

And stiffly, "Thank you for your service, sir."

Through it all, Fawn stood beaming like a kid who'd brought her shiny new pony to the fair, and Griff realized why she was suddenly interested in him. He was a trophy date. As long as she clung to his elbow, Fawn could bask in some sort of reflected glory. She didn't know he didn't deserve it. Didn't know they had it all wrong.

Once he managed to extricate himself from the crowd, Fawn steered him toward the booths that lined the back wall, but he resisted. They were dim and private, and he didn't want to be trapped there with Fawn in case she started with the Dr. Phil stuff again. Instead, he led her to a table near the bar. Fawn happily hiked herself up onto one of the tall chairs and smiled, patting the seat beside her.

"See? I told you everyone would be glad to see you." She beamed. "When we heard you were back, a lot of people thought we should have a parade, but some of the older guys said it wasn't a good idea." Her pretty eyes softened, and she gently touched his arm. "It might remind you of…things."

He nodded, doing his best to look soulful and damaged. If she thought he was a basket case, she might get bored and leave him alone.

He was relieved when the house band hit the stage at nine and played rock-laced country songs loud enough to make conversation a challenge. Griff watched a smattering of couples make their way to the dance floor and sensed Fawn casting him meaningful looks as if she wanted to get up there and join the two-steppers, but he wasn't in the mood.

He wasn't in the mood for any of this, and he was starting to feel sorry for Fawn. She seemed genuinely concerned about him, but her approach was all wrong somehow. Maybe she was right and he was afraid to get into the water or whatever.

He resolved to try harder as a waitress approached. Griff recognized her, but danged if he could remember her name.

"Well, hey, look who's here! What can I get *you two*?" She emphasized the last two words, touching Fawn's arm, widening her eyes, and giving her a not-so-subtle congratulatory nod.

"Hey, Lucy," Fawn said. "A cosmopolitan for me."

Lucy George. Griff remembered her now. She'd dated one of his friends, but asking about that would probably be awkward.

"Beer." He looked down at the table. "Any kind."

A shadow fell over the table and Griff looked up warily, expecting another well-wisher he barely remembered, but he actually smiled when he saw who it was.

"Matt Lassiter." He stood and shook the newcomer's hand. "Long time, buddy."

This time, the handshaking and backslapping felt good. Lassiter had been a fellow contestant on the rodeo team and the ultimate troublemaker all through high school. If a relatively harmless prank involved fireworks, spray paint, or wayward animals, Matt had been the man for the job.

Obviously, things had changed. Somehow, Grigsby High's most notorious prankster had gotten himself elected town marshal. Lean and sinewy, with piercing brown eyes, he looked like a worthy adversary for Wynott's criminal underworld—if only there were one. As far as Griff knew, the town's isolated location had kept it clean and innocent, without the taint of drugs or crime—so far. It was Matt's job to keep it that way.

"How are you?" Matt pulled out a chair and joined them. A slight frown tugged at the corner of Fawn's polite smile, but Griff was relieved. Having Matt here made the whole "date" thing a lot easier.

"I'm good. You know Fawn, right?"

Matt nodded, and they made small talk for a while, talking about Matt's job, some incidents at the high school, and a robbery at the convenience store at the edge of Wynott. Griff was starting to enjoy himself, but his mind kept wandering back to the ranch, back to Riley and the sorrowful look in her eyes just before he'd left—the look she'd covered up with that phony pasted-on smile.

He'd honestly forgotten about the date with Fawn. If he'd remembered, maybe he wouldn't have kissed Riley.

Yeah, right.

Who was he kidding? Nothing could have stopped him out there on the truck. But he could have explained the situation in advance. Or called Fawn and canceled.

He couldn't believe Riley had suggested he and Fawn go down to the quarry. That was the last place he and Riley had been intimate—or was it? He'd woken this morning with her snugged up against him, enjoyed the warmth of her body, and heard the soft whisper of her breath. That was intimate, wasn't it?

Suddenly, he missed her with almost a physical ache.

"Hey, buddy," Matt said. "You here with us or on another planet?"

"Sorry." Griff gave him a rueful smile. "Another planet, I guess."

Fawn reached over and took his hand, her eyes shining with compassion. She was a sweet, kind woman, and Griff was sure her kindness was genuine. He just wished it wasn't aimed at him.

"He's been through so much," she said to Matt. "Sometimes he just gets lost in his thoughts." With a winsome smile, she nudged his arm. "You're surprised I know that, aren't you? Well, I've been doing some reading about soldiers coming home from war. And I'm not a professional or anything, but I think I have a good understanding of what you've been through and what you need."

Oh, sweet Jesus, get me out of here. Now.

He gave her a sickly smile. "Sure, Fawn. But I'm okay. Doing fine."

He wasn't, though. The din in the bar was clanging inside his head, and the dark corners, together with the milling crowd, made him nervous.

He cleared his throat and tossed a desperate look at Matt. "So what's it like patrolling the mean streets of Wynott?"

Matt laughed. "It's even worse than you'd imagine. Mostly, I get old ladies who mistake stray cats for stalkers and complaints about barking dogs." He sobered. "But trouble's coming. I partnered with the state police busting up a meth factory out in the county, and somebody was selling pills at the high school in Grigsby. We've got so many different types of community—the ranchers out in your area, the little downtown area, the trailer parks, and the mountains, with who-knows-who squirreled up in those remote cabins. We've been having issues with squatters."

"Are you the only law in town?"

"Might as well be." Matt sighed. "Jim Swaggard ran against me, and he was so crushed he didn't get elected that I took him on as a deputy. Trust me, I need another one. He still hasn't qualified to carry a weapon, and it's been three years."

Griff chuckled, and it was real humor this time. Jim was Wynott's one-man volunteer police force before the town could pay for a full-time law-enforcement officer. They'd chosen to elect a marshal, like the Wild West town they were, but Jim had more enthusiasm than skills, and his law-enforcement education came from *Law & Order* reruns rather than the police academy. He'd been dedicated, riding a bicycle around town in a uniform he'd fashioned for himself that boasted a marshal's star that looked like it came from a Toys"R"Us Western Lawman kit. Nobody took Jim seriously, but he'd considered himself the only man standing between Wynott and the lawless wilderness.

"Hey, I heard Riley James is working on your house," Matt said. "I haven't seen her for a while."

"Yeah, my dad has her staying out there." Griff felt Fawn stiffen slightly. "She's torn everything apart, so now I guess she's putting it back together."

"Yeah, well, Riley's really good at fixing things," Matt said.

Things like me.

Suddenly, the din of the bar seemed to roar in Griff's ears and he wanted, *needed* to be back at the ranch with Riley. Fawn thought she could fix him, but only someone who'd been through fire themselves, who'd had to conquer her own demons, would understand what it was like.

He thought of Riley's blunt, nonjudgmental ways, her hoarse, boyish voice, and her tool belt—well, not really the tool belt itself, but the way it slung around her hips, making her look strong and capable even as it emphasized her delicate femininity—and the need to go home hit him like a freight train. He put a hand to his forehead.

"What?" Fawn put her hand on his arm. He resisted the urge to shake her off. "What's the matter?"

"I'm just…" Griff did his best to give her an apologetic look. "I get these headaches."

He wasn't entirely fibbing. She'd given him a headache the other day with all her lectures about closing himself off and jumping into the deep end of some pool, and another one was coming on fast.

"I think I'd better go home." He stood clumsily, almost knocking over his chair. "They can get pretty bad."

"Really?" Fawn looked woefully disappointed, and he suddenly realized what a heel he was. She was only trying to help him as best she could. Sure, she was clueless, but it wasn't like she'd ever lived in the real world. She was a Wynott girl, safe and protected. And while his interest in her was waning, he wouldn't want her to be any other way. The world needed girls like Fawn—pure of heart, transparent of motive, and not too complicated of mind. *Normal* girls, for normal guys.

"I thought… Well, I thought we'd talk more," she said. "I really think I can help you, Griff."

Then take me home to Riley.

"Maybe another time," he said. "Matt could drive me now, though, so you can stay. The band's pretty good."

"Griff Bailey." He winced. Her tone reminded him of his third-grade teacher. Mrs. Sabellico had been as strict as she was tiny, and she'd held even the biggest boys—who happened to be Matt and Griff—in check. "I am your date for the evening, and I will take care of you." She turned to Matt. "Excuse us, please. I need to take him home."

Matt, looking concerned, tried to get a look at Griff's face. "You going to be okay, buddy?"

Griff hated this—being the center of attention, making his friends worry. But he needed to get out of here. "I'll be okay. Just need to get home."

"I'll get you there." Fawn stroked his arm, giving him a worried look. "Don't you worry about a thing."

CHAPTER 21

By the time Fawn pulled into the Diamond Jack, Griff had gone completely silent. He didn't dare say a word, because Fawn seemed convinced the passenger seat of her Subaru Outback was a therapist's couch. Worse yet, she thought she was the therapist.

"You need to talk about it, Griff," she said for the umpteenth time as they turned into the Diamond Jack. "These things just fester inside you like infected wounds."

So far, she'd compared his thoughts and memories to infected wounds, birds in a cage, and even rats in a trap. No wonder he had a headache. It was busy in there.

But the comparisons weren't far off. In fact, her willingness to take on his unspeakable memories would be funny if it wasn't so awful. He never wanted those thoughts, or anything like them, to touch sweet Fawn or anyone else in Wynott.

"Thanks," he said as she stopped the car. "Sorry to end things, you know, prematurely. It's just... I'm not ready to talk about this stuff. Plus there's a lot there that I can't tell a civilian."

Her eyes widened. "You mean it's classified?"

He nodded, looking somber. "Top secret."

He wasn't lying. Some of his activities overseas *had* been confidential. He wished he'd thought of that sooner.

"Why didn't you tell me?" she asked. "Oh, Griff, here I've been asking and asking, and you've been so strong and brave. Some men would have spilled their secrets to me, I'm sure."

Griff was sure, too. She was lovely and sweet and very, very kind. Here in the close quarters of the car, he'd realized she smelled like flowers, sunshine, and a sort of innocence that was rare in this world.

But he and Fawn didn't fit together. It was like they were dolls from two different manufacturers. He was a GI Joe, he supposed, while Fawn was one of those old Kewpie dolls, all curls and cuteness.

"Good night," he said. She leaned in for a kiss, but he took her hand instead. "It was too much, going to the bar tonight, but I know you were trying to help."

"There are other ways I could help," she said.

Before he could bail out of the car, she lunged toward him, pressing her face to his. He had no choice but to return the kiss, but it was so deep he felt kind of violated.

He sure hoped Riley wasn't looking out the window.

—◆—

Riley was working on a particularly stubborn pipe fitting when Bruce let out a warning *woof*. Glancing out the window, she saw Fawn's car turn into the drive. She ran into Jess's bedroom to hide, since she was dressed for hard work in a cheap man's undershirt from Kmart and her oldest jeans, which were wildly out of style and downright indecent, with holes in both butt cheeks and flared legs that made her look stuck in the sixties. Her tool belt tugged down the waistband, making the jeans hang indecently low on her hips, and the weight of it stretched the undershirt to reveal every bit of her nonexistent cleavage.

She couldn't help peeking out the window. Griff was home early, which shouldn't have surprised her. He and Fawn probably couldn't wait to be alone together.

She wondered if he'd kiss Fawn the way he'd kissed her.

He'd better not.

No, stop it. Just stop it. It's not like he's yours. He has every right.

Griff was a soldier home from war. He probably hadn't kissed a woman in a year, and Riley had to admit she'd asked for it. Or at least she would have if she'd known she'd had a chance of getting it.

And boy, oh boy, she'd gotten it. Griff gave the kind of kisses that lasted a lifetime. Smiling, she touched her lips as she tilted the curtains in Jess's bedroom and looked out. Griff and Fawn hadn't gotten out of the car yet. They must be talking. Or doing something else.

She froze as the passenger door swung open and the dome light flickered to life, revealing the two of them pressed together so passionately it was hard to tell where Fawn ended and Griff began. They were sharing a warm, passionate kiss that left no doubt as to what would happen next.

Riley turned away, feeling sick. When Bruce padded into the room, she knelt to ruffle the fur around his ruff and kiss the top of his furry head.

"Griff's my friend," she whispered to the dog. "I should be happy for him. A kiss doesn't mean I own him, right?"

The dog's amber eyes stared steadily into hers, filled with adoration.

"Oh, sure, you're easy. A kiss and some kibble and you're mine. But men are different."

She couldn't tell if it was jealousy, embarrassment, or fury that was making her burn from the inside out, but whatever it was, she needed to drown it. She didn't drink, so she'd have to use the bathtub. Fortunately, Jess's room was the first where she'd installed an en suite bathroom for future dude-ranch guests. The rest were all plumbed and mostly done, but this was the only one with flooring.

As soon as she heard the front door open and close, she turned on the water full blast. After witnessing that kiss, she definitely didn't want to hear the sweet nothings they'd be babbling at each other. She needed to scrub off her selfishness and find some happiness for her friend. Her *friend*.

"I just wish I *liked* her better," she told Bruce. "There's really nothing wrong with her. *Nothing.* Considering how pretty she is, Fawn's a really nice person."

And unlike Riley, she was a perfect match for Griff. Like him, she was heir to a ranching family, the product of generations of cowboys who'd found their cowgirls. And while Griff might think he was through with ranching, she'd seen his heritage in his eyes every time he worked with the horses.

"He'll figure it out," she told the dog. "He'll marry her and raise a nice family right here on the Diamond Jack. And I couldn't do that. I wouldn't be any good at it."

She just wasn't mother material. For one thing, she might as well have been raised by wolves for all her own mother had cared. For another thing… Well. The past was past, and she didn't like to think about it.

With Bruce passed out on the bath mat, snoring like a sailor, she managed to soak away her jealousy, along with the sore muscles she'd earned from a day's hard work. Once she'd towel-dried her hair and donned her favorite pajamas—pink stripes and kittens— she slipped between the sheets with her book. Bruce joined her, leaping up on the foot of the bed.

"This is great," she told the dog. "It's about a fictional city girl and a fictional cowboy, and they're having fictional torrid sex every five fictional pages."

She flipped the pages, reading every word but failing to string them together and give them meaning. When she did, she pictured Griff as the cowboy, which worked, but then she imagined herself to be the city girl, and that was ridiculous. She should picture Fawn in that role, but that would be ooky, because the sex scenes were pretty hot.

Between thinking about Griff naked and remembering the fudge-dipped Oreos she'd left on the counter downstairs, she was dying of intense, unyielding needs. She should have grabbed those cookies before she came upstairs. They were the next best thing to sex—except for chocolate cake. Cake was even closer.

Moving the curtains aside, she glanced out the window. A crescent moon was riding high in the sky, hooking a wreath of wispy clouds. The shadows of the tall pines stretched across the lawn, and the barn was a featureless hulk except for the golden squares of its lighted windows. The driveway was rutted, and footprints led up to the door—but there was only one set of prints, and no car in the turnout.

She's gone.

Riley knew Fawn had insisted on driving Griff to the bar, probably because once she'd tracked him down, she wanted to keep him under control. That meant she must have left. And unless she'd taken Griff with her, he must be down there alone.

Riley pressed her hands to her heart, trying to squelch the leaping, spinning puppy-dog antics that were stealing her breath. She wished her heart could have some dignity, like Bruce, who had fallen asleep and was breathing slowly, steadily, with one leg twitching as he chased imaginary rabbits.

It was no big deal that Fawn was gone. Griff had probably hated the bar. All the people had probably exhausted him, so he'd gone to bed.

Take that, puppy dog.

Her heart whimpered and settled down, but its tail was still twitching hopefully. Then she remembered how Griff had looked the night before with his hard features gentled by sleep, that lock of hair dangling over his forehead, his lips slightly parted…

Up jumped the puppy dog, dancing.

"Stop it," she whispered. "*Down.*"

Casting her an aggrieved look, Bruce slid down from the bed.

"Not you, doofus."

Sighing, the dog tossed himself on the floor and seemed to fall instantly into a deep sleep. Riley giggled at his snores as she tiptoed to her door and strained her ears for some indication that the man of the house was awake. She was about to give up when there was a clang of the woodstove door and a thump that sounded like a log being tossed on the fire.

So he *was* down there. And Riley needed those cookies, she really did. If she ran into him on her way to get them and he wanted to talk, well, it would be rude to leave, wouldn't it?

Elated, she bent down and kissed the dog on the head again, then trotted down the stairs. She was halfway down before she remembered the kitten pajamas, but hey, they were better than the worn, see-through tank top.

CHAPTER 22

GRIFF CLOSED THE DOOR OF THE WOODSTOVE AND WIPED HIS mouth for the umpteenth time. Fawn had totally stunned him with that kiss, and the sheer seductive heat of it made him wonder if she'd changed since high school. She'd had a reputation as a flirt who'd touch and tease, then dance away at the last minute, but that kiss had invited much more. It had implied a certain sly knowing, and he had a feeling Fawn didn't dance away anymore.

Once, his hands would have been all over the lithe, athletic body he'd dreamed of all through high school, but tonight, he'd just wanted to be alone. Going to bed with Fawn meant waking up with Dr. Phil, so he'd begged off, citing the headache, and sent her off a little hurt and a lot confused.

He was confused himself. Riley had gone to bed, which left him flat and deflated yet relieved—because what would he say to her?

Well, she was Riley, so he'd have to tell her the truth.

I sat there with her, and all I could think about was you.

I missed you the whole night.

But if she'd seen that kiss… Lord, he hoped she hadn't seen it, because how could he explain that?

I didn't want to do it. She overpowered me. I was just being polite.

She'd never believe that.

The truth was, he shouldn't have kissed anyone, let alone Riley, as long as the bees were still buzzing inside him. He'd lost his temper in her truck, and he never wanted to do that to her again. She'd made some mistakes in her life and been mixed up with some pretty bad people, some of whom had hurt her badly. While she'd bounced back from all that remarkably well, the last thing she needed was a mess like him riding shotgun.

Opening the woodstove, he poked at the fire, then slouched down in the chair and bent his head over his book, but the words danced on the page. With a curse, he threw the novel down and ducked his head into his hands.

"Griff?"

He lifted his head, blinking, and there she was, dressed in the most adorable pajamas he'd ever seen. Her long hair spiraled down her back in silver tendrils, and he had a crazy notion that if he opened his arms, she would run to him, let him hold her, let him whisper in her ear that Fawn was nothing to him, nothing, and she was everything.

Because she was.

But he knew she deserved better—so he stared at her, wordless, with his mouth hanging open, the words he needed to say all jumbled up and caught in his throat.

Something must have gone wrong on Griff's date, because Riley found him sitting with his head in his hands, looking like his world had ended—which was strange, considering that kiss. It had looked like love to her, or at least a whole lot of lust.

The fire he'd built warmed the room, and the twinkle lights tucked into the garland on the mantel were reflected in the red balls on the tree, warming the room with the serenity of Christmas. But Griff looked anything but serene. Riley didn't know what had happened, but she had a sudden urge to race down the road, haul Fawn out of her car, and bust her lip for hurting him.

Griff was a good man and a strong one, but he'd been through a lot and didn't need some woman messing with his head. Everybody knew he'd always yearned for Fawn, and no doubt Fawn knew it, too. Had she led him on and then smacked him down? The man was a war hero. He'd been through hell. How *could* she?

"Riley." Griff looked up, wiping his face as if he could erase his emotions—sadness, regret, with some anger underneath. The Christmas lights, along with the flickering firelight, made his face a study in light and shadow. "I didn't hear you come down."

"Didn't mean to sneak up on you." She stood by the mantel, fooling with the twinkle lights as if Molly Bailey hadn't arranged them perfectly.

"It's okay." He tried to smile, but it slid sideways and faded fast. "My warrior skills are letting me down, that's all. Or maybe you're a ninja master spy who missed her calling." He dropped his voice and put on an English accent. "Bond, Jane Bond."

She couldn't help grinning. She'd never seen Griff try to be funny before, and while the joke was kind of lame, it made her think he might be all right despite whatever Fawn had done.

"My ninja skills are a little weak," she said. "For instance, I can't figure out why you let Fawn go home. I thought sure you'd invite her in."

"No." He rested his elbows on his knees, keeping his eyes fixed on the fire. "Fawn's not…she's not who I thought she was."

"Fawn hasn't changed."

He looked up, his eyes filled with an intensity that surprised her. "Maybe I have."

Riley frowned. "So the girl you always wanted is chasing after you, and you're not into it. Are you trying to punish yourself?"

"No." He chuckled. "No, I'm not that noble. It's just… It's not going to work with Fawn. You know what she did? She read all sorts of books on the military, combat, PTSD, you name it, thinking she'd help me heal from some terrible trauma. But she's never been through anything worse than a hangnail herself, so it just won't work." He sighed. "You were right when you said she hasn't changed. She's still perfect, the heart of this little town. But I don't want perfect."

He leveled a gaze at Riley that seemed oddly heated,

considering they were talking about how much he *didn't* want a woman. Unless… No. He couldn't mean that.

"What *do* you want, then?" She tried to keep her tone light, but her voice broke on the last word. His affect didn't change. She was probably imagining the faint flame that rose, then fell behind his stony expression.

"I want somebody who can find her way through the dark," he said. "Somebody who knows what it's like to fail and have to claw your way back to life after the dust settles. Somebody who's been through the fire."

"That's what I thought." Riley didn't think Fawn was the right woman for Griff, either, and it wasn't just jealousy. Griff had put into words exactly what was bothering her. "You need somebody who's seen the bigger picture. Somebody tough. But I don't know why you'd want somebody who *failed*. I was thinking somebody strong, like you—a kickass Army Ranger girl, or a real Jane Bond."

Because if you want someone who failed, I'm it. I don't know why you'd want that, but here I am. I've crashed and burned a dozen times. Is that what you want?

He reached out and took her hand to pull her down beside him. "It's a phoenix, right?"

She stared at him, confused by the total change of subject.

"Your tattoo." With a faint smile, he stroked the curling inked tail that coiled up from her collar. "It rises from the fire, and it's stronger for it, right?"

His hand followed the feathers that coiled around her neck, while his eyes glowed with reflected light from the tree. A Christmas hush fell over the room, and the scene felt somehow holy—so she didn't pull away when he cupped the back of her head, those eyes on hers, sleepy, smiling. He'd just kissed another woman, and now he was—what was he doing?

She didn't care, because hey, it was the season of giving, not the season of asking questions.

"Come on," he said softly. "Come here."

Drawn by that flame, she closed the distance between them, and their lips met in a kiss that seemed to change the texture of the night, binding them together in a sweet, clandestine dream. She closed her eyes, feeling dizzy, disembodied, as if she'd stumbled into Alice's rabbit hole and lost all sense of time and self. All that was left was sensation—the questing press of his lips, the tangle of their tongues, his fingers forked in her hair as he took her so thoroughly she was sure she'd be changed forever.

Except for that night at the quarry, she'd kissed all the wrong men for all the wrong reasons. There'd always been an equation, a transaction. *You do me and I'll do you. I need this, I'll give you that.* But kissing Griff wasn't about giving or taking. It was about finding a place to belong.

It had taken a long time to find that place, and that was fine with her. She never wanted to leave this kiss. Never wanted to come back to the real world.

But all good things come to an end, and she wanted that to be on *her* terms. Finally, regretfully, she pulled away, but he held her close, and she couldn't help it. She let him. She rested her head on his chest and breathed in the scent of him.

"This is what I came back for." The rumble of his voice vibrated through her body, and she shivered. "I told her some story about an old war wound acting up, but I came back for you."

Riley closed her eyes, absorbing the words, holding them in her heart, treasuring them—but then she remembered that kiss.

She'd just seen it, so how could she fall for this? Griff wasn't being sneaky; he was just trying to let her down easy to protect her self-esteem. She'd only believed him because he'd kissed her and shorted out her brain.

Pushing off his shoulder, she stood and shoved her hands in her pockets. She gave him a cockeyed smile to soften the blow, but she didn't soften her words.

"You're busted, Griff," she said. "I saw you kiss Fawn out there."

He looked stunned. He'd thought she wasn't watching.

Rising, he stood with his hands loose at his sides. As she watched, he clenched his fists, then unclenched them. "It wasn't what you think, Riley. *She* kissed *me*."

She laughed. "Griff, it's okay. I know it's been a while since you've had, you know, women around. You get overexcited—like just now, or this afternoon on the truck. I know it didn't mean anything."

"Maybe not to you."

"Maybe not to you, either, since you left with Fawn, like, half an hour later," she shot back—but she was still smiling. He was just back from Iraq, after all. The man deserved a break. "Look, I know how you've always felt about her, and it's great she finally realizes what a great guy you are."

"I'm not a great guy, Riley. I'm a mess." He spread his hands helplessly. "I mean, look at this moment. I've completely screwed up."

She did her best to laugh. "If you're a mess, the world needs more messes. You're a war hero, for heaven's sake."

"I'm no hero." He took her hands and drew her toward him. Resting his forehead against hers, he forced her to meet his gaze. "Trust me, all those reports are wrong. If there's a hero in this room, it's you. You're the one who's been through the dark and come out strong." He smiled gently. "That's why you light up every room you walk into."

"Only when I bring the wiring up to code." She smiled and gave his hands a gentle shake. "I got myself into trouble. I'm not a hero for getting out. And trust me, I had help."

"We all need help. I think you're mine."

She slid her gaze sideways, trying to avoid the intensity of his stare. She wanted to shake off his hands, spin around, and flee, but she knew he needed to talk. Hero or not, he'd been prepared to give his life for his country. The least she could do was listen.

"I made mistakes, and it cost some men their lives," he said. "I feel like a fraud with all Fawn's hero crap, but if I tell her the truth, she'll never let it go." The flame in the depths of his eyes rose even as he seemed to relax. "You're the only one who gets me at all, Riley. It's always been that way." He looked down a moment, and it was clear whatever was coming next was costing him. He wasn't a man who talked about emotions easily.

"It wasn't her I thought about over there in the desert," he finally said. "Those long nights—it was *you* I remembered. *You* that got me through. Just you."

CHAPTER 23

RILEY MELTED. SHE COULDN'T HELP IT.

Men were always full of flattery when they wanted something—and Griff definitely wanted something he probably wouldn't get from Fawn. Not yet, anyway. Sweet Fawn Swanson wasn't going to hop into bed with him after one date—not even after that kiss. Romance for girls like her wasn't about hot, sweaty, honest sex; it was about candlelit dinners and diamond bracelets, and then she *might* give in. Tonight, she'd given him that one wild kiss and sent him on his way, crazy with need. A need Riley could satisfy.

Lord knew she wanted to. Heck, she almost *had* to. The butterflies in her nether parts were having a hoedown, and only his touch, his hand right *there*, would make them stop.

He was still staring at her, waiting, she realized, for an answer.

And the answer, despite the warning lights in her brain, was rising from her heart—and it was *yes*.

It wasn't like Fawn owned him. As a matter of fact, she doubted Fawn could even handle him. As he loomed over Riley like the powerful animal he was, she figured Fawn would squeak like a mouse and run away at the sight of him. It had been a long time since Griff had been with a woman, and it showed—in his kiss, in his eyes, in the waves of heat that were about to carry her away.

She smiled up into those eyes and had one last semirational thought. If innocent little Fawn wanted to ride a riled-up stallion, somebody ought to tame it for her, right? A few rolls between the sheets would smooth his rough edges, make him safe enough for Wynott's sweetheart.

Maybe.

He was so big, so strong, with so many dark secrets, she was almost scared herself. But while female power might be delicate, it was still power. With a flutter of her lashes and a come-hither smile, she called him to her. He lunged for her, clasping her in his arms, pressing his mouth to hers, and they lost themselves together in a darkness all their own.

There was no going back now. Leaning into the kiss, she gave in to the urges coursing through her, sending her inhibitions off to keep her rational mind company where it cowered at the back of her brain. She was going to let the old Riley James come out to play—the Riley who was a bad girl deep inside, always had been. She knew what bad girls were for.

So did Griff.

Deep down, she was sure this wouldn't end well. It was going to hurt someday when Griff and Fawn Bailey hired her to renovate their house. They'd probably want her to build on a nursery for them. That was how things went for girls like her.

But until then, why shouldn't she enjoy herself?

―――

All those years ago, during that night at the quarry, Griff had discovered the real Riley.

Behind her husky voice and blunt way of talking, there'd been a fragile soul. He'd had to move slow, making sure he soothed her and earned her trust.

But there was no fear tonight, no wary eyes or fight-or-flight tension. She'd drawn him in with a flutter of her lashes and a sexy smile. If he'd been able to breathe, he would have laughed, because who knew Riley James could flirt? Somehow, she'd lost her fear and grown into her outsized personality to become, through and through, the woman she appeared to be. It was as if she'd called her own bluff and won.

Despite all that, he still had to be careful. He'd never forgive himself if he hurt her.

"You okay with this?"

"It's got to be done," she said. "You're a cowboy, right?"

"Was. Sort of." He frowned. "What does that have to do with anything?"

"A cowboy has to get back on the bucking bronco, right?"

"What are you talking about?"

He was being stupid, but his brain was absolutely fried by hormones, and he couldn't work out what she meant.

"The metaphorical one, silly." She gave his arm a playful slap. "You've been terribly, terribly traumatized by Fawn's ferocious attack, and you need help or you'll be scarred for life. You might never be with a woman again if I don't save you." She grinned and slid her hands up inside his shirt. "I need to save you right *now*."

He smiled but hesitated. "I'm not the same guy I was that night. You know that, right?"

"I know." She pulled his head down and kissed him again, softly this time. "But the real you is still there. The cowboy." She smiled. "I do love a cowboy. Remember when you used to ride real bucking broncos? You were really something."

He was surprised at the sting of tears that rose behind his eyes. He had loved high school rodeo. He'd missed the ranch, too, and he wondered if he'd been a better man when he'd worn the hat and boots. He'd definitely been happier, but back then, he hadn't had the smarts to appreciate it. He'd wanted to see the world, be a hero. Dammit, he never should have left.

Great. Go and cry all over her. Yeesh, she'll never look at you again.

Her eyes flicked to his, and he knew she'd caught his sadness because she brightened immediately, lifting his mood with hers. "It would be a shame to waste this opportunity," she said with an exaggerated sweep of her hand. "We have this nice house all to ourselves, snowy night, warm fire…"

He sat down beside her. "Warm woman," he joked.

"Warm and willing."

She proved it, making the next kiss harder and needier, a wild, blazing glory of a kiss that continued when he pushed her down onto the cushions. He was on top, he could have sworn he was, but somehow she ended up there, straddling his hips, unbuttoning his shirt and running her hands over his chest.

There was one thing the military had done for him. He had nothing to be ashamed of in the fitness department. The blast that had led him home might have damaged him in a dozen invisible ways, but muscle and sinew and bone were intact.

Others hadn't been so lucky. In the hospital, he'd kept in shape, spending hours in the gym, working off the stew of anger, angst, and anxiety with reps and sets, lifting more and more weight, taking long journeys, up and up and ever up, on the StairMaster as if working out for his whole unit, for all the men who would never run or climb again.

Riley flipped her long hair to one side so he could see her face. She was biting her lip, and those pale eyes glistened with heat.

Maybe he could finally stop thinking about the past for a while. The explosion, the impact, the order he'd given. The way he'd said it. It was his duty to remember it every day, to relive what had happened every night, but he could put it away just this once. Just for Riley. She'd fought her own war and deserved his full attention.

She was already barely dressed. It was easy to unbutton her pajama top and cup her small breasts. Throwing her head back, she squeezed her eyes closed, her expression blissed out and wanton. His thumbs found her nipples and teased them, and she shook the top off without a trace of shyness, revealing the pale stretch of her torso, the soft mounds on her chest with their perfect pink tips hard under his hands.

He pulled her down and changed positions, lifting himself above her to take one into his mouth, running his tongue over the nub. She moaned, arching her back, and suddenly he wanted her so desperately he could hardly stand it. He needed to strip her pajama bottoms off and have her, right now, right away. It had been a long time, too long, and he had so much emotion, so much need built up…

No. No. Slow down.

He turned his face into the soft curve of her neck and shoulder and breathed in her scent, his body shuddering with need.

"You smell real," he muttered without thinking. "None of that lilies-of-the-valley crap or whatever it is girls wear."

She laughed. "Is that a compliment?"

He flushed. "It is from me. I like women who do stuff, not women who sit around primping all day. You hammering away at nails, tearing walls apart—that turns me on, you know. Especially the tool belt."

She cocked her head and smiled. "You want me to go get it?"

"Nope." He grinned wolfishly. "No additional clothing, please."

She laughed again, and he wondered at how easy this was, how natural.

"I'm pretty sure the hammer would get in the way anyway. But"— she bit her lip and gave him a wide-eyed, flirty look as she snapped the elastic—"without the belt, there's nothing holding these up."

"That's a shame." His voice came out in a low growl, and he glanced at her face, worried she'd notice how much trouble he was having holding himself back, but she was smiling down at him without a trace of nerves.

"Griff," she said.

"Hmm?" He ran one finger across her waistband, savoring the smooth skin of her belly. The pj's were low-slung, and she shivered when he tucked the tip of his finger inside.

"We don't have to go slow," she said. "I'm dying here, okay? Girls like to have fun, too."

Hooking her fingers into her waistband, she shimmied her

way out of the pj's. They were loose enough to slide off but tight enough to drag her panties along for the trip, and in a half second, she was naked, gloriously naked, that pale, lean body spread out on his sofa, his for the taming, the taking, the tasting.

Riley looked up at Griff, who didn't seem to know where to look. It wasn't that he was shy. He just couldn't seem to decide where to stare: her face, her breasts, or a little lower down.

To his credit, he settled on her face.

"Jesus, Riley." His gaze swept down the length of her again. "You're beautiful."

She couldn't help laughing. She was no beauty, but she was female, and she was naked, and Griff probably hadn't seen a woman's body in a long, long time. The realization made her fiercely glad she was the first since his long drought. Her, not Fawn. There was a part of him in this room that would die tonight—the towering need, the deprived soul, the soldier obsessed by a certain kind of thirst—and she'd take that for her own. No matter what happened later, he'd never forget it. Not even Fawn would be able to drive this night out of his memory.

"Beautiful?" She put a finger to her lips, considering. "You're not bad yourself. But you're not nearly naked enough."

He made a short, strangled noise. "Let's keep the beast under wraps for a minute," he said. "You let him out, I can't guarantee he'll behave."

"You call him 'the Beast'?"

He flushed. "Trust me, it fits."

Laughing, she reached down and unsnapped his jeans. "What makes you think I want him to behave?"

"He moves too fast," Griff said. "There's scenery along the way we don't want to miss."

"Scenery, huh?" She watched him slide his hands down her body, stroking her curves, and tried to steer him where she wanted him to go, but when he resisted, backed away, and knelt at her feet, she felt dizzy. "Griff, do you think you can... I mean it's been a long time, and I... This is about you, not me, so..."

"This is about *us*." He parted her legs and touched her center, just touched it, and whispered "*Oh, man*" with such breathless admiration that she thought she'd die right there. She was afraid all her butterflies would spiral up through the ceiling and into the night sky, never to be seen again. But when the warmth of his mouth and the questing velvet of his tongue touched her, they celebrated, wild wings fluttering as she savored Griff's mouth, his tongue, his touch.

Throwing her head back, she let out a sound, half cat in heat, half Riley. He paused, and she knew he was watching her, enjoying her helpless ecstasy. If it had been anyone else, she would have been embarrassed. But she wasn't—and she didn't want to explore just what that meant. Not now.

"It's you, Riley," he whispered. "It always was."

She didn't know what he meant by that, but when his tongue touched her there, right *there*, it wasn't what launched her into space. It was the emotion behind those words that sent her, wild and helpless, into the limitless sky. Closing her eyes, she clenched her fists, clutching at the cushions and struggling for breath. He held her and she rose, rose, and flew, certain she'd rocket off into the cosmos if he ever let her go.

But he did at last. Rising up, he unzipped his pants and stepped awkwardly out of one leg, then the other. Then he was all grace again, a feral, muscled man making her need him in a way she never had before. She reveled in being feminine. Being delicate. Being taken by a man, a real man, who was stronger than a thousand storybook heroes in her eyes.

CHAPTER 24

GRIFF CLOSED HIS EYES. IT WASN'T THAT HE DIDN'T WANT TO look at Riley. He did, but the blissful expression on her face was enough to make him embarrass himself. He needed to think about something else, something ordinary, even ugly. Otherwise, he was liable to explode.

But this moment was too precious to waste on anything but her.

A picture of Fawn flashed into his head, and he shook it away. Fawn was all tidy, like a Persian kitty at a cat show, but Riley was an alley cat, lithe and powerful, a survivor like him. She was what he needed, what he wanted, and what he'd have—for tonight, anyway, and a whole lot longer if she'd let him.

Deep down, though, he wondered if that was even possible. Riley was a loner. Even now, she was giving him everything but her heart, and he wondered if she'd ever give that to any man. He couldn't blame her for being cautious after all she'd been through, but maybe he could change her.

No, not change her. *Heal* her. He hoped she'd always be Riley, but he wanted her to be happy, free from that fear he saw under her bold facade. Like when he'd hit the dashboard that time.

He remembered the expression on her face, the way she'd twitched as if to run. The way she'd scanned his face, searching for the right response.

Obviously, he'd have to heal himself first, before he could do anything for her. To his surprise, the thought energized him. He had a goal now—a reason to find his old self buried under all the painful memories.

For once, the picture that flashed into his mind wasn't smoke and flames or faces wrenched with pain. It was Riley, dressed in white, carrying flowers. Daisies, or those little mini-roses, walking, slow and stately as music played...

"Griff? Hello?"

"Sorry." He wouldn't tell her he was picturing her in white, considering a forever life together. It was way too much, too fast. Besides, Riley had enough problems. She didn't need one more.

And so he lied.

"I was busy trying to figure out how we could do this again and when," he said.

"Not a tough problem." She shrugged. "I'm here. You're here. We might as well play house."

"Okay." He lowered his voice. "But just so you know, I'm not playing."

He didn't want to scare her, but he needed to tell her this wasn't a game. It was real—but she might not have been listening, because she pulled his head down and kissed him, hard and wild, and he lost it, totally lost everything in the world. Everything but her.

<center>~~~</center>

Riley closed her eyes and kissed Griff, letting her inner alley cat out of the bag. She hadn't let anyone touch her in a long, long time. In fact, she avoided most men, except for people like Ed and her friends' husbands. Men she could trust.

She didn't know if she could trust Griff, but she sure couldn't resist him. Those big hands, that broad chest... When he held himself above her, the muscles in his arms and shoulders bulged. It made her feel small, but not in a bad way. In a delicate, feminine way. A beautiful way. And he looked at her like he'd never seen anything he wanted more.

Right now, she wanted him to do more than look. *Much* more. She was afraid she'd make a fool of herself if he didn't just *do* it already. The Beast was ready, and reaching down, she showed him the way, showed him how easy it would be, with her so slick and willing. With a gasp, he let himself push, but he held back again, not even halfway there.

"Now," she said. "Hard. *Please*."

"Wait."

When he stood, she felt suddenly naked, lost, and she had a moment of horror when he fished his wallet from his jeans. Was he going to *pay* her? She almost laughed when he flourished the condom.

She was more than ready once he'd put it on, but one glimpse of his face made her look away. His eyes were too tender, staring straight into hers. She was afraid she'd give something away if she looked back—but then he stopped again and touched her chin, and she knew he wanted her to look. Shaking inside, she tried.

His eyes seemed so impenetrable sometimes, but now they were warm, like deep, rich chocolate, and she forgot to hold herself back as he slid inside. It hurt—it had been a long time—but in a good way, and as she rocked against him, it stopped hurting and she decided what the heck. She'd made a fool of herself already. She trusted Griff. Why not let loose?

That was her last thought before the two of them became one creature, one body, one mind fixed on one pleasure. They rocked together, wild and thoughtless as the firelight flickered on their naked skin, touching them with magic. Need licked at her body as the flames licked the logs, and she heated, burned, then collapsed beneath him, sending up sparks.

Merry Christmas to me.

Lacing her legs around his waist, she threw her head back as he bit at her throat like an animal, taking her. Those crazy thoughts about wild stallions weren't far off the mark. She felt more and more a part of him, and when he gasped out something incomprehensible, she gasped, too, and the two of them flew off together this time, rising like the flames, floating like the smoke, changing shape like a cloud, changing forever as they rose up into a velvet night sky scattered with stars.

—◦◦◦—

Riley woke to Griff's face focused on hers with unnerving concentration. She rubbed her nose, wiped her lips.

"Do I have something on me? Did I drool?"

"No." He shook his head as if he'd just woken up. "No. I was just…looking."

She flushed, wondering why. All her life, she'd been told how odd she looked. Often it was under the guise of admiration—*you're so different, your eyes are so weird, you hair's such a strange color*—but she'd have given a lot just to be normal. It was lonely, being different and unable to hide it. In Wynott, she felt like the only one of her species, one who wanted nothing more than to mingle with the other animals. To fade into the crowd.

"Thanks," Griff said. His somber expression transformed into a smile, and she couldn't help smiling back.

"No, thank *you*."

"I'm serious," he said, looking wounded as she laughed. "I know we weren't planning on that, but it's good, right? I feel… I feel human again."

Riley remembered his comment the day before, when he'd slipped and said he felt "almost human." She'd vowed then to do her best to make him better, make him part of the fabric of life again. And hey, look, she'd succeeded—and had fun doing it.

That was what it was, she reminded herself. Just *fun*.

"Happy to help," she chirped.

His brows arrowed down. "So are we good?"

"Sure." She sat up, puzzled by the question. "Why wouldn't we be? Good for you, good for me, good all around."

"Good." He put an arm around her, and she curled against him, loving his strength, the safety of his arms. "So that means we'll do it again?"

She laughed. She couldn't help it. He was so awkward.

"I guess. I don't know." She gave him a gentle punch in the arm. "Let's just let things happen naturally, okay? What happens happens."

"Okay." He grinned. "But I gotta warn you, it's going to happen."

He tugged her close and kissed her. This time, it was a tender kiss, one that warmed her to her toes. But she heard warning bells in the back of her busy brain, telling her to go slow, be careful. Part of her heart belonged to Griff now, and she wasn't comfortable with that.

With an act of will, she pulled herself out of the kiss and looked at him as if from the outside. He smiled, his eyes still closed, his forehead unlined, his expression relaxed.

And there he was, her cowboy, the one she'd held in her heart all those years he'd been gone. He was still in there. She just had to find him and coax him out.

But this is for Fawn, she reminded herself.

No, it's for Griff.

She'd seen how his memories overwhelmed him and worried it was more than she could handle, but with all he'd given for his country, for the men who served him, and for this small town and all the others like it, she ought to do her part to help him. It was her patriotic duty. She smiled at the seriousness of her thoughts. Everyone served their country in their own way, and she'd found hers. What a sacrifice, right? She'd fix him all up, and then she'd have to pass him on.

It would be like the house she'd renovated to earn her certificate. It had been an old farmhouse, homey, solid, and strong, but damaged by water and wind and tasteless tenants. Once she'd peeled away the layers of ugly wallpaper, the hideous vinyl flooring, the trendy paint, and taken it down to its bones to reveal its beating heart, she'd fallen in love with it—only to have to pass it on to the real owners.

Griff was like that house. He was a cowboy down to his bones, but a cowboy was a simple man, and he'd become complicated, with a whole lot of layers built up that obscured the man inside. She'd find that man—and, inevitably, pass him on.

She just had to remember how big a sacrifice that would be. Ever since she'd thought of the nursery scenario, she'd known she wouldn't want to stick around and watch Fawn enjoy the fruits of the renovation. But that was okay. It was time for her to move on. She'd never expected her stay in Wynott to last forever, especially since the Harpies and the Only Heir had shown up.

Pulling away, Griff smiled and gently tapped her forehead. "What's going on in there?"

"Nothing." She rose and stretched, laughing when his eyes widened. "Want to go to bed?"

He grinned. "Do I ever."

He laughed so low she barely heard him, and at the sound, her body softened, ready all over again for whatever this man wanted.

Oh lord, she was in too deep. This wasn't going to end well.

CHAPTER 25

THREE DAYS LATER, RILEY WASN'T SURE PLAYING HOUSE WITH Griff was working for her. She kept busy all day with the bathroom renovations, but instead of playing house like newlyweds or at least like *I Love Lucy*, Griff spent all his time holed up playing video games. Thursday morning found her standing, again, in the doorway to the family room, where there were no lights but the flickering video screen. She could hear the click of guns cocking, the blast of shots fired, over and over, despite the early hour.

"Hey, Griff," she said. "We should probably get out of the house."

"Uh-huh." *Bang. Bang.*

He'd been playing for days. She'd tried to distract him. She'd reset the timer for the Christmas lights, so when dusk fell, the tree in the corner would light up, cutting through the video game's blue light with something warm and bright, but he didn't seem to notice. She'd cooked the most tempting meals she could, even replicating the coq au vin she'd made for Ed's sisters, but although he ate, he barely seemed to notice what she'd made. He wasn't rude, but he wasn't appreciative, either.

She'd even left for a while—not that he'd noticed. Ed had picked her up and taken her back to her truck, and they'd had it towed to a garage in town. It was all fixed now. Ed claimed the damage hadn't been bad, just a crumpled fender, but since the vehicle looked far better than before the accident, she wondered what he'd spent. He wouldn't show her the bill, said it was nothing, but she knew better.

She'd helped Ed out in the store for a while that afternoon, but after they closed, she went back to the Diamond Jack. Griff might care about a video game more than he cared about her, but at least he wasn't actively hostile like Ed's sisters.

In spite of all this, their nights together were still magic. At ten o'clock sharp, he'd find her, wherever she was. He'd take her hand, and they'd go upstairs to practice being human together. They'd climb into bed, she'd meet his eyes, and together they'd dive down deep into the wild, rocky river of their feelings.

She didn't fool herself by thinking his feelings were for her. She gave him something he needed—a release, a safe place to let his emotions loose. Eventually, he'd find himself again, the old Griff, and he'd remember he was crazy about Fawn.

But on these nights, he was hers, and she loved the long hours before sleep when they explored each other wordlessly. She'd learned how he liked to be touched, and he'd learned what she needed. They twisted together in the moonlight that slanted through the window, giving, taking, stoking the flames of need until they rose together in ecstasy, their spirits rising up into the night.

Afterward, his sleep was sound. There was no shouting, no clutching at the sheets, no sudden leaping from the bed. Nobody could tame Griff himself, but she was working on the demons she'd seen lurking in his gaze—the ones that urged him to shoot, shoot, shoot in that danged game.

He was like an ogre in a fairy tale who only turned into a prince at night. In the morning, he'd be back to grunting words of one syllable while he shot at virtual soldiers. She couldn't cut through his concentration, not with food, not with talk, not even with a skimpy tank top and her tool belt slung low on her hips the way he liked it.

She almost wished they weren't so isolated. If they lived in town, there'd be people around, walking past the windows, stopping by. But obviously she was hiding as surely as he was, because when the doorbell rang late Thursday morning, she felt almost violated. And when Bruce let out a low growl from his spot on the hearthrug, she was almost scared.

Opening the front door just a crack, she peered out at their visitor, then opened the door wide and did her best to smile.

"Fawn," she said. "Come on in."

She glanced at the arched door to the family room. It was dark, with only silver flickers from the screen hinting at Griff's presence.

"You probably want Griff," she said.

Who doesn't?

She turned to get him, and there he was, big as life or maybe bigger, standing in the doorway. He'd run his fingers through his hair and smoothed it down, and he looked almost civilized, despite the stubble from not shaving.

"Hey, Fawn."

His smile looked completely normal, as if he was really glad to see Fawn. And of course he was, Riley reminded herself.

It looked like she'd done her work too well. Griff was a tame horse now, and she could turn him over to Fawn like she'd intended—except she still saw the darkness in him every day when he played that stupid game. Was he reliving some event from his service? Was he replaying it over and over on the screen? Or was he just bored with her company unless they were in bed?

Whatever the answer, he looked fine now. Obviously, Fawn could bring him out of his depression in a way Riley never could.

"What's up?" He gave Fawn a grin, like he was genuinely interested in real life.

"I wondered if you wanted to go to lunch at the diner," she said. "Matt's going to meet us. He wants to talk to you."

"About what?" There was a wariness in Griff's eyes, as if he thought Fawn wanted to trick him into something.

"I don't know." She shrugged. "You'll have to ask him."

Griff nodded and paused a moment, his eyes on Fawn. Finally, he relaxed. "Okay. I'll meet you there. Give me a half hour, okay?"

"Okay." Fawn gave him a kiss on the cheek, kicking one foot up behind her as she hopped to reach him. "Oh, I'm so glad. We've missed you. We were worried when you left the other night."

"I'm fine," he said.

"Are you?" She stroked his rough cheek. "You look like a mountain man."

Apparently Fawn liked mountain men, because she snuggled against him for a moment, her smile blissful.

Riley turned away, her stomach roiling, but Griff touched her arm.

"Riley, you want to come?"

She shook her head, backing away into the hallway and tripping over a throw rug. She barely caught herself on the banister.

"No," she said. "You go ahead. I've got work to do." Her heart squeezed hard, and she did her best to ignore it. "A lot of work."

She needed to work on packing her stuff. That was what she needed to do. And once she got that done, she needed to unpack her heart and jettison all the fond feelings she had for Griff Bailey. Because she'd been kidding herself. He didn't need her.

He needed Fawn, and Riley needed to get out of the way.

CHAPTER 26

ED SLUMPED INTO THE ARMCHAIR HE CALLED OLD FAITHFUL, setting a glass of Riley's Jack Daniels on the table at his elbow. Closing his eyes, he clasped his hands to his chest and sighed. Sharing a meal at the Red Dawg with his sisters had been too much for him.

It was bad enough they bossed him at home. For them to harangue him in the Dawg the way they had, with everyone around them listening, was too much. He hadn't wanted to spread their family issues all around town, so he'd stayed mum as they'd gone on and on about how the "family" business should be passed down to Trevor. About how Ed "owed" the boy.

He'd wanted to tell them it wasn't a family business. He'd started Boone's Hardware himself, with money saved from a stint in the navy plus Ruth's small inheritance. The two of them had lived on beans and rice in the early years, putting every dollar they earned back into the business. They'd started out with one room, selling feed and some essential ranching equipment, then expanded gradually, buying the current building after five hard years of sacrifice.

Now that his sisters were upstairs and he was alone with his thoughts, his anger rose. His sisters had contributed nothing to the store. *Nothing.* If Riley hadn't come along after Ruth got sick, there wouldn't *be* any store. He would have gone broke paying for nursing care.

And the things they'd said about Riley—well, it literally made his heart hurt. They wanted her gone so Trevor could step in. They didn't understand that she'd earned her place. If anything, *he* owed *her*.

He downed another gulp of whiskey and coughed. He wasn't

used to the way it burned, but when the heat rose to his head, it felt good. A little more, and he might be able to say some of these thoughts out loud.

Carol bustled in from the hallway. She bustled everywhere, which was strange because she didn't seem to accomplish anything. She just bustled hither and yon, making everybody nervous.

"What are you doing?" she asked. "Why are you sitting here in the dark?"

Ed sighed, and that hurt, too. "Just thinking."

"Good." She sat down and tucked her legs under her, and for a moment, he saw the girl she'd been. "There's a lot to think about, but I can help. Do you want me to go up and get that book? It really is good."

She'd talked about nothing but "that book" at dinner. Apparently it had tear-out forms for creating partnerships.

"Getting everything in place now will make the transition easier when you…" She had the decency to blush. "Well, you know. You're not getting any younger."

Ed stared at her over the rim of his glass. He'd tried to put a happy face on things for Riley, but he was starting to realize he couldn't stand his sisters. He and Ruth had been thrilled to move away from Wisconsin, and now he remembered why. Carol and Diane had interfered constantly, offering advice, harassing Ruth about every little thing.

"*Riley's* my partner," he said now. "She's earned it."

"Trevor's your grandnephew."

"I realize that, and if he works hard, he might earn a share, too. But so far…" He splayed his hands rather than say the words. Surely Carol had noticed the boy had been useless.

Taking a Kleenex from her pocket, she dabbed at her eyes. "Oh, Ed. You have to make allowances. His parents are gone, and we're all he has. The rug was pulled out from under him when they died."

Carol's only daughter and her husband had been killed in an

accident with a drunk driver. It was a tragedy, especially for the boy. Carol had taken over parenting him, but she'd been grieving the loss of her daughter and was hardly capable of helping a young boy deal with such a great loss.

"He's not feeling well or he'd be helping more," she said.

Ed sat up. "Not feeling so hot myself." He gasped as something squeezed in his chest, stealing his breath. His whole left side hurt—his arm, his chest…

"Are you all right?" Carol hopped up and slapped him on the back.

"It's not… Stop hitting me! I'm…I'm not choking," he managed to squeeze out. "Heart attack. Again. Call 911."

"Oh, for heaven's sake." She headed to the kitchen, clearly more annoyed than concerned.

A half hour later, he was strapped to a gurney, bouncing over the uneven sidewalk on his way to an ambulance. He wasn't aware of the passage of time, only a dark spell before waking into a world of frightening whiteness. Snow whiteness would have been fine, but this was hospital whiteness—white walls, white sheets, white everything. The smell of disinfectant stung his nose, reminding him of the long hours he'd spent in the Grigsby hospital when Ruth was dying.

"Well, look who's awake!" A busy blond in what appeared to be pajamas decorated with dancing snowmen bopped into the room and began fussing with his sheets. "I just need to take your vitals, Mr. Boone. How are you?"

Ed didn't much want to talk, and he was pretty sure he needed to hold onto his vitals. But when he turned his head away to stare out the window, he realized he had questions. There were tall buildings, parking lots, and industrial-looking factories as far as he could see. This wasn't Grigsby.

"Where the he—heck am I?" Obviously, he wasn't himself. He'd almost cursed in the presence of a lady. "This isn't Grigsby."

"You're in Loveland." She laughed. "Guess you missed all the excitement. You were life-flighted in. Don't you remember?"

He shook his head, which seemed to scramble his brain and make him tired again.

"I'll bet that was some helicopter ride, with the snow and all."

Ed twisted the sheet between his hands and stared out the window. He felt old and scared and alone. "Did somebody call Riley?"

"Is that your sister? She's here with you. She just went downstairs to get something to eat. She'll be so thrilled to see you're awake."

"Riley's my—my friend." He was betraying her. He used to call her his daughter, but with his sisters around, he didn't dare. "Somebody needs to call her."

"Well, your sister's devoted to you. I'm sure she'll call anyone you want. She's been just beside herself with worry."

Ed remembered a conversation about partnerships and transitions and figured his sisters would probably stay devoted as long as it took for him to sign those handy tear-out pages in their precious book. He hoped they didn't nose around the office back at the store and find the will he and Ruth had made up. That had come from a book, too, and it left everything to Riley.

"I need to call her. Riley, I mean."

The nurse was fiddling with an IV bag that hung above his bed. "Now, you just leave that to us. I'll let your sister know. What was your friend's name? O'Reilly?"

Ed managed to croak out a *no* before something swept over him, a sweet, all-encompassing sleepiness that fogged his mind and smothered all his worries, sending him off to dreamland.

But there were voices. He managed to open his eyes a crack. The nurse was talking to someone—a woman. Tall. Brunette.

Diane.

He tried to speak but only croaked. Lifting one hand, he waved it feebly in the air. The woman turned.

"What do you want?"

The voice was harsh, the tone abrupt. Definitely Diane.

"Riley." Ed could barely speak, his lips were so dry.

"Water," he said.

"Here." Diane grabbed a mug from the table beside his bed. It had a bendy plastic straw in it, and he managed to drink a few sips while half the water in the mug dribbled down the front of his— not his shirt, that wasn't his shirt. He was wearing one of those hospital gowns. The loose kind that flapped around and let your heinie hang out.

"We haven't seen your Riley in days," Diane said. "I suppose she's busy with that Gruff man, out on that ranch. Trevor's been handling the store all by himself."

Ed felt suddenly dizzy as a monitor across the room began to beep frantically. The nurse came back and fussed around him, pulling a pillow out from under his head, easing him down on the bed.

"Now, Mr. Boone, don't get yourself all upset." The nurse shot a slitty-eyed look at Diane. "Don't you upset him," she said. "He's very fragile."

Fragile. He sighed. Why did he inspire all the wrong adjectives? Fragile. Kind. Nice. Just this once, he wished he could be tough. Tough enough to overcome this sleepiness, find out what had happened, and make sure Riley knew where he was. He wanted to see her, but she'd say the store needed her more. She was responsible like that.

But Diane said she hadn't been there.

"Did you call her? Tell her what happened?" His words sounded muffled in his head, and he wondered if Diane could even understand him.

"Oh, I'm sure she knows," Diane said. "But we haven't heard from her." She pursed her lips. "You'd think she'd at least want to send condolences."

"Condolences?" He tried to sit up on his elbows, but his head seemed to weigh more than his old bowling ball—the one he couldn't lift anymore. "Am I dying?"

"No, you silly man. You just had a heart attack." Diane said. "All this drama, and this Riley, Riley, Riley. You need to calm down."

Riley, Riley, Riley. It echoed in his head, Diane's voice saying Riley's name, echoing until the sound had no meaning. He tried to speak, but the white walls, white lights, and white sheets blended together into a cold and empty nothingness, and he slept.

CHAPTER 27

As Griff bounced the Jeep down the highway to the diner, he hoped Riley understood why he had to go. If he begged off, Fawn would set the whole town buzzing about how *damaged* he was. Despite all the research she'd done, she didn't seem to understand a thing about him.

Riley, on the other hand, accepted him as a work in progress. She didn't complain when he forgot to shave and shower, and she didn't demand that he come to the table for those delicious dinners she cooked. Obviously, she knew how much the video game helped him—how much he needed to practice every scenario, to save his virtual soldiers over and over.

And when night came, he didn't have to say a word. They went upstairs and straight to heaven every night. He hadn't had a nightmare since.

He should probably show her more appreciation, though. Now that he thought about it, the relationship seemed a bit one-sided, and Riley had been kind of quiet lately.

At the diner, he found Matt and Fawn seated in a corner booth. They looked good together. He'd have to mention that to Matt. If Matt made a move on Fawn, Griff wouldn't have to be psychoanalyzed anymore. Surely the marshal would be hero enough for her.

There was the usual handshaking and backslapping before Matt slid onto the bench across from Fawn. Griff tried to do a subtle do-si-do so he wouldn't end up sitting with her, but Matt was wily. Evidently the make-a-move-on-Fawn thing hadn't occurred to him yet.

Griff wasn't hungry, but when he ordered two eggs and toast,

Fawn made a tsking sound, called the waitress back, and ordered him biscuits and gravy, a cinnamon roll, and a side of bacon.

"You need your strength," she said.

Her blue eyes shined, and he reminded himself that she meant well, so he gave her a smile, pretending he actually enjoyed eating in public and talking to people. In truth, he had no idea how he'd choke down the eggs and toast. He thought about raking the whole mess into his lap and hiding it in his napkin, like a kid who hated broccoli.

Shoot, he was a grown man. Why couldn't he just say his appetite was gone?

Because they need to believe you're okay. He needed a lot of people to believe that, including the U.S. Army, so when the food arrived, he shoveled a few bites into his mouth. Finally, he put down his fork to search for a topic of conversation.

"So how do you like being marshal?" he finally said.

Matt greeted the question with a smile and a glance at Fawn that made Griff wonder if he'd stepped into some kind of trap.

"It's a good feeling," Matt said. "Remember when you made up your mind to enlist? You were talking about how you wanted to make a difference, serve your community."

"My country," Griff growled. When he'd left, his community had seemed like the dullest, slowest-moving place on earth.

"Wynott's part of that, remember?" Matt said.

"Yeah," Griff admitted. "A big part for me. I didn't realize that then."

It was funny—he'd enlisted to get away from Wynott, only to discover that for him and many of his men, preserving the innocence of the Podunk hometowns they came from was their reason for fighting. They kept evil at bay so folks could believe in the essential goodness of the world the way kids believed in Santa Claus. From what they'd seen overseas, it was about as real.

"There's more action here than you'd expect," Matt said. "Right now's a crucial time. Opiates, meth labs—all that's starting to come to Carson County, plus Springtime Acres keeps me busy."

"I thought Shane and Lindsey Lockhart bought the trailer park."

"They did, and it's a lot better than it used to be. They hired Ozzie Wells to manage it, and he keeps folks in line, but there are still a lot of domestic calls there, drunk and disorderlies—that kind of stuff."

Griff gave a noncommittal grunt. Matt looked down and cleared his throat.

Here it comes, whatever it is.

"I finally got the funds from the county to add another squad car, and I need a deputy." Griff's old friend met his eyes with a frank and friendly look. "I can't think of anyone I'd rather put in the job."

He paused as if to let that sink in for a while.

It sank in all right. Lots of things were sinking—Griff's heart, his mood, everything.

Because to his surprise, the offer sounded good, but it could never happen. For one thing, Griff needed to go back to the military and redeem himself. He wasn't sure how he'd do that. He couldn't change the mistakes he'd made.

And even if he'd wanted to take the job, it was impossible. His commanding officer didn't feel he could trust Griff in a combat situation. What would he say about letting him loose with a sidearm among innocent civilians?

"Sorry. Can't," he said. "I'll be going back to my unit as soon as I can."

He wasn't really lying. It might be true. He hadn't freaked out in days, but that was because of Riley, and he doubted the army would let him bring her along. He pictured her decked out in fatigues, giving that sloppy salute, and smiled.

Fawn smiled back, assuming he'd meant that look for her.

"Matt, you know Griff has issues, but he doesn't want to talk about them. And that's his choice."

"I just wondered what the situation was," Matt said sharply. He seemed to be getting annoyed with Fawn's constant pity party for Griff, too. "We could make the job temporary."

Griff shifted in his seat, feeling trapped. In a way, the job would be perfect for him. His unit had been a police unit, guarding troops, upholding the law. But he had no idea how to even start rehabbing his traitorous mind. Give him an enemy combatant or a village full of hostiles, and he knew exactly what to do, but he was powerless against his own mind.

"Just think about it," Matt said. "You could use all your military skills in the job."

Griff grinned. "We don't get much experience driving around eating doughnuts."

Matt punched him on the arm. Fawn laughed, and this time, Griff did smile at her. He'd made a joke, cut the tension. He *was* getting better.

"Seriously, thanks," he said. "It would be great to protect and serve with you and all that, but I'm just on a break."

Matt shifted uncomfortably and fooled with his french fries. "You told me when you left your enlistment was up before Christmas."

He was right. Griff would have to reenlist before he could go back, and his application was in limbo, pending a clean bill of health from the shrink at Walter Reed.

"Yeah, well, I'm planning to re-up."

Fawn and Matt were looking at him as if he had two heads.

"*What?*" Griff set his fists on the table and looked from one to the other. "You two act like I'm lying or something."

"It's just… We heard what happened, that's all," Matt said. "I don't see how somebody could go back after that."

They hadn't heard what happened. Nobody had, and he

supposed he was grateful for that. He was even more grateful when Fawn changed the subject.

"I'm just glad you'll be here for the Red Dawg Christmas party," she said. "You can't miss that."

He didn't want to talk about that, either, even though he'd loved that party as a kid. Ranchers from far-flung homesteads mingled with the folks from town, enjoying the one day they could get together without calves to brand or stock to move. The folks from the trailer park came, too, and one of the ranchers would dress up as Santa Claus in a moth-eaten costume with a cheesy cotton beard taped to his face. The kids would gather round, wide-eyed with rapt belief. Griff had figured out the truth about Santa by age six, but he'd let the other kids have their illusions.

Come to think of it, that might have been the first time he'd felt like he was outside the circle looking in. Jaded by age seven, he'd made himself responsible for guarding his friends' innocence. Which was ridiculous and kind of sad.

Still, the party was a big deal. Maybe Riley would go with him. They could sit together and watch everybody else get drunk and celebrate. It would be like that night at the quarry—the two of them on the outside, looking in, but looking in together.

"I thought we'd go together," Fawn said.

"Um, we'll have to see," Griff said.

"Oh, good," she said as if she hadn't heard him. "Remember we have to bring a toy. There are lots of kids in Springtime Acres this year, and a couple of the ranchers had their crops fail with that hailstorm last summer. There's a real need."

Griff remembered the kids who poured in from the trailer park for the party—kids who got free lunch, who never had quite the right clothes, who acted out and cursed and kept secrets about what happened at home. They never stuck around Wynott for long; their dads worked the oil fields, and they moved before they could really settle in. But when Santa showed up, their eyes would shine with happiness and hope.

"Yeah, thanks for reminding me," he said. "I'll be sure to bring some toys."

"Good," Fawn said earnestly. "It'll be good for you to get out. We worry about you, holed up out there on the ranch. I mean, what are you doing all day?"

He paused. Saying "I play *Call of Duty* and sleep with Riley" just didn't sound good. They wouldn't understand that the game relieved the helplessness that had plagued him since the explosion, and Riley—well, he wasn't sure he understood that himself.

"I've been helping Riley with the renovations." He should be, anyway. "She's putting in some extra bathrooms, doing some upgrading."

"Oh yeah," Matt said. "I heard about that. Guess things'll be different around there once your sister gets home."

"Uh-huh." Different? Well, yeah, they'd have a lot more bathrooms, but that was about it, right?

For the first time, he had some uncomfortable thoughts about the renovations. He'd figured his dad just wanted to help Riley out, give her some work, but there were an awful lot of bathrooms going in.

Fawn looked sweetly sympathetic. "A lot of changes happening at home."

He nodded. Jess had written him a letter, just before he came home, telling him about her wedding to his friend Cade and some of her future plans. She and Cade were eventually going to live at the Diamond Jack, while Griff's dad, Heck, and his new wife, Molly, moved to Cade's farmhouse. Griff was surprised his sister was settling down; she'd always seemed to love working in the travel industry, but it was nice to think of the ranch staying in the family. Still, the bathroom thing was weird. Jess wanted a big family, but they were up to five bathrooms and counting. Riley was tiling the last two and had only a few fixtures to install. Just how many nieces and nephews was he going to have?

"So you're helping Riley get that stuff done?" Matt grinned. "Didn't know you were handy with a hammer."

"I'm not," Griff said. "She's teaching me."

Fawn's eyes narrowed momentarily, and she looked away. Matt shot her a glare, and suddenly she was herself again, smiling sweetly.

"Well, that's great," she said. "It's nice of her to help you keep your mind off—you know, what happened."

Griff clenched his fists at his sides and stared down at his food. He was tired of Fawn's constant references to his service. He wasn't going to talk about that stuff, no matter how hard she pushed.

Suddenly, his head was about to explode and the bees filled his chest. They weren't panicked now; they were angry, and he couldn't stay a second longer.

Shoving back his chair, he rose abruptly. Most of his food was still on his plate, but he wasn't hungry, and he needed to get out of there. Shadows were gathering, ghosts stalking and waiting. He needed to take them with him back to the dimly lit family room at the ranch. Back to the game and a world he could control. Back to Riley, who seemed to be the only person who understood him.

"I need to go," he said. "Got to get back to… You know."

"Sure." Matt stood. "I'll walk you out." He flashed a look at Fawn, and to Griff's relief, she stayed put.

When they reached the door, Griff turned to the marshal. "Look. I appreciate that offer. But I'm going back to my unit if I can. If I can't, it'll be because they don't trust me to stay sane enough to do my duty."

"Sane how?" Matt asked.

"Sane like calm," Griff said. "Sane like not ripping somebody's head off because they looked at me sideways." He sighed. "I can't help you, bud. Not if I don't get a handle on things."

Matt looked him in the eye but seemed lost in thought. Griff was starting to feel uncomfortable when the marshal finally spoke. "I think you can," he said. "But it's up to you."

CHAPTER 28

Riley heard Griff's Jeep outside, then Bruce's happy *woof* of greeting. She paused with a stack of clean laundry halfway in her duffel bag. She'd been hoping he'd stay out longer, because she wasn't sure she could stand to say goodbye to him without embarrassing herself. She could pick a fight, make him punch a wall or something. Then it wouldn't hurt so much to leave.

She wondered, for the thousandth time, if she should stay. Sure, the days were dull, when he played that danged game over and over. Sure, he hadn't shaved, had only showered when she pushed him out of bed and demanded it. But at night, they made love like—like they loved each other.

She was going to miss having a prince, even one who only showed up at night. But he'd never face the real world if he spent every day playing games and every night playing *her*. Plus he'd miss his chance with Fawn. Much as it hurt, she knew that was what he really wanted. And much as she wanted to think she was helping him find his way back to humanity, she was only helping him hide.

The front door slammed, and the *rat-a-tat-tat* of gunfire filled the air almost immediately. He hadn't looked for her, hadn't even yelled a hello.

So there was her answer. He didn't care if she stayed or not.

She trotted down the stairs and stood at the door to the family room. The dog *woofed* again, wanting to come in, but she was afraid the conversation she and Griff were about to have would upset him, so she left him outside.

"Griff?"

"Just a minute." He kept his eyes glued to the screen where two shadowy figures slunk into position behind what appeared to be machine-gun nests. Narrowing his eyes, he pressed the control, and they exploded in fountains of blood.

Gross.

"Okay, what?"

She sighed. "Don't you think you ought to do something else?"

Dammit, she sounded like such a whiner—but to his credit, he put the controls down and turned away from the game.

"Like what?"

"I don't know." She should have thought this through. It was an important moment, and she needed to play it just right. Ask him for help with a project or guide him to some alternate activity. But her brain was blank and filled with static, like a television on the fritz. "You've been playing that game all day every day," she said. "Sitting here in the dark isn't good for you."

He rolled his eyes. "I just spent lunch listening to Fawn tell me what *she* thinks is good for me. Now *you're* going to boss me around?"

She leaned a hip against the doorframe and sighed. "I'm trying to help."

"I don't need help."

He turned back to the game, aimed, and fired. Another fatigue-clad man blew up, and she felt sick inside. The house was so filled with the sounds of battle that she could almost smell the cordite.

He shifted his shoulders as if her watching made him itch and finally turned. "What?"

She lifted her chin. "You're hiding. That's what you're doing. Hiding from the real world."

He stared back, his brown eyes nearly black. "And what are you doing, Riley James? If anybody's hiding, it's you. You've worked with Ed for years, but you're giving up the place you earned without a fight."

"I'm not hiding." Her last thoughts of staying rolled over and died. What he'd said amounted to a dare—and she always took a dare. "I'm going back. That's what I came to tell you."

"Do what you want," Griff mumbled, turning back to the screen. "Just don't come down here and try to tell me what I need. I'm on leave, and I'm done taking orders."

Riley raced upstairs, tears burning at the backs of her eyes. He didn't want her here. He'd just been using her, comforting himself with her just like he entertained himself with the game. Lunch with Fawn must have gone well, and now he wanted Riley gone.

Besides, he had a point. It was past time for her to go back to Ed's and face his sisters—and her future—head on. She needed to make herself a life that was truly her own. One that didn't depend on anybody else—because if she couldn't rely on Ed or Griff, the two men she cared about most, who could she depend on?

—⁓—

Griff listened to Riley running up the stairs and knew he'd won; she wouldn't try to tell him what to do anymore—but was that really a good thing?

No. You're an idiot. You're going to lose her, and then what'll you do?

Shutting off the game, he scrambled to his feet and went looking for her.

She stood in the mudroom, tugging on that absurd hat and pulling the earflaps down. She looked so small, dwarfed by the furry hat and the bulging duffel bag at her feet.

"Hey," he said. "I'm sorry."

"It's okay." She sniffed, then shook her head as if to erase the sound. "You're right. I shouldn't be lecturing you. At least your fears are genuinely scary. Mine are just a couple old ladies and a troubled kid."

"He's not a kid. What is he, twenty?"

"However old he is, I can't let him run me out of my home. I'm heading back to the store and making things right."

The bees stirred, but he did his best to swallow them and smile. "You've got reason to be scared of those old ladies. Hell, they scare *me*, and I'm a goddamn soldier. We can hide together."

He was relieved to see a quick smile flit across her face, but it didn't reach her eyes.

"They're just people," Riley said. "And let's face it, we're not helping each other."

"You're helping me." His throat was aching and his voice sounded strangled. "I think we're doing each other a lot of good."

The corner of her mouth quirked up in a smile that looked a little more genuine. "Like how?"

He forced a smile of his own. "I think my excess testosterone is leveling out."

She barked out that peculiar laugh, just as he'd hoped she would.

"I'm just not sure I should be the one doing that for you," she said.

"What?"

She shrugged. "Fawn doesn't seem real happy to have me here. And I'm sure she'd be glad to help with your testosterone."

He squeezed his eyes closed, then opened them and struggled to keep his cool. "What does Fawn have to do with anything? It's my house. I think it's up to me who stays here." He took a step closer. "Look, I'm sorry about today. I didn't want to go with her, but she's so persistent. And Matt…"

Riley held up one hand like a policeman stopping traffic. "It's okay," she said. "I know how you feel about her."

"No, you *don't*." He clenched his fists, struggling to stanch the rising tide of dread that threatened to overwhelm him. He couldn't let her leave. He *couldn't*. "She's always poking at me, like she's trying to find what hurts. She drove me nuts the whole time we were at the diner."

"Sure." Riley laughed as if he was joking. "Give her some time, Griff, and maybe talk to her. Or don't talk." She raised her eyebrows suggestively. "I'm sure she can make you all better."

She pulled her coat from its hook and started to swing it on. He reached for it and she smiled, turning, expecting him to help her like a gentleman, but instead he pulled it away and hung it back on its hook.

"I'm not looking for advice about Fawn, okay?" He set his hands on her shoulders and turned her to face him. "I'm trying to tell you how I feel."

"I told you, I already know," she said. "You've been crazy about her half your life. Why would you stop now? And it's fine with me. You need to move on with your life. and so do I."

She reached up and patted his cheek. He couldn't help himself; he closed his eyes and leaned into her touch. She smiled. "Oh, Griff, don't worry. You'll be fine. I'm glad Fawn will be here for you. Honestly, she's what you need."

The words bit like a knife. He'd thought the sensations that enveloped them at night were something very close to love, but apparently he'd read her wrong. What he'd thought was love coming into bloom was simply casual sex for her.

"What?" She was staring at him, and no wonder. He'd been standing there like a big, dumb oaf, opening his mouth without making a sound.

Words. Find the words. Tell her how you feel. Just pull out your heart and hand it over.

He closed his eyes again, searching the darkness inside him, but what was left of his charred, blackened heart wasn't much of a gift.

"What about the job?" He hated his accusatory tone, but how else could he keep her? If he couldn't be her lover, than dammit, he'd be her boss. "It's a mess up there."

He expected her to argue, but she just shrugged. "I'll be back to get it done. You don't use that back part of the house anyway, and I'm way ahead of what your dad expected. I worked it out in my head last night."

"You did?"

It was a good thing he hadn't told her what he thought about at night. While he'd been dressing her in white and choosing flowers, she'd apparently been planning her escape.

She gentled her tone. "Griff, I have to go. You were right. I need to face the Harpies, win my future back."

What was that old saying? If you love something, let it go? Yeah, right. That was fine for butterflies and horses. But if he let Riley go, she'd be gone for good.

He moved right into her personal space. They'd been closer than this every night for almost a week. He hoped she'd remember what that had felt like.

But she retreated as if threatened.

"Come on, Griff. You'll be fine. Once you stop hiding out here, you'll find out there's a lot more to life than shoot-'em-up video games. You've got to know Fawn wants…"

"I don't *care* what Fawn wants." He wrapped his hands around her biceps and gave her a gentle shake. "I want *you*, don't you get that? Not Fawn."

He stared her straight in the eye, trying to see straight into her heart, but what he saw was fear, not love. Panic rose again, swelling in his chest, and he gave her another gentle shake.

"Don't go, Riley. Please."

She put her hands on his, tugging at his fingers, her eyes wary and wide. Her expression was calculating, as if she was trying to figure out how long she had to endure him, how soon she could escape. She thought he was one of those men, he realized. The ones who abused women, held them against her will.

That's not what I'm doing. I'm just trying to make you see…

He was an idiot, or something worse. Instead of telling her he loved her, he'd frightened her. Furious with himself, he let her go.

She staggered back, stumbling over the threshold to the mudroom and catching herself with one hand on the wall.

He hadn't meant to push her, dammit.

"I'm sorry, Riley. I didn't mean to do that."

"Okay, sure. I'm going, all right? Take care of Bruce for me. I'll be back to finish working on the house, but it might be a couple days. It might be…longer. I-I might wait until your dad gets back."

She grabbed the duffel bag and backed out the door like she was afraid to turn her back on him. Like he was a wild animal or something and might attack her at any moment.

He clenched and unclenched his hands, trying to hold the bees that were building up inside, buzzing beneath his desperation. As her boots hit the porch steps, he rushed outside. He couldn't let her go.

"Riley."

She didn't turn, just waved, as if this was some ordinary good-bye.

"Riley, I'm sorry," he said. "You're not hiding. You're the bravest woman I know, and you're dealing with things the best you can."

She'd made it to the truck. She was opening the door.

"I don't want Fawn, Riley. I want you." He stopped at the edge of the porch, knowing he'd only scare her more if he ran after her. The bees pressed against his heart, squeezed out the words, and for once, finally, they were the right ones.

"I love you. Please, Riley. Stay."

She stopped a moment, one foot in the truck, the other in the snow, and he thought he'd gotten through to her. But she didn't look at him, and after a second or two, she pulled the other leg in and started to close the door.

He ran down the steps, feeling something winged and desperate rise in his throat. "Marry me, Riley," he shouted.

She probably hadn't heard him. Slamming the truck door, she started the engine. Bruce raced to the truck, following as it careened down the drive, his barking fading behind her.

Griff stood there in the cold for a long time, thinking about what he'd done and what he'd said. He regretted most of it. He never should have grabbed her like that. Never should have pushed her.

But as the dog trotted back to him, there was one thing he didn't regret.

He really did love her. And he'd marry her this minute if he could.

Returning to the family room, he slumped down on the sofa and put his head in his hands. He'd told her all that too late. After he'd manhandled her, how could she believe him? He'd erased every bit of the trust he'd earned.

She was afraid of him. He'd made her that way. And he deserved to be alone.

CHAPTER 29

RILEY PULLED INTO HER USUAL PARKING SPACE BEHIND THE hardware store and sat behind the wheel, struggling to compose herself. She didn't know if she was crying from fear, from anger, or from sorrow, but she needed to stop. Checking the rearview mirror, she winced at her red-rimmed eyes. then opened the truck door to plunge her foot into a drift nearly a foot deep. Trevor obviously hadn't shoveled the lot or even the sidewalks.

Griff was right—the kid was useless. But at least Ed hadn't tried to shovel and given himself a heart attack. With her gone, something like that could happen. Another reason she never should have left, no matter what his sisters wanted.

Hoisting her duffel bag from the truck bed, she tramped around the side of the building to the front door. She'd drop her belongings in the office, then get to work. The Harpies might not want her around, but somebody had to shovel the sidewalks and parking spots, check inventory, and keep the place clean, and obviously Trevor wasn't up to the task.

At least she could be useful. With a surge of determination, she grabbed the handle on the old front door to yank it open—and almost dislocated her arm.

The door was locked.

She looked around at Wynott's other businesses and the old Victorian homes that lined Main Street. Their sidewalks were shoveled, and the street was plowed. It was a Thursday afternoon, and the sun was shining. Folks would need shovels, and kids would come in and buy the plastic sleds she'd ordered. So why wasn't the store open?

She glanced at the show window and felt butterflies in her belly again, but instead of fluttering with anticipation, they were plain dang nervous, because the lights were out, the Styrofoam snowman's hat had fallen over one eye, and the scrapers and boots she'd carefully arranged were in disarray. Ed's cardboard Closed sign was stuck in one corner.

Maybe the sisters had insisted on some sort of family outing, like shopping in Cheyenne or going to see the Christmas lights in all the subdivisions scattered around the town. But why wouldn't Ed have called Riley and asked her to watch the store? Staying open during his appointed hours was practically a religion for him. He believed a hardware store was like one of those urgent care clinics but for houses instead of people. Folks depended on them to be there with first aid for stopped-up plumbing, broken washing machines, and busted irrigators. He'd even been known to open in the dead of night when one of their regulars had an emergency—but judging from the depth of the snow on the sidewalk, Boone's Hardware had been closed for more than a day. Something was wrong.

Riley glanced up the street, then down. The town was quiet, with few cars braving the slushy, slippery roads. High drifts were heaped on each side of the street, spilling snow out onto the sidewalks. Giant plastic candles surrounded by evergreen boughs graced each lamppost, and lights were strung on wires that crossed the street from building to building. Some people might think their tacky holiday decor was kind of sad, but it warmed her heart with small-town Christmas spirit.

She made up her mind. She'd go over to Wynott Willie's, the diner that served as the town's gossip center. Whatever was going on at Ed's, someone there would know.

The buzzer on the door that announced new customers had been replaced by a strap of jingle bells, so it sounded like Santa Claus was coming to town when Riley stepped into the old-fashioned chrome trailer. She was immediately engulfed by delicious scents—brown gravy, roast turkey, hot grilled cheese, chicken Parmesan.

"Riley!" Willie himself was at the counter, filling ketchup bottles from a big industrial-sized jug of the stuff. "Sure am glad to see you. Boone's has been closed for two days, and let me tell you, folks are really worried. How's Ed doing?"

Riley hopped onto the cracked vinyl seat on one of the old chrome stools that lined the counter. "That's what I was going to ask *you*."

His eyes went wide. "You don't know?"

Gooey red ketchup dripped unheeded from the jug, sliding down the outside of the smaller bottle and pooling on the counter like blood.

"I've been gone." She grabbed a few napkins and helped him dab up the mess. "I was, um, working out at Heck Bailey's place. Since Ed's sisters were here, I let them use my apartment."

"Huh. Well." Willie mopped up his mess, refusing to meet her eyes.

"What happened, Willie?"

He cleared his throat. "He... Actually, I'm not sure. There was an ambulance there the other night, and his sisters followed it, I reckon to Grigsby. That nephew was back for a day, but he didn't open the store. Not sure where he went, but there hasn't been a sign of life around the place since."

"Oh, no. No." Riley had been thinking about ordering a hot turkey sandwich, but her appetite suddenly vanished. "He must have... Oh, no. His heart. He has trouble with his heart."

"Are you telling me those women didn't call you?"

She sighed. "They don't like me much."

Willie, who was filling another ketchup bottle, gave the jug a shake. A massive red blob blooped out onto the counter and spattered his white apron. Ignoring the mess, he shook his head. "I can't say I'm surprised. They were over here most every night, ordering stuff fixed special and being rude to my servers. I always say you can tell a person's true nature by the way they treat a waitress." He grabbed a rag and wiped his hands. "Those women came straight from the devil, and as far as I'm concerned, they can go right back to hell. They should have called you."

"It's not their fault. Well, not completely. I should have called Ed. Checked on him," Riley said. "I was…busy."

While Ed suffered, she'd been sleeping with Griff, conning herself into thinking she was helping Wynott's hometown hero heal from his war wounds. The truth was, she'd been having an awfully good time and completely ignoring her responsibilities.

Hiding, just like Griff said.

"I've got to go," she said. "I need to find Ed, and then I'll come back and open the store."

"Thanks, Riley." Willie screwed the cap on the ketchup jug and eyed the mess he'd made. "Businesses here depend on one another, and we miss the place." Grabbing a wet rag, he began mopping up the counter. "We've missed you, too, hon. It's good to see you back."

"It's good to be back," she said reflexively.

But she was lying. It wasn't good at all. She didn't know where Ed was. She'd abandoned him, and the worst possible thing had happened. If he'd had another heart attack, it could be really serious.

She needed to find him, and fast.

———

Griff was tired of sleeping alone.

Well, not really *alone*. A serenade of snuffling and snorting reminded him that Riley's dog, who'd moaned and whined for half an hour after she'd left, was sleeping on the rug beside his bed. She'd said Bruce belonged to his dad, but it was clear where the dog's loyalty lay.

"Come on." He nudged the dog. "Misery likes company. Talk to me." The dog let out a sigh. "Oh, that's right," Griff said. "Guess I'll have to do the talking. Want to hear about all the mistakes I've made in my life?"

The dog sat up, ears perked. He was a good listener, as somber and attentive as any of the shrinks at Walter Reed.

"Iraq was the biggie." Griff buried his hand in the deep fur over the dog's shoulders and closed his eyes tight, squeezing out memories of smoke, flames, and the kind of screams you never forgot. "See, I dragged a couple guys out after the first explosion. That's the big hero deal everybody talks about. But there was a private standing there flat-footed with his mouth open, and I yelled at him to quit standing around and help somebody, dammit. He did, and he stepped on a wire, and then—well." Griff took a deep, shuddering breath. "It should have been me, buddy. He was just a kid, and the last thing he heard was me, yelling at him. Telling him he wasn't good enough, like my dad always told me."

The dog stood and shook hard, his ears flapping against his head. He probably just had an itch, but Griff preferred to think he disagreed.

"I guess I couldn't have known what would happen. But that kid... I've done some stupid things in my life, but that's the one I regret the most. I'll never forget his face." He sighed. "I saw that same look on Riley's face the other day. I didn't hurt her, I swear, and I never would. But I scared her."

Bruce sat up and put first one front paw, then the other, on the edge of the bed so he was sitting up like a rabbit, and he looked up at Griff with hooded amber eyes that clearly believed in Griff's innate goodness. The dog's tail slowly swept the floor behind him.

"You wouldn't wag your tail if you'd been there," Griff told him. "You probably would have bitten me. I guess I deserved it."

The dog sighed and set his paws back down. Griff lay there stewing in regret until Bruce hoisted himself up onto the foot of the bed. The dog walked up to sniff Griff's face, then groaned and collapsed, falling hard against Griff so he was pressed as tight as possible against his back. He seemed to fall asleep as soon as he hit the mattress. After a while, his steady breathing lulled Griff into sleep as well.

An hour passed, maybe two, before Griff woke to the sound of an explosion. When he sat up, he saw nothing but moonlight coming through the window, creating dancing tree shadows on the wall. A poorwill sang its monotonous song, and he knew he'd been dreaming. He was home. He was safe.

Hey, that was progress. A week ago, he'd have rushed out and fallen down the damn stairs trying to rescue people who weren't there.

Bruce, who had lifted his head the moment Griff woke, settled down and was snoring again in seconds, but Griff stayed awake a long time. When he'd had dreams like that in the past, he'd simply turned and looked at Riley, fast asleep beside him, to soothe his nerves. He'd listen to her slow breathing, and if the moon was out, he'd watch her face, lovely in the silvery light. He'd think back to their lovemaking, and soon those thoughts became dreams, good dreams, and he'd sleep through the night.

But she was gone now. He'd blown it, and he probably couldn't talk her into coming back.

Probably. That was the magic word. There was still a chance, and he had to take it. If he could conquer his demons and unwrap the man he'd been before he'd left—the cowboy whose hopes and dreams she'd admired all those years ago at the quarry—she might come back.

Hopes and dreams. That was what he needed. Whether a man dreamed of winning a football game, saving the world, or winning back a girl, that dream was what kept him alive. Sitting up on the side of the bed, he rested his elbows on his knees and his chin on his hands as he planned the laborious resurrection of his former self and the re-romancing of Riley James.

He needed a goal. That was the problem. When he'd come home, he'd been determined to rejoin his unit, but he was starting to rethink that choice. Going back wouldn't change what had happened, and running headlong into his own death wouldn't help the men who'd died that day. Slowly, his goal was shifting. He wasn't sure yet what it was, but he knew it had a whole lot to do with Riley James.

The dog woke and wriggled to the edge of the bed. His eyebrows twitched as he rested his chin on Griff's leg and scanned his face.

Griff stroked Bruce's head. "She said broken-down old houses were her favorite kind, remember?" Griff smiled at the memory. "She tears up the linoleum, scrapes off the wallpaper, rips out the drywall, and opens the place up to the sun. What was it she said?" He pictured Riley's face, so animated when she talked about her work. "She peels back all the layers and finds 'its honest old-time heart.'"

He scratched the dog behind the ears and spoke into those trusting eyes. "What do you think, buddy? Do I still have an honest old-time heart?"

If he did, he'd hand the whole thing over to Riley.

The dog looked up at him with eyes that believed. Griff had his doubts, but he had to try. It would take more than power tools or a crew of carpenters to get it done, and there was nothing he could buy at Boone's Hardware that would help. But somehow, some way, he was going to find his inner cowboy and win her back.

CHAPTER 30

RILEY JAMMED THE BUTTON THAT SUMMONED THE HOSPITAL elevator and shifted from foot to foot, watching the lighted numbers fall, one by one, to her floor. It opened to reveal an orderly guarding a gurney that carried a patient-shaped mound, a nurse guiding an IV stand, and another pushing a cart loaded with complicated tech equipment. The group stared at her as if daring her to try to squeeze inside.

"Never mind," Riley said. "I'll take the stairs."

She'd had to park on Level 5, so by the time she bounced down the stairs and racewalked to the information station on the ground floor, she must have looked a sight. The elderly woman wearing a volunteer badge gave her a slit-eyed look that was anything but welcoming.

Maybe it was her tattoos or the single silver ring on the arch of one eyebrow. She'd always considered her body art a tasteful expression of who she was, but older folks didn't see it that way. Even Ed had taken a while to come around, saying he'd always associated tattoos with sailors.

"I'm looking for Ed Boone," she said. "He's a patient here."

The woman blinked slowly, like a lizard. "Relation?"

"He's my... He's my dad." Riley had never said those words out loud to anyone before, but she knew them to be true. Ed was her real dad, not the stranger who'd played sperm donor at her conception, not the various stepdads and so-called uncles who'd made her childhood a misery.

So why couldn't she say the words out loud with more conviction? The woman was giving her the side-eye. "Really?"

"He's... We live together. I took care of his wife, and now we take care of each other."

The woman's side-eye turned into downright disapproval.

"Shoot," Riley mumbled. "That didn't come out right."

She'd never had trouble saying it before. She and Ed agreed that was the way their relationship worked, and nobody in Wynott questioned it. But somehow, Carol and Diane's suspicions had made it into something ugly.

"Patient information is strictly confidential," the woman said.

"Oh, I know." Riley bounced on her toes, pleased she and Ed had prepared for this very situation. "But we filled out a form—a living will. He named me as his power of attorney."

The woman narrowed her eyes behind her wire-rimmed glasses. "I wouldn't know about that. I suggest you speak to his physician."

"I think it's on file. If you just…"

The woman stared Riley down. "Speak to his physician. Or perhaps a family member."

"All right. I'll…I'll just go."

Riley strolled as casually as she could to the big hospital directory. It looked like a menu board, but instead of listing turkey sandwiches and the soup of the day, it listed medical specialties she hoped she'd never need.

Urology, proctology… There. Cardiology.

That was where Ed would be. Second floor.

This time, the elevator was empty and waiting. Stepping inside, Riley checked out her reflection in the stainless-steel walls, which were warped like a fun-house mirror. Raising her coat collar, she tugged down her sleeves to cover her tattoos so she'd look more… normal.

When she reached the second floor, she started toward the nurses' station. Then she realized they might refuse her, too, so she strolled down the hall, trying to look as if she knew what she was doing as she ducked her head into each room to look for Ed.

What she saw didn't make a hard day any better. Old men,

old women, all looking sad and sick, their skin gone gray, their eyes rheumy and unseeing. It hurt her heart to think of Ed being among them, but it hurt a lot worse when she finished the floor and hadn't found him. Where could he be? Pausing in the hallway, she thought about her next step.

She hated hospitals—the lights, the sounds, the smells. She'd never been sick a day in her life, but she'd been injured more times than she liked to remember by people she liked even less. Back then, she'd been a street-smart waif with a mouth like a sewer and an attitude to match. She'd held off the pity and compassion of the nurses with an iron hand and checked herself out before anyone could ask any questions.

All around her, in the unforgiving white light, bells chimed mysterious warnings. A PA system barked out incomprehensible instructions buried in static, while the scent of bleach tried and failed to obscure the odor of hurt humanity. Nurses and doctors flowed around Riley, and an orderly pushing a mop bucket mumbled as he passed. She was pretty sure he was swearing at her. She didn't blame him, but she couldn't seem to move.

Maybe Ed had left already, and they'd crossed paths on the road to Wynott. She'd head home, and later they'd laugh about the way she'd poked her head into all those rooms, probably scared those old folks to death.

But that notion couldn't conquer the worries that made her drive too fast down the spiraling concrete parking structure. And it fled her thoughts entirely when she got back and found the hardware store still closed.

Pulling out her key, she decided she'd have to open the store and wait for news. Much as she wanted to see Ed, there'd be bills to pay, so that would help him more than anything.

She began the routine she'd done a hundred times before— turning on the lights, counting out the cash, touching up the window display, and tidying up the store. She was getting started a lot later than usual, but the old routine was still a comfort.

She took down the Closed sign, unlocked the doors, and shoveled the sidewalk and the three parking spaces out front. Back inside, she strolled the aisles with a pad and pencil, doing a quick inventory, and confirmed Trevor was useless. It wasn't that hard to pull gloves and hammers and chain-saw oil from the back room and restock the shelves.

When the bell over the door rang to announce a customer, she hustled to the front, wondering who it was. Maybe Devon Walters had finished painting her ceilings and was ready to move on to the walls. Maybe Sierra over at Phoenix House had another craft idea for the kids. Or maybe that rancher from out beyond the Baileys needed more supplies for running electricity to his barn. She was worried about that guy. He was getting on in years, and it wasn't an easy job. She should probably stop out there and…

"*You.*"

Riley stopped fast, noticing grit beneath her shoes. Trevor hadn't kept up with the sweeping, either, and now here were his grandmothers, calling her names again.

Well, "you" wasn't exactly a name, but Carol sure made it sound like one.

"Carol. Diane. Oh, my gosh." In spite of their hostility, she was so relieved to see them, she wanted to hug them—but that probably wouldn't go well. "Where's Ed? Is he okay?"

The Harpies looked at her like most folks looked at cockroaches.

"Where's Trevor?" Diane asked.

"Not my day to watch him," Riley snapped. Regretting her tone, she eked out a polite smile. "I mean, he's a grown man, right? He doesn't have to tell me what he's up to."

"Of course he doesn't," Carol said. "But he'd be right here, watching the store, if you hadn't barged in."

"Listen." Riley didn't regret her sharp tone anymore. "I found the store closed, so I opened it. I don't know where Trevor is. I also didn't know anything about Ed being gone. I still don't, because nobody thought to call me."

"We don't have to call you," Carol said.

"No, you don't, but it would have been common courtesy." Riley folded her arms over her chest and stared the women down. She'd been down on herself since she'd been such a mouse leaving Griff Bailey's and had enough anger simmering from that encounter to take on a dozen Harpies. "Plus, I would have been glad to come and keep the store open. You know, so Ed could pay his bills?"

"Trevor was doing that."

"No, he wasn't. I got here and the place was dark. The Closed sign was up. Nothing was shoveled, either." Carol started to speak, no doubt to make excuses for the Only Heir, but Riley held up a hand for silence. "I did all those things, and I'm here, ready to work the way I always do. You haven't had the courtesy to let me know where Ed is, but that's okay. I'll just keep working. If taking care of the store is all I can do for him, it's what I'll do, but I'd sure like to see him. Is he okay?"

The women glanced around the store as if expecting a new and improved Trevor to leap out of the back room to assure them he was doing his grandnephewly duty, but no luck.

"He will be," Diane said. "His heart isn't good, you know."

Carol frowned. "It's probably the drinking."

Riley folded her arms across her chest and glared. "Ed doesn't drink."

She remembered the night she'd met these people: the bottle of Jack Daniels that Trevor had helped himself to. The coq au vin with its wine-flavored sauce. Apparently, that had been enough to convince the Harpies that Riley and Ed had been holding one long, drunken hoedown until the sisters had shown up to put a stop to it.

"Just tell me where he is." Riley was doing her best to be polite, but anger was stewing in her chest, threatening to burst out. "I went to the hospital in Grigsby as soon as I heard, but I couldn't find him."

"Maybe he doesn't want to be found." Carol tossed her head, making her sprayed-in-place hair wobble like Jell-O.

Diane piled on. "Maybe he's upset that you abandoned him for that *man* who came here and left him to run things all by himself."

"Ed knew where I was, and he knew I'd come if he called." Riley kept her voice calm, but she was hanging onto the edge of the counter to keep her hands from shaking. She shouldn't have gotten so caught up in her fling with Griff Bailey. She should have checked in with Ed sooner. She'd been childish, sulking because he hadn't stood up for her to these women.

"Well, while *you* were off with your boyfriend, *our brother* was airlifted to Loveland," Carol said.

"Oh, no." Riley couldn't imagine poor Ed so far from home, sick and alone. Somebody should be with him—preferably *her*. "Are you going down to see him? Can I go along?"

"I thought you were going to watch the store. *Finally*." Carol said.

"I am. But I thought you said Trevor was in charge, so I thought—but never mind." Riley busied herself rearranging the blanks on the key lathe. Thinking of Ed in the hospital had made her eyes tear up, and she didn't want Carol to see. Like any other predator, the woman would strike at any sign of weakness. "I'll figure it out, okay? But if you see him, could you just tell him I'm here?"

She didn't know how she'd get to see Ed. She might protest when people like Griff made fun of her truck, but the truth was, she didn't like to drive it too far, especially after its collision with the ditch. The thing had always been rickety, and now its rattles had rattles, and it developed palsy if she took it over forty miles an hour. It would be a hazard on the interstate.

"What I want to know is where Trevor went." Carol's voice had turned high and fretful, reminding Riley she was an old lady, like all the other old ladies Riley knew. An old lady who loved her grandson.

"Check upstairs," she suggested.

"He's not there. I don't understand. He was with us in Loveland, and he was heading straight up here to open the store." Carol lifted a hand to her mouth as if to nibble on a nail, then dropped it to her waist and grasped it tightly. The slight tell made Riley smile. A woman who chewed her nails was at least half-human, right?

"We're staying in a hotel near the hospital, but we came to pick up some clothes for Ed and check on Trevor," Diane said.

Riley simply smiled and shrugged in an effort to make light of Trevor's failure, but the women turned and stalked off, and while they didn't slam Ed's door, they didn't say goodbye, either.

Riley shrugged and went back to straightening the store. She'd give the women time to calm down while she made some sales and showed the good people of Wynott that Boone's Hardware was here for them. There was a new Home Depot in Grigsby, and she didn't want people to get in the habit of shopping there.

She wished her truck was in better shape so she could go down to Loveland, but it was just as well. Ed needed her to keep the store open, so here she would stay. Literally. On a cot in the office. She didn't have anywhere else to go.

CHAPTER 31

RILEY HEAVED A SIGH OF RELIEF WHEN THE HARPIES HEADED back to Loveland in the morning. Work had always been her salvation, so she puttered around the store, dusting, sweeping, restocking shelves, and ringing up an occasional sale. Nobody mentioned that the store had been closed, so she hoped nobody had noticed. It was getting close to Christmas, and their business always fell off that time of year, although the power tools normally did well.

Power tools.

She ought to make a window display, give people some gift ideas.

Doing the displays was one of her favorite jobs, so the rest of the day flew by. By closing time, she'd posed the Styrofoam snowman with a table saw, cut his carrot nose in half, and placed the cut-off tip on the saw. Giving Mr. Styrofoam a tragic frown, she stepped back and surveyed the effect. It made her laugh, which meant it would make people talk—and that was always the goal of her window displays.

As she began her closing routine, her thoughts wandered to the ranch—to her cozy blanket and favorite chair, the warm woodstove and the even warmer Griff Bailey—but she couldn't go back. Griff wasn't abusive, but he got mad too easily, and Riley couldn't deal with angry men. That was one reason she wasn't looking for a relationship; it wasn't fair to love somebody but not allow them to have negative emotions. Griff was fine for somebody like Fawn, who still believed the best of everyone.

Glancing up at the clock, Riley saw it was closing time. She thought of her apartment upstairs, so cozy with its slanted ceilings, its cunning dormer windows, and the comfy old sofa she'd trucked home from Grigsby's Goodwill store. Even the thought of the cramped shower, where she was always banging her elbows, caused a pang of regret. Even though the Harpies had left, it was still their space as long as they stayed. And she was starting to think they planned to stay forever.

It was her own fault. She should have developed a life plan that went beyond helping Ed and hiding—yes, hiding—in an attic apartment for the rest of her life. She needed to find some other option quick, before the Harpies threw her out. If Ed thought it was her choice, he wouldn't feel so bad about it. He'd helped her when she needed it; now it was time for her to move on so he could help his grandnephew. His real family.

She counted out the register and made up a bank deposit and balanced everything. As she tucked the bank bag under one arm and locked the big front door, she looked over at the window, where the sad snowman stood regarding his broken nose. It was cute, but she didn't feel like laughing, because she was a little broken herself. Just over a week ago, she'd been excited about Ed's sisters coming. Now, she was an orphan again, striking out on her own.

As she walked to the night deposit, she considered her options. She really didn't want to sleep in the office again. Maybe she could stay with Sierra for a couple days. Her friend could always use a hand with the foster kids at Phoenix House, and Riley was betting the part-timers there would be glad to get some time off before the holidays.

She dropped off the deposit, then crossed the street to Phoenix House. Sierra answered the door looking frazzled. Behind her, Riley heard a boy shout, "Bring on the Exploding Kittens!" The shout drew a massive cheer from what sounded like a crowd.

"You're not really letting them play Exploding Kittens, are you?"

Sierra looked abashed. "It's a G-rated version."

Another shout rose from the lounge.

"I thought you only had six kids right now," Riley said, grinning. "It sounds like a hundred."

"They have friends," Sierra said. "Jeffrey's staying the night. Isaiah, too, and a couple other kids from school."

"Sounds like they're doing okay."

Sierra beamed. Phoenix House was a last-chance foster home for kids who'd run through all their other options. The boys, aged mostly eight to twelve, had been moved from one foster family to another without success. Sometimes they ran away; other times they were tossed back into the system for being "too difficult," "too troubled," or simply "too loud."

For Sierra, no child was ever too difficult or troubled. Though she privately admitted that "loud" drove her crazy, Riley knew her friend worried about the boys fitting in. The school system in Grigsby had been welcoming and flexible, but the small-town kids had sensed these boys were different. For a long time, the Phoenix House kids had stuck together as a unit to defend themselves, making the situation worse, but judging from the racket in the lounge, they'd found their place in Wynott.

"What's going on with you?" Sierra asked as Riley followed her into her office. It was a tiny room the size of a closet, but it muffled the shouts of the boys enough that she and Sierra could carry on a conversation.

"Too much." Riley had already told Sierra about Ed's sisters. Now she explained Ed's illness, Trevor's issues, and the challenge of keeping the store going while Ed was in the hospital.

"But you're staying out at the Bailey place, right? How's that going?" Sierra waggled her eyebrows suggestively. She knew Riley had a crush on Griff before he left for the military, but she didn't know what had happened since.

Riley caught her up, sparing nothing. When she explained what had happened when she'd left—how he'd gripped her arms, shaken her, shoved her—Sierra's eyes grew wide.

"You can't stay there," she said.

"Oh, I know it." Riley sighed. "The trouble is, that leaves me sleeping in Ed's office on a cot. Which is fine." She lifted a hand to stop Sierra's protests. "Except I don't really want to share the kitchen with Carol and Diane, let alone the bathroom."

"You can stay here," Sierra said. "The back bedroom's open."

Riley's heart warmed. Sierra was basically the mother of a pack of difficult, lost boys, at least half a dozen but sometimes more, and yet she was always there for Riley. As a junior in high school, Sierra had been assigned to middle-school Riley as a mentor, and she'd had a lot to do with Riley's recovery. When things had gotten difficult down in Denver, Riley had followed Sierra to Wynott, and the rest was history.

She might not have a home right now, but she was still better off than she'd been. She needed to remember that.

"I was thinking I could watch the boys some nights. Or days," Riley said. "Whatever you need. Your part-timers might want some time off around Christmas, and I could help."

"You sure can," Sierra said. "Plus the Christmas party at the Dawg is tomorrow night, and we have an open spot at our table. I thought you might be going with Griff, but..."

"I'm definitely not doing that," Riley said. She tossed her head like it didn't bother her, but her heart was aching.

Sierra's all-seeing eyes narrowed. "You miss him."

"Sort of." Riley sighed. "I care about him. A lot. But I know he's too much for me to deal with. It's just... My mind keeps scrambling for excuses, trying to justify the way he acted. I can't shut it down."

"Well, the party'll take your mind off it."

"I'm not really in a mood for social stuff," Riley said. "I'd rather stay here and watch the boys."

"They're going, too," Sierra reminded her. "Plus my husband was asking about you just the other day. He said he misses seeing you, and you know Ridge never says anything he doesn't mean."

Riley had to smile at that. Sierra's husband never wasted a word, so his compliments were high praise.

"Besides, you know as well as I do that when life gets stressful, you have to be vigilant." Sierra touched Riley's arm, her eyes wide with concern. "If anyone has ever fully recovered from addiction, that would be you, but you know the danger's always there. And with everything in upheaval…"

"I should go to a crowded bar and drink beer?"

"You should fill your time with friends and community. You know how much that helps. Plus Santa will be there. You know who it is this year?"

Riley shook her head.

Sierra glanced around as if the walls had ears. "Brady Caine," she whispered.

Riley laughed. Brady Caine was Sierra's brother-in-law, a larger-than-life rodeo star who had found fame endorsing western wear and riding gear before he'd buckled down to business—literally—and ridden his way to the National Finals Rodeo in Vegas. He'd settled down after marrying a champion barrel racer, but he hadn't lost his rowdy, boyish heart. That made him a favorite with the Phoenix House kids.

"Maybe they'll find some bucking reindeer somewhere," Riley said.

Sierra laughed. "You won't want to miss it."

Riley smiled. Sierra was right; she needed to keep busy. But she was sure Griff would be at the party, probably with Fawn at his side. And even though she was sure he wasn't the man for her, even though she'd entered into their relationship for the sole purpose of turning him over to Fawn once he was "tamed," she wasn't sure she could stand to watch the two of them together as their perfect, storied romance lit up the town of Wynott with love and holiday cheer.

Sierra was a good friend, yet Riley had never felt so alone. She'd felt that way a lot back in the bad old days, and loneliness had led her down a dangerous path. This time, she'd have to find a new way to cope.

CHAPTER 32

SATURDAY MORNING, GRIFF DECIDED HE WAS DONE WITH video games. He wanted something real, and there was no better place to find it than the riding arena that adjoined the barn. He wanted the blue sky overhead, the cold air in his lungs, and a horse's muscles shifting beneath him. Leaving Bruce on the porch, he headed for the horses.

They clearly hadn't been ridden in a while. Thanks no doubt to Cade Walker's training skills, most were well behaved, but not every ride went smoothly, which was just as well. Griff had to wipe away his memories and fears so he could watch each horse's ears for signs of rebellion and catch every quick flick of its heels, every sideways crow-hop or rebellious toss of the head. There was no time for his mind to run in circles around Riley James.

He looped the horses in circles and figure eights, finding their strong points and weaknesses. It was as fine a string of cow horses as his father had ever had, and again he wondered. All these horses. All those bathrooms. Yet a small herd of cows that looked strictly ornamental. What was Heck Bailey up to?

He shook away the thought. What his dad did with the ranch had nothing to do with him. He might be enjoying the cowboy life a lot more than he'd expected, but he'd left abruptly, barely saying a word to his dad. It would be a long time, if ever, before the two of them could carry on a civil conversation, let alone work together.

As a matter of fact, Griff wondered why his mind was even heading in that direction. Up to now, his whole life had been about escaping his father's control. Hadn't it been his father's demands that had sent Griff's mother, Dot, into the arms of another man? She'd explained it all the first time teenage Griff, wounded by her seeming abandonment, had visited her at her new husband's swanky log home up in Montana. She'd told him how Heck wouldn't listen to her, wouldn't see things her way. She'd said she'd hated being a rancher's wife. Now that he looked back on it, Griff realized that was about the time he'd resolved never to take over the place and to escape as fast as he could.

Yet his mind was like a barn-sour horse, always hightailing it for home. Once he finished grooming his last ride and sent it back to its herdmates in the snowy pasture, he discovered aches in muscles he'd forgotten existed—but he felt better somehow. He'd had to clear his mind for the sake of the horses, and to his surprise, it hadn't been that hard to forget the past and live in the moment—mostly.

He'd managed to push away thoughts of his men, the explosion, and his time in the hospital, but Riley had taken their place as his new obsession. He'd gone from searching his memories of the explosion for something he could have done to change the course of events to reliving his last conversation with Riley and wishing he could find a road to forgiveness.

He heard the phone ringing as he returned to the house. He doubted Riley would call, but that didn't stop his heart from goading him into a run. Dashing up the stairs to the front door, he tripped over the threshold, caught himself on the heels of his hands, scrambled upright, and grabbed the phone halfway through the umpteenth ring.

"Hello?" He was panting from the run, but he did his best to sound cool and casual.

"Hey."

That's not Riley.

"It's Matt."

"Yeah. Yeah, I know." Bending at the waist, Griff struggled to round up his renegade thoughts, which had scattered like spooked horses in a storm. "How's it going?"

"Fine. I'm just calling to keep you out of trouble. Fawn says you promised to take her to the Christmas party tonight at the Dawg."

"No, I didn't," Griff growled. "I told her I'd try to come, but I never said I'd take her. And anyway, I've had enough of the Dawg for a while."

"Understandable." Matt paused just long enough for Griff to feel awkward. He liked Matt and hated to say no to everything.

"How 'bout if I pick up a six-pack?" Matt suggested. "We could drive down to the quarry, like old times."

The weather was hardly right for outdoor beer drinking, and yet it sounded like a good idea. Griff needed to work out his future plans, and it would be good to bounce some ideas off Matt without Fawn analyzing every word.

But the Christmas party was a big deal in Wynott, and the marshal would have to be there.

"Another time," Griff said. "Don't you need to show up at the party to kiss babies and charm the old ladies?"

"Sure do, but it doesn't really get going until after seven."

"Oh." Griff thought a moment. "Okay. The quarry, then."

"Bundle up. I'll be there in a jiff."

By the time Matt arrived, Griff had pulled on a clean thermal Henley under a red flannel shirt. Heavy wool socks demanded a pair of his father's cowboy boots, which were a half size larger than his own. It wasn't hard to find some; the difficulty was finding some his dad would wear in this weather. The man was cowboy as they came, with little regard for his appearance, but when it came to boots, he was the cowboy version of a Hollywood starlet. His collection of fancy footwear covered every known maker and every type of exotic leather, with tooled designs ranging from cattle skulls to American flags.

Griff shoved his feet into a pair of unadorned Ariat work boots just as Matt pulled up and tooted his horn. Griff was glad to see his friend had driven his old beater Ford instead of his municipal

SUV. As soon as Griff had fastened his seat belt, he reached for the six-pack of Coors on the floorboards, popped a can open, and took a slug. Wiping his mouth with the back of his hand, he shot a troublemaker's grin at his old drinking buddy.

"There's an open container law in this state," Matt said.

"Yeah." Griff shrugged. "But I've got an in with the town marshal."

"You'd better hope Jim doesn't show up." Matt pulled out of the drive onto the highway. "He'd like nothing better than to haul my ass off to jail or at least give me a ticket. He thinks he ought to have my job."

"Can't believe you took him on as a deputy." Griff laughed. "Don't go napping after lunch. He'll kill you in your sleep."

"Naw, we get along," Matt said. "He has his quirks, but nobody cares more about this town. Folks might laugh, but they're fond of him. He's kind of like a mascot."

They fell silent as Matt headed for the quarry. No plows maintained the roads, but the wind had obligingly swept most of them clean. Everything looked unfamiliar to Griff—he'd been gone a long time, and the snow was disorienting—but he figured out where Matt was headed soon enough to stop him.

"We don't have to go all the way to the lookout," he said.

"Sure we do. You chicken?"

Griff actually *was* chicken, though not in the way Matt thought. He didn't mind the danger of the slick, snow-covered roads, but he did mind the emotional minefield waiting for him at the turnout where he and Riley had spent that long-ago night. He was sure the spot was haunted, not by the legendary ghosts of leaping lovers or suicidal outlaws but by his old self and a younger version of Riley.

"I've changed my mind," he said. "Let's go to the Dawg."

Matt turned his head so hard Griff worried he'd get whiplash. "You sure?"

Griff nodded. "Yeah, I'm sure."

A slow smile spread across the marshal's face. "You're thinking Riley will be there, aren't you?"

Griff shrugged. "I doubt she'll talk to me."

He didn't tell Matt that watching her spread her quirky version of Christmas cheer to everybody else would be better than not seeing her at all. Nor did he admit even to himself that he was hoping she'd remember the message of the season included forgiveness as well as joy and goodwill.

CHAPTER 33

ED'S NECK ACHED. HE'D HAD HIS HEAD TURNED TO ONE SIDE ever since he woke up so he could look out at the slice of blue sky beyond all the complicated vents and chimneys on the roof below his window. Somewhere to the north, that same sky arched over Wyoming. Over Wynott. Over Boone's Hardware store, and over Riley.

Once in a while, he'd turn his head to stare at the phone. He knew it worked, because he'd called Carol and Diane. They'd said she was busy with Griff Bailey and made *busy* sound like a dirty word, so maybe she didn't have time for him. New love could be like that. And hadn't he always hoped Riley would find love with a man like Griff—a man who'd take good care of her?

He felt useless lying there, missing her, worrying about the store. Carol and Diane were sure Trevor was ready to take over. Ed was sure they were wrong.

"How hard can it be?" Carol had asked. "There's a price on the merchandise. He rings it up, he takes the money. It's not exactly rocket science, is it?"

Ed didn't want to tell her he was afraid Trevor really *would* take the money—and put it in his own pocket. He'd been trying to see the good side of the kid, but it was tough to look past the laziness, the lying, and the snide remarks.

He closed his eyes and tried to shut out the noise from the hospital corridor, but something cut through the bells and mutterings and footsteps and made him lift his head from his pillow.

"Ed Boone?" said a female voice. "Yes, he's in room 214, on the left. He'll be happy to see you."

Relief washed over him, making him feel better than he had in days. It had to be Riley. He hadn't wanted her to drive that rickety pickup of hers all the way to Loveland, but his blood warmed his veins for the first time since he'd arrived, and that sliver of sky seemed bluer and brighter.

Hoisting himself up on his elbows, he reached for the remote to crank up the head of his bed, chiding himself for being so lazy. He'd been moping all day. He could have at least combed his hair. He swiped at the few strands with his fingers, hoping he didn't look too old, and smiled expectantly as the door creaked open. His heart leapt—only to plummet when Trevor's wan, spotty face appeared.

"You decent, Uncle Ed?"

Ed sighed. "Decent as a man can be in this dress they make me wear."

"What, the grandmas didn't get you any clothes yet?"

Ed shook his head. His sisters had moaned and groaned about having to stay in a hotel last night and made out like his request for a pair of pajamas wasn't a welcome excuse for a shopping trip. Evidently, the trip was a success, because it was nearly noon, and they still hadn't found those pajamas. If they'd even looked.

"You want me to go pick up something for you?"

"No, Son, that's okay. I'm sure they'll be along." He eyed his grandnephew suspiciously. "Weren't you supposed to go back and open the store this morning?"

"Yeah, Uncle Ed, I was. That's why I'm here. I messed up—again—and I wanted to say I'm sorry. I'll head up there right now."

Right now? It was already noon. Had the store been closed all morning?

"Okay." There wasn't a danged thing Ed could do about it now, so he swallowed his anger and tried to drum up some understanding. "What happened, Son?"

"I stopped to see some friends and things got…complicated."

The kid had the grace to be ashamed, anyway, and stared down at his toes. "I had too much to, um, drink and fell asleep."

Ed didn't know what to say, which was fine, because silence seemed to deepen the boy's shame more effectively than anything he could have said.

"I think I've got a problem, Uncle Ed. I'm going back to Wynott, and I'm going to try to do better. Nothing good happens when I'm, you know, *drunk*."

Ed had a pretty good notion drink wasn't the issue. He'd seen enough problem drunks in his life to know Trevor wasn't just hungover. For one thing, drink didn't hang over every day of your life, but Trevor was always struggling to stay awake. Drink didn't usually make someone lose weight, either, and Trevor was thin as a rail.

Ed was angry that the store was closed and customers who'd relied on him for years weren't able to buy the nuts and bolts they needed this morning. But he couldn't help feeling sorry for this sad, slouching, white-faced boy.

He cleared his throat. "Can I give you some advice?"

Trevor nodded, sinking into the chair beside the bed. He actually seemed eager to listen. Something bad must have happened.

"Go back and take care of the store. Do your best," Ed began. "Hard work will help distract you from whatever ails you, and I'm not just saying that because you're working for me. It's its own reward, Son. You'll see."

Trevor nodded, looking thoughtful. "It's just... I never thought I'd end up working in a store."

"Not many people do," Ed said. "But it's what we've got. Can you do it?"

"I think so." The kid picked at a loose thread on his shirt, unwilling to meet Ed's eyes. "I think... I wondered... Can I ask you something?"

"Sure."

Ed figured the kid was going to ask for money, but instead Trevor asked, "Have you talked to that girl?"

"Riley? No." Ed swallowed and hoped the boy couldn't see how much that hurt him.

"I don't know why my grandmas don't like her," Trevor said. "I have a lot of questions about the store, and they won't let me call her." He glanced up at Ed. "I don't think she even knows you're here."

"What?"

"I don't think they told her," Trevor said. "I bet she doesn't even know you're sick."

Anger struck Ed's soul like a bolt of lightning, but it left a smooth stretch of blue sky in its wake. Riley hadn't called because she thought he was home, having some sort of family Christmas with his sisters. She tended to exaggerate the value of family—and to forget that she herself was the heart of his.

He had to let his heart slow down before he dared to speak. "Thanks for letting me know that, Trevor. I appreciate it. Can you do me a favor?"

"Sure."

"Get hold of her when you get home, no matter what your grandmas say. Have her answer your questions about the store, and tell her to call me, okay? The number's in my…" He realized he hadn't seen his cell phone since he'd arrived. "I guess my phone's back at the store."

Trevor shook his head. "My grandma has it."

Ed's throat tightened. His phone was private. There was nothing bad on it, but he hated to think of them going through his photos. He and Riley had done some jokey ones around the store, just for fun, and stuff like that wasn't any of his sisters' business.

"Is it password protected?" Trevor asked.

Ed shook his head. "I don't know how to do that."

"I can fix it for you," Trevor offered. "Then they won't be able to snoop."

Ed felt a bit more of that blue sky, just knowing there was an innate decency in his grandnephew's heart after all. "That would be helpful, Trevor. Thank you."

"Sure." The boy stood, glancing around the room. "You got a pen?"

"I think there's one in that drawer over there."

Trevor rummaged through the few things Ed had brought—his wallet, a handkerchief, a pocketknife—until he found a ball-point pen with the hospital logo on it. Taking a napkin from a forgotten cafeteria tray, he tore it in half. On one half, he wrote the number of the phone on the bedside table. On the other, he scrawled another number. That part, he handed to Ed.

"That's my cell number, okay, Unk?" The boy flushed, as if embarrassed at assigning a new nickname, but Ed kind of liked it. "If you need anything, just call me, okay? I'll head up there now and get the store open." He flushed deeper. "I'm sorry I messed up."

"First step is admitting it," Ed said. "I know you'll do a good job once you put your mind to it. And Riley will help you a lot. You give her a call."

"You bet. Thanks, Unk." The boy started to leave, then paused awkwardly, bent down, and kissed Ed's forehead. Surprised by the gesture, Ed reached up and patted the kid's head. His hair was greasy and unwashed, and he smelled of cigarettes, but he'd said he'd do the right thing and Ed believed him.

No fool like an old fool. But Trevor had owned up to his mistake, and for that he deserved another chance.

"Hey, could you hand me that phone?" he asked.

"Sure." Trevor carefully draped the cord over the side of the bed and set the big landline phone on his uncle's lap.

"Can you look up a number for me?"

Trevor nodded, and Ed had him look up the number for the Bailey place and write it down. He should have called Riley there sooner, but he'd assumed she was so busy with Griff she didn't want to hear from him. She was probably wondering why he hadn't called.

Once Trevor was gone, Ed pressed the numbers into the phone. The ringing sounded tinny and far away, and Griff's voice sounded scratchy and gruff when he answered.

"Baileys."

"Griff, it's Ed." Ed was a little awkward around Griff Bailey. Word around town said the man was a genuine war hero, and that was something Ed himself would never be. "I wonder if I could speak to Riley, please."

"Riley?" Griff sounded surprised, and Ed's heart dropped in his chest like a stone in deep water. "I thought she was with you."

"No." Ed remembered the last time they'd spoken. They'd gone through this same routine, and it had turned out Riley was in danger.

"I'm in the hospital down in Loveland," he said.

"Hospital?" Griff cleared his throat. "You okay?"

"Sure," Ed said. "I'd be better if I knew where Riley was."

"Well, she's not here."

War heroes were apparently kind of blunt and not terribly comforting.

"She must be at the store," Ed said.

If she was, she'd have found the place closed up, the apartment empty. She must be worried sick.

"You want me to go check on her?" Griff asked. "Not sure she'd be real glad to see me, but…"

It sounded like there was trouble in paradise, which made one more reason Ed wished he could be there for Riley. Folding the napkin, he ran his finger across Trevor's number.

"I'll take care of it," he said.

"Okay." Griff sounded relieved, and Ed wondered again what had happened. But Griff wasn't Ed's problem; Ed's sisters were the problem, and as long as he was here in the hospital, they held the upper hand.

The situation had become truly dire. He dialed Trevor's number and was gratified when the boy picked up on the first ring.

"Hello?" Trevor's voice sounded rushed and quivery. "I'll have it for you, I promise. I just need to…"

"Trevor? It's Unk."

"Oh." There was a long, embarrassed silence while Ed wondered who the boy thought was calling. What he thought he needed to "have" for someone. But he didn't have time to think about that now.

"You in my truck?" he asked.

"Yep. I'm just about to get on the highway," Trevor said. "I'll get up to the store as fast as I can, I promise."

"There's been a change of plans." Ed swung his legs out of bed and glanced around the room, wondering where they'd put his clothes. "Turn around. You're taking me with you."

CHAPTER 34

LIKE EVERY OTHER RESIDENT OF WYNOTT, RILEY FELT RIGHT at home in the Red Dawg Bar & Grill. Housed in a squat, square building coated with stucco painted the color of adobe, it had no architectural pretensions except for two large windows hung with neon beer signs and a crude, crooked porch roof over the door. The name was painted across the front in large, clumsy red letters that were beginning to peel.

Inside, the age of the building showed in rustic exposed beams that supported a colorful assortment of whimsically posed taxidermy—a lynx reaching up with one snowshoe paw to snag a duck flying past on a wire; a curious otter wearing a cap decked with trout flies and holding a fishing rod; and the obligatory jackalope—a large brown rabbit topped with a truly impressive rack of antlers. In a corner by the entrance, an enormous bear stood upright, roaring silently and lifting a welcoming paw at the patrons as they entered.

This being Christmastime, the bear wore a Santa hat and held a wrapped present in his upraised paw, the jackalope's antlers were wrapped in twinkle lights, and the lynx wore a green singlet, a pointed cap, and the curly-toed shoes of an elf. All around the walls, multicolored lights were draped in patterns that had more to do with enthusiasm and excess than decorative skill, while a ten-foot Christmas tree in the back corner by the bandstand was lavishly bedecked with western-themed ornaments—tiny cowboy boots and hats, miniature elk pulling toy sleighs, and a collection of cunning western birds ranging from Steller's jays to Clark's nutcrackers, all of them cleverly formed of feathers and looking remarkably real.

The party was just getting started when Riley and Sierra arrived with their charges, a group of boys aged eight to twelve who were barely held in check by Sierra's frantic promises of Jell-O Pudding Cups for breakfast for good behavior. The kids raced to the tree, admiring the many presents mounded beneath it. Those who had been at Phoenix House for more than a year whispered the tradition to the newer kids: Santa would appear at some point in the evening and distribute the gifts to all the good kids. And somehow, nobody had ever been too bad to receive a gift—or if he was, this Santa didn't know it.

"Roads are pretty bad," said Isaiah, his eyes lighting up with covetous joy. "Maybe not too many kids'll show up. Santa won't be able to take these presents back with him, so we'll have to help him out. Lighten the load."

Isaiah was a Phoenix House alumnus, having been adopted by Brady Caine and Suze Carlyle soon after their marriage. He'd always been a natural leader—or naturally bossy, depending on who you asked.

"Isaiah, you wouldn't want other kids to miss out, would you?" Sierra asked gently.

"Sure I would." Isaiah grinned. "More presents for me. That's the Christmas spirit, right? Gimme, gimme." His dark eyes gleamed as he grinned impishly at Sierra. He pretended to have an Isaiah-centric view of the world, but his humor shielded a tender heart when it came to the littler kids. It was hard not to ache for the lost boys, tossed away by parents with drug problems, jail terms, and violent propensities—especially for Riley, who'd been there herself.

"Don't forget, I'm expecting you to be Santa's helper tonight," Sierra said.

"Oh, I'll help him," Isaiah said. "Can't wait to see old Santa."

Riley grinned, wondering if Isaiah would be a help or a hindrance to his adopted dad in his new role as a first-time Santa.

"He wanted me to dress up as an elf, you know that?" Isaiah grimaced. "I said noooo way. So then he tells me I should bring all our games and sh—and stuff." He pointed toward a table laden with board games. "Some of those were *my* Christmas presents last year, but I gotta share and help keep the kids busy 'til he comes." He shoved out his lower lip in an exaggerated pout. "Thought Santa was supposed to spread joy, not boss everybody around."

"Well, it's nice of you to help," Sierra said gently. "I will, too, okay? We want to give Santa time to get dressed."

"Well, all right." Isaiah brightened. "But we're gonna start with a snowball fight. I promised the little kids."

"Okay, but be gentle." Sierra gave him a stern look. "And do it in that empty lot to the side of the bar, okay? Santa's going to enter from the back door."

"Okay. You know you can count on me." He tried for a wide-eyed, innocent look, but his elfin brows and the mischievous glint in his eyes gave him away. When they laughed, he looked indignant and pointed at the crèche that topped the upright piano by the stage. "You know I'm like one of those sweet baby lambs over there, hanging out with Jesus."

Laughing, Riley and Sierra headed for the Christmas tree, winding through the tables that had been arranged in long rows to facilitate community dining. Red candles nestled in wreaths of real pine branches every few feet. The ceiling lights had been dimmed to let the dancing flames give the room a festive look.

Clutches of kids were huddled around the tree whispering about the presents mounded under the boughs. It looked like the community had really stepped up this year. Riley figured there were at least two or three gifts per child under there. She'd contributed a half-dozen kiddie tool kits, and Griff had wrapped several sets of green plastic army men.

Griff. He'd probably be here tonight. Riley tamped down the puppy dog's joy, reminding her heart Griff would be with Fawn.

Riley might be all for their inevitable coupling, but watching them fall in love over Christmas dinner was not her idea of a good time.

Scanning the tables as they walked, she nodded and smiled at people she knew. That made for a lot of nodding and smiling, since most everyone came into Boone's Hardware. It made her feel good to know so many people, to have them smile and nod back. In her pre-Wynott life, a lot of people had known her, but half of them had been social workers or cops, and the rest hadn't smiled much.

She reached up and lightly smacked the side of her head, trying to reset her brain. Tonight was about Sierra and the kids. She wasn't even going to *think* about the past. *Or* about Griff.

"Look out." Sierra pointed at the door, where people were shedding their heavy coats. "There he is."

Riley tried not to stare. From all the way across the room, she could still somehow sense his size and strength as well as his confidence as he spoke to various friends and neighbors. As he hung up his Carhartt jacket, she saw he was wearing a red shirt in honor of the holiday. He had on black boots and that black cowboy hat, too, and his walk, a surprisingly graceful swagger, reminded her of that day he'd come in from riding. Plus, miracle of miracles, he was smiling.

It seemed like less of a miracle when she saw who he was smiling at. Bending, he cocked his head to let Fawn, dressed in a classic "ugly" Christmas sweater, whisper in his ear. She swept her golden hair to one side, then reached up and touched his shoulder as she stood on tiptoe to tell him some secret.

As Riley watched, Griff straightened, still smiling. Fawn giggled, then scanned the room. When her eyes lit on Riley, all the humor in her expression evaporated. Despite the hardness in her eyes, she still looked so perfect she made Riley feel skinny and scarred and dirty.

Squeezing Griff's arm, Wynott's golden girl gave him an apologetic smile, then headed across the room to Riley's table.

"Sierra," she said. "Hi."

Well, good. Maybe she's not aiming for me after all.

"Hi, Fawn," Sierra said. "Nice sweater."

"Oh, thank you!" Fawn patted the puffy knit reindeer that crossed from hip to shoulder in front of a chimney that emitted equally puffy smoke. Each wore a silly grin and a Santa hat, and when Fawn turned to show Sierra the back, she revealed a puffy Santa with googly eyes and a miniature pack stitched to his hand. "There's a contest, you know. I'm hoping to win."

You probably will, Riley thought. *Why not? You win everything else.*

"I just wanted to say, I think it's so wonderful what you do for these poor disadvantaged children," Fawn told Sierra. "I just don't know how you do it."

"It's not hard," Sierra said. "They're good kids."

Fawn laughed her tinkling laugh. "That's not what I've heard."

Sierra's eyes narrowed at Fawn's singsong, finger-wagging response. "Well, most kids are good once you get to know them."

"I suppose," Fawn said. "I just don't know many poor kids."

Riley stood. "I should go help Isaiah," she said, starting for the side door, but she wasn't fast enough. Fawn grabbed her sleeve.

"Oh, Riley, I wanted to talk to you. Could we go sit down?"

Giving the bartender a little finger-wave, she started for the booths.

"I guess," Riley mumbled.

When they reached a booth at the back of the room, Fawn slid inside and motioned toward the bench across from her. "Have a seat," she said as if she owned the place.

Riley sat.

"First of all, Merry Christmas. How *are* you?"

"Fine." Riley slid into the booth, feeling self-conscious. She'd thought about dressing up but had settled for clothes that made her confident: jeans that really fit, tooled cowboy boots, and a red-plaid button-down shirt that was her only concession to Christmas. It hung open over a T-shirt that advertised DeWalt power tools. She was hoping that would give somebody a gift idea and garner some business for Ed.

The outfit had seemed right when she'd chosen it, but now she felt like an ugly caterpillar next to Fawn's colorful butterfly.

"You look fantastic," Fawn said, smiling as a server delivered some fruity, girlie drink. "But you always do."

"You too," Riley said, and at least *she* was telling the truth. Fawn really did look fantastic, but while Riley had put on some eyeliner and lip gloss, she knew that only brought her up to acceptable.

Fawn cleared her throat and squared her shoulders.

Here it comes, thought Riley.

"We need to talk about Griff." There was a light in Fawn's eyes that told Riley this was *it* in her mind: a showdown over the man she wanted, Riley guessed. She didn't think Fawn loved Griff. Not yet.

But you do.

She shook off the thought.

"There's nothing to talk about," she said. "It's not serious between us."

"Are you sure? Because he's been avoiding me for some reason, and every time we go out, he seems awfully anxious to run home."

"He's not running home to me," Riley said.

But he was. He'd said so.

She squelched the protests that were coming from her puppy-dog heart, which thought everybody loved her. More likely "everybody," a.k.a. Griff, just loved sleeping with her.

"He's got a lot of issues to work through, and I don't think he wants you to see him struggle, you know?" Riley sighed. "You're a forever kind of girl, and he wants to be worthy of you."

Her heart churned at that last bit, but it was true. Naturally, Fawn preened a bit, but it turned into a pout soon enough.

"He'd be a lot more worthy if he wasn't fooling around with you."

"We're not," Riley said.

And it was true. She'd never been just "fooling around" with Griff. But she couldn't speak for him.

"We had a fight," she said. "So it's over."

But was it really a fight? It wasn't like he'd hurt her. He'd just been frustrated—but she had Sierra on one side, disapproving because she believed Griff might be abusive, and Fawn on the other, disapproving because she wanted him for herself. There was no reason to keep seeing him. Absolutely none.

Oh yes, there is, said the puppy dog. But the puppy dog had had terrible judgment in the past, and Riley didn't trust it one bit.

"I care about Griff, and he deserves somebody like you," she told Fawn. "He'll figure that out eventually, but you have to give him time."

Fawn sighed. "It's just that I've already waited so long."

What, a week?

When life handed a woman everything she wanted, that probably seemed like a long time to be denied. Or maybe absence had made the heart grow fonder. So said the angel on Riley's shoulder—but the devil on the other one told her Fawn hadn't given Griff so much as a thought until he'd been labeled a hero.

All the time he'd been overseas, working his way up to that status, Riley had thought of him just about every night. She'd sent hundreds of messages into the void, hoping to help him through a tough day. Her heart had twisted every time she heard of a casualty overseas, but had Fawn ever worried about him?

The little devil said no. It said Riley surely deserved him the most, but it was, after all, a devil, and she was done being led astray. She might not have been a good girl all her life, but she was good now—or as good as she was able to be. So she smiled at Fawn.

"I know how it is. But whatever happens with you and Griff, you don't have to worry about me."

"I wasn't *worried*," Fawn said.

"Oh, I know. Why would you worry about me?" Riley tried to laugh, but it came out sounding like a death rattle. "And anyway, I'm leaving town soon."

She hadn't known it until that moment, but it was suddenly the absolute truth. She wasn't going to stick around and watch Griff and Fawn fall in love. She remembered the nursery renovation she'd seen in their future and shuddered.

"You're leaving? Oh, that's right." Fawn nodded like she'd known this all along, her eyes dewy with liquid pity. "Because of the situation at the hardware store, right?" She rested one perfectly manicured hand on the table. "I'm so sorry about that. It must be hard."

Riley shrugged. "It's okay. I've been planning to leave for a long time."

By your standards, anyway. A whole week.

Fawn sighed. "I guess it'll be up to me to help our wounded soldier, then." She sighed. "It's a challenge. He keeps so much bottled up inside. But I plan to be there for him and help him let it all out."

"Right." Riley felt uneasy. "It's just… You have to let *him* decide when that should happen."

"Hmm. Well, that's your opinion. And I think that's why he's still so troubled." Fawn stood, brushing off the front of the short plaid skirt that made her look like a sexy schoolgirl. "Well, I appreciate this little talk."

She took a sip of her drink, smiling around her straw like a schoolgirl sipping a Shirley Temple. Reaching the bottom, she made a sucking sound with the straw and turned wide eyes on Wayne, who waved and began taking down bottles and setting up the blender.

Of course he did. Ordinary Wynottians were lined up three deep at the bar, but Fawn only had to bat her lashes to get an instant refill.

Riley rose, thinking she'd leave right after the party, sneak out the back door, and take off. Nobody needed her anymore—not Griff, who had Fawn now, and not Ed, because the Harpies wanted the store for Trevor and she had no doubt they'd get it. Griff was right. She wasn't going to fight. But she wasn't going to hide, either. She was going to run away.

After all, it was Christmas—a time for giving—and the only way Riley could give anybody what they wanted was if she gave up something she loved. The hardware store. Her apartment. Griff.

They said the more it hurt to give something away, the more generous the giver. By that metric, she was just loaded with Christmas spirit.

CHAPTER 35

THE MINUTE RILEY RETURNED TO SIERRA'S TABLE, AN ITCH
started between her shoulder blades, like somebody was watching her. Turning, she saw Griff's eyes fixed on her so intently she
swore they burned her soul.

"Look out," Sierra murmured, touching Riley's arm. "He's
coming over. Remember what happened now. I know he's attrac-
tive, but…"

Riley stood. "I have to go to the ladies' room."

"Atta girl." Sierra patted her arm.

Riley slipped through the crowd, moving fast, smiling, nodding.

"Gotta go," she said, nodding toward the restrooms. "Sorry.
Excuse me. Gotta go."

She was halfway to her destination when a broad expanse of
red shirt loomed into view.

Uh-oh.

"Excuse me," she said. "Um, sorry. Gotta go."

"Where?"

She looked up, which was a mistake. Griff had shaved—for
Fawn, of course he had—and he looked happy. Relaxed. Like his
old cowboy self.

See how good Fawn is for him?

Her heart suddenly ached so much she touched it and squeezed
her eyes shut for a second. Why was Fawn always the lucky one?

Because she's always been a good girl. That's why.

"You're not babysitting the Only Heir tonight, are you?" he
asked.

"No," Riley said. "I doubt he's even here."

"He will be." Griff nodded toward the stage. "Wayne said the kid talked him into hiring some band from Denver. Said Trevor's their manager."

"Good for him." Riley shrugged. "It's not my job to watch him."

"Good for you," Griff said. "We're here to celebrate Christmas, not watch the kid."

We? Riley looked up at him and blinked a moment, lost in the depths of his eyes. They grew serious, and she wondered if he was going to kiss her.

Push him away.

That's what Sierra would say. And Fawn. Fawn would *definitely* say that. In fact, after the conversation they'd had, Fawn would probably take Riley out back to be drawn and quartered if Griff kissed her.

But the butterflies had formed a gang and were bashing their wings against her belly, pushing her toward him, making her stare up at those eyes, those lips, that strong, stubble-free jawline, and the puppy-dog heart was dancing like a hippie at Woodstock.

It was hard to swallow that much joy, but she managed. "I-I have to go. I need to help Sierra."

She fled to the table without looking back and found Sierra chatting with Eleanor Carson, who'd made Riley's scarf—the one Griff thought was too long.

"Hey, Mrs. Carson." Riley gave the old woman a gentle hug. "I wore that awesome scarf you made me tonight. It's my favorite."

"That's wonderful, dear." The old woman was holding a plate of tiny sandwiches, which must be her potluck offering. She peeled back the Saran Wrap that covered them and held the plate out to Riley. "Have some chicken-salad toasties. I made them myself."

The chicken looked slightly brown around the edges, but Riley would never hurt Eleanor's feelings. She'd just picked up a piece when Isaiah came flying out of the restroom marked "Cowboys." He skidded to a stop just in time to avoid plowing into Mrs. Carson and her chicken sandwiches and knocking Riley's selection out of her hand.

"Hey!" He could barely catch his breath. "Santa—you know, *Santa*?" He gave them an exaggerated wink, as if they might not remember Santa was actually his dad. "He's in the bathroom and he's *puking*. You gotta help him!"

"The men's room?" Riley asked.

"I'll check on him," said a low voice.

She hadn't realized Griff had followed and was right behind her.

"Maybe it's nerves," Riley said.

"No way," Isaiah said. "My dad—I mean Santa—he's *never* nervous."

He was probably right. She'd seen Brady ride some mighty tough broncs, and lately he'd played rodeo clown at Wynott Days, facing down angry bulls before they could impale fallen riders on their horns. He'd entertained the crowd by vaulting over their backs or doing handstands on their horns.

Playing Santa was a whole different ball game, though. Between the kids from Phoenix House and the tough little nuts from the trailer park, he was facing a challenging audience. Bulls might be easier.

After Griff charged through the restroom door, Isaiah stood nearby, wringing his hands, clearly worried about his dad.

"Why don't you go in and check on him, too?" Sierra asked.

"I can't," Isaiah said. "I'm a sympathetic puker. See, if I see somebody throw up, I'm liable to… Oh, no." He covered his mouth and leaned in to Sierra, sweat forming on his brow.

"Where's your mom?" Sierra asked, glancing around for Brady's wife, Suze.

"I dunno," Isaiah moaned. "She went into the cowgirls' room about the same time. She's supposed to be putting on her elf costume."

"Suze? Elf costume?" Riley's eyes widened with surprise. Suze normally focused on two things: her family and her barrel racing. She wasn't supersociable like Brady.

"She wasn't too happy about it, but Dad said he wouldn't do it 'less she helped," Isaiah said. "She's been in there an awful long time, though. Probably embarrassed to come out. Unless…"

Sierra took him by the shoulders. "Unless what?"

"Well, they both ate some chicken salad when we first got here. Suze says it might've been in Mrs. Carson's car too long, but she and Dad ate it to be polite." He thumbed toward his own narrow chest. "*I'm* not polite," he said. "So I'm not puking." He glanced toward the men's room as the unmistakable sound of retching grew louder and frowned. "Yet."

Riley and Sierra shared a glance, then slipped into the women's room. Sure enough, the sounds of a stomach in full revolt emanated from a closed stall door.

"Suze?" Sierra called. "Are you okay?"

"I'm *dying*," came a faint voice from the stall. "Here." She slid a plastic grocery bag under the door. "That's the elf costume. Somebody else is gonna have to help Brady."

"You've got that right," Sierra said. "He's throwing up, too."

"Oh, no." The door cracked open, and Suze poked her head out, looking like a zombie version of her healthy, athletic self. She wasn't the type to fuss about her appearance, but she was sweating profusely and her hair hung lank around her pale face. "Can you do it?"

Sierra shook her head. "I've got the boys. But Riley…"

Riley backed away, lifting her hands to ward off the bag Sierra was holding out. "Oh, no. I'm not the elfin type, okay?"

"Nonsense," Sierra said. "Who's always complaining people say she looks like a fairy? You'll be perfect."

Riley looked down at the cheap, tattered velvet elf suit, then back up at Sierra, who gave her a pleading look.

"The kids need this," she said. "*I* need this."

Riley sighed. Sierra knew just what buttons to push.

"Okay. But somebody better step up and be a really good Santa, because an elf can't carry Christmas on her own."

———∿∿∿———

Griff stood at the men's room sink, listening as Brady Caine emptied the contents of his stomach into the toilet.

"You think you're going to be okay, buddy?"

"First kid that bounces on my lap is going to get a dose of half-digested chicken salad." Brady retched again and moaned. "There's almonds in it. They hurt coming up."

Griff blanched. "Are your brothers around?"

"Ridge is helping Sierra with the kids." Brady staggered out of the stall, snatching a paper towel and wiping his face. "Shane isn't coming 'til later, plus he's got Cody. That kid still believes, and he'd recognize his dad for sure." Brady nodded toward the Santa suit, which hung on a hook behind the stall door. "It's gotta be you, bro, and it's gotta be *now*. We don't have time to mess around. The longer those kids wait, the crazier they get. You'll have a full-on riot pretty soon."

Griff eyed the suit. "Probably won't fit me," he said. "I'll check around. There's gotta be somebody."

He stepped out of the men's room as Brady raced into the stall to start another round of retching and almost ran over a svelte, silver-haired elf who was standing in the vestibule between the restrooms. He couldn't help admiring the way Santa's slender helper filled out her soft green suit or the shapely legs that disappeared into her pointy shoes. When she turned and fixed wide, other-worldly eyes on him, a shiver raced along his spine, as if he'd actually happened on a being from some magical land.

Riley had been born for this.

Slumping back against the wall, she frowned. "Shit," she said.

Well, that wasn't very elfin. But even with the illusion shattered, she looked good in that suit.

"What are we gonna do?" She glanced over at the Christmas tree, where Sierra was leading the kids in a carol. "Those kids look forward to this all year." Her pale eyes glistened. "Some club in Denver put on a Christmas party when I was in foster care, and I swear it was the highlight of my childhood. Santa Claus was there, and I thought he'd come straight from the North Pole." She smiled sadly. "He was probably just some reluctant volunteer in a smelly old costume. It was the wonder that made it work. The way kids see things—that's the magic."

Griff pictured little-girl Riley, her eyes wide with wonder, her heart still tender with hope.

He sighed. "I'll see if the suit fits."

"You will?" She looked up at him, her eyes shining, and for the first time in forever, he felt like a genuine hero.

"I'm not sure I'll be any good," he said. "I'm not really the Santa type."

"It'll be fine," Riley said. "It's just acting, and you've only got one line."

He wrinkled his forehead, feeling stupid.

"Ho, ho, ho," she said, poking his chest with each repetition. "How hard can it be?"

Matt hurried up to them. "Heard what happened. You stepping up, Griff?" Playfully, he poked Griff's stomach. "You've got the size, all right."

"Hey, you'd be better," Griff said.

"Nope." Matt waved a cowboy hat with antlers stitched to the sides and tossed a red rubber ball in his other hand. "I can be Rudolph for you, but I can't serve and protect in a Santa suit." He grew serious. "This party's fun, but there's always a lot of drinking. I'm liable to have to break up a fight, so it's all you, my friend."

Putting an arm around Griff's shoulders, Matt pulled him aside and lowered his voice. "Hey, Fawn can't psychoanalyze you when you're in a crowd of kids. And did you see that elf?" He shoved Griff toward the men's room. "I'll get the two of you out the back door so you can make your entrance, okay?"

"Okay," Griff grumbled. But Riley smiled, and a flood of warmth filled his heart. Was it love or Christmas spirit? He wasn't sure, but it came with a shot of courage that helped him through the door marked Cowboys, vowing that he and Riley would give the kids a Christmas they'd never forget.

CHAPTER 36

ED HAD RANSACKED HIS ENTIRE HOSPITAL ROOM BY THE TIME Trevor returned, but his clothes were nowhere to be found. His sisters must have taken them, leaving him trapped in the ridiculous blue cotton hospital gown. It had blue flowers on it and no back.

"Just act like we know where we're going," he said as he shuffled down the hallway with Trevor in close pursuit.

"Where *are* we going?"

"Home. But if they ask, I want to see the fish tank in the main lobby."

Trevor nodded. "Sure, Unk."

"And for God's sake, help me hold onto the back of this danged dress." Ed reached back and struggled to pinch the back of his gown closed. "My whole backside's hanging out."

They headed down the hall, moving as fast as Ed could manage. Just hours before, he'd been too weak to get out of bed, but his adrenaline was pumping and he felt like a new man, probably because he had a purpose. He was going to find Riley and make everything right for her. No matter what it took, he wasn't going to let his sisters chase off the little girl who'd done so much for him and for his Ruth.

He and Ruth had always talked about having a family, but those dreams had never come true. They'd never found out where the problem lay—with him or with her—but they'd agreed they didn't need to know. God hadn't seen fit to give them children, and they'd had to accept that back then. They'd sent money every month to three children overseas, paying for food and schooling for kids who couldn't afford it, but it wasn't until Riley came that they got their little girl.

He smiled. He'd never call Riley a little girl to her face, but that was what she was—their sassy, stand-up, independent, tattooed cuss of a little girl. She wasn't what they'd expected, but she'd turned out to be as fine a human being as anyone he knew, and he was proud of her. Ruth had been, too, and it would have broken her heart to see how his sisters treated her.

Not that she'd have been surprised. Carol and Diane hadn't liked her, either.

Nurses stopped him and Trevor several times, and once a busy doctor eyed them through half-glasses with a frown and asked where they were going. Each time, the fish-tank lie worked perfectly, but when they passed it and headed for the parking garage where Trevor had parked Ed's truck, there were no more excuses.

"Stay here, Unk," Trevor said as they entered the cold, grimy parking garage. "Right in front of this car. Crouch down some so nobody sees you, and I'll get the truck."

Ed crouched, praying nobody would drive by. His billowing cotton gown would fairly glow in the darkness of the parking garage, not to mention the full moon hanging out the back.

Hiding by the bumper of a full-sized Chevy van, he thought about his mission. Finding Riley was number one. Well, actually, finding some clothes was number one. But after that, things were going to be complicated—and hard. Ed was going to have to stand up—for himself, for Riley, and for what was right.

Finally, Trevor pulled up in the truck. Ed toddled out from behind the SUV, gown flapping, and climbed in.

"Thanks, Son," he said.

But although he was grateful to Trevor for executing his escape plan, the boy had to come second to Riley. It was good to see the boy stepping up, but that didn't mean Ed wasn't going to throw the kid out of Riley's apartment the minute they got home. That was Riley's home, and he never should have let her leave.

It was a long drive. Trevor offered to stop at a Walmart and pick up some pants and a shirt, but Ed wanted to get to his own place and wear his own Wranglers. Getting Riley back into his life would mean a confrontation with his sisters, and he didn't want to face them in polyester pants.

When they passed the Red Dawg, the parking lot was packed with every sort of vehicle, from gigantic ranch trucks to the seventies sedans some of the old folks drove.

"It's the Saturday before Christmas, isn't it? There's a party at the Dawg tonight."

Trevor nodded. "Yeah, the band I manage is playing it."

"You manage a band?"

"The Iron Kings. They're really going places, Unk."

"Hope they know some Christmas carols."

Trevor looked worried. "They said they'd learn some."

Ed opened his door the minute Trevor pulled into a parking space. As soon as he stepped out, the wind caught his gown and dang near ripped it off. He clutched it around himself and shuffled to the back door.

"Um, do you think you'll be okay on your own?" Trevor gestured toward the bar. "I'm supposed to be helping the band set up."

Ed sighed. Trevor was a disappointment after all. He could at least make sure his uncle got inside.

"It's a responsibility, Unk," the boy said. "They're depending on me."

"All right."

Ed stepped inside, looking forward to wearing real pants. Then he'd head to the party and watch Trevor's band. He had no doubt that was where Riley was.

And wouldn't she be surprised to see him?

Riley staggered backward when Santa stepped out of the men's room. The moth-eaten suit was stretched across his broad shoulders, but the lower hem hung loose over his slim hips.

"What's the matter?" he asked.

She laughed, shaking her head. "It's unnerving, that's all. I'm having X-rated Santa fantasies."

For heaven's sake, don't tell him. You promised Fawn.

Matt, obviously immune to the fantasies, eyed him critically. "You need a pillow. Santa's supposed to have a belly."

"I know, but the one they gave me is too big. It won't fit," Griff said.

"We'll fix it." Riley shoved him into the men's room and grabbed the pillow he'd left on the counter. "Hold on." Ripping the stitching at one end, she began tearing out handfuls of puffy white down. When it was about half-full, she handed it back to Griff. He shoved it up the suit, then stood sideways so she could admire his silhouette.

Riley grinned. "That should slow down the fantasies a bit."

"Really?"

"No." She shook her head, smiling down at the floor. "Not really."

When she looked up, meeting his eyes, she couldn't breathe. Their memories of those nights they'd spent together hung in the air between them, heating it, pulling them together.

You promised.

Quickly, she looked away. "Hey, did anybody ask Fawn to be the elf? She might want to do it."

"Too late," Griff said. "Those kids can't wait much longer. Besides, you're perfect." She looked up in time to see his eyes soften. "Perfect."

Isaiah stuck his head into the room. "Is my dad okay?" He glanced around at the mounds of white feathers scattered around the room. "Whoa," he said. "What happened? Looks like an angel exploded in here."

"Yeah, and it's a shame." Brady was leaning against the counter, and while he was no longer vomiting, he looked a bit green. Still, he managed a smile. "She was bringing glad tidings."

"That's what angels do," said Isaiah.

Riley and Griff laughed, and when she smiled up into his eyes, they were suddenly a team. And that was okay, she told herself. He was Santa and she was an elf, so when he put an arm around her, she sighed and let it stay.

Perfect.

"Okay." Matt was in full law-enforcement mode, which made Riley giggle because he was wearing the absurd antlered hat and had the red ball stuck on his nose. "We'll get you two outside. There's that sort of sled thing, remember? With wheels and that old Chevy bench seat on the back? You'll ride in on that—I'll pull, being Rudolph—and when I shake the jingle bells, I want to hear some ho-ho-ho-ing, bud." He grinned at Griff, then tweaked Riley's elf hat, making the little bell on the tip ring. "And Griff, try to look jolly, okay? You give those kids your usual look, you'll scar them for life."

CHAPTER 37

As the sleigh wobbled its way into the Dawg, Riley fell against Griff. He held her against him, and she let him, because holy cats, where had all those kids come from? The crowd had seemed manageable when she and Isaiah and Sierra had divided them up in groups, putting older boys in charge of various games and activities, but now they were a sea of faces—expectant faces, looking to Griff and Riley for...for what?

For presents, sure, but when she scanned their expressions Riley didn't see greed. She saw wonder and hope and a longing for the magic of Christmas to be real. They were counting on her and Griff to make it so.

"Ho, ho, ho." The voice behind her was so hearty and, well, *jolly* that she had to look back and make sure Santa himself hadn't shown up. But it was still Griff, and as he belted out another round, he winked, then bent and whispered in her ear. "Look at them. They think we're real. They think we're *magic*."

Riley thought they might be right. She sure *felt* magic. And what else would explain how good Griff looked with a pillowy belly and dirty cotton beard?

Matt pulled the sleigh up to the Christmas tree, then stepped aside as a burst of static sounded from his hip. "Shoot," he muttered, then grinned and waved at the kids. "Rudolph's gotta go. See you later!" He made a weird neighing noise that made everyone laugh and galloped out the door, his boots clippity-clopping across the wooden floor.

Once they were inside, Griff settled into a red wing chair that had been decorated as Santa's throne. Standing beside him, Riley was almost as filled with wonder as the kids to see her grim, dark-eyed soldier become a real Santa before her eyes. He was jolly and kind, bouncing kids on his lap and making them smile, promising he'd try to give them what they wanted, reminding them to be good to their parents and do well in school. Every now and then, he'd glance at her and wink.

It wasn't always easy to smile, though. So many kids asked for things no Santa could ever give, like for Daddy to come back from the war or for Mom to return from wherever she'd gone when she'd run off with some other man. One wished he could be good so his dad wouldn't hit him anymore, and Riley memorized the innocent face so she could tell Sierra and Matt about it later.

As she handed out gifts and smiled for the volunteer who was taking pictures, she knew the magic of this night would get these kids through the year to come. For one night, bullies would make peace with their victims, and their victims would forgive them. Hostilities in broken families would cease for the day, and parents who fought grinding poverty all year would somehow treat their kids to a family meal and a few treasured gifts. Quiet kids learned to laugh and even shout, while kids who couldn't seem to do anything right sensed love and approval from Santa, from partygoers, and maybe even from their parents for once. Meanwhile, carols drifting from the speakers in the ceiling made everybody feel holy inside.

Soon the carols were drowned out by the sound of paper tearing and the oohs and aahs of children—along with a few moans of disappointment.

"I got a stupid doll," said a boy with curly hair. He held up a plastic baby doll that wore a look of stunned surprise, and no wonder. Its new daddy looked like a miniature auto mechanic, with greasy black hair and grit under his fingernails. Riley searched under the tree for a different present for him, like one of those tool sets, but they were all gone.

"I'll trade with you," said a small voice, and she looked down to see a little girl holding out a box. "I love baby dolls."

Riley looked at the box. It was a My Little Pony playset, full of pink and purple horses with long flowing manes. There was a comb to style their hair with, and Riley couldn't think of anything most boys would want less, except for the baby doll.

"That's okay, honey. We'll find something…" she began.

"Cool!" exclaimed the mini-mechanic. "I love My Little Pony! You *sure* you want to trade?"

The child beamed down at the baby doll cradled in her arms. "It's going to be all right," she crooned, and Riley could have sworn its look of surprise calmed a bit.

She basked in the lights, the scents of pine and roasting turkey, and the happiness of the kids as the warmth of the holiday danced all up and down her spine—but then a red-clad arm pulled her close, and she realized Griff was standing behind her, a wall of warmth that had nothing to do with the holiday.

She looked around for Fawn, who was still over at the bar. She wasn't looking, but Riley still felt guilty when she leaned back against her Santa's soft belly. She'd made a promise, but then again, she wasn't Riley right now, and he wasn't Griff. They were a wayward elf and her Santa trapped in a sea of torn paper and discarded ribbons. As they watched the kids exclaiming over their toys, she twisted to look up at him and smiled.

He smiled back, pulling her close, and she was just starting to wonder how she'd kiss him through that cottony beard when the back door burst opened, slamming against the inside wall like a gunshot.

Isaiah appeared in the opening, his eyes darting frantically around the room.

"Where's the marshal?" he asked.

"He got a call," Griff said. "Why?"

Isaiah's narrow chest rose and fell rapidly. "There's a fight out back," he said. "Well, not really a fight. More like some dude got his lights punched out."

"Who?"

"Some guy with the band. Blond guy. I think he had glasses before, but he doesn't have 'em now. Not sure he's got a *pulse*, either. Some big guy worked him over *good*."

Rushing across the stage, Riley stepped out the bar's back door and almost tripped over the prone body of the Only Heir, who looked so much like a broken doll that she almost panicked. Kneeling beside him, she was relieved to see his eyes were open, watching her from behind a whole lot of swelling and two matching bruises.

He'd lost that cynical sneer, along with a couple of teeth. In the fan of light that stretched from the bar's back door, she could see his nose was bleeding, his jeans were torn, and his clothes were soaked with snow. His shirt was hiked halfway up his back, revealing muddy boot prints where someone had kicked him in the kidneys. He started crying when Riley took his hand.

"What happened?" she asked.

Trevor lifted his head to look at her, winced, and fell back into the snow.

"Is anybody in there an EMT or anything? A nurse?" Riley asked.

"I'll check," Isaiah said.

Griff, who had been kneeling beside Riley, stood. "I'll dial 911."

While he answered the dispatcher's questions, a curly-haired young man dashed out the back door, bringing several long-limbed, skinny boys with rock 'n' roll hairstyles with him.

"Trevor. What happened, dude?" Curly asked.

"Looks like You Know Who tracked him down and got him good," said a tall, emo-looking guy decked in head-to-toe tattoos. Riley guessed he was probably the lead singer, judging from the way he tossed his hair and ended every movement with a pose.

"Send the marshal," Griff told the dispatcher. "Somebody just about killed this guy."

"Oh, hey, don't call the marshal," Curly said.

"I already did." Griff flashed him a grim look. "And he's going to want to know who You Know Who is."

Curly snorted. "Don't worry about it, *Santa*. Come on, guys. Let's get Trev out of here."

One kid grabbed the Only Heir's legs, while two others took his arms. They started to drag him toward a battered van half-loaded with amplifiers and instruments, but Griff blocked their way.

"Stop," he said.

Shocked by the voice of command coming from the supposedly jolly old elf, they dropped their burden in the snow.

"Oof," said Trevor.

The musicians turned to walk away, but Riley grabbed the back of Emo Boy's shirt along with Curly's and tugged them backward.

"Tell me who hit him," she said.

"What, little elf, is he your boyfriend?" Curly sniggered. "I don't think you want to mess with the guy who did this." He looked her up and down, leering. "He might want to mess with you, though."

A man loomed up out of the shadows. "I did it. Who wants to know?"

The guy was huge, but he looked soft, like a prizefighter past his prime. Riley looked at the skull and snake tattoos, the lowering forehead and the jutting jaw, and wondered why she felt compelled to protect the Only Heir, who'd been nothing but nasty to her.

Griff stepped up beside her, and her stomach clenched. The stranger topped him by a couple inches in height, and his arms were so long his knuckles almost dragged the ground, but that wasn't what worried her. It was more that if Griff released the violence festering inside him, he might kill the guy.

Griff's hand fell heavily on her shoulder, and she knew it was too late.

"Don't push the elf," he growled. Anger pulsed through his

grip, but he bent and whispered, "I pushed her once, and I've never been sorrier. Biggest mistake I've ever made."

Surprised by the sudden dose of sweetness where she'd expected a burst of temper, stunned by the arousal sparked by the tickle of his fake beard and the warmth of his breath against her ear, the butterflies formed a conga line and started dancing up and down her spine.

Stop it. You promised Fawn.

Riley squeezed her eyes shut, then opened them to see a half-dozen trucks swing into the space where the sleigh had been, spinning skilled doughnuts on the ice to shine their headlights on Trevor and his attacker. Truck doors slammed like muffled gunshots as a circle of shadowy men armed with long guns stepped out to stand silhouetted against the glare from their headlights. It was just as well their faces and figures were obscured by the bright light, since most of them were hardly spring chickens.

A few more men spilled out the bar's back door, including a very pale Brady Caine, his brother Shane Lockhart, looking dangerous in hat-to-boots black, and Sierra's husband, Ridge, whose slight limp only made him look more dangerous. Wayne came next, carrying the shotgun he always kept under the bar. He'd never used it, but he'd named it Emmy Lou and caressed it lovingly with a bar rag, whispering sweet nothings, whenever anyone threatened to start a fight.

The stranger put his hands up, but he didn't back away from the prone form of the Only Heir. "Listen, this has nothing to do with any of you."

"If it has to do with Trevor, it has to do with me." Riley felt a bit self-conscious in her elf suit, but she stood tall, hoping Trevor's attacker wouldn't realize that the constant jingling of the bells on her hat and pointy slippers meant she was trembling from head to toe.

"Well, that's good, honey." The big man's smile revealed the jagged, stained teeth of a meth user, which should have scared Riley but only turned her stomach. "Guess I'll just take *you* in payment then. That okay with you, Santa? Your elf can be my Christmas present."

This was just what Riley had been dreading. The man might as well have poked a grizzly bear with a stick. Griff stood firm behind her, a wall of red-velvet Santa suit, and she knew there was too much tension here, too much at stake.

A crowd of kids stood wide-eyed in the doorway, watching the showdown. If Santa and his elf got hurt, they'd be scarred for life. But if Santa killed somebody, it would be even worse.

Where the heck was the marshal?

CHAPTER 38

GRIFF DIDN'T HEAR EXACTLY WHAT THE BIG MAN SAID TO Riley because the bees were swarming, taking over his brain, clouding his thoughts, and making the cold air hitch in his chest.

He glanced over at the kids gathered in the doorway and remembered he was still Santa. Just moments before, he'd been soothing little kids who were scared to sit on his lap and listening to the hopes and dreams of the older ones. He could smell the dinner Wayne and the women were preparing—roast turkey and stuffing, pumpkin pie and other sweets—and the cold, crisp air bore a hint of pine. It smelled like Christmas, and that seemed to satisfy the bees. They slowed and finally went still—really still, for the first time in forever.

Just then, a series of clicks sliced the air—guns cocking, one after another, all around the circle of trucks that surrounded them.

The stranger turned and scanned the circle of men standing in front of their trucks. "Go ahead," he sneered. "Hain't you never heard of a Mexican standoff? You'll all shoot each other."

"Not if we shoot off your feet," somebody shouted.

The voice sounded high and cracked with age, but the stranger lifted his hands in the air anyway. He looked like he was surrendering, but his attention was still darting around the crowd as if looking for a weak spot.

Enough.

Easing Riley behind him, Griff grabbed the stranger's arm. All that clenching and unclenching was apparently paying off, because the guy turned white when Griff tightened his grip. He wanted to deck the guy, twist his arm behind his back and break it, stomp him into the ground, but he swallowed his temper as a tall, stooped man shuffled out of the crowd. Shadowed against the headlights, only the newcomer's hair, a few reddish strands stretched across his scalp, caught the light.

Ed. It's Ed Boone. What the hell…

"Leave Riley alone." The old man's normally gentle voice was a venomous hiss, like Clint Eastwood on a bad day.

Riley staggered backward into Griff. "Ed! What are you doing here? Aren't you supposed to be…"

Griff tugged her close with his free arm, hushing her. The stranger didn't need to know the man confronting him was supposed to be in a hospital bed. But wonder of wonders, that was what Ed was doing—confronting the man who was threatening Riley. He stood toe-to-toe with the stranger as if he'd fought tough guys all his life, his normally watery eyes steely with determination.

"I'm just trying to collect on a legitimate debt here," the stranger whined. "This kid stole from me, and I'm tryin' to make things right."

"Is this how a real man makes things right?" Griff tightened his hold on the big man as Ed poked him in the chest. "Harasses innocent, um…" He glanced back at Riley, looking confused. "Innocent *elves*? Is that what real men do?"

The crowd erupted in nervous giggles.

"Yeah!" somebody shouted. "Leave the elf alone!"

"Don't mess with her," shouted somebody else. "That's one tough elf!"

"What does he owe you?" Ed helped Trevor to his feet. "And what's it for? Drugs?" He turned and spat on the ground.

Ed. Spat. Had the world turned upside down?

"Well, yeah." The man twisted a foot in the snow in an oddly childlike gesture. "I'd say he owes about three hunnert dollars."

"You did *that* for three hundred dollars?" Ed pointed at Trevor, who looked like a character from *The Nightmare Before Christmas*, with bruises ringing his eyes and his clothes all torn. His nose streamed blood, and his arms were scraped and bloody.

"Pick on somebody your own size next time," Ed sneered.

Ed. Sneered. Griff had never seen anything like it, and judging from the nervous hush that gripped the crowd, they hadn't either.

"What's your name?" Ed asked.

"Um, Darrell."

"Okay, Darrell." Ed spit the name out like it was *worm* or *earwig*. "Tell you what. I'll get you your *three hunnert dollars*, and you can go back to the rat hole you came from and leave my family alone." He paused and scanned the crowd. "My *family*. That's this boy *and* the elf, okay?" He turned to Riley and instantly turned back into the old Ed as if someone had thrown a switch. "Can you go get the money, sweetheart?" He glanced at the stranger and lowered his voice. "There's plenty in the safe."

"Sure." Riley twisted to look up at Griff. "I'm going to go get it, okay?"

She looked strangely wary, and he wondered if she was still afraid of him until he realized he was squeezing her much too hard. He relaxed his hold and smiled tenderly at this brave woman, this fearless warrior, this defender of the lost. The woman he loved.

Yes, *loved*. Who wouldn't love a woman who could face down a devil twice her size, standing ramrod straight with fire in her eyes and her loving heart leading the way? Who wouldn't love her for protecting Trevor of all people—the Only Heir who was taking away her rightful place in the world?

"Take care of Ed and Trevor, okay?" she said.

Griff wanted to take care of *her*, but if taking care of people she loved was all she asked, he'd do it.

"I'll protect them with my life."

"I know you will." Bouncing up on the tips of her pointy shoes, she kissed his cheek, the bells on her hat jingling as they brushed his face. "That's what you do."

He touched his cheek as she turned and walked away, then turned to Ed. "You want to sit down for a bit? I can take care of this guy." He shook the big man's arm, then nodded toward the ambulance that had just turned into the lot. "The EMTs can take care of the Only… Trevor."

Right before Griff's eyes, Ed seemed to deflate, becoming his gentle self, shoulders hunched, gaze soft and dreamy. "I guess that'd be good," he said. "I'm kind of tired now."

He wandered off after Riley. Griff looked down at Trevor as the EMTs approached.

"Don't hurt me," the boy squeaked.

"I won't," Griff said. "Because Riley doesn't want you hurt. You need to think about her, though, and think about the person you are. Look what she's doing for you and look what you're doing to her. You might be Ed's Only Heir, but she's worth ten of you. A hundred."

"I know." The kid sniffled and wiped his nose on his sleeve, leaving a streak of blood behind. "I already talked to my uncle. I know it's not right."

Griff nodded, distracted as he made a quick internal inventory. The bees were still silent. He pictured the swarm escaping like a black cloud rising into the night sky, taking all his anger with them, and was surprised to find they hadn't taken away his strength. He still gripped the lunkhead's arm, and the spindly musicians hovering in the background ducked when he turned their way. His free hand hung idle at his side, but his fingers were relaxed. He didn't have to make fists to calm himself.

He smiled. He couldn't help it. And when the marshal, who'd followed the ambulance into the lot, joined him, he savored a new kind of kinship. They were both strong men. *Good* men, who could handle the tough stuff without violence. Men strong enough to wear Santa suits, red noses, and hats with antlers. Griff wondered what the folks on Matt's last call had thought of his Rudolph costume.

"What's going on?" Matt asked.

"Not much." Griff stared cross-eyed at Matt's nose until the marshal reached up and removed it, looking sheepish—or at least a bit less reindeerish.

"Did you explode?" Matt asked Griff. "Hit anybody? Kill anyone?"

"No, it's pretty much over, except Riley's going to give this guy three hunnert dollars."

Matt lifted a skeptical eyebrow.

"I mean three *hundred*."

"Okay." Matt was wearing a shit-eating grin that made Griff realize he'd fallen into a trap. He'd told Matt he couldn't handle this, and here he was, handling it just fine. He wondered if the call that took Matt away had even been real.

"It was just a fender bender," Matt said, reading his mind. "I knew I didn't have to hurry back with you here. Now I'll just interview some witnesses and then talk to your friend there." Matt nodded his antlers toward Darrell. "Make sure he doesn't leave, okay?" Turning away, he flashed Griff one last smile. "Thanks, *Deputy*."

CHAPTER 39

RILEY JOGGED DOWN THE SIDEWALK TOWARD THE HARDWARE store. Darrell didn't deserve his ill-gotten gains, but if she paid him off, Trevor would have a chance. Recovery made a person vulnerable, and he wouldn't be able to heal unless he was free from fear.

She was so lost in thought she forgot to pay attention to the icy spots. Twice, she slipped and caught herself. She'd completely forgotten about the elf costume until the bells jingled. Glancing up, she spotted her reflection in a shop window dancing a slippery little jig and laughed.

When she reached the store, she glanced left and right to make sure Darrell didn't have any buddies lurking in the shadows, then unlocked the door. As she flicked on the night light by the counter, she inhaled the store's nostalgic scent. Fresh-cut lumber, dust, and something else—something old-fashioned and very dear to her. This place was her sanctuary, and she was going to miss it.

She was kneeling behind the counter, dialing the combination into the safe, when the lights came on. Leaping to her feet, she almost bumped heads with Carol and Diane.

"What are you doing?" Carol asked.

"You can see what she's doing," Diane said. "She's stealing from our brother."

Carol nodded. "The question is *why*."

"Because she can," Diane said.

"To buy drugs, I'll bet," said Carol.

Riley stood, brushing off her elf pants. Glancing from one sister to the other, she noted the expressions on their faces. Distaste, distrust, dislike—they were the Dis Sisters. Or maybe the Dis Sasters.

She smothered a smile. Ed would like that one.

"You think this is funny?" Diane asked. "I suppose you thought that disguise would fool us. We know you're anything *but* Santa's helper."

"Actually, I am," Riley said, remembering the kids—the babies, soft and powder-scented as she set them in Griff's gentle arms, the kids she'd comforted when waiting in line got too hard. "I've been his helper all night."

"You'll wipe that smile off your face when we call the police," Diane said.

"The marshal? He knows what I'm doing." Riley turned back to the safe. "Go on and call him."

She was making a good show of strength, but while facing Carol and Diane should have been way easier than facing hulking, criminal Darrell, it seemed a lot harder—mostly because she shouldn't have to fight them. She was on their side, trying to help Trevor, yet they just assumed she was stealing. People like them made her wonder if she'd ever outrun her past.

As the safe swung open, she turned back to the Harpies, and her anger burst out.

"You know, I could have robbed Ed blind over the past few years," she said. "I must have been in and out of this safe a thousand times." She gave them a phony, wide-eyed look. "Oh, but you don't know that, because you *weren't here*. Not once." Grabbing the zippered bank bag and the bundle of keys beside it, she stood. "You never visited Ed. Not when his wife died, not when we held her funeral, not when he had his first heart attack." She set the bag on the counter. "So why are you here now? Because you want the store. *You* want to steal what he built—not me." She snorted. "Some *family*."

Unlocking the bag, she pulled out a stack of bills and began to count, slapping them down on the counter with her thumb. *Ten— slap. Twenty—slap. Thirty…*

"But I don't understand." Carol's voice quavered, reminding

Riley they were old ladies and unlocking her heart—a little. "What are you doing? It's the middle of the night. We came home to get clothes for Ed, and here you are, taking money."

Riley set the bills on the counter and sighed. It probably wasn't their fault. Something in their lives must have twisted them into all this meanness.

"In a way, you're right," she said. "I *am* getting money for a drug dealer."

"I knew it," Carol said fiercely.

Riley kept counting. *Sixty—slap. Eighty—slap. One hundred.* "I'm paying him because Trevor owes him three hundred dollars. The dealer's from Denver, but he's at the Red Dawg now, waiting for the money. He beat Trevor up, and I'm paying him to keep it from happening again."

Diane narrowed her eyes. "Don't you claim that money's for Trevor," she said. "Where would *he* meet a drug dealer? You must have introduced them."

"Trust me, Trevor screwed up all by himself." Riley laughed, sharp and mirthless, but she really wanted to cry, for herself, for Trevor, even for the Harpies, who had so much to learn about the world. "He's managing a band, and there are always drugs around musicians. Something got ahold of him, that's all. It doesn't mean he's a bad person."

She recounted the money, then set the stack on the counter. "If you don't believe me, just follow me over to the Dawg and see for yourselves."

"We have no desire to follow you to a *bar*." Diane said the word as if she hadn't eaten at the Red Dawg just the day before.

"Well, you should. Tonight's the Christmas party, and once we get all this straightened out, there'll be music and stuff." Riley smiled down at the counter. "Probably not from Trevor's band, though. But you can ask Ed what's going on. He'll tell you."

"We know you're lying," Diane said. She sounded desperate

but triumphant, too. "Ed's in the hospital. You can't even keep your lies straight."

"No, he's not. He's here." Riley frowned. "You brought him home, right?"

The bell on the front door jingled, and a tall, spare figure entered, stomping snow off his boots.

"Ed!" Carol lifted a fluttering hand to her chest, and Riley thought Ed should have brought the EMTs with him.

"What are you doing here?" Diane asked.

The old man glared at Carol, then at Diane. He was looking peaked; his hair was straggly and his face lined and tired. Riley's heart ached. It was Christmas. He shouldn't be dealing with all this trouble.

"I had Trevor bring me home," he said. "Seems there's some nonsense going on around here I need to take care of."

"You don't have to take care of anything," Diane said. "If that boy is into drugs, that's *his* problem. We've given him everything, and this is what we get in return?"

Riley looked away as a fat, embarrassing tear wobbled past her defenses and splotched onto the stack of bills. She was crying for Ed, who was spending his holiday dealing with a drug-addicted nephew and a couple of Harpies instead of celebrating at the Red Dawg. Or maybe she was crying for the two old ladies, who were so confused and disillusioned by Trevor's situation. But mostly, she was crying for Trevor. He had the family she'd always wanted, but they weren't offering anything close to unconditional love. Sure, he'd messed up. And he was kind of a jerk. But the Harpies were ready to abandon him just because he'd made a mistake.

No wonder he'd turned to drugs. It wasn't an excuse, of course, any more than Riley herself had had an excuse. But it was a reason, and she understood him better now.

Swatting her tears away, she shoved the three hundred dollars into her back pocket, scribbled an IOU on a sticky note, and pasted it to the remaining bills. She shoved them back into the bag, locked it back in the safe, then looked up at Carol and Diane.

They didn't look like Harpies anymore. They looked like a couple of scared old ladies who'd just had their world turned upside down.

"Why don't you come with me?" she asked. "The marshal's over there, and he can explain what's going on. Or if you'd rather, I'll take care of things and bring Trevor back. I think you ought to hear about the situation from him."

Carol opened her mouth to speak, but no sound came out. Likewise, Diane lifted an admonishing finger, but it slowly dropped to her side as she seemed to realize that for once, she had nothing righteous to say.

Riley turned and gave Ed a gentle but fierce hug, pressing her cheek to his. He seemed so fragile, like a man made of paper that might crumple at any moment. But he'd been brave, so brave. He'd stood up for her—and she loved him so much.

"You okay, Buddy?" she whispered.

"I am now." He rubbed her back the way he always did, in a soft, comforting circle, and she nearly burst into tears, it was so good to have him back. "You go take care of things, honey. I appreciate it. And bring Trevor back here, okay?"

"I will," she promised.

And she would. Because she'd do anything for Ed Boone while she had the chance. He wasn't well, and the thought of losing him—her buddy, her hero, her *dad*—was almost unbearable.

CHAPTER 40

RILEY GLANCED UP AND DOWN WYNOTT'S CURVING MAIN Street. Snow fell gently from the night sky, but the town was aglow with colored bulbs that bordered awnings, rooflines, and windows. Snowflakes caught the light, glittering like diamonds scattered in the drifts, and the faint sound of Christmas music wafted from the bar. The town's familiar Christmas decorations glowed from every lamppost, cracked and ancient but familiar and beloved. She'd always seen Wynott as a Wild West Brigadoon, a magical place where nothing bad could happen—but here she was, headed for a standoff between old men armed with shotguns and a hulking drug dealer.

It won't ever happen again, she thought fiercely. She'd pay off Darrell and send him on his way. Griff and Matt, along with the Decker Ranch cowboys, would make sure he and the Iron Kings spread the word that this was a law-abiding town.

The ugliness in the Red Dawg parking lot could not be the first step in the death of yet another small town in the West. In so many others, jobs had dwindled and despair had flowed in, followed inevitably by addiction. The few young folks who stayed turned to drugs that seemed to shield them from hopelessness and shame—until the drugs killed them or ruined their lives.

That wouldn't happen to Wynott. It was a community that stood together. She smiled, remembering the absurdity of the standoff over Trevor. He was an outsider who'd brought them nothing but trouble, but he was Ed's, and that made him family to all of them.

She'd longed to be family, too, but if Carol and Diane turned their backs on Trevor, he'd need to stay with Ed, and it made sense for him to take her place at the hardware store. That just confirmed her resolution to move on. Ed would be sad, but the Harpies would be happy. So would Fawn.

How come she couldn't do that for anyone she *liked*?

Whatever happened, she'd be okay, because a hometown wasn't where you happened to be born. It was the place that formed you and made you who you were. For her, that was Wynott, and the memory of this town would give her a solid place to stand no matter where she went.

Halfway across the street, she noticed the falling flakes turning from green to yellow to red and back again in the light of the town's single traffic light. She glanced right, then left. Nobody was watching, so she spread her arms and turned in a slow circle, delighting in the way the falling snow changed colors as it fell through the beams of colored light.

She'd forgotten she was wearing the elf costume until she tripped and jingled her bells. The realization made her laugh and wonder if anyone was watching. If so, they might believe a little more in the magic of Christmas.

After one last spin, she hurried down the street and back to the Red Dawg Bar to rescue the kid who was going to ruin her life.

Griff was starting to worry about Riley. Leaving Darrell with Matt, he headed for the edge of the parking lot and peeked around the corner. He could see up and down Main Street, including Boone's Hardware, and was relieved to see Riley come out the front door. She was still dressed in the elf suit, and the pointy shoes made her walk with long, loping strides that only emphasized her otherworldly charms.

As she crossed the street, the traffic light changed to green, lighting up her costume so brightly she cast a chartreuse reflection on the icy street. Stopping, she looked up at the falling snow and then turned, slowly, like a ballerina in a wind-up snow globe. He knew she was looking at the snow and the lights, but most of all at Wynott. As the light turned yellow, then red, it looked like the town was being blessed by a genuine Christmas elf.

Finally, she stopped and trotted toward the Dawg again, so Griff hurried back to Matt and used his newly discovered hand strength to resume possession of Darrell. Matt moved away to wander up and down the rows of trucks and the few cars in the lot. When he got to a turd-brown Buick in the back row, Griff felt Darrell tense.

Matt meandered back and gave the big man a grin. "That your Buick?"

The big man jutted out his jaw. "None of your business."

"I can always run the plates." Matt's tone was pleasant and conversational, as if he was doing the guy a favor.

Darrell hung his head and kicked at the snow. "Okay," he said. "It's mine."

"Well, good." Matt took Darrell's hands like a dance partner, executed a rapid do-si-do, and snapped a pair of handcuffs on his wrists. "You must have been in a hurry to get your *three hunnert dollars*, because you left about that much *product* in plain sight on the passenger seat," he said. "You're under arrest, my friend, for that and for assault. We'll be confiscating your vehicle, too."

The big man struggled to wrench his wrists apart as Matt recited a Miranda warning. Griff gave him a shake, and he finally slumped, defeated.

Matt turned to see the so-called Iron Kings watching wide-eyed from the parking lot. "You there, boys. Is that your van?"

Leotard Boy's eyes widened. He nudged Curly, and the two of them dashed toward the battered vehicle. As they piled into the front, the other two Iron Kings, looking anything but royal, raced after them and leapt into the back, slamming the doors behind them.

They'd almost cleared the lot when the side door slid open and Curly tumbled out. He raced back to the bar, grabbed a guitar, and leapt into the sliding side door of the van with it tucked under his arm machine-gun style as the vehicle careened out of the lot. Sliding on a patch of ice, it nearly hit the side of the building, then spun its wheels and tore off into the night.

"Hey," Matt said mildly. "They forgot the rest of their equipment. Guess they're donating it to the Dawg." He set a hand on Griff's shoulder. "Watch our friend Darrell, would you?" he said. "I need to notify dispatch."

Griff glanced at their prisoner. Cuffed, he looked somehow diminished, like a sulky child caught red-handed at the cookie jar, but this was the man who'd given Riley that slimy, predatory stare and talked about her being his Christmas present. Again, Griff thought about grabbing the guy's shackled wrists and slamming him into the ground. He wanted to smash his fist into that sulky, stupid face, beat the guy black and blue. The dark, demon-haunted part of him wanted to kill the guy—and yet the marshal was walking away without a backward glance, confident his prisoner would live.

Griff waited for the bees to swarm, but instead, Matt's words rose in his mind. *I know who you are. Whatever happened, you're still that person.*

Apparently, the marshal was right, because the buzzing was really gone. The law would take its course and make Darrell pay, and somehow, that was enough.

Not long ago, that would have been cause for celebration. With the anger beat, his self-control restored, he could go back to the military. That had been his only goal not too long ago, but now his goal was Riley James—her respect, her love, her heart.

If only he'd found this peace before he'd gone and blown it by pushing her around. He'd give anything to undo those moments that had brought fear into her eyes, but it was too late to undo the damage he'd done. Still, dealing with Darrell was a good start. And he planned to stick around and keep going.

He was sure of that now. He'd take the job Matt offered, get his own place. Better yet, he'd move into the forest-service cabin on the ranch's back forty. His dad had traded some forested land for the place, and Griff had loved to go bird hunting with his grand-dad there. It sat on a wide sweep of prairie, backed by pine trees that stood out almost black against the golden plains. There were just two rooms, plus a small stable for horses, but he knew a kick-ass contractor who could fix the place up, maybe add on a nice kitchen.

He'd still be around the ranch. He could mess around with horses in his spare time and be with his family again. He could get to know his new stepmother, even mend things with his dad. Best of all, he'd have the time to redeem himself in Riley's eyes.

In the parking lot, the men of Wynott had relaxed. Leaning against their trucks, they talked and laughed softly. Some cradled their long guns in their arms; others rested them in the snow while they talked casually with their neighbors. Occasionally, one would glance over at Griff, see him still holding the drug-dealer prisoner, and nod.

It would feel good to do this every day. To be a man they depended on. To keep this town safe.

It was funny how you couldn't wait to leave a place, and then the loss of it grew and festered until it ached like an abscessed tooth. In the army, he and his men had spent long nights talking about home, and he'd learned most of them fought to defend the places they'd come from—their towns, their families, their way of life. Wynott had hovered in his mind all along, the image of it driving everything he did.

He looked around at the tacky Christmas decorations, the quiet men at the ready with their guns, the gossipy girls clucking like chickens under the streetlamp. A familiar high-pitched laugh cut through the night, and he noticed Fawn Swanson standing with a few friends in a pool of light cast by a streetlamp. Her pretty eyes kept flicking toward Griff, and she'd toss him a flirty smile now and then, but he didn't return it.

Funny how things could change. He would have slayed dragons for one of those smiles when he was a kid, but now he knew they were only skin deep.

He'd continue to fight for it all—the dusty pickup trucks, the lined faces of the old men, the hopeful spark in the eyes of the kids from Phoenix House, even Fawn Swanson's all-American beauty. But he'd fight his battles here, where he belonged.

He'd learned at great cost that he couldn't save the whole world. But with Riley as a guiding star, maybe he could help save Wynott.

CHAPTER 41

RILEY PAUSED JUST BEYOND THE LIGHT THAT STREAMED FROM the bar. People like Darrell tended to travel in packs, so she wasn't about to dash in waving a bundle of money.

But everything looked okay. Matt was in his Explorer, talking on the radio with Trevor beside him in the passenger seat. The kid was staring through the windshield as if seeing his future spread before him, an endless road leading to an unknown destination. He didn't look terribly happy, but he looked thoughtful, which was good.

In the center of the circle of light stood Griff, looking solid and strong with one big hand wrapped around Darrell's arm. The guy wasn't bruised or battered, so nobody'd lost their temper.

She was almost ashamed at how surprised she was. She knew Griff was a good man. Matt knew it, too, and she wondered if he'd left on purpose to let Griff prove himself. It made her wonder why she'd taken a few moments of frustration as proof he was irredeemably violent.

Probably it was because he'd believed it of himself—but he looked confident now. Confident and calm and in charge.

Most of the residents of Wynott had come out to watch the excitement, creating a party atmosphere. Sierra had taken the kids back to Phoenix House for a movie, but the Decker Ranch cowboys sat on the tailgate of somebody's pickup truck while a couple of Ed's friends sat on a bench outside the bar's back door. She spotted Fawn Swanson standing under a streetlamp, watching Griff, and glowing with… What was that? Pride?

Riley ignored the pain that pierced her at the thought. She'd lost a lot of things in her life, and Griff would just be one more. She'd get over it. She always did. But he'd be the toughest yet.

As she stepped into the light, all eyes were on her. Well, let them watch. She'd give Darrell his money and get him out of town so they could somehow save Trevor. Her part in that project would be leaving a place for him—a healing place.

Boone's Hardware had healed her. She'd been lucky to find it. And good luck wasn't something you owned. You couldn't keep it to yourself. You had to pass it on.

A hush fell over the crowd. Griff turned to see Riley in the circle of light, heading right toward him. Maybe he hadn't blown it as badly as he'd thought—but as she got closer, he saw her eyes were on Darrell, not him. She was fishing for something in her pocket when Matt stepped out of the cruiser and stopped her.

"What are you doing?"

She eyed him warily. "Paying off Trevor's debt."

"Didn't you see Darrell's fancy new bracelets?" He nodded toward the cuffs. "Trust me, he's not collecting any debts." He nodded to Griff, who walked the man to the cruiser. Matt loaded him in the back seat, motioning for Griff to help Trevor out of the front.

Griff didn't know quite what to do with the Only Heir. The kid was pretty beat up and probably ought to go home. The hardware store wasn't far, but it seemed heartless to make him walk.

The kid glanced around. "You know where Riley went?"

"She's over there. You know she brought money over to pay off your drug dealer?"

Trevor sniffed, hanging his head. "Yeah." He kicked at the snow with the toe of a very damp sneaker. "Riley's the best. All that stuff my great-aunts say about her… It's bullsh—wrong." He glanced around. "Where's the band?"

Riley joined them. "Yeah, what happened to the band?"

Griff smiled. "They skedaddled. Apparently the marshal made 'em nervous."

"Shi—shoot," Trevor said. "That was our first paying gig in months."

"I thought you said they were some hot Denver success story," Wayne said.

"Well, they're pretty good," Trevor said. "They just—they kind of burned a lot of bridges in Denver. Sometimes the lead singer throws up onstage, and one time, the drummer fell asleep."

Slowly, the crowd was beginning to file back inside. Griff made as if to follow, but he halted just outside the door and leaned against the building, obscured by shadows. Riley, still talking to Trevor, didn't seem to notice.

"So the Iron Kings kind of squandered their talent, huh?" Riley said.

Trevor grimaced. "Yeah, it's frustrating. I keep telling 'em not to party until after the show, but…"

"But they can't control it," Riley said.

Trevor shoved his hands in his pockets and stared down at the snow, poking at it with one foot. "No, they can't."

"You're not having much luck controlling it, either."

She didn't ask him; she told him. The kid nodded, his shoulders slumping.

She didn't respond right away, just stood there, watching him. Griff knew what it was like to be watched by those eyes.

The woman could make a rock confess.

When Trevor's shoulders began to shake, Riley gave him a side hug, kind of rough but, she hoped, big-sisterly. "Hey, some of what your aunties said was true, okay? I was as messed up as you. More, probably. I know how easy it is to fall and how hard it is to climb out. But it can be done, okay?"

He nodded, still staring down at his toes. "I've tried a bunch of times, but all my friends are into it, and I end up caving every time."

"Your friends are in Denver, though, and you're here. That really helps, believe me."

"I can't stay, though." He finally looked up. All the nastiness had left him, and what was left behind was a wayward little brother who needed her help. "I'm not going to take your apartment away or your job. I don't care what my aunties say." He sighed. "They're probably going to disown me anyway."

"About that," Riley said. "They already know what's going on."

Trevor's eyes widened. "What? You told them?"

"They saw me getting money out of the safe to pay Darrell. I tried to explain it wasn't your fault. Not entirely, anyway."

Trevor grimaced. "Don't know why you're helping me. I haven't been very nice to you."

"This kind of thing's a bond. We'll help each other. Friends, right?"

Trevor gave her a quick, shy smile that fled his face so fast she almost missed it.

"Family," he muttered.

Her heart ached. It was a sweet sort of ache but deep, so she changed the subject before she embarrassed herself by crying.

"If you work hard for Ed, you won't have time to even think about drugs. That's what helped me. But your aunties might want to pay for some cushy rehab joint."

"No." His chest heaved as he swallowed a sudden sob. "They won't pay to help me. They probably won't even let me go home."

"Then it's good you've got Ed."

Trevor shook his head, hard. "But you live there. You work there. Your boyfriend—he said I'd better think about what I was doing to you, and he's right."

"Griff's not my boyfriend. And I don't live here anymore. I'm leaving." Riley swallowed hard as she said it, but it was true. Fawn had helped him, made him leave the safety of home and get out among people, where he could heal as she had. All Riley did was... Well, all she did was love him. And that wasn't smart. As it turned out, he could keep his temper leashed, but she'd been much too ready to believe the worst of him. Besides, she'd promised Fawn.

She turned to give Trevor a hug, and there was Griff, right behind him.

Speak of the devil. Or Santa, or whatever.

Her heart fluttered—or was that the butterflies waving goodbye? He looked away, but she was pretty sure he'd heard.

"Where are you going to go?" Trevor asked.

"Back to Denver." She glanced up at the star-strewn sky as she led him back inside. She should feel sad. There weren't this many stars in Denver—but there were more opportunities. A whole universe full. "I went through a program there that helped me, and I always said I'd go back and pass it on, you know? So I'm going to work for them."

I hope.

"You'll see," she said. "You'll get better, and you'll want to do the same kind of thing someday."

CHAPTER 42

RILEY STOPPED AS SHE AND TREVOR REACHED THE BAR. "Hey, did you want to go home and clean up?"

"I'll do it in the restroom," he mumbled. "Don't want my aunties to see me this way."

Riley started to tell him that was a good idea when she realized Griff had followed them inside. He didn't look happy, so she turned away, pretending she hadn't seen him.

Somebody in the bar plinked a high note on the piano, then a low one. A couple experimental chords followed, finally forming themselves into a song. Riley smiled. It had to be Eleanor Carson, who played the piano at the Lutheran church in Grigsby.

Sure enough, Eleanor's thin, high soprano commanded all the merry gentlemen in the bar to let nothing them dismay. Riley wondered what the merry women were supposed to do, but she still couldn't help chiming in on the chorus.

Oh, tidings of comfort and joy…

She was surprised when Trevor harmonized with a serviceable tenor and even more stunned when Griff joined in, his voice low and masculine but soft, as if he was singing to himself. He probably thought no one could hear him, but the rich, tender tone melted something inside her.

…comfort and joy, oh tidings of comfort and joy.

Their voices balanced so well—Riley's whiskey-laced alto, Trevor's sweet tenor, and Griff's baritone. Around them stood their neighbors; the men who had so recently armed themselves and surrounded Darrell now held their hats to their chests and sang. The women smiled up at their men and at one another, their smiles linking each to each, saying they were one, they were community, they were family.

Riley wished she could put the scene in a snow globe, preserve it forever in a glass dome with a key on the bottom so she could wind it up and hear the sweetness of the carol anytime she wanted.

As they swung into the next verse, most of the men dropped out, and Riley found herself singing almost alone, with only Eleanor Carson's thin voice joining her. It was embarrassing, but most folks didn't know the later verses, and somebody had to help Eleanor out. Riley had loved the classic carols ever since she'd found a ragged paperback as a kid that showed all the lyrics. She'd memorized every one. "Joy to the World," "Hark, the Herald Angels Sing," "Away in a Manger"... She loved them all, and that little book had been like a bible to her, teaching her about love and giving all year round.

When the comfort-and-joy part came around again, Griff put his arm around her but in a nice way. Brotherly, she told herself—as if it were possible to be brotherly after the nights they'd shared at the ranch. She looped one arm around his waist and drew Trevor in with the other, and as they sang the chorus, she felt a tenderness she couldn't quite identify. It was almost like they were a family—she the mom, Griff the dad, and Trevor their troublemaking son—but that was silly.

There'd be no family for her. Not with Griff. That was over. And she couldn't imagine wanting one with anyone else.

Everyone clapped at the end of the carol. Griff figured they were clapping for Riley, whose singing had stood out so on the last few verses. She really did have a lovely voice, sweet but low, with a Janis Joplin rasp that made it unique.

But when Riley smiled and turned to him, he realized she was clapping, too, her hands high. He shrugged and joined in, and she laughed, her face alight with joy.

"They're clapping for *you*, doofus," she whispered.

"What?"

He thought she had to be mistaken, but he stopped clapping as Wayne came up and smacked him on the back.

"That was something out there," he said. "Thought somebody was going to get hurt, but you and Matt sure took care of things."

Someone he didn't even know shoved a beer into his hand. "Good job, buddy."

Next thing he knew, he was at the center of a group of men, all of them talking at once about the drug dealer, how dangerous he was, and how Griff had, in the words of various men, "taken care of him," "shown him who was boss," and "defanged that MF-er."

"Some guys come back from overseas all messed up," somebody said. "But I heard you were a hero over there, and I guess you're not done yet."

Another smack on the back gave Griff a reason to grimace, which was just as well. He hated the "hero" label. It didn't fit, and he knew he was still messed up—but he didn't want to talk about what had happened.

His stomach started to hurt as the crowd lifted their plastic cups of beer, because he hadn't been a hero tonight, either. He just hung onto the guy while Ed, Riley, and the marshal took care of business, but everyone seemed happy and a little drunk, so he didn't protest. After a while, they turned to other things, and he found himself enjoying the Christmas joy that hung in the air like the green and red crepe paper streamers that swayed in the breeze from the heating vents. Every face gleamed with happiness—although the effects of Wayne's famous Black Russians and the mulled cider he had cooking in a Crock-Pot contributed quite a bit to the festive mood.

Bucky Maines from the feed store shook Griff's hand. "Matt said he offered you the deputy position," said Bucky. "I hope you're going to take it."

"Thinking about it," Griff muttered.

Riley turned, wide-eyed. He wished she'd smile, but she just looked shocked.

"Matt's going to run for the legislature someday," Bucky said. "That would give you a chance at being town marshal. We'd sure like to see that." He gave Griff a nudge and a crafty grin. "Saw you with Fawn Swanson. Now, that's the kind of woman who'd be an asset to your campaign. You need to think about that kind of thing, you know."

Bucky had it all wrong. There was only one woman Griff wanted, and he needed to convince her that he was, in fact, her boyfriend and talk her out of leaving town.

As the crowd around him thinned, she put a hand on his arm. He smiled down at her, hoping she wanted what he did. If she went home with him, maybe she'd change her mind. There was a lot of comfort and joy to be had back home at the ranch.

But she nodded toward the bar and gave him a push. Looking up, he saw Fawn Swanson perched on a barstool, looking right at him.

She looked adorable but like she was trying a bit too hard, with every hair in place and perfectly applied makeup. She was wearing one of those ugly Christmas sweaters, but you could tell it was one that had been made to order, not something cool she'd found in a Goodwill store. In contrast, Riley's hair was tangled from her run to the hardware store, her cheeks pinked by the cold, her eyes alight behind lashes still damp from the snow. And she was still wearing the green felt elf costume. How could Fawn compete with that?

When Fawn caught Griff's eye, she patted the stool beside her. All the seats at the bar were taken, but that one was occupied only by her purse.

Dammit, she was saving him a seat.

"Go ahead," Riley said. "She's been watching you all night, and you know *she's* hoping you'll say yes to Matt. If you're really going to do that, you two have a lot more than Christmas to celebrate." She bumped his shoulder with her own and gave him a wink. "Go get her, tiger."

"What are you talking about?"

"Griff, come on." Riley rolled her eyes.

"I'm with you tonight," he said. "Fawn came on her own."

Riley laughed. "Come on. I saw her whispering sweet nothings in your ear when you walked in. You were together. And honestly, I don't mind."

"I was just being polite," he said.

She gave him an eye roll. "I've seen you be polite to her before."

"That wasn't…"

"Never mind. That was catty." She shook her hair out of her face, making the elf bells ring. "I'm heading back to the store with Trevor. The sooner he faces Carol and Diane, the sooner he'll be able to get on with his recovery."

Griff took a sip of his beer, then set it on a nearby table. "I'll go with you."

"No need," she said. "Fawn's waiting, and you don't owe me a thing, okay? I know you two belong together, and so does everyone else. You heard Bucky, right? And *you* know you've been crazy about her half your life." She punched his arm. "So go. Have fun."

He looked down at her. His mouth was moving, but no sound would come out. Why did she keep shoving him at Fawn? Was it her way of saying she didn't care? He didn't believe that. He'd felt the emotions that surrounded them when they… Well. Those feelings were real, and he'd been sure they went both ways.

At least, he'd been sure until Riley went to leave the ranch. Maybe he'd killed any love she had for him when he'd manhandled her.

Maybe.

But he didn't think so. There was still an openness in her gaze, an honesty in her smile, so maybe it was just that she was so used to loss that she expected him to move on. Sometimes she seemed to see herself as less than Fawn, which was ridiculous. Or maybe she was punishing herself for past misdeeds and thought she didn't deserve happiness.

But she did. And Fawn Swanson would have to enjoy the company of her purse until she gave up on Griff and let some other man sit beside her.

CHAPTER 43

WHEN TREVOR CAME OUT OF THE MEN'S ROOM, RILEY GAVE him a smile and a thumbs-up. Smiling wasn't easy after what she'd heard Bucky say. He'd looked right at her when he'd said it, and some of the men with him, the ones congratulating Griff, had looked at her, too. She understood those looks. She got them all the time.

Griff needed a woman who was more like Fawn—one who'd been born in this ranch community, with a background that was blemish-free. One who'd be "an asset to his campaign." But knowing it was true didn't make it hurt any less, so Riley was glad to have Trevor's troubles to distract her. There was no hiding that shiner, but he'd combed his hair and washed his face, and he looked…better. She slung an arm around his shoulders and gave him a friendly shake.

"Cheer up."

He hung his head. "Can't."

"Come on. It's Christmas. I'll buy you a Coke."

"No, thanks." He stared over at the bar, then down at his feet. "I should go home. I mean, back to Uncle Ed's. I want to get things over with."

"Good for you." She gave his arm a gentle punch. "I think that's best, too. Do you want me to come along?"

"*Yes.*" He clutched at her arm. "That's why I want to do it now. I need you with me."

He squared his shoulders as if preparing for a fight, and Riley's heart broke right in half. Any kid should feel relieved when he was about to come clean to his folks on such a big problem. But it was obvious he was dreading it.

"Where will I go?" he asked.

"What do you mean? Home, right? To Ed's."

"They'll throw me out."

"No, they won't. Did you see Ed stand up to that guy? He won't allow them to throw you out."

"Yeah, well, that guy was a mouse compared to my aunties," Trevor said.

Riley laughed, pretending he'd made a joke, but he had a point. She just hoped the women would surprise him. Sometimes, a real family emergency made people pull together in surprising ways—at least, it did in books and movies. Riley had no idea what happened in real life, because her own family had been shattered as long as she could remember. Nobody had ever been angry with her; no one had cared enough to bother.

As they left, Griff followed. "If you think I'm going to let you face those women alone, you're crazy."

Riley turned to protest, but he shook his head.

"I won't interfere, I promise. But if I'm there, they'll think twice about hurting you the way they do."

"They don't hurt me." Riley shook back her hair and tried to look like she didn't care. "They can't."

Deep down, though, they could. They *had*, and she was glad he was coming along. His presence alone made her stronger—not just because he was big and strong but because he represented all that was good and brave.

Plus he chose you, not Fawn.

She smothered that thought, shutting down the butterfly dance. Griff would choose whoever needed protecting. That was his nature. If Fawn smartened up and played damsel in distress instead of town sweetheart, he'd probably choose her.

Maybe Riley should tell her, help her out—because the longer it took for Griff to figure out where he really belonged, the more Riley's heart yearned for him. And the harder she fell, the worse she'd suffer when he finally figured out his place in the world.

Marshal's deputy, probably marshal someday, with a pretty, golden-haired wife at his side—not a tattooed lady with a checkered past.

Walking behind Riley and Trevor like a volunteer security guard, Griff caught himself clenching and unclenching his fists and shoved his hands into the pockets of his Santa pants. Riley needed his support, not his anger. The scene when she left the ranch played in his head over and over, with a soundtrack of *if onlys*—if only he hadn't shouted, if only he hadn't grabbed her, if only he hadn't shoved her.

He'd gotten his anger under control with Darrell. Why hadn't he been able to do it earlier with Riley?

Probably because there was so much more at stake.

He followed his favorite elf and the Only Heir across the snowy street and down the slippery sidewalk to the hardware store. Riley went around the building to the side entrance that led to Ed's door, and Trevor took her hand like a child.

Griff might not like the kid, and he resented the way Trevor had upended Riley's life, but the gesture made him feel sorry for him.

Riley tapped on the door, then went inside without waiting for an answer. The three of them stamped snow off their boots and wiped their feet in the foyer.

"It's about time," Carol said as they entered the living room.

"Now, Carol," Ed said. "It's Christmas."

The room certainly looked like Christmas. In fact, the room was so beautiful that the two women standing by the fireplace looked oddly out of place with their folded arms and grim expressions. Ed, kind-faced as always, sat in the glow of the tree's twinkle lights.

Riley led Trevor to the sofa and sat down while Griff remained in the doorway, looming. He was good at looming.

"I was sitting there," Diane said.

"Oh, I'm sorry." Riley started to stand, but Trevor gripped her hand like he was drowning and she was his only lifeline, and Ed stood up, offering his chair to his sister.

"There are plenty of places to sit." He didn't sound like Dirty Harry anymore, but he didn't sound like his old self, either. There was a firmness in his tone that even Griff wouldn't want to challenge.

"How are you feeling, Uncle Ed?" Trevor asked.

"Three hundred dollars poorer, that's how he's feeling," Diane said before Ed could answer. "*If* that woman is telling the truth, you have a lot of explaining to do, young man. But I really doubt her story."

"You shouldn't doubt her," Trevor said. "Riley tells the truth. I'm the one who lies. I…" The kid stared down at his lap, then looked up at Riley with a look so desperate Griff almost felt sorry for him. "Can you tell them?"

"No." Riley patted his knee. "You need to do it."

The kid looked from Carol to Diane to Ed and back again.

"Tell your uncle," Riley said.

"Okay." Trevor took a deep breath. "Uncle Ed, I-I started doing drugs. Things weren't going right, and I never fit in, not even with my friends, and I just… I thought it would make me feel better, but then I couldn't seem to stop. I mean, I could have, but for some reason…I just didn't. I couldn't. I don't know." He paused, opening and closing his mouth like a gasping goldfish.

"What Trevor's saying is that he got addicted. He didn't realize what was happening until it was too late." Riley squeezed the kid's hand. "Is that right?"

Trevor nodded and seemed to find some courage at last. His voice was stronger, and he looked Ed in the eye.

"I tried to get off it a bunch of times, but I couldn't seem to do it. Since I came here, I've been clean, though. It's the longest I've gone without taking anything. That's why I was so sick, because it—it makes you sick."

Riley was dismayed when neither sister appeared to unbend. With folded arms, they faced Trevor like jailers dealing with a prisoner gone wrong. But she noticed Carol's hands were trembling, and Diane was clenching her jaw so hard it had to hurt.

"What are you going to do about it?" Carol's voice was high and querulous.

Trevor looked down at his clenched hands. "I thought if I stayed here…"

"Stay here?" Carol looked outraged. "Being here is the problem. Being here with *her*. We all know she's the *expert* on taking *drugs*."

Griff took a step forward and was rewarded when Carol stopped midtirade.

"It wasn't her," Trevor said. "Actually, she's the only one who's helped me. She figured out what was going on, and…"

"Well, if someone had told us, we could have helped. But of course, no one had to tell *her*. She…"

To Griff's surprise, Diane interrupted.

"Let Trevor tell it, Carol."

Pressing her lips together, Carol settled back in her chair, but her flashing eyes made it clear she wasn't done with Riley.

"I started in Denver," Trevor said. "I'd never even *met* Riley then. Once we came here, I couldn't get the stuff so that's why I was so sick. If I'd just stayed clean another day or two, I might have been all right, but when we went down to the hospital in Denver, I went to see some of my friends and…"

"They're not friends," Riley said gently.

"I should say not," said Carol. "And neither are you, young lady, sitting there holding his hand like you're actually *helping*. Trevor can speak for himself. Sit up, young man. Look us in the eyes and tell us what you did. And don't keep looking at *her*."

CHAPTER 44

TREVOR LOOKED FROM CAROL TO DIANE. FINDING ONLY stares of disapproval, he turned to face his uncle.

"I messed up, and I know I disappointed you." Griff could tell Trevor was trying to keep his voice steady, but there was a shaky undercurrent he couldn't control as he turned to the Harpies. "You gotta lay off Riley. She's really nice. She helped Uncle Ed, and she's really nice to me and to him. She'd be nice to you if you let her, but…"

"That's enough," said Carol. "She has taken over this store and all but stolen it from your uncle." She flashed Riley a furious look. "I've talked to people in town, young lady, and I've been told over and over that you're my brother's *daughter* and should actually inherit the store. They'd never even *heard* of Trevor." She gave her brother a reproachful glare. "Obviously, she has taken over your life."

Ed stood up. "She *saved* my life. That's what she did. And I'm tired of hearing you two harpies go on about something you don't understand."

Carol and Diane gasped in unison at the word *harpies*. Griff wanted to laugh, but he was too busy watching the drama play out.

Ed seemed stronger, more upright, as if he'd literally grown a spine. "All those folks are right." His gaze lit on Riley and warmed. "Riley's the daughter I never had, and you can bet she'll get the store when I'm gone." He turned to Trevor, looking benevolent but stern. "Trevor might get a share of it, but he'll have to earn it, just like Riley did."

Carol began to speak, but Ed wasn't done.

"And as for me talking about Trevor—why would I? I haven't

seen the boy since he was knee-high to a sparrow. I'm glad to get to know him now, but you two..." He glared at his sisters, surprising Griff with the sudden force of his anger. "You two need to get out."

"No, Ed." Riley stood and went to his side. "It's okay. They've had a shock and they need to adjust. Plus Trevor needs them." Griff saw the women soften at that.

"As you know, I'm an addict myself," she told the sisters. "I've been clean for years now, but I failed, too, at first—a bunch of times. Trevor won't be able to do it alone. He needs family support."

Griff wondered how Riley had managed. As far as he knew, she hadn't had a family since she was thirteen.

Riley explained addiction and recovery to the Harpies in simple terms. She told them about withdrawal, about the importance of cutting old, destructive ties. She talked about the meetings she attended in Grigsby once a week—Griff hadn't known about that—and let them know Trevor wasn't strung out anymore—that he'd gone through withdrawal alone, and that took courage. That was why he'd been so sick, she said.

"It's hard, and the fight is forever," she said. "But fighting gets to be a part of you and makes you stronger. Trevor will have reason to be proud, every day, as long as he stays clean."

She didn't tell them about the drugs the marshal had seen in the Iron Kings' van or the fact that Trevor had been hoping to get more. He hadn't managed to do it, and Griff figured that was what mattered—to Riley anyway. And for the moment, the kid seemed sincere.

The women listened with twin lemon-sucking looks on their faces. By the time Riley was done, they were no longer actively spouting hatred, but that was only because they were so confused and upset. With her quiet recognition of their pain, her refusal to take offense, but most of all her genuine desire to help Trevor, she'd done all she could to help them—but they still shot venomous looks her way when she wasn't looking.

Griff looked up at the ceiling. He hadn't prayed in a long time, but he needed to pray now—for Riley, who was the strongest person he'd ever known. Not only had she overcome her demons, she still fought them to a standstill every single day. He needed to pray for himself, too, in the hope he could become the kind of man she needed, one who stood beside her and helped make the fight worthwhile.

He was working on it. He'd started controlling his anger, and he wasn't bushwhacked by loud noises anymore. He'd stopped clenching and unclenching his fists so much—probably because he'd stopped clenching his heart and let somebody in. Love was what had ambushed him, as fully formed and overwhelming as those demons Riley fought.

But he wasn't going to fight it. Whether Riley returned his affection or not, he was going to love her and do all he could to win her. If that didn't work, he'd somehow be whatever she needed—a friend, an ally, or, if things went south, a dimly remembered stranger.

He'd take whatever she offered, because the smallest crumb from her table meant more than a banquet from anyone else.

Riley stood. She'd done her best. She felt sorry for Trevor and sorry for his aunties, but she'd done all she could.

"You probably want to discuss this as a family," she said. "I'll…"

The words faded away as she realized she didn't know what she was going to do. Stay in the office on that cot, she guessed. She had to admit she wasn't looking forward to it, but she had to rest somewhere, and it was too late to go over to Phoenix House. If Sierra had gotten the kids to go to bed, company would only start them up again.

"You're family, too," Ed said. "We want to discuss it with you."

Riley looked at Carol and Diane and could see they definitely didn't want to discuss the weather with her, let alone something so personal. She didn't want to make them any more miserable than they already were, so she had to get out of there somehow.

Griff took her hand. "We want to go back to the party," he said. "I don't want her to miss all the fun."

Ed smiled indulgently. "Go, then, you two," he said.

Griff more or less hauled her off to the foyer. He presented her with her boots, and she stepped into them and out the door—but as soon as he took her hand, she shook him away.

"Look, I can't go back there with you," she said. "Fawn's there."

"I'm not with Fawn," he said. "And I can't leave you here," he whispered. "I worry about you with those women."

"You shouldn't," she said. "I stood up to big, fat Darrell, so I can stand up to anything. No old-biddy church ladies are going to get the best of me, you know."

He chuckled. "I *do* know. So does everybody else around here." He slung an arm around her shoulders and steered her toward the sidewalk. "You're the only one who doesn't know how strong you are."

"So why are you so worried?"

He laughed. "I'm not worried for you. I'm worried for *them*." He did his best to look somber and official. "The marshal trusts me now, so it's my job to protect old-biddy church ladies and keep you from killing them like they deserve."

"But they're old ladies," she protested. "They can't help who they are."

"Somewhere along the way, they could have learned to be decent human beings."

She sighed. "Some people never get the chance."

He shot her a penetrating look. "And yet they do it anyway. But here's the thing. I'm Santa and you're my elf, and I can't let you sleep on a cot. Plus you know it would break Ed's heart. He'd have to stand up for you again and throw his sisters out."

"That would probably give him another heart attack." Riley sighed. "Cheap shot, Griff, but you win."

Maybe she could glance over at Phoenix House on the way to the bar, see if the lights were still on. If they were, she could go join the kids.

Griff tugged her hand through the crook in his arm, helping her across the ice as if she were an old lady. She didn't need the help, but Griff needed to give it, so she let him.

"I can't believe you helped Trevor like that," he said as they cautiously navigated the ice. "He's been nothing but rotten to you."

"He's a kid," she said. "He's still learning from the people around him, and they were the wrong people. He got in deep before he knew what was going on."

Griff nodded. "But when you got into drugs, you were different. You knew what you were doing."

She gave him a wry smile as he helped her off the curb as if she were ninety years old. "Well, yeah. I was old enough to know better."

She wondered why he was taking so long to cross the street. There was such a thing as being too careful, and she was anxious to get back to the party. Anxious to be anywhere but alone with Griff and his questions.

"How old were you when you started using?" he asked.

"Thirteen, I guess."

"And Trevor's how old?"

She sighed. "It's not about age, it's about experience. So many of the adults around me were addicts that I understood the consequences. He's been kind of sheltered."

They continued past a few shuttered buildings before they reached the bar. At the corner, he stopped, pulling her to face him and holding her arms in his big hands while he looked searchingly into her eyes.

She froze. She was sure he wouldn't shake her again, but she was afraid he'd kiss her. And she'd promised Fawn.

"Listen to yourself, Riley," he said. "Being exposed to drugs and violence at that age wasn't an advantage, okay? Kids imitate the adults around them. And I'll bet a lot of them encouraged it, didn't they?"

She shook her head, even though it was true.

"Here you are, saying *you* should have known better while you're making excuses for a kid who's older, who's had every advantage and all kinds of role models. Why?" He pulled her closer, but there was nothing sexual going on—no kiss hanging in the air. He was just being caring, darn it. And nosy.

"Why are you so hard on yourself?" he asked.

She opened her mouth to answer, then closed it because she didn't know. She'd just figured since the things she'd done were bad, then *she* was bad, but he had a point. She wouldn't label Trevor bad, after all.

Oh, she was so mixed up! Why wouldn't he just leave her alone? *Alone.*

At the thought, she was suddenly desperate to lean on him, since it was probably the last time. Resting her head against his chest, she closed her eyes and cherished the steady beat of his heart. She would have stayed there all night if he hadn't gently pushed her away and taken both her hands in his. Again he was looking down at her, this time with infinite tenderness.

"Forgive yourself," he said softly. "If Trevor deserves it, so do you."

She looked up at him, and the world fell away. If only she could shed the past so easily, along with the burden of guilt she'd been carrying for so long. All her mistakes, all her struggles, all the ugly things that had happened—she looked up into his dark eyes and wanted to let them all go.

"You're a good person," he said. "The best. You have a kind heart, and you do your best to do the right thing. That's *in* you and always was. It's who you are."

She looked down at the ground, biting her lip. Every day, she thought of the mistakes she'd made, the things she'd done—but she'd always tried, hadn't she? The thought made her feel better than she had in a long time. People like the Harpies might never forgive her, but she could forgive herself.

They were just outside the Red Dawg's back parking lot, and she could hear Christmas music streaming from the bar's back door. It was one of her favorites—"Hark, the Herald Angels Sing."

Griff pulled her closer and began to sway, humming the melody. His voice vibrated deep in his chest, and she swayed along until they were slow dancing to the ancient carol, just the two of them under a lonely streetlight on the edge of town, beneath a cracked plastic candle propped in a Christmas wreath. The low hum of the crowd drifted from the party, but it had nothing to do with them. This was their world. Their time.

She joined in with the lyrics.

"Peace on earth and mercy mild, God and sinners reconciled."

Griff joined her, his voice strong enough to lift hers higher, and the song rose into the night.

"Joyful all ye nations rise, join the triumph of the skies…"

And then she was crying for real, because he was so sweet, and she was so happy, and everything was going to be okay. She might lose Griff. She knew she would. But after what he'd said, she felt for the first time in her life that she might deserve to be this happy.

CHAPTER 45

GRIFF HAD HEARD A LOT OF CHRISTMAS CAROLS IN HIS LIFE, but he'd never understood the words the way he did when Riley sang them, and he'd certainly never *meant* them the way he did now. The words about reconciliation and redemption, forgiveness and a higher power—they spoke to him, and he hoped they spoke to her.

After the music faded away, he held her as long as she'd let him, knowing by the shaking of her shoulders that she'd been moved by the carol, too. When she pulled away, she had to swipe away tears, but the smile she gave him was real as if…well, as if she'd joined the triumph of the skies. Dramatic as that sounded, he couldn't think of a better description.

He looked down at her, and her eyes were so trusting, he realized he was getting that second chance. Cupping her face in his hands, he did his best to be gentle, to prove that business in the mudroom would never happen again, to let her know that he treasured her, cared for her. Would *take* care of her, if she'd let him.

Riley relaxed on a sigh, and then he didn't have to think so hard. The rest of the world receded, the sounds of the bar going faint, and the cold creeping into his coat was conquered by the warmth that started in his heart and spread to every part of him.

"Come home with me," he murmured when they stopped kissing and stood face-to-face, a bit breathless. "Quit all this nonsense about Fawn. I don't want her, I want you. So don't go back to Ed's. Come to the ranch. It's all I want."

He'd have to find out who turned on the Red Dawg jukebox just then. Wayne always stocked it with Christmas classics, and now Mariah Carey started warbling about how all she wanted for Christmas was *you*. Riley smiled.

"I can't hit those high notes," she said.

"Honey, you *are* a high note." He waved her toward the truck. "Let's go."

Riley looked up at Griff and remembered the nights they'd spent together—the gentle look of his face in sleep, the way his lashes flickered when he was dreaming, and the way they'd stop when she stroked his brow. The surprising softness of his skin in the hollow of his shoulder. She remembered how it felt to know this big, strong man, this warrior prince, needed her to get through the darkness of his dreams, and a wave of tenderness knocked down all her defenses.

The two of them were magic together. She could tell Griff sensed it, too, but he'd find it again with Fawn because he *was* the magic. He just didn't know it yet, and he apparently wasn't ready for a forever girl like Fawn yet. So going home with him just this once wouldn't change anything, would it?

She thought of the promise she'd made to Fawn, but then she remembered the hard, lumpy cot in Ed's office and the way the old radiator woke her up with its harsh clicking in the night. Lots of people had slept in worse places, including her. But it was Christmas, and she longed for some hint of warmth and family. And the Bailey house had that aura about it—something settled. Something warm.

She'd go, she decided when they reached her truck. It was all she wanted for Christmas, too.

Sorry, Fawn. You'll have to wait a little longer.

This would be the last time, but she wouldn't think about that. For now, she hoisted herself into her truck, leaned over, and unlocked the passenger side door for him. How many times had she driven down the highway behind a pickup and seen the silhouette of a cowboy driving, a girl snuggled up in the middle seat? She wanted to be that girl, just this once. That girl with the gearshift between her knees and the cowboy's arm across her shoulders.

Griff slid over to the middle seat now, and she savored his strong profile, silhouetted against the streetlight where they'd danced. It lit a swirling cone of falling snow, and she wished she could run over there and stand in the light, because she'd been busy dancing and hadn't paid attention to the private world they'd made there. Things were easier in that world, where there was no Fawn, no Trevor, no trouble. So while she settled into the seat with a sigh of satisfaction, there was a touch of longing, too.

Merry Christmas, Riley. Enjoy it while you can.

She smiled up at the man she…loved. Yes, loved. It was okay to admit it to herself.

He didn't have to know.

When Griff had left the ranch, he hadn't figured Riley would ever come back, so he'd turned off the timers for the twinkle lights, leaving the place lit only by moonlight. And yet as they pulled into the drive, the house, nestled in moonlit drifts on the silver plain with just one lamp burning, still looked like Christmas.

Once they'd found their way inside and given Bruce the fur ruffling and smooching he demanded, Riley raced around flicking on all the Christmas lights she could find.

"Thanks," Griff murmured, ashamed of his Scrooginess. "It didn't make sense to keep them lit just for me."

As he fed the woodstove and started a fire, he enjoyed the glow of a new kind of happiness. Back when he was a kid, he hadn't enjoyed life much. He'd just gone through the motions, doing the chores he'd hated, watching his parents' marriage fall apart, and dreaming of seeing the world. But he hadn't been able to see the most important world of all—the one that had made him who he was.

Always warring with his dad, he'd been desperate to escape the ranch. He'd found kinship with the men in his unit, but with that fateful explosion, all the pieces of his new family had scattered and his future had gone up in flames. He hadn't really believed he could find another one until tonight in the standoff with Darrell, when the men of Wynott had arrived with their guns, asking no questions, spouting no braggadocio or hard words. He doubted half of them could shoot straight, and the guns probably weren't even loaded. Outside of hunting season, nobody ever shot anything unless somebody found a rattlesnake in the road or gophers taking over a pasture.

Something about their quiet courage had helped him harness his anger. He'd felt less alone, less like he had to save the world on his own. That was what had been giving him nightmares—being alone, more than he'd ever been in his life, but with the same impossible tasks to accomplish.

While he'd been staring at the fire like a dumb old cow, Riley had shed her coat, kicked off her boots, and fed Bruce before settling into an armchair, pulling her feet up, and clasping her knees like a child as she admired the Christmas tree. The dog lay on the floor beside her, drooling over memories of kibble. Riley was still wearing the elf suit, and she looked like the real thing when she glanced up at him with her eyes alight.

"Hey, Santa."

He glanced down at the costume and gave her a rueful grin. "Guess I'd better get out of this suit."

She nodded. "Guess you'd better."

He gave her a hopeful look. "Want to help?"

She looked at him a long time, her expression serious beneath the elf hat, with its jingle bell dangling over her head. He wondered what was going on inside her heart.

"Yes," she finally said. "I do."

He stood, holding out his hand, and she took it and followed him up the stairs.

CHAPTER 46

ON THE WAY UPSTAIRS, GRIFF TORE OFF HIS BEARD AND ditched his pillowy belly, or what was left of it. He seemed unaware of Bruce, who'd climbed the stairs behind him and now grabbed the poofy mass and carried it back down.

When he reached the landing and turned, he'd shed the suit, and Riley had never seen him look so serious. His gaze was so... devoted, almost. As if there was something more between them than this bed, this room, those nights. Maybe there was, but it was nothing she wanted to talk about. He'd never wanted to talk about it, either—the dreams, the nights he'd start awake shouting, the times she'd come in here to comfort him.

That was what she was here for. Not for herself. Not with any thoughts of the future. Just for him.

He helped her with her green velvet jacket, the absurd slippers and pants, and leaned in to her. This was where she belonged—on this bed, between these sheets, where they could come together without speaking. Removing a stray shred of cotton from his cheek, she kissed him, and he returned it with so much passion that her whole body warmed as if her bones had turned to liquid, as if every part of her was readying itself to open for him. She pushed him back onto the bed and pressed against him, rolling them over until he rose above her and their hips pressed tight together. Closing her eyes, she rocked against him, and a sweet release began to build.

"Riley."

He sounded serious. Gripping his hips, she tugged him against her, hoping he'd lose whatever he wanted to say in the sensation, but when she opened her eyes, he looked serious, too.

"Stop talking," she said. "Come on. I need you."

"I will," he said. "But just one thing." He hiked himself up on one elbow. "You don't know much about elves, do you?"

"I read Lord of the Rings," she said. "Twice. So I bet I know more than you."

"Nope. That was fiction. I'm talking about real elves here."

"Okay." She grinned. "Tell me about elves."

"They don't have pasts," he said. "They're born anew every morning. Clean slate."

She stared up at him, and something inside her rose and flew away. Maybe it was the butterflies, but it felt like something bigger. Like fear or guilt or the past itself.

"Really?"

He nodded soberly. "Really."

She looked up into those eyes and realized he knew her better than anyone in the world. Knew what she needed—what she wanted most of all. "A fresh start," she said. "I think that's the nicest Christmas present anyone's ever given me."

Seeing herself through his eyes, she felt the burden of her misdeeds leaving her, and when he bent down and kissed her, hard and long, it made the whole world go away except for *now*. There was no past to regret, no future to fear. She was alive in this present moment, and it was everything—their own world of touch and sensation and love.

Yes, love. *Just for now.*

This bed was her happy place. *He* was her happy place, so she'd remember this night the way some folks remembered a beach or a lake when they needed to calm down. She'd take out this memory like a smooth stone from her pocket and trace its gentle curves, caress its soft, smooth surface. She'd be able to find an echo of this moment anytime she wanted. That was all she needed from Griff Bailey.

He'd stopped talking now, which allowed her to concentrate as he dipped his hand into her panties—bad-girl panties, black and silky with a scrap of lace. When he touched her, she was already wet, so his finger slipped inside as he bent his head to her breasts.

She'd never let a man control her the way he did. He mastered her, holding her arms while he touched and sampled, stroked and licked. She'd never trusted like this.

Pulling her panties down her legs, he slid his fingers inside and…

Merry Christmas.

He hit all the right spots. *All* of them. Wrestling her arms free, she clung to him and tensed, her eyes squeezed shut, wanting to hold on to every bit of this pleasure.

But if she wanted to remember, she should look. Opening her eyes, she found him watching her face, so serious, so earnest, so *loving*, that her heart flew to him—and that was the best feeling of all. Helpless, wild with need, she bucked against his hand. She almost lost it then but caught herself and reached down to stop him.

"It's Christmas," she said. "So we give *and* receive."

He opened the drawer in the nightstand and made short work of a condom while she watched with greedy eyes. He was so beautiful, his body big but spare. She loved the strong column of muscle that defined his thighs, the broad spread of his shoulders, the square, muscular chest and narrow hips. But the best part was who he was and what was between them.

He was Griff, her Griff. For tonight, anyway. For *now*.

He looked into her eyes, his expression questioning. "Now?"

She laughed. Had she said it out loud? "Yes, now!"

She pulled him to her, into her, and everything inside her opened to take him in. Now he was the one who closed his eyes, and she watched him, gathering images to savor later. She memorized the bow of his back, the way his big hands gripped her hips, the way his jaw clenched when their bodies met and meshed.

She could tell he was afraid he'd hurt her, but he never did. She urged him on, and when they found their rhythm, he opened his eyes, and she loved him looking at her. She felt nothing but beautiful for the first time in her life.

Reaching down, he touched her right *there*, still watching her eyes. She didn't know whether it was his touch or the intensity of his gaze, but she broke apart, crying out, leaving nothing behind as her spirit soared to the stars. Her body seemed to melt away into a smoking puddle of sensation.

Just as she started to spiral down to earth, he closed his eyes and thrust hard, letting go, and that sent her skyward all over again, so they both rose to the stars and fell together, a tangle of limbs and lust and love.

They were one at this moment, this precious now. She wanted to close her eyes, but she didn't want to miss so much as a second. This was her treasure, the smooth stone that fit her palm, the precious gem she'd take out and turn over in her mind when she needed something good in her life.

CHAPTER 47

GRIFF LOVED RILEY'S BODY. SPARE AND SMALL-BREASTED, SHE was nothing like the swimsuit models and movie stars who were supposed to be ideal. She was ideal for an elf, though. With that pale skin and silver hair and the tattooed vines climbing her arm, she had him believing such beings were real. It was like making love to a sprite, a nymph, an illusion—but her strength, her toughness, was human.

When she threw her head back and lifted her hips, crying out, he watched her rise to the heights and hang there, taking everything he could give, and then he was with her and they were both rising, losing themselves in the stars.

If only they could stay. If only she could give herself to him like this, without reservation, without holding back. She thought he should be with Fawn, which was a joke. As far as he could tell, it was just because they'd both been born in Wynott, both to ranching families. She thought Fawn was a "good girl" and she wasn't— but that depended on your definition of good. For him, good meant compassionate, kind. Making an effort, always, to do the right thing. Thinking of others and not just yourself.

That was Riley. And while he didn't know Fawn all that well, she simply couldn't compete.

What if Riley had been born on a better day, in a better place? What if she'd been spared whatever ordeal had made her flee to Wynott? He might never have known her—but surely she'd be even more remarkable, even more special.

Or would she? Wasn't it the past she'd overcome that made her Riley? Conquering her troubled past had given her a killer combination of toughness and vulnerability that made her irresistible.

He admired her. Everyone did. How could he make her understand that? It wasn't that he wanted to give her happiness. She seemed to do that for herself.

He wanted to give her the safe and certain knowledge she deserved it.

When she opened her eyes and met his, he knew she felt the love that had built up between them—the sense of soul meeting soul, of finding home in the heart of someone you loved.

But she was holding back. She wouldn't open the door, and if she did, he doubted she'd stay.

Not until he convinced her she belonged there.

Riley awoke curled in a pool of moonlight, stroked by the swaying shadow of a windswept pine. She listened to the deep, even breathing of Griff beside her, and she'd never been happier in her life. Sighing, she shimmied backward on the bed until she was snugged up against him, safe in the circle of his embrace.

"Love you, Riley," he muttered.

She stilled, afraid to move. She didn't want to wake him in case he took it back.

She knew she shouldn't take it seriously. She knew how men were, how they mistook an orgasm for love and said things they didn't mean.

But then he opened one eye and gave her a sleepy smile. "Really. Just you."

She didn't answer. He was half-asleep, and she'd seen him jump out of bed and take a swing at the wall in that state. Muttering words of love was nothing compared to the delusions of his nightmares. She was just another dream, but at least she was a good one.

For now, she decided, she'd pretend he'd meant it. The words had made the butterflies wild with joy, and for once, she wouldn't try to stifle them. She'd treasure his words, believe in them for one night, and deal with reality tomorrow.

Closing her eyes, she rested her head on his outstretched arm and basked in the moment. She had one last thought before she dropped off to sleep, feeling strong, trusting, and loved.

This must be what it's like to be somebody else.

The next morning, Griff heard Riley coming down the stairs and clenched the old landline phone harder. He wanted to go to her, make sure she knew the night before had been for real, but apparently Bruce had spent the night looking for Isaiah's angel. Feathers were scattered all around the room, and Griff had been busy cleaning them up when the phone rang.

His stepmother had freaked out the second he answered, and she hollered for his dad to pick up the extension, so the jig was up. His family had found out he was home. He didn't know if they were cutting their vacation short or if they'd planned to be at the ranch for Christmas, but they were on their way.

"How long will you be home, Son?" his dad asked.

"Not sure." Griff's old resentment rose at the sound of his father's voice, and he searched for a safe topic of conversation. He didn't find one.

"Hey, what's with all the bathrooms?" he asked.

Riley stopped at the bottom of the stairs. He saw her eyes widen slightly, though she tried to cover the reaction by faking a yawn. He'd been right, then. She'd always changed the subject when he'd asked about the renovations because she had something to hide.

"We're making some changes," his dad said. "Nothing you have to worry about. Your sister's got things all planned out, and of course we didn't know you were coming home, so..."

"Just tell him, Heck." Griff didn't know his stepmother very well, but he was glad she'd interrupted. "Or I will. Griff, you know we thought about selling the ranch a while back. Your dad's health hasn't been so good, and…"

"What's wrong with his health?" He barked out the words before he could think. His dad was never sick. He was always hale and hearty, ready to outride, outrope, and outwork anybody—and he'd made sure his son knew it.

"A little heart trouble," his dad said. "Nothing to worry about."

Molly cleared her throat. "Jess came home to help us get the place ready to sell, but then she had this fabulous idea." Her voice quavered. "She and Cade are going to help us make the place into a guest ranch. Isn't that…great?"

Griff heard the plea in her voice and realized they were worried about his response. But he didn't care what they did with the place, and really, the idea was brilliant. His dad loved people, and from what Griff had heard, people loved his dad's new wife. Jess had a degree in hospitality, and Cade… Well, Cade could be in charge of the horses. Griff was glad they had someone to take tourists on trail rides, because he wasn't about to volunteer.

"Sounds like a good idea. Guess that means Jess will stick around?"

"She and Cade will live at the ranch and run the operation." Molly was talking fast now, the tension in her voice giving way to enthusiasm. "Heck and I are moving over to Cade's place, but you know, we love this RV thing, so we won't be around much. Jess will be the manager, Cade's going to run horse clinics, and when we're home, I'll be in charge of children's activities."

"I'll be chief wrangler," Griff's dad said.

He sounded happy. From what Jess had said in her letters, he'd been tamed by Molly, who more or less ran his life. Their dad had been domesticated, she said. *Mollified.* Even he'd had to laugh at that.

"Is Riley around?" Molly asked.

He started to hand the phone to her, but she shook her head, waving her hands. He didn't know why she didn't want to talk, but he respected her wishes. "She's busy, I guess," he said.

Smiling, she bent and began picking up Bruce's mess, gathering feathers in her hands.

They chatted a little more, but when he hung up the phone, Griff realized he'd better make the most of the time he and Riley had left. Once his family came, she'd probably stop sharing his bed—at least until they had a chance to reveal their relationship.

He turned to find her at the kitchen counter, watching him with big, apprehensive eyes. She was wearing one of his old T-shirts, but she still looked like an elf somehow. When he bent to kiss her, she seemed surprised.

"What do you think?" she asked.

He grinned. "I think that was our best night yet."

"About the dude ranch, I mean. I was afraid you'd be mad."

"Why would I be mad? It's not my ranch."

She was dumping sugar into her coffee—one spoonful, two, a third. Her sweet tooth always made him smile.

"It could be," she said. "Someday."

"Not interested. It's perfect for Jess. I want a different kind of life."

One with you.

She sipped her coffee, those pale eyes regarding him steadily over the rim of her cup, and he realized this wasn't the time to say that out loud.

"This place is good for you," she said. "Whenever you come in from the barn, you're like a different person."

He shrugged. "The horses are good for me. The rest of it—I can take it or leave it."

"No, you can't." He was relieved to see her smile. "You're a cowboy at heart. Under all that tough-guy stuff, you're happiest shoveling horse apples."

"No." He leaned against the counter next to her, letting his hip bump hers. "I found out last night I'm happiest being Santa. I think I have another present for you."

Riley edged away. After last night, the move surprised him. "They're coming home, then?"

He nodded. "They're on their way. Should be here this afternoon."

"Hadn't Jess told you about your dad's heart?"

"No, she was probably too busy mooning over Cade. I got a wedding invitation out of the blue, like I could drop everything and come home. That was it. Do you know what happened? He didn't seem to think it was serious."

"He had two heart attacks. He almost died."

Griff's own heart stopped for a moment. He pretended to fuss with the coffee maker to cover up his emotions. Heck Bailey was a force of nature, always the strongest, the bossiest, and the best. It had never occurred to Griff that he was mortal.

He turned to say so, but Riley had already slipped out of the room. All he caught was Bruce's long tail, wagging its way out the door in her wake.

CHAPTER 48

RILEY KNEW GRIFF WOULDN'T BE HAPPY WHEN SHE LEFT. BUT she wasn't about to horn in on yet another family celebration. Griff had been gone for years, and he needed to reconnect with his dad. Riley liked Heck Bailey, and reconciliation would mean a lot to him.

The Baileys would make her welcome at their family holiday, but then, so had Ed—and look how that had worked out. She needed to go and let them be a family. She'd finished the tiling and painting and had only a little bit of cleanup left to do on the bathrooms. The porch—the porch would have to be turned over to a contractor to finish in the spring. There was a guy over in Lackaduck she trusted. She'd email him the plans and let Heck know he could be trusted.

As for Griff, she hadn't promised him anything beyond going home with him last night. If everything went her way, he wouldn't know she was leaving until she was already gone. She barely knew what her plans were herself, but they didn't involve Griff Bailey.

Oh sure, the butterflies and the puppy dog thought Griff should be in her future—but she knew better. They'd be happy together for a while, but she was sure something would happen. Maybe the Harpies would dig up some issue from her past and make it public, or someone from her previous life would surface. He'd lose his election and start to resent her. They'd fight, and that would destroy that smooth stone of memory she treasured.

After dressing hurriedly in jeans, a button-down shirt, and her cowboy boots, she checked the drawers in Jess's dresser to make sure she hadn't left anything behind. She thought of the elf suit and tiptoed to Griff's bedroom. Picking up the crushed velvet jacket and pants, she held it to her chest.

Come on. Don't cry, stupid. It was magic, and magic doesn't last.

Blinking herself back to business, she found a hanger and did her best to smooth out the wrinkles before hanging the suit on the hook at the back of his door. He'd see it when he closed the door, and he'd remember. He'd have a smooth stone to treasure, too, but he'd forget eventually, when life got busy, when he was running for marshal with Fawn or someone like her by his side, when he had a home and a family and…

Stop it.

Hurrying back to Jess's room, she glanced around, knowing she'd miss the safety she'd felt here, the frilly little-girl bed and fussy furniture. She'd never had a childhood bedroom, and it had felt like the lap of luxury to her.

She turned back to the door to find Griff leaning there, watching her. She straightened her shoulders and jutted out her chin, firming her resolve. He wasn't going to make this easy.

"Your sister's going to need her room," she said.

"So move to a different one. There are plenty." His lip curled in a wry smile that didn't reach his eyes. "With bathrooms."

"There aren't any beds, though. Jess and Molly are going to shop for furniture after Christmas." They'd said she could come, too, but that wouldn't happen now.

Riley stepped closer, willing him to get out of her way and let her go. She wasn't staying, no matter what he said. She could tell he'd been shocked at the news of Heck's heart attack, so hopefully he'd find forgiveness for whatever was wrong between them.

"You can't go back to Ed's," he said. "Those women…"

She wasn't going back to Ed's, but she wasn't going to tell him that.

"It's Christmas," she said. "I'll be fine."

Griff followed Riley out to her truck, his heart pounding. Bruce padded behind him, his furry forehead wrinkled with concern.

Griff couldn't figure out what he'd done wrong. Didn't she realize how much she mattered to him? It couldn't be his family. They'd always made her welcome. So it had to be him.

One thing was certain—he wouldn't let frustration get the best of him. Like a kid, he'd remember to use his words. He wished he was better at that, but he'd have to learn on the fly.

He watched her climb in, fasten her seat belt, and start the engine. It was time to say something or she'd be gone. He tapped on her window. Grimacing as if he was just too much trouble to deal with, as if last night had never happened, she rolled it down.

"Why are you doing this?" He realized he sounded angry and tried to modulate his voice. "I thought last night meant something."

"It did. In the moment, I mean." She rushed to explain. "Remember you said that thing about elves being born every morning? The clean-slate thing?"

He nodded, but he still looked mad.

"Well, that was n-nice," she said. "B-but it wasn't real."

Why was she stammering? He looked down and realized he was clenching his fists and leaning forward, looming over her. Quickly, he took a step back.

"It all felt real to me," he said. "Everything. And I meant what I said."

She looked down, fiddling with her seat belt.

"Sorry." She busied herself with the car, checking the lights, running the wipers. He noticed she needed new ones. "I meant to tell you I told the women at Climb Colorado I'd come back and work for the program. Teach some classes, mentor the new girls, help them see they can lead a normal life. Elves keep their promises, right?"

"When did you arrange this?"

She looked left, then right, like a kid caught in a lie. "A while back."

He clenched his fists again, and this time, they didn't unclench. The bees didn't rise. They were well and truly gone. But that didn't mean he wasn't angry.

"How are you going to convince them they can lead a normal life when you refuse to do it yourself?" He set his hands on the sill of her open window and ducked down so he could see her. His head and shoulders filled the window, and he was probably scaring her again, so he spoke softly. "A normal life has love in it, Riley, but every time somebody gets close to you, you shut it down."

"That's not true. Ed has a real family, and they…"

"They're wrong, and you know it. But you stayed with Ed until the going got tough, and then you sacrificed yourself, right? Well, you didn't do him any favors. You should have stood up to those women. He would have backed you up if you hadn't been so dead set on running away. You saw that at the Red Dawg."

She revved the engine so it roared, then turned to glare at him. "What's your point?"

"My point is you can't call yourself recovered until you can stand up for yourself."

"Yeah, well, as soon as I find a place to stand, I'll do that."

"You *have* a place. All you have to do is claim it." He reached past her into the truck, shut off the ignition, and pulled out the keys. "You have a place at Ed's. You know that. And you damn sure have a place with me."

"I have a place in Denver, with the program," she said. "They made me what I am."

"*You* made yourself what you are." He was trying to seem less aggressive, but the fact that he still held her keys in his fist probably didn't help, so he shifted his hand to her wrist. It seemed impossibly fragile, birdlike in his clumsy grip, and he reminded himself to be gentle. "Riley, you're who you've always been, inside."

Staring straight ahead through the windshield, she spoke while barely moving her lips. "Let me start my truck. I can't stand being trapped."

"I'm not trapping you." He let go and handed her the keys. "You've trapped yourself."

She started up the truck, then paused. A surge of hope rose in his chest.

"You'll take care of Bruce for me, right?"

He glanced down at the dog, then back at Riley. Seeing her in the front seat of the truck made him remember another night when she'd been lying there helpless, snow all around her, the truck's headlights staring sightless at the sky.

"No," he said. "You need him. Take him with you."

"I'm going to the city," she said. "He won't be happy there."

"Neither will you." Griff rounded the car at a run, patting his thigh. The dog followed. "You'll be a lot safer with him along. Hop in, buddy."

He opened the passenger door, and the dog came as close to hopping as he could. Once in the passenger seat, he glanced over at Riley, then stared solemnly through the windshield.

"Griff…"

"I'm serious," he said. "I won't take care of him."

Blowing out a furious breath, Riley reached over and tugged the seat belt across the dog's chest, clicking it closed. Griff couldn't help smiling. Even now, at this moment, she thought of the animal's safety.

She still had the truck in park, but she pressed the accelerator so it roared, and he had to shout to be heard.

"I love you, Riley," he said as she shoved the truck into gear.

The dog glanced at him, but Riley didn't hear. Or if she did, it didn't stop her.

CHAPTER 49

When she reached the end of the driveway, Riley had no idea which way to turn.

She'd lied to Griff. She had no idea if the program had a place for her. Yes, they'd told her they wanted her to come back—but that had been over five years ago. For all she knew, they said that to all the graduates.

In any case, she could hardly go there tonight. They closed for a week over Christmas, and she didn't know how to get in touch with the program director. For that matter, she wasn't sure if her program director even worked there anymore.

She turned at the bottom of the driveway, dreading the drive through Wynott. She had to go through the town to get anywhere, and memories would attack her at every turn. She wanted to fly down the quiet streets and get it over with, but Matt Lassiter would issue a ticket no matter who you were, so she drove a sedate 35 miles per hour to the town's single stop-light. Despite the total absence of traffic, she stopped and looked around one last time, remembering the way it had looked the night before in the snow, with the light going green to yellow to red.

With jolly plastic Santas on doorsteps and the town's cheesy decorations lashed to every lamppost, Wynott looked like an old-timey postcard, ready to welcome visitors from a future it would never know. The town was an oasis of the past, adrift in a sea of modernity it had rejected.

It was hard to say goodbye, so Riley pretended to herself she was just taking a little trip. She did her best to be excited about the future instead of scared.

Wynott was her true hometown, and she'd always carry it in her heart.

—∽∿∽—

Griff was relieved when the emotional greetings were over and his family settled back into their normal affectionate bickering. It had been a long time since he'd been around, and coming back from his deployment was a big deal to them, but his sister acted like he'd risen from the dead, and her new husband, Cade—who'd been Griff's best friend all his life—seemed overcome as well. And though his dad had been hearty and stoic as usual, Molly, the step-mother he barely knew, had actually cried.

"It's for Heck," she said, wiping her eyes. "I'm just so happy he has you back." She'd embraced Griff, then pushed him out at arm's length and looked him up and down. "I'm just making sure you came back in one piece, honey. Your dad worried about you every day, you know that? Every day."

Griff had been planning to dislike his stepmother. Molly had been a substitute teacher at the high school, so he'd known who she was. He knew her reputation, too; word was she'd auditioned the husbandly skills of every man in Wynott before she settled on Heck. But Griff found her remarkably easy to be with and ended up sitting at the kitchen table while she bustled around baking Christmas cookies.

It almost distracted him from missing Riley, but he was starting to wonder if you could have a toothache in your heart. The pain was like an abscess—constant, deep, and impossible to ignore—but he did his best to pay attention to his family.

"Have you seen your mother yet?" Molly asked.

He shook his head. "Maybe after the holidays. You know how busy she is, entertaining and all that."

Dot Bailey had run off with a slick politician from Jackson Hole when Jess and Griff were teens. She'd pretty much ignored them ever since, dedicating herself to nurturing her husband's career instead of her kids. But she was still his mother, and he'd resented his dad for years, blaming him for her departure.

"We'll share you if we have to, but it sure is nice to have you here." She took a cookie sheet from the oven and began stacking the warm gingerbread men on a plate. Lifting one to her mouth, she bit its foot off and stared at him, chewing, looking like a thoughtful squirrel.

"What?"

She smiled, which seemed to make her cheeks even plumper and pinker—if that was even possible. "Did something happen between you and Riley?"

He shrugged, glowering. Usually that was enough to shut down any conversation, but Molly just stood there, resting her hip against the counter with a gleam in her eye that looked dangerous. Or motherly. Or both. Either way, she was a threat he wasn't prepared for.

"Riley talked to your dad about you while you were gone."

He looked up. "Why would she do that?"

"She said she texted you while you were away."

He nodded, struggling to work his way through a sudden onslaught of memories.

"She was the one person who kept in touch," he said. "She'd text me gossip about Wynott—nothing I really cared about, but it was nice, you know?"

The truth was, he hadn't expected to come back, not alive, so he hadn't dared to care, but that night at the quarry, together with her texts, had made that almost impossible.

"And since I got home…" His throat constricted, and it was suddenly hard to breathe. Sorrow hit him like the anger, like the fear, but it was worse, because it came from a deeper place.

His shoulders heaved as he struggled to master himself. "She saved me. Dammit, she talks about how she's not whole, and she's so damn *complete*, you know? She fixes everybody else. Why can't she see that?"

"She will." Molly set the plate of cookies in front of him, then sat down herself. Resting her elbow on the table, her cheek on her palm, she gave him an impish smile. "We just have to find her first. Did she go back to Ed's?"

He shook his head. "Ed's sisters are here with their grandson. They pretty much pushed her out of the hardware store."

"You're kidding. And Ed let them?"

"He's trying to stop them, but Riley seems to think family is all that matters."

"She's right," Molly said. "But there are different kinds of family, and Ed and Riley were definitely kin." She ate her cookie's other leg. "So where was she going?"

"Denver."

Molly gasped. "Oh, no. You have to go after her. If she goes down there, who knows what will happen? That's where… Well, it's where all her trouble started."

"If you're thinking she'll fall into her old ways, you're wrong." He was almost grateful Molly had made him mad, because the anger blotted out some of the sorrow. "Riley's the strongest person I know. The only thing she can't take is the way everybody still looks sideways at her, like she's going to whip out a crack pipe or cook meth in their bathroom."

Molly was smiling, which seemed strange until he realized how hotly he'd defended Riley.

"You love her, don't you?"

He didn't know what to say, so he shrugged again. That should have shut down the conversation, but not with Molly. She seemed impervious to even his best avoidance strategies. She was still smiling, still staring at him with her fluffy head cocked. She looked like a squirrel again—a magical talking squirrel.

Sheesh. Riley had him thinking in fairy tales again.

"Have you told her?" Molly asked.

Swallowing hard, staring down at the table, he nodded. "She left anyway."

"So you have to go after her." Molly stood, tugging her purse from where she'd left it on the counter and looking down at him with an expectant glint in her eyes. "You ready?"

He looked up at her, confused. "For what?"

"We're going to go find her, silly. You can't just sit here."

Griff thought about refusing. But then what would he do? Go upstairs and sulk in his room? Go out to the barn and tell his troubles to the horses? Talk to his sister?

He'd take his chances with Molly. Maybe he'd get one of those Christmas miracles everybody talked about, and they'd find Riley and bring her home.

CHAPTER 50

MOLLY HIKED HERSELF UP INTO THE JEEP LIKE SHE RODE shotgun in monster four-wheelers every day. She and Griff bumped down the dirt road and hit the highway, heading for town. As they passed the marshal's office, she bounced in her seat, pointing. "Matt Lassiter, the marshal! He'll help. He might have seen Riley."

"He won't be there," Griff said. "It's almost Christmas."

"Matt's always there," Molly said. "That boy's a great town marshal, but he needs to get a life. Once we have you and Riley settled, we need to find a girl for him."

Griff couldn't help laughing at Molly's confidence.

"What's up?" Matt leaned back in his chair and grinned when they walked in. "You come to give me a Christmas present?"

"Sure." Griff couldn't help smiling back. "Got you some baby powder and bubble bath."

"That's not what I wanted." Matt scanned Griff's face, his expression somber. "I was hoping for a deputy."

Griff glanced at Molly. He'd mentioned the job to Cade but hadn't discussed it with anybody else in his family. He wasn't sure he was ready, but when would he be? And if he accepted it now, made it official, he'd have everything settled if—no, *when*—he found Riley.

"You got one," he said. "Merry Christmas."

Molly clapped her hands like a child. "Oh, Griff! That's wonderful. I thought you were going back to the army."

"So did I." Griff grimaced. "But it's not going to happen."

"Well, I'm sorry if that's hard." Molly patted his arm. "But your father will be so pleased. Everybody will."

"I need lots of hours, okay?" he said to Matt. "I want to work all the time, learn a lot."

"That's not necessary," Matt said. "Besides, you'll need plenty of time to spend with that awesome girl of yours."

Griff grunted. "That would be nice, but the awesome girl isn't mine. I can't even find her. So when do I start?"

Matt sobered. "Seriously, you can't find Riley?"

"She left this morning. Said she's moving back to Denver." He looked down at his hands. "She thinks she doesn't belong here."

"She's wrong about that." Matt stood, hiking up his pants like an old-time lawman in a movie. "Guess you've got your first assignment."

"What?"

"Track her down like she's an outlaw on the run and bring her back alive. Preferably to your place." He tossed Griff a radio. "You cover the east side of town, I'll cover this end. Radio me if you spot her. I'll do the same."

Griff stared down at the radio. "I don't know if she'd want me to set the cops on her."

"It's okay when the cop is you," Matt said.

"Let's go." Molly turned to Matt. "It's okay if he has a sidekick, right?"

"Sure." Matt clipped the radio to his belt, grabbed his hat—which still had antlers on it—and gave her a grin as he held the door. "Every lawman needs one, and you'll do fine."

———

Riley leaned against the side of her Chevy LUV and watched the lighted numbers on the gas pump count up the gallons.

"Don't you eat my snacks, Bruce."

The dog ducked his head, panting. She'd taken him for a long trot, and he'd watered all the weeds behind the dumpster. Now he was belted in again, so hopefully he couldn't reach the grocery bags.

"That's Christmas dinner," she said. "And don't worry. I'll share. And there's a bag of kibble in the back."

Maybe gummy bears, Cracker Jacks, and Cool Ranch Doritos didn't sound like Christmas dinner to most people, but she had Mounds bars and Little Debbies for dessert. Besides, giving in to her urge for junk food might help her avoid any other temptations she might find closer to the city. She needed all the distractions she could get to make it through the days before she had a job.

She was glad she'd remembered to grab her portable DVD player from Griff's place. She'd brought it over to help with lonely nights at the ranch, but then Griff had turned up. She probably would have been better off watching the old romantic comedies she'd brought along, but she'd seen them over and over.

That was why she'd been pleased to find a five-dollar DVD bin beside the mini-mart's candy racks and Twinkie displays. She'd found a few older movies she hadn't seen in ages—*Dirty Dancing*, *Music and Lyrics*, and a Sandra Bullock boxed set that included *Miss Congeniality*. She could drool over Patrick Swayze, Hugh Grant, and Benjamin Bratt while she stuffed herself with junk food. That would keep her from missing Griff.

Yeah, right.

She adjusted the nozzle, listening to the gas chugging down the line and praying the truck would make it to Denver. It would be awful to break down the day before Christmas. Even if she could get a tow truck, where would she tell them to take her?

She imagined standing by the side of the road, telling some hairy trucker dudes to tow her precious Chevy LUV to the lot of the nearest cheap motel. They'd know then that she had nowhere to go. And maybe up to that point they'd have been nice to her, because of the holiday and all, but then that wall would go up. They'd look at her with pity, and she'd be one of *them* again. The poor. The homeless. The unloved. She shuddered at the thought.

A vehicle pulled up to the tank beside her truck. It shuddered and roared, tossing great diesel farts into the clear, cold air. She turned her back to it, not wanting to start a conversation. The way she felt, she was likely to burst into tears if somebody so much as said Merry Christmas.

The Jeep's door slammed, and she heard the driver opening the gas cap. As he—she could tell it was a he—notched the hose into place, she could sense him staring at her. It was like a sixth sense for her, the knowledge a man was giving her the eye. It had meant danger at one point in her life. Now, without the protection of the good people of Wynott, it would mean that again.

Bruce's tail was wagging like crazy, which made her wonder just how much protection he'd be. She tried to concentrate on the tinny Christmas music coming from the speakers under the canopy. It was Wham! singing that corny song about giving someone your heart for Christmas and getting it back. She could identify with George Michael on that one, except he was planning to give it to somebody else instead, while she was on her own from here on.

Finally, she turned to the other motorist, ready to shout an exasperated "What?"

But the words balled up in her throat, and all she could let out was a croak as Griff Bailey crossed his arms over his chest, leaned back against his Jeep, and gave her a lazy, self-satisfied smile.

—⁓—

Griff did his best to stay calm, to make sure the bees didn't rise again. This was his last chance with Riley, and if he got nervous, he was sure to blow it.

The smile was real, though. Between the ancient, absurd pickup, the enormous dog filling up the front seat, and the slight, spare figure with the long, silvery hair spilling out from under a Carhartt baseball cap, she cut quite a distinctive figure. She looked remarkably delicate, but she had a spine of steel and a stubborn streak a mile wide. Somehow, he needed to bend them both.

"You got me in trouble," he said.

She looked puzzled. "Trouble?"

"Everybody was expecting you to spend Christmas at the ranch. You're half the reason they came home early."

"Why would they expect me to do that? Why wouldn't they think I'd be with Ed?"

"I guess because I told them."

"Told them…"

"Pretty much everything. So now they know I'm the reason you left."

"No, you're not. Tell them it's not your fault. I make my own decisions."

"I tried that." He shrugged. "Didn't work. I need you to tell them yourself. Come on. Let them see you're okay and I didn't send you sobbing off to Denver or anything."

"No." She tilted her chin up and stared into his eyes—an expression he'd learned meant for sure she was faking it. "I'm not going to horn in on your family Christmas, okay? I'm always doing that. Besides, I have obligations."

He strode over and leaned on the hood of her truck. "Obligations to who?" He peered in at her grocery bags. "Little Debbie? Mike and Ike?"

She grimaced. "No, just—to people in Denver, okay? And to myself."

"Yourself."

"Yes, myself." She took a deep breath. "Look, everybody's been really nice, but I'm sick of being the third wheel every Christmas. Or the fifth wheel, or the seventh. I'm not doing that again."

"You wouldn't be a third wheel. You'd be with me. My wheels came off." He smiled, realizing that was true. "You *are* my wheels."

"No." She avoided his eyes. "I'm not…I'm not the right girl for you."

"Are you back on that Fawn thing?"

"Maybe," she said. "I know you said you're not interested, but you loved her for so many years. Now you can finally be together. How can you not want that?"

He made a gagging sound.

"Come on. Feelings like that don't just evaporate."

"How do you know?"

"I just do, that's all. Once you love somebody, it's forever. It doesn't change, no matter where that somebody goes or what he does." She turned away abruptly, pretending to concentrate on the gas pump's digital readout, but the pump turned off just then with a loud *thunk*, and there was silence, making her next words seem much louder. "Even if he loves somebody else, it doesn't change. That's how I know." She waved her hands as if she could erase the words before they reached his ears. "Or her. If *she* loves somebody else. That's what I meant. Or him. Not me."

"Right. So you're saying once you fall in love, that's your happily-ever-after, and you can't have it with anybody else?"

She looked away. "I don't think happily-ever-after's going to work for me."

"Seems to me it never works for anybody—until the last, best time. And then it does."

Shrugging, she opened the passenger door of her truck and tossed her purse inside.

Dang it, she was going to leave. He shot an SOS look at his truck, then winced when Bruce, who'd somehow slipped his seat belt, dove for the Little Debbies and sent some stuff clattering to the pavement from the open driver's side door. Griff dodged around the truck to pick up whatever it was.

DVDs. A bunch of them. As he helped Riley pick them up, he couldn't help smiling at the titles. They were all romantic comedies, old ones. The kind they sold for five dollars at mini-marts.

"Look, here's proof." He gathered up three titles and fanned them out in front of her like a poker hand. "You think Hugh Grant found love on the first try? How about Matthew McConaughey?" He picked up another DVD and squinted at the title. "Patrick Swayze? He and Baby—they had a rough time, right?" He set the last one on the seat and turned to face her.

"Those are stories," she said. "Life's not like that."

"Not yet," he said. "But it could be if you'd let it."

CHAPTER 51

RILEY LOOKED UP AT GRIFF AND WISHED THINGS WERE SIM-pler. She wanted to climb up into his Jeep—because that was what he was driving, that was why she hadn't realized it was him—and go home with him. And once they got there, she wanted to go upstairs and lose herself in his bed for the next two days. They could forget about Christmas, forget about other people, and go back to that safe space they'd found together—the one where she wasn't the damaged one. The one where *she* helped *him*.

But instead, he'd come charging to her rescue in that big, old truck, like a knight galloping on a white horse, and he wanted to drag her back and shove her into the bosom of his family, and he thought she'd belong, just like that. But if she didn't belong with Ed, where she'd been happy for so many years, she'd never belong with anyone.

"Riley James."

Riley knew that voice, and she knew it meant trouble.

Molly Bailey stood on the curb that held the gas tanks, her cheeks pink from the cold, her hands, clad in red mittens, fisted on her plump hips. She was normally a kittenish kind of woman, but right now, she reminded Riley of a rodeo bull.

"Heck and I rushed all the way here just so we could spend some time with you," she said. "Jess and Cade can't wait to see you, and Griff… Well, I think you know how Griff feels." She raised a hand, and despite the mitten that obscured her raised finger, she made her point. "I guess our friendship doesn't mean much to you if you'd rather spend Christmas in Denver than spend it with us."

She wagged an admonishing finger. "Not only that, but you stole Heck's dog."

"I didn't mean to," Riley said, horrified by the thought. "Griff made me take him, honest. But you can have him back."

"I don't think so." Molly smiled at the dog, who was gazing lovingly at Riley with drool dripping from his jowls. "You stole his heart." She glanced over at the gas pump and smiled. "Seems to be a habit of yours."

Thus far, Riley could handle the lecture—but then Molly swept her into her arms.

"We love you, honey, and we're so sorry about what happened with Ed's sisters. We wish you'd stay with us. I always thought we were like another family to you. We sure want to be."

Riley sniffed, inhaling the motherly scents of White Shoulders perfume and perm lotion. Griff's stepmother felt comforting and pillowy in her arms, and she was horrified when the tears she'd been holding back all day burst the dam to wet Molly's shoulder.

"It's not that." She kept her face buried in Molly's sweater so no one would see her cry. "It's just that this is your first Christmas with Griff in so long. It'll be just like old times, and I don't want to spoil that."

Molly backed off, giving Riley a gentle shake. Wiping frantically at her face, Riley took off her cap so her hair would fall forward and hide her face.

"Old times are nice and all, but there are always changes. *I* was a big change," Molly said. "And I can tell you, I was the third wheel for a while. A stepparent is always on the outside looking in. But if you love folks enough, you become family. That's why the present matters more than any old tradition, and we want to share *our* present with you."

Riley was crying again, so she jammed the cap back on her head and pulled the brim down.

"We love you, honey. Me and Jess and Heck." She thumbed toward Griff. "And that one, too." She held up a hand to stop Riley from protesting. "I don't know what kind of love, whether it's friendship or, you know, *love* love, but there's no escaping the truth." She smiled, kittenish again. "Heck is just dying to see you and tell you how much he likes those bathrooms, and he's already got a half-dozen new projects lined up. We stayed in some really nice places on the road, because that RV shower is a little cramped for him. He got a lot of good ideas."

She turned to nod at Griff, who was hanging up the nozzle while studiously avoiding them. Riley could tell he knew darn well it hadn't been fair to sic his stepmother on her. Molly was like a plump, pleasant steamroller who managed to flatten anyone who disagreed with her while somehow making them feel loved.

"I'm making cookies tomorrow, and you know *this* guy won't be any help," she said now. "Plus Jess can't wait to see you. You were her maid of honor, Riley! How could you be a bigger part of our family?"

The question hung shimmering in the air as Molly looked over at Griff, who'd hung up the nozzle and was climbing back in the truck.

"Well, there might be a way," Molly continued. "But we can talk about that later. I have to tell you, we were so glad when Griff said…"

The roar of a diesel engine drowned out her next words. Griff leaned out the open window of the truck, which was belching black smoke from the tailpipe. "Are we going back or not? Because I'm ready."

He didn't say exactly what he was ready for, but his eyes lit on Riley's, and more than anything he or Molly had said, the look he gave her said going back wasn't such a bad idea after all.

She didn't want him to think she was easy, though, so she pouted. "I was looking forward to spending Christmas with Hugh Grant."

"He can come, too," Griff grumbled. "But I don't think he's your type. Hope not, anyway."

Riley giggled. She couldn't help it. Comparing Hugh Grant to Griff Bailey was like comparing a cocker spaniel to a grizzly bear.

Griff waved toward her truck. "You lead the way. I'll follow and make sure you don't get stuck."

"I won't get stuck," Riley said. "Don't underestimate my truck. It's…"

"I know. It's a collector's item," Griff said. "But I'm still glad I've got a tow strap."

The next morning, Griff stood in the barn's open doorway, leaning on a manure fork, supremely satisfied with the world. He and Riley were together now. He wished he was sure of that.

Well, he'd *make* sure of it. Riley didn't seem to be sure of anything—yet.

He was surprised to find he didn't mind the work he'd resented so much as a boy, even when doing it with his dad. Though horse leavings were hardly fragrant, he liked the rhythm of the work, the glide of his muscles, and the slight ache in his shoulders at the end. And he loved knowing Riley was inside talking girl talk with his sister and helping his stepmother with the baking.

But he still wasn't sure he liked his father. He loved him, sure, and he'd been hoping those health scares would mellow the old man some, but the old resentment was like a wire strung tightly between them, strangling them so they couldn't talk like a normal father and son, so they couldn't relate the way they should.

Beside him, Heck cleared his throat and kicked at the old wooden floorboards before speaking. "I want you to know I respect the decision you made when you enlisted, and I'm proud of what you did." He looked down at his toes, clad in a pair of fancy tooled Durango boots. "Not very proud of myself, though."

"What? Why?" Griff had to say something, but he didn't know

how to respond to that. His father had always been supremely confident that his way was the right way. That was the problem.

"I never wanted anything but this place," his dad said. "This land. Horses and cattle. The riding, the roping, the branding—it's in my blood." Heck's voice grew husky. "I thought it would be in yours, and when it wasn't... Well, I thought I could make you a rancher anyway. Thought you'd change your mind sooner or later."

Griff shrugged. Once again, he'd disappointed his dad. He was used to it now.

"I thought there was nothing better for you to be." Heck waved an arm at the view, then let it fall limply at its side. "Not many men grow up with the promise of twenty thousand acres of prime grazing land, you know?"

"I know." Griff gazed across the landscape from the distant hills to the tilted fence posts that bound the corral, from the crazy old house with its turrets and gables to the barn itself, built to last with thick beams hewn from native trees. "I always knew I should appreciate it more. Cade would have given anything to have the luck I did. But it wasn't what I wanted."

"Well, I'm proud of what you chose to do," Heck said. "People in town compliment me all the time, like I had something to do with it." His laugh sounded bitter. "Like I made you what you are, when all I did was fight you. I know you deserve all the credit for the man you've become."

"I don't know." Griff warmed toward his dad in a way he never had before. It had never been easy for the old man to apologize. "I think you prepared me for combat pretty well."

Heck looked wounded. "I know we fought, but..."

"No, that's not what I mean." Griff gave his dad an affectionate cuff on the arm. He should just give the old man a hug and get it over with. He'd been shocked to see how his father had aged. But that affectionate punch was the best he could do for now. "What I mean is, ranching's a lot like combat. Remember what you used to say? How it's 'long periods of sheer boredom punctuated by moments of panic'? That's what they say about combat, too, and it's true."

His dad's eyes took on a faraway look. "Moments of panic," he said. "Remember when Jess roped that randy bull-calf back when she was—how old was she, ten?—and the rope got under her horse's tail?"

Griff chuckled. "Never saw such a rodeo. She hung on tight, and we got things straightened out, but I couldn't do a thing to help her, 'cause my horse was bucking in sympathy or something."

Heck grinned. "Wondered if I'd get you kids out of there alive, but we managed," he said. "Your mother wasn't too happy with me."

Griff sobered. "My mother wasn't too happy with anything. She hated ranch work." He thought a moment. "She was determined we'd hate it, too."

Heck turned so fast Griff was afraid he'd wrench his neck. "She was?"

"Sure. You didn't know? She always told Jess she could do better. Watched those shows with her, about the Karklashians or whatever, talked about hair and makeup. Why do you think Jess wanted to move to the city so bad?"

Heck nodded. "Jess said something about that. That she was trying to please her mother."

"I was, too." Griff shoved his hands in his pockets. "Don't get me wrong, I'm no rancher. I'd be happy if I never saw another cow in my life. But mostly, it was Mom. She made it seem like ranching was a low-class occupation that didn't do anybody any good."

"That's not true," Heck said. "Ranchers feed the nation. We…"

Griff laughed. "I know that, Dad. I'm just telling you what she said."

"All right." Heck set a hand on Griff's shoulder. "Just so you know, I'm proud of you, Son. Proud of the way you carry yourself, the things you've done. You can bet I won't try to boss you any-more. You've done fine. More than fine."

Griff was surprised to find his breath shuddering in his chest. He'd apparently wanted his father's approval more than he realized.

"It's not for everybody." Heck waved at the landscape again. "Dot didn't like it, and neither did you kids. Thought I could make you somehow, but I went about it all wrong."

Pressing his hat firmly onto his head, he headed for the house. Griff called after him, shouting over the wind.

"Dad?"

Heck turned.

"Turns out I liked it more than I thought. I missed it like crazy after I was gone, and now that I'm back, the horses... Well, they're the best part, aren't they?"

Heck grinned, then sobered. "Almost, Son. Almost. But not quite." He kicked at the snow, suddenly shy. "It was always you kids that were the best part. Family's what it's all about."

"Well, just so you know," Griff said, "it turns out I was a cowboy after all. I'm not planning on hitting the rodeo again anytime soon, but I know I was lucky to be raised here. And I was lucky to be your son."

His father's eyes, already rheumy, filled with tears as he turned and clasped Griff in a hug. They patted each other's backs, then parted awkwardly, shoving their hands in their pockets, glancing around to make sure nobody'd seen them.

"Come on inside," Heck said gruffly. "Got something for you."

As they returned to the house, Griff couldn't help noticing how slowly his father moved. Now he had another reason to stick around—to spend some time with his father now that they under-stood each other better.

Heck held up one finger, asking Griff to wait while he hobbled off to the bedroom. Griff could hear drawers opening and shut-ting, then a muffled curse before his dad returned, carrying a little box in one hand. When he opened it and presented it like a magician revealing a rabbit, Griff couldn't help laughing.

"I love you, Dad, but I'm not going to marry you."

"Shhh." Heck put a finger to his lips. "It's not for you, stupid. It's for Riley."

"She won't marry you, either."

Heck cuffed his shoulder. "Now you listen to me. This ring was your grandmother's. My daddy gave it to her when they'd already been married ten years because up until then, all he could afford was a plain gold band. It wasn't fancy enough for your mother, but I always kept it, thinking maybe someday I'd have a daughter-in-law who'd wear it. You know how much Molly and I think of Riley."

"I know, Dad, but…"

"That little girl could bring a sparkle to any diamond," Heck said. "You give her this for Christmas, seal the deal. Don't let her get away."

Griff took the ring. The box seemed fragile in his big, clumsy hands, but the stone had plenty of sparkle. "Dad, I think she already did."

"We got her back here, Son." Heck gave him a glare that brought back old times—and not the good parts. "We did our part, and now it's up to you. Don't be telling me she doesn't want you. That girl's so in love she don't know which end is up. You love her back, right?"

Griff nodded.

"I know I promised I wouldn't boss you anymore, but I've got one last order for you," Heck said.

Griff sighed. "All right. Go on."

"Try again," his father said. "And don't quit trying 'til you win." His tone softened. "She's worth it, Son. I can see what's between you. Don't let her get away."

CHAPTER 52

RILEY WOKE WITH A START, GLANCING AROUND WILDLY BEFORE she remembered where she was.

It was finally Christmas. Molly and Heck were still in bed, and Jess and Cade had returned to Cade's old place, which they were going to fix up for Molly and Heck so they could move into the ranch house. There was room for Riley in Jess's old room after all, at least temporarily, so she wasn't homeless, and she had even more work to do than she'd thought. Jess wanted to fix up Cade's old place so Molly and Heck could grow old there. Heck had grumbled at the idea of grab bars in the bathroom and other adjustments, but Riley figured the world would end if he ever admitted he was getting old.

That would mean staying here and close to Griff, but she knew he didn't want to live with his folks, so she might be able to avoid him, along with whomever he chose to share his life with. Because it would not be her.

Even if she hadn't cared about him and his future, she wasn't sure she had the courage to face people like the Harpies. She'd rather be alone so she could remain on the edges of Wynott's version of high society, keep her head down, do her work, and leave the moving and shaking to people like Griff and Fawn, who belonged here.

People like the Harpies were everywhere. They made up their mind about you based on rumors and half-truths, and no matter how nice you were, no matter how hard you tried, you could never, ever change their minds. Griff didn't understand that and never would. He actually seemed to believe she was an elf, waking every morning with a clean slate.

The thought made her smile. It *was* Christmas, after all. She'd try to stop thinking these serious thoughts and enjoy it. The Baileys had made her so welcome during their raucous Christmas Eve dinner that she hadn't felt like a third wheel once.

She moved slowly and quietly, swinging her feet to the floor. She'd meant to sleep in Jess's room, but it had seemed natural to share Griff's bed, as she had so many times. It wouldn't seem natural for her to emerge from his room in front of his family, though, so she'd better keep moving.

As she opened the bedroom door, a snippet of song floated up the stairs. Molly was up already, busy in the kitchen and serenading the day with Christmas carols.

Well, Christmas songs, anyway. "Grandma Got Run Over by a Reindeer," sung slightly off-key, wasn't exactly a carol.

Riley washed up, then hurried into Jess's room and dressed hastily, popping the elf hat on her head at the last minute so the jingle bell dangled just above her nose. As she trotted down the stairs, she caught the scent of cinnamon, and when she reached the hall, she glanced out the windows to see snowy fields stretching out in every direction under impossibly blue skies.

She stood there a moment, savoring the scent of fir and cinnamon and vanilla, listening to Molly warbling happily in the kitchen, and feeling a peace and promise she'd always believed Christmas morning should hold but had never found. Her world felt new, as if the warmth and love of the holiday was about to change everything. As if the world might be a better place from this moment on.

She'd never had one of those exciting Christmas mornings where she rushed down the stairs to see what Santa had brought. Usually, Santa was an old drunk on the corner in a ragged suit and soiled beard who tried to get little girls to sit on his lap. She never got presents or sat around a loaded table smiling at a family of her own.

When she stepped into the kitchen, Molly turned to her and

smiled. Riley smiled back, and there it was, warm and bright as a string of twinkle lights—the magic. It had always been there, even on the worst of Riley's many disastrous Christmases. Always, there'd be a moment of warmth when she could remember. It made her think of the carol about the "merry gentlemen": *Let nothing you dismay.*

On this day, she would let nothing dismay her. Even if she only got a moment, just a ragged scrap of Christmas, it still made life silvery, magical, and full of promise.

Molly had outdone herself with breakfast, creating a delicious sausage-and-potato casserole to go with eggs, French toast, and her famous cinnamon rolls. Once breakfast was done, the family opened gifts. Mostly they were little things, many of them jokes, like the Christmas tie Jess got for Heck. The man hadn't worn a tie in ten years, but apparently Jess always got him one. This one had Santa in a cowboy hat riding a bucking reindeer.

Even Bruce got presents—a great big bone to chew and a big, fluffy bed they'd set by the fire. He looked happy, gnawing his bone and enjoying his warm bed.

They'd gotten through all the packages and were laughing over a sexy apron Heck had given Molly when Griff stood up and fished a tiny beribboned box from the branches of the tree. A hush fell over the room as he presented it to Riley. It was small, square, wrapped in silver paper and decorated with a beautiful red-plaid ribbon, shot through with silver threads. If she didn't know better—if she hadn't discouraged Griff at every turn from planning any sort of future for them—she'd have thought it was a ring.

Maybe it is.

Her heart danced, but she reminded it that a ring wouldn't be good news. It would force her to break Griff's heart again by telling him no, and that would ruin his Christmas, and probably everyone else's too. Especially hers, because she wanted Griff so much that… Well, she wouldn't think about how much.

"Okay, Heck and I had better do the dishes," Molly said.

"What?" Heck looked up from his chair. "Why? I want to see…"

Molly made a "scoot" motion with her hands. "Come on, old man, let's go."

"I should help." Riley hopped to her feet.

"No, honey, Heck and I are looking forward to doing dishes in a full-sized kitchen, aren't we?"

Riley didn't know why. She'd had a tour of their fifth-wheel trailer, and its kitchen, with its shiny stainless-steel appliances, definitely outranked the aging ranch-house kitchen's seventies-era harvest-gold range and avocado refrigerator. The RV even had a dishwasher. The ranch kitchen was still stuck in the hand-wash era.

"You wash, I'll dry," Heck said.

Molly laughed. "And then you'll hide the dishes in all the wrong places so I can play treasure hunt the next time I cook."

Heck looked a bit hurt, then grinned. "It's a time-honored tradition."

Jess rose, too. "Tell you what. I'll try to pay attention, so I can tell you where he put them."

Cade was still sitting on the sofa, tracing the tooling on a new pair of boots Heck had given him. Riley didn't blame him for losing himself in admiration of the fine leatherwork, but Jess kicked his foot, jerking her head toward the kitchen.

"What?" He looked up as if she'd caught him sleepwalking. "Oh. I-I'd better go out there, too, because…" He looked helplessly at Jess for a hint, but she just jerked her head again. "Because Jess wants me to."

"Reason enough," Griff said.

"Seriously, I can help, too," Riley said. "I'll put away the cookies."

"Don't you dare." Griff grabbed a gingerbread man and bit off the head. "I'm still eating them. Besides," he said, his voice muffled by the cookie, "you have to open your gift."

As the others left the room, she stared at the package. She was about to tear the paper when Griff reached out and clasped her hand, box and all, in one big hand.

"I need to tell you something before you open that."

CHAPTER 53

GRIFF OPENED HIS MOUTH TO SPEAK, THEN CLOSED IT WHEN someone pounded loudly on the front door.

"Company?" He groaned. "On Christmas morning?"

Bruce looked up from his bone and growled softly.

"I should get that," Riley said, but he grabbed her wrist as she tried to flee.

"There are how many people in the kitchen?" He lowered his brows, puzzled. "I thought you liked presents."

"I like Christmas," she said. "But getting presents—it's kind of embarrassing."

He started to speak, but then Heck let out a grunt of surprise, and all hell broke loose.

Griff wondered if Santa had brought a sack full of cats and they were fighting in the foyer—fighting to the approximate tune of "Joy to the World." The caterwauling set his teeth on edge. Heck emerged from the kitchen, plugging his ears—and Molly had just told Griff he was getting hard of hearing. Bruce had retreated, leaving his warm bed to cower behind the stove, his bone clutched in his jaws.

Jess shouted above the yowling, sounding confused.

"What are you doing?"

"We're caroling," said a pair of familiar voices.

The sound was like fingernails raking down a blackboard. Griff had already heard those voices too many times, and he'd vowed Riley would never have to hear them again if he had his way.

But for some reason, Carol and Diane had pursued her all the way to the Diamond Jack, no doubt in order to torture her some more.

CHAPTER 54

RILEY'S HEART DROPPED DOWN INTO HER SOCKS. SHE couldn't imagine why Carol and Diane would come all the way to the Bailey ranch to sing Christmas carols unless they'd decided to blame her for Trevor's troubles after all, and this was a sneaky way to get inside and ruin her Christmas.

She headed for the hallway, hoping she hadn't brought chaos to the Bailey family and spoiled their Christmas, too.

The women launched into another song as she approached. Riley wasn't sure, but it sounded like "Away in a Manger," if the ox and ass were singing it themselves.

Griff stood stolidly in the hallway with his hands shoved deep in his pockets, wearing a frown that would have chased ordinary mortals from the door in seconds. The Harpies were oblivious, though, so Riley figured they must be really determined to crash the party.

As soon as the song ended, Molly asked if they wanted to come in.

"Oh, no," said Carol. "We're just going around the neighborhood, caroling."

"*What* neighborhood?" Griff asked.

Riley knew he was trying to stand up for her, but being hostile wasn't going to help. She was about to offer the ladies some gingerbread men when she noticed two more figures coming up the walk and squealed, hitting a higher note than either of the Harpies had managed—and that was saying something.

"Trevor," she said. "And *Ed*!" She just about knocked the women over rushing to greet her buddy, her best friend, her *dad*. The Baileys were a hugging kind of family, but she'd still been longing for one of Ed's special Christmas hugs all morning. That had been the gift she'd always treasured most, no matter what presents he'd given her. Ed made her feel like family, and that was better than any power tool invented. Which, for Riley, was really saying something.

"Riley, honey." He hugged her all right, but it was disappointing. Kind of hasty, like he was hoping the Harpies wouldn't notice. "Carol? Diane? What are you two doing?"

"Caroling," Diane said, but she looked down at the floor like a sulky child.

Ed suddenly channeled Dirty Harry again. "That's not what we came here for, and you know it."

Riley had never heard Ed speak to anyone like that. Not even Darrell had merited that sort of scorn. The ladies shuffled around, looking cowed.

"Go on," Ed said. He reminded Riley of a really mean teacher she'd had in sixth grade. "Say what you came to say."

The women glanced at each other, then fidgeted some more.

"You say it," Carol muttered.

"No, you," said Diane.

"Why don't you *both* say it." Ed waved his fingers like an orchestra conductor. "One, two, *three*."

"*We're sorry*," the sisters said, squawking the words in unison.

"Sorry, *who*?"

Riley couldn't believe the change in Ed. He seemed taller and was carrying himself with an almost martial air—shoulders back, chin down, eyes flashing with anger.

"Sorry, *Riley*," said Diane.

"Yes, Riley. We're sorry," Carol echoed.

"We were wrong about you," said Diane. "We realize now what a good person you are."

"The best," Carol said. "Because it's a lot harder when you have so much to overcome."

Diane frowned. "You make it sound like she had some sort of character deficit or something. But she's a fine person, deep down, to have come so far in life."

Riley stared at them, openmouthed. Was Diane actually fighting for her? She turned to Ed.

"What did you do? Pay them?" she asked.

"Nobody paid us." Diane laced her fingers together, posing like a top Sunday School student trying to get her way. "We're just telling you how we feel. We were wrong, Riley."

Ed poked her in the back. "And?"

"And we heard you were thinking of leaving, but we wanted to ask you to please stay and help Trevor," said Carol. "He told us how much you've done for him already."

"And we need you at the store," said Diane.

"Trevor can bunk with me," Ed said, "and you can have your apartment back."

"Oh." Riley thought for a moment. She thought about how these two women had come into her home and chased her out of it. She thought about how they'd never come to help Ed, not even when Ruth died, but now they wanted the store for Trevor. She thought about how rude they'd been and how they were only being nice because they needed her.

She thought about telling them to get lost, but then she looked at them, and they were just two old ladies. Not Harpies—just sad old ladies who'd been disillusioned by the boy they loved like a son. And they needed her.

"Of course I'll help."

She was relieved when Molly appeared in the kitchen doorway. "Come on in, everyone," Griff's stepmother said. "Riley and I made cookies, and we have eggnog." She beamed. "It's just wonderful to have carolers clear out here."

The women entered, followed by Ed, followed by an almost unrecognizable Trevor. The Only Heir had taken a shower and cleaned up. Dressed in clean jeans and a shirt he must have borrowed from Ed, he looked like what he was—a young man visiting family for the holidays.

Molly bustled around, pouring eggnog and plating cookies. Riley moved in to help her but was shushed away.

"Go sit with your family," Molly said. "I was hoping you and Ed could get together today, and now isn't this nice."

Amazingly, it was. She was a little curious about Griff's gift, but then again, she was amused by his frustration. He kept flashing meaningful looks her way—looks that made the butterflies dance.

Quelling the butterflies, she headed for the living room to sit beside the man who'd been a father to her for so many years. When Molly set two pitchers of eggnog, she started to reach for one, but Griff was already filling up a glass mug for her and one for Trevor from a different pitcher. So she handed her pitcher to Carol and Diane, who served themselves brimming cups full. Griff poured another cup for Ed, and everyone lifted their mugs in the air.

"To Riley," Ed said. "The heart of our family."

"To Riley," chimed the sisters.

Tears sprang to Riley's eyes as they clinked their mugs together. Kind smiles transformed the Harpies into humans. They looked grandmotherly now, like nice old ladies instead of—well, instead of Harpies.

"Oh, this is good," Carol said.

"Really good." Diane drained her mug and held it out for more. "What's your secret ingredient, Mrs. Bailey?"

Molly smiled. "It wouldn't be a secret ingredient anymore if I told you what it was."

Riley didn't really like eggnog, and she wasn't sure any secret ingredient would change her mind. It seemed kind of bland, actually, but she drank hers to be polite. The talk turned to the new year and some ideas Trevor had for the store—good ideas, Riley thought. She'd finally found the Christmas she'd dreamed of when she'd first heard Ed's sisters were coming.

Trevor caught her eye and leaned over to whisper in her ear. "I know what the secret ingredient is."

"Really?" Riley wasn't sure Trevor was any sort of eggnog expert, but she humored him. "What?"

"Booze," he said. "That's why Griff poured ours from that other pitcher, I think. My grandmas always get red noses when they drink, and look."

The two did have a Rudolphian flush. Riley didn't believe in slipping drinks to folks who disapproved of alcohol, but the sisters seemed to be having an excellent time, and she didn't want to spoil their fun.

Once everyone finished their eggnog, Ed and the Harpies got up to go. Riley saw them to the door and was stunned when both sisters hugged her goodbye. She stood in the doorway, watching them pile into Ed's truck, and hugged herself, holding the most surprising gift of all—the warmth of unexpected understanding and forgiveness.

Could there be a better Christmas present?

CHAPTER 55

When Ed's taillights had disappeared into the night, Riley turned to find Griff leaning on the newel post and holding a familiar-looking silver box. The rest of the Baileys had once again escaped to the kitchen.

"Open it," he said.

Riley took the box and carefully unwrapped it without tearing the pretty silver paper. Inside was a velvet box with a hinged lid. Huh. If she didn't know better…but surely Griff did. She'd made things very clear.

It wasn't until she opened it and saw the beautiful, old-fashioned filigree setting with its sparkling diamond that she realized it *was*. It really *was*. And it wasn't until she looked up at Griff's face and saw the tenderness there and the hope that she realized how much she wanted this ring. How much she wanted to say yes.

"I didn't expect this."

Suddenly, he was kneeling right in front of her, and he took the ring in one hand and looked up in her face, and oh, she could get lost in those eyes. But they were different this morning. Where before she'd seen a darkness in their depths, the darkness of his past, his tortured memories, today they looked warm and loving. What she saw there was a future—one she could reach out and take if she only dared.

"Riley." His eyes were fixed on her with so much intensity she had to look down at the sparkling ring, because their tenderness overwhelmed her. "You told me how you like renovating old houses—how you peeled away the layers and found their… What was it you said? Their heart?"

She nodded.

"Well, that's what you did for me. When I came back, I wasn't sure I had a heart left to give, but you found it, and you made me want a new kind of life. I let go of the need for a do-over. I learned to forgive myself and found my real purpose." He paused, his chest heaving, and she realized how hard it was for him to express himself like this, to dig out these emotions and hand them to her.

"Remember how we were talking about happily-ever-after, and I said it only works the last, best time?" he asked. "Well, last night—that was the last, best time for me. And if you don't say yes, nothing will ever beat it. I'll never get my happily-ever-after if it's not with you." He took a deep breath. "I love you, Riley James. I want to marry you. I want us to have a home and a family and a normal, happy life in Wynott. Is that so hard?"

She looked down at the ring, dazzled and confused. It didn't sound hard. Why had she thought it was? Her mind scrambled for her reasons. The Harpies? They'd obviously come to terms with her place in Ed's life. And if they could forgive her, surely anyone could.

Then again, she wasn't sure that mattered, because the man she loved was smiling at her with so much love it made her dizzy.

"Come on, Riley," he said. "Take a chance."

The words reminded her of something Sierra said once: *Leap and the net will appear.*

She'd made a lot of leaps in her life, and the net had always appeared. One had been following Sierra to Wynott. The next had been to jump in and help Ed and Ruth when they needed her. Those leaps had worked out. Why not this one?

She looked down at the diamond sparkling in the lights from the tree. That diamond had a lot to say. Its sparkle reminded her of Christmas lights, and when she looked up at Griff's eyes, there was a sparkle there, too, one that said he was happy, truly happy. Her grim, haunted soldier had found his place in the world, and that was what she wanted most. He'd still have those dreams, but he was staying, letting Wynott heal him the way it had healed her.

Maybe she could help, not hinder. Maybe this was the start of her outrunning her past. She'd thought the Harpies were proof some people would never forgive her, but the warmth of their goodbye still lingered, and she felt like she really was an elf, newly risen on Christmas morning. And she was done punishing herself for the past.

Maybe magic *did* last, after all.

With a tearful *mew* that was kind of embarrassing, she reached for Griff, and he rose to sit beside her and wrap her in his strong arms. Resting her head against his chest, she nodded, just the slightest bit. When he kissed the top of her head, she knew he'd heard her say yes.

And just like that, in a silvery Christmas moment, she had the life she'd always dreamed of and a cowboy to make it come true. She almost lost herself in his kiss, but then she caught Molly's sob of joy from the kitchen doorway and a quiet cheer from Jess as well as Heck's sniffles as he tried to hide the fact that he was a sentimental old fool. Bruce ventured out from behind the stove and stood there watching them, a loving light in his eyes, drool dripping from his chin.

Reaching out one arm, she motioned for the Baileys to gather round and hoped Griff didn't mind sharing. Finding herself the center of the circle, she savored a new sense of peace and belonging. Finally, she had the one thing she'd always wanted in the world—a family where she belonged and a love that would last forever.

THE END

There's nothing better than celebrating Christmas with Joanne Kennedy's cowboys, but if you're ready to heat things up, don't miss the first book in the Blue Sky Cowboys series. Keep reading for an excerpt!

COWBOY SUMMER

Available now from Sourcebooks Casablanca

CHAPTER 1

JESSICA JANE BAILEY CRANKED DOWN HER CAR WINDOW AND let the scents and sounds of Wyoming sweep away the stale city funk of her workaday life. While the wind tossed and tangled her blond curls, she sniffed the air like a dog, savoring the familiar mix of sage, pine, and new-mown hay.

It was August, so the plains had shed green gowns for gold. Brilliant yellow rabbitbrush blazed against red rock outcroppings, and cattle, corralled behind rusty barbed wire, shared forage with herds of antelope. The cows only lifted their heads as she passed, but the antelope startled and raced away, flowing over the coulees like schools of fish.

A fox dashed into the road and paused, one paw upraised. Hitting the brakes, Jess met its eyes for one breathless instant before it darted into the underbrush.

There was something in that gaze she recognized—a kindred soul. It had been years since she'd encountered anything wilder than a pigeon, and the thrill of it surprised her. So did the swelling of her heart as she turned onto a red dirt road and felt the real Wyoming pummeling her little Miata's muffler without mercy.

Her love for this land had lain in ambush all these years. The place was so stunningly wild, so unique, so home, it hurt—because she was going to lose it. Every branch and flower was waving goodbye.

She'd given herself two weeks to live it, love it, and learn to let it go.

And she wouldn't let anyone see how much it hurt.

———

Jess's dad was like a well-oiled chainsaw; pull the cord, and he was raring to go. No one ever had to wait for him to get to the point, so Jess hadn't been surprised when he'd launched into conversation the moment she'd answered her phone.

It was what he'd said that made her clutch her chest and gasp for breath.

"I'm selling the Diamond Jack," he'd announced. "Know anyone who wants to buy a ranch?"

The words had sent her white-walled office spinning like a manic merry-go-round. Backing toward her desk chair, she missed the seat and landed with a spine-rattling *thud* on the floor. The phone flipped out of her hand and bounced across the floor with all the cunning of a fresh-caught fish while she bobbled it and dropped it again.

She had no reason to be so upset. She was on the verge of a promotion at Birchwood Suites, one that would take her to their new Maui location and put Wyoming firmly in her rearview mirror.

White sand beaches. Sunset on the water. Crashing surf. And surfers...

She'd been to the ocean once in her life, and it had awed and entranced her. The vastness of it and the big sky overhead reminded her of home, and the thundering roll and retreat of the waves answered a longing deep inside her. Living and working near a beach sounded like heaven, and it was Birchwood's ultimate prize.

She'd vowed to win it, but first, she had to deal with her dad. By the time she caught the phone, he was cussing like a bull rider with a porcupine in his pants.

"Dag nabbit, Jess, you 'bout broke my corn's-a-poppin' eardrum."

"I just—I couldn't—what did you say?"

"I said dag *nabbit*. And I *meant* it."

"No, before that."

"Oh. I said I'm selling the ranch. It's not like you want the place," he said. "You take after your mother."

She bristled. "Do not."

Dot Bailey had run off with a slick politician from Jackson Hole when Jess was sixteen, leaving Heck with two kids to raise and a ranch to run. He'd been hurt all over again when his son chose the army over ranching and Jess took her mom's advice and moved to Denver after high school. Lately, his resentment had risen between them like dust on a dirt road, clouding the closeness Jess had always treasured.

"You know what I mean." He sounded sulky. "You like people better'n you like cows. And your brother's too busy chasin' terrorists to even think about it." He sighed. "Always thought you and Cade might get together, take the place on. That boy would've made a fine rancher if his daddy hadn't sold so much land out from under him."

"Cade got *married*, Dad, and not to me. Don't you think it's time to let go?"

"You're the one who let go. What was the boy supposed to do?"

"Well, he wasn't supposed to marry Amber Lynn Lyle."

Jess didn't like to say she held hatred in her heart, not for anyone, but Amber Lynn Lyle had always inspired some awfully strong feelings. And that was *before* SHE'D MARRIED CADE WALKER.

Heck grunted, which sounded like agreement, but Jess sensed there was something he wasn't telling her.

"Is this Molly's idea?"

"Sort of," he said. "She's tired of ranching."

"That didn't take long."

"Now, you be nice. It's a hard life for a woman."

Jess knew her dad deserved happiness, and she wanted to like her new stepmother. But rumor had it Molly Brumbach had auditioned the marital skills of every man in town before she hit on Heck at a church pie sale. Oblivious as he was to the wiles of women, he'd probably fallen in love with her coconut cream before he'd even looked at her face. With her too-blue eye shadow and penciled brows, she looked as out of place on the Diamond Jack as a rabbit at a rodeo.

"She's looking at some retirement communities," Heck said. "You know, for the over-fifty set."

Jess winced. Her dad wasn't part of any "set," and Molly didn't know him if she thought he'd retire like some normal old man. Cowboy to the core, he sat a horse like most men sat a La-Z-Boy recliner and cared more about his livestock than his own sunbaked skin. Without horses to ride and cattle to tend, he wouldn't know who he was.

"Dad, you can't sell the ranch. You just *can't*."

"Sure I can. Molly's got it all worked out." He coughed, a brutal, phlegmy sound, and Jess wondered if he had a cold. "She sent for five brochures from retirement communities in Arizona. Now she's lookin' at floor plans and measuring the furniture."

"But what would you *do* all day?"

"Guess I'd finally have time to fix stuff around the house. Get your evil stepmom to stop nagging me."

Even Jess knew Molly was about as evil as a golden retriever, and any nagging was well-deserved. Her dad's cowboy work ethic meant everything was shipshape in the barn, but the house was a festival of deferred maintenance. The dripping faucets, sagging stair treads, and wobbly doorknobs had all dripped, sagged, and wobbled for decades. He preferred what he called "the real work of ranching," which was any job that could be performed on horseback. If he could figure out a way to get a quarter horse into the bathroom, he might get those faucets fixed. Until then, they'd continue to drip.

"What about your horses?" Jess asked.

"Molly says they can come, too. These places have community stables and riding trails."

"Yeah, for sissies." She snorted. "They probably all ride English."

She tried to picture her father's finely tuned cow horses prancing around groomed riding trails with a bunch of show ponies. For some reason, the image pushed her over the edge. She tried—and failed—to stifle a sob.

"I know you're a city girl now, with a fancy apartment, cable TV, air-conditioning—hell, I hate to ask you to leave home."

"The Diamond Jack is home, Dad."

The truth of that statement hit her heart so hard, it left a bruise. She'd been dead set on leaving the ranch when she'd graduated from high school, but Denver hadn't been the big-city paradise she'd hoped for. She'd felt closed in, trapped by the looming skyscrapers.

Home in her heart was still the ranch, with its horses and cattle and miles of fence, its endless pastures and dusty dirt roads. It was blushing-pink dawns and tangerine sunsets, the misery of riding drag and the triumph of roping a scampering calf. Home was sagebrush and wild lupine, the bright sheen of mountain bluebirds by day and coyote yodels spiraling up to the moon at night. She might not want to be there every minute of every day, but the ranch was her roots and supported her still.

"If you care so much, how come you never come home?" he said. "Molly loves you, you know, and she worries she's keeping you away."

Jess couldn't tell her dad he was right. Molly tried too hard to make Jess like her while Jess struggled to pretend she did. The tension stretched tight as the duel in *High Noon*, but Heck, who could tell a cow had a headache from thirty feet away, wasn't much good at reading women.

Molly wasn't the only problem, though. Jess had no desire to watch Cade Walker squire Amber Lynn Lyle around town in the beat-up truck where he and Jess had run over so many of life's milestones—first kiss, first promise, first…well, first everything. That truck was practically sacred, and she couldn't bear to think of Amber Lynn Lyle sitting on the bench seat, cozied up to Cade with the stick shift between her knees.

She sniffed, blinking away tears.

"Now, Jess." Her dad's voice dropped into a parental baritone. "What did I tell you 'bout crying?"

She recited one of the mantras he'd taught her growing up. "'Cowgirls don't cry, and tantrums are for toddlers.'"

It was true. Cowgirls didn't cry—but they didn't just lie down and die, either. Not without a fight. The ranch was her heritage and her dad's lifeblood. No oversexed pie lady with poor taste in eye shadow was going to take it away.

"I need to be there," she said. "I'll take vacation or something."

"I'd sure like that," he said. "Molly's just crazy 'bout these brochures, but I don't see why. The folks all look like the ones in those vagina ads."

"Dad, what are you talking about?"

"The vagina ads. On TV. For that medicine men take when they can't—oh, you know."

"It's *Viagra*, Dad."

"That's what I said, dang it. They look like the folks from the Viagra ads."

"Well, I guess they won't be bored, then."

"Nope. According to those ads, their erections last four hours or more." He snorted. "No wonder they're skin and bones. Bunch of silver foxes, like that newscaster on TV. The women are foxes, too, so Molly'll fit right in."

Jess smothered a snort. Molly was hardly a fox. In a Beatrix Potter story, she'd be a lady hedgehog, one that baked pies and seduced all the old man hedgehogs.

"You there, hon?"

"Uh-huh. I'll come home soon as I can, Dad. I miss you. And I miss the ranch."

He sighed. "We'll all be missing it soon. I'll be playing canasta with a bunch of the vagina folks in Sunset Village every night. When the game gets slow, we'll watch the ladies fight off those four-hour erections."

She laughed despite her fears. "Sit tight, okay? And don't do anything crazy."

That was like telling the sun not to shine. Her dad was always up to something, and that something was usually crazy.

If those folks at the retirement home thought a four-hour erection was trouble, wait until they met Heck Bailey.

CHAPTER 2

CADE WALKER'S PICKUP LET OUT A METALLIC SHRIEK AS HE downshifted into his driveway. The old Ford, persnickety as a maiden aunt, had been raiding his wallet for months with its nickel-and-dime demands. He'd bought it a fuel pump just last week, and now it wanted a transmission. Dang thing was starting to remind him of his ex-wife.

He thumped the dashboard with his fist. "I'll trade you in for a Dodge."

It was an empty threat. He couldn't afford a new truck now. Not with the mortgage to pay.

The mortgage. The thought of it plagued him ten times a day, hammering shame into his heart so hard it felt like a railroad spike in his chest. One missed payment and the place would be gone, a hundred-acre rug ripped from under his feet.

Not even his dad, with his taste for bourbon and high-stakes gambling, had managed to lose the ranch itself. Pieces of it, sure. Tom Walker's bad habits had chipped away an acre or two at a time, until Walker Ranch was more of a ranchette than a working cattle spread. But Cade had only himself to blame if he lost what little was left.

You don't have to stay, Son. Cut your losses and get out if you're so miserable. You always were a quitter.

Cade tried to shake off the voice in his head. Maybe he was losing his mind. His father's legacy wasn't just the leavings of their once-great ranch; his voice remained as well, delivering a never-ending harangue about Cade's incompetence, his stupidity, his uselessness and bad decisions.

But Cade wasn't a loser like his old man said, and he had proof.

He'd worked his way out of the mess his father made, sold off the cattle, and gone all in for training horses. Just last week, he'd gotten a job offer from one of the country's top clinicians. Most of the famous so-called horse whisperers knew more about self-promotion than they did about horses, but John Baker was one of the greats. After hearing raves from some of Cade's clients, he'd sent a letter offering the opportunity of a lifetime.

It was a chance to learn from a legend, and Cade felt validated by the compliment. But accepting the offer would mean leaving the business he'd worked so hard to build. Worse yet, it would mean leaving Jess Bailey. She was finally coming home, at least for a while, and Cade couldn't help but stay. His chance to win her back had finally come, and he had to take it.

As he neared the house, a shard of light distracted him, arcing up from behind a shed. He'd cleaned up all the old machinery and car parts his dad had left behind, along with a rusty seized-up tractor and a fifty-gallon drum full of broken glass, so there shouldn't be anything back there but weeds.

As he pulled past the shed, he saw a black car parked by the pasture fence. Long and lean with a predatory sheen, it sure didn't belong to any of his friends. Cowboys drove pickups, most of them rusty. A truck wasn't supposed to be pretty, just functional, so when a paint job surrendered to Wyoming's brutal climate, they slapped on some primer and kept going. But this vehicle was some fool's pride and joy. Beneath the dust from the dirt road, it was waxed to a shine.

Stepping out of the truck, Cade peered through the weeds at the car's back end. When he saw the crest on the trunk, an eerie silence settled over the landscape, as if the birds and the breezes were holding their breath.

Cadillac.

His ex-wife drove a Caddy, but hers was an SUV—an Escalator, or something like that. This was a sedan, something her daddy would drive, and that couldn't be good news. Amber Lynn's daddy owned the bank in Wynott, and the bank in Wynott owned Cade's ranch.

He glanced around, unnerved by the silence. Where the hell was his dog? Boogy should be bouncing in the front window, barking his head off. The bandy-legged, brindled boxer cross was supposed to guard the house.

He was probably hiding behind the sofa.

Cade sighed. He didn't need trouble right now. All day, he'd been looking forward to stopping by his neighbor's place—casually, of course—to see if Heck Bailey needed a hand with anything.

Like maybe his daughter.

Jess Bailey had always been the first to climb the highest tree or ride a forbidden horse when they were kids. Her sexy, reckless courage had whirled like a tempest through Cade's life, and her smooth-muscled cowgirl body, laughing blue eyes, and wild blond curls had filled his dreams, right up to the day she left him behind.

Actually, that wasn't true. She *still* filled his dreams.

But she'd put much more than miles between them, following a star he couldn't see from Walker Ranch—a star that told her a high-powered job in the city was worth more, somehow, than an honest country life.

She was wrong, but a life without her hadn't been worth a dime to Cade. Maybe he should have followed her. If his father had left him with anything to offer, he might have convinced her to stay.

There you go again, blaming everything on me.

Cade shook his head hard, but the voice droned on.

I warned you it wouldn't work out with the Bailey girl, but would you listen? Not a chance. And then you up and married that other bitch. Dumbass. You should have…

A sudden clash of hooves on steel shocked the voice into silence. Jogging back to his horse trailer, Cade flung open the battered door to find his wild-eyed, tangle-maned gelding flailing toward a full-on mental breakdown.

"Easy, Pride. Settle down."

He might as well tell the horse to turn a somersault. The only thing that calmed the nervy Arabian was work, the harder the better. They'd enjoyed a busy day chasing feral cows through the canyons and coulees of the neighboring Vee Bar ranch, but the ride home had set off a collection of twitches and itches the horse needed to shed with a little bucking, a lot of crow hopping, and a gallon of high-test attitude.

Once Cade swung the butt bar aside and clipped on a lead rope, Pride calmed. Tossing his head, swishing his tail, he pranced down the ramp with the hot feline grace of a flamenco dancer.

The horse had belonged to Cade's ex, but she'd lost interest in riding like she'd lost interest in her other expensive hobbies, which had included fine wine, ballroom dancing, and sleeping with men who weren't her husband. Amber Lynn had left a mess in her wake, but he could almost forgive her, since she'd left him Pride. The horse was responsive as a finely tuned sports car, and working with him was a challenge Cade enjoyed.

What if Amber Lynn's daddy thought Pride still belonged to him?

Cade released the horse into the pasture and slammed the gate, letting the chain clang against the metal rails. Spooked, the horse pitched along the fence like a demon-driven rocking horse, then rocketed over a hill, out of sight and hopefully out of everybody's mind.

Returning to the shed, Cade strode through the tall grass and peered into the Caddie. Candy wrappers and fast-food containers littered the floor, and a bottle of wine sat on the passenger seat, cork askew.

Amber Lynn.

Sure as claw marks on a tree trunk spelled bear, junk food and expensive booze spelled Amber Lynn Lyle.

Crossing the parched lawn, he jogged up the porch steps and flung the door open, letting it bang against the wall. Boogy skulked in from the kitchen, staggering sideways like a sorry-ass drunk, his jowly face eloquent with doggie remorse.

"Aw, Boogy." Cade bent to rub the dog's ears. They stood up like satellite dishes, swiveling toward whatever Boogy was looking for—which was sometimes Cade but usually bacon.

A ripple of tension ran down the dog's back.

"She's here, huh? You're scared," Cade whispered. "It's okay. Me, too."

Sliding to the floor, Boogy rolled over, gazing up with adoring eyes as his tongue flopped out the side of his mouth. Cade had been looking for a cow dog when Boogy had turned up homeless. He'd fallen for the sturdy, smiley critter and told himself any dog could learn to herd cows. Unfortunately, he'd been wrong. Boogy couldn't grasp the difference between herding and chasing, so the folks at the Vee Bar asked Cade to leave him home.

A faint squeaking sound came from the kitchen. Standing slowly, Cade peered around the doorframe.

Amber Lynn Lyle, formerly Amber Lynn Walker, crouched in one of the battered captain's chairs at Cade's kitchen table. Her feet rested on the rungs, and she'd thrust her hands between her knees like she was cold. Dark hair hung knotted and limp around her hunched shoulders, obscuring her face.

Cade stilled, chilled to the bone. His ex had broken their vows so hard and cleaned out his bank account so thoroughly, he'd assumed she was gone for good. There was nothing left on the ranch but him, and she'd made it clear he wasn't what she wanted.

Yet here she was, looking almost as sorry as poor old Boogy. Her pose was calculated to inspire pity; with Amber Lynn, every move had a message, and every position was a pose. There was always an equation behind those green eyes, and the answer was always Amber Lynn Lyle.

He knew, sure as he knew his own name, that her timing was another calculation. Gossip spread across the county fast as wildfire in a high wind, and everybody knew Jess Bailey was coming home.

So here came Amber Lynn, staking her claim like an old dog peeing on a tree.

"Amber Lynn?"

She shivered dramatically.

He glanced up at the cabinet over the refrigerator. Hadn't that bottle of Jim Beam just called his name? Maybe he should offer his ex-wife a shot, pour one for himself. Calm things down.

But no. It was whiskey that had led him to Amber Lynn and sobriety that had set him free.

"What are you doing here?" He pulled out a side chair and straddled the seat, resting his forearms on the back. "You wanted to get married; I married you. You wanted me to pay off your bills; I hocked my ranch to pay 'em. Then you wanted Drew Covington, and I gave you a divorce." He splayed his empty hands. "What's left?"

"I'm s-sorry." She hiccupped, then dropped her voice to a whisper. "Drew was a mistake."

"So was I. Or so you said." He hated to be harsh, but hey, at least he was talking to her. He'd much rather take her upstairs and throw her out a second-story window. "How is your boyfriend, anyway?"

"Drew? He's not my boyfriend. Not anymore." With a dramatic sniff, she tossed her hair aside, revealing a nasty black eye. The skin around it looked like a stormy sunset, purple with streaks of red.

"*Drew* did that to you?"

She nodded.

Cade couldn't believe it. Drew had been a jerk, but he'd been a civilized jerk. In their only confrontation, he'd been scared as a skinny second grader facing the school bully. Cade had waved him away, told him to go on and take her. But if he'd known the man would hit her...

This is your fault. You should've seen he was a hitter. Not like you never knew one, right?

For once, Tom Walker's voice made sense. Poor Amber Lynn.

But as pity clouded his brain, his ex-wife bit her lip and looked away, as if something outside the window had caught her eye.

The woman was as transparent as a toddler. Cade leaned a little closer.

"Seriously? Drew?"

Squeezing out a tear, she shook her head. "No." She shot him a sulky glare, as if the lie was his fault. "Not Drew. It was another guy."

"Jeez, Amber Lynn. It's serious stuff, accusing a man of something like that."

"Well, it was Drew's fault." Her voice rose to a whine. "He locked me out of his house, and I didn't have anywhere to go. I knew this other guy liked me, so I went to his place, and then—he hit me."

There was something missing from that story. His ex blinked up at him with red-rimmed eyes. "Aren't you going to ask who it was?"

"I don't fight your battles anymore. I stopped that when you started sleeping around."

"I had to do *something*. You never paid any attention to me." She pointed toward the barn the way another woman might point at a bar or a strip club. "You were always out there with the horses, and I was always *alone*."

He'd heard this song before. She'd demand his attention, then leave in a huff just when he made time for her. Usually, she'd gone shopping for revenge, spending what little money he had. When that ran out, she'd forged his name on credit applications and spent money he didn't have. When he'd been forced to take on extra work to pay the bills, she'd hurled herself into storms of weeping—because he never spent time with her.

"Cut it out, Amber Lynn. We've been over this."

"All right." With a final sniff, she straightened her shoulders, took a deep breath, and blew her nose with a honk that would have impressed a Canadian goose. She was trying, at least, and that was all it took to make him feel pity again.

She couldn't help who she was. Her folks had given in to every tantrum instead of taking the time to teach her right from wrong. Now, she survived the only way she knew how—by manipulating people.

"I'm s-s-*sorry*, Cade."

With one more comical goose honk, she dissolved into tears, crying so hard, he was afraid she'd pull a muscle.

Wait. Did sobbing require muscles?

He had no idea. He'd never cried like that in his life. Not when his dad smacked him around, not even when cancer took his mother. The only time he'd cried had been when Jess left, but even that hadn't been an all-out, shoulder-heaving show like this.

"I had such a bad night." She hiccupped, then burped, and he smothered a smile. "I s-s-slept in the c-c-*car*."

She blinked her sorry sheep eyes, clueless that the burp had made him feel closer to her than any of her womanly wiles.

"I have n-nowhere to go." The blinking turned to all-out lash fluttering. "Can I stay here? Just tonight?"

Boogy whined and crawled under the table.

"Why can't you stay with your dad?" Cade asked.

Amber Lynn slumped like a puppet whose strings had snapped. "That would be the first place that jerk would look. Besides, Daddy won't even talk to me because I left you. He said you're a g-good and decent man."

"Yeah, right. Last I knew, I was a low-class, redneck, white-trash bum who'd forced his precious daughter to live in a hovel. I believe that's a direct quote."

"He knows better now. You're a good man. You *are*." She choked on another burp and hiccupped. "My own daddy disowned me, 'cause I'm nothing but a tramp."

"You're not a tramp, Amber Lynn. You're just confused."

"I *am* confused." The storm cleared as suddenly as it had begun, and Amber Lynn smiled. With her face all pink from crying, she looked pretty as a prize piglet at the fair—except for that eye. "I need to get a good night's sleep and figure things out. Can I stay here? Please?"

"Why don't you get a hotel room?"

"I l-l-left my purse back at—back where…" She pointed toward her black eye, then pushed her chair back. "You're right, though. I should go back and get it." She sighed. "I don't *think* he'll hit me again."

Cade felt his resistance waning, then thought of the Cadillac parked behind the shed. It had to be her father's car, and if Jasper Lyle would loan her the car, why wouldn't he give her a place to stay?

Cade was pretty sure she was lying. Matter of fact, he was sure of it, because her lips were moving.

"I'm sorry, but no," he said. "You can't stay."

The sniffling started up again. He raised a hand, palm out, as if it could hold back her tears. "I need to go out. You can rest a little. Take a nap and maybe a shower, okay? But then you have to go."

She opened her mouth, no doubt to ask where he was going, but Cade wasn't about to tell her. She'd throw herself on the floor and pitch a fit if she knew he was helping out at the Diamond Jack and hoping to see Jess Bailey.

"You can use my soap, okay? Shampoo, too. But be gone before I get home, around sundown, okay?" He answered for her. "Okay. Come on, Boogy."

When they reached the truck, Boogy jumped up into the shot-gun seat while Cade gripped the wheel, his head spinning. Had he been firm enough? Would Amber Lynn be gone when he got back?

Probably not. When Amber Lynn wanted something, she was stubborn as a rusty gate. But he couldn't deal with her right now. He'd made a promise to Heck Bailey—one that just might put him in place to welcome Jess back home where she belonged.

Turning to Boogy, he rubbed the dog's flat head. "You're a good dog, but you're useless, you know? I ought to replace you with a Rottweiler."

Boogy panted and grinned, oblivious to the threat, his mind on the wonders of truck riding.

"I'm not any better, though. We're both softies at heart, and you know what?"

The dog perked up, as if Cade had said "ball" or "play."

"It's going to get us in trouble, Boogy. All kinds of trouble."

ACKNOWLEDGMENTS

How do I thank thee? Let me count the ways.

Actually, I should count the people! I've needed a lot of love and encouragement through the writing of this book, and I've been lucky enough to get it from the best friends and family anyone could ask for, as well as publishing professionals who are a joy to work with.

First of all, the Joanne Kennedy Books Facebook page has taken on a life of its own this year. I love sharing my life on the wild edge of Wyoming, with all its mountain lions and bears, wildflowers and waterfalls, big skies and stunning landscapes. I also post about my dogs and cats, who feel quite famous thanks to their many fans. It's a positive place to be, thanks to the many Facebook friends from all over the country who have become real and very dear friends. Kristine Anderson, Murlene Crowley, Karen Hackett, Kay Mills, Paula Neel, Mary Warschun, and so many others have been my inspiration. Knowing they're out there waiting for the next book keeps my fingers tapping the keyboard, and I look forward to their comments every day. I used to want to go to England or Chile or France, but now my dream trip is to pack up the dogs in the RV and go visit all my far-flung Facebook friends!

I especially want to thank Kathy Everingim of Cheyenne for naming Bruce, Riley's dog. Bruce is based on my big dog Jesse, who didn't want his real name used; he's shy and was worried about being mobbed by female stalker dogs. Bruce is a perfect name for a lovable but very protective pooch.

I have a lot of old and very dear friends who have had my back for years. Amanda Cabot and Mary Gillgannon are like sisters to me, while the Cheyenne contingent—including Jaren Artery,

Mike Bleakley, Lori Brand, Wendy Soto, and Kate Wright—is always supportive even when I'm not around. Jeannette and Neil Gallagher are always there to offer tea and sympathy all the way from Maine, and my good friend Jeanette Daly is my role model for living in this wild place forever with courage and independence.

Then there's my family. I was lucky enough to marry a man with terrific kids I love and admire. Scott and Aminda, Alycia and Ryan and their kids, and Jackie and Brian are all successful, hardworking, and best of all kind. We also have a new baby in the family. I can't wait to watch Alan grow up!

Last but not least, I really don't know how my husband, Scrape McCauley, manages to live with me every day without losing his mind. His patience and support have been incredible this past year, and he's always there to help me through the plot twists in real life as well as fiction. He is *still* the reason I write romance novels.

Joanne Kennedy
Stillwater Sanctuary
Colorado
September 22, 2019

ABOUT THE AUTHOR

Joanne Kennedy is the RITA-nominated author of ten contemporary western romance novels, including *Cowboy Trouble*, *Tall, Dark and Cowboy*, and *Cowboy Tough*. The first book in her Decker Ranch trilogy, *How to Handle a Cowboy*, was named one of *Booklist*'s Best Romances of the Decade. She lives in a secret mountain hideout on the Wyoming border with too many pets and a retired fighter pilot. The pets are relatively well-behaved.

Joanne loves to hear from readers and can be reached through her website, joannekennedybooks.com.